Chicks and BALANCES

Baen Books by Esther Friesner

Chicks in Chainmail
Chicks 'N Chained Males
Did You Say Chicks?!
The Chick is in the Mail
Turn the Other Chick
Chicks Ahoy! (omnibus)
Chicks and Balances

Witch Way to the Mall
Strip Mauled
Fangs for the Mammaries

Chicks and Balances

Edited By
ESTHER FRIESNER
JOHN HELFERS

BAEN

CHICKS AND BALANCES

This is a work of fiction. All the characters and events portrayed in this book are fictional, and any resemblance to real people or incidents is purely coincidental.

Introduction copyright © 2015 by Esther Friesner.

Copyright © 2015 by Esther M. Friesner and Stonehenge Art & Word.

A Baen Books Original

Baen Publishing Enterprises
P.O. Box 1403
Riverdale, NY 10471
www.baen.com

ISBN: 978-1-4767-8063-4

Cover art by Tom Wood

First Baen paperback printing, July 2015

Distributed by Simon & Schuster
1230 Avenue of the Americas
New York, NY 10020

Library of Congress Cataloging-in-Publication Data

Chicks and balances / edited by Esther Friesner and John Helfers.
     pages cm. -- (Chicks in chainmail ; 7)
ISBN 978-1-4767-8063-4 (paperback)
1. Fantasy fiction, American. 2. Women heroes--Fiction. 3. Women--Fiction. I. Friesner, Esther M., editor. II. Helfers, John, editor.
  PS648.F3C48 2015
  813'.08766083522--dc23
                              2015011950
Printed in the United States of America

10 9 8 7 6 5 4 3 2 1

Contents

Dedication

This book is dedicated to Sir Terence David John Pratchett, OBE

Though Y'r Humble Editrix is always pleased to think of him as Terry,

Master of the *Monstrous Regiment,*

He who always Remembers the Ladies,

And who is proof positive that the Good Guy also wears the Black Hat.

Post Script

I am deeply sorry to say that Sir Terry Pratchett
left us on March 12, 2015.

He did know that this book was going to be dedicated to him,
for which I am glad.

His wisdom, insight, and humor live on.

Chicks and
BALANCES

"The enemy isn't men, or women, it's bloody stupid people and no one has the right to be stupid."
                              —Terry Pratchett, *Monstrous Regiment*

Introduction

by Esther Friesner

Congratulations, you've just picked the sixth slick *Chicks shtick*.

Now try saying that perfectly, ten times, *quick*! If you fail (epically, as is the custom nowadays) you owe me a drink.

Yes, you do. It's a proven fact that whenever I include a request, suggestion, pipe-dream or Imperial Command in the Introduction to one of the *Chicks in Chainmail* books, someone somewhere out there in GentleReaderLand always seems willing to take care of fulfilling that li'l ol' *wouldn't-it-be-nice-if . . . ?* for me.

Case in point: Ages ago, the Introduction to an earlier *Chicks* anthology contained my simply *dreadful* doggerel poem in praise of Lucy Lawless, then starring in *Xena, Warrior Princess*. (No, I don't remember which volume contained said poem and my home library is in a permanent state somewhere between Category and Chaos, so I am unable to ferret out the hard data. Deal with it.) I also voiced the hope of someday acquiring an autographed picture of Ms. Lawless inscribed "To Binky." (I am unable to explain *why* I wanted that particular personalization. I just did. What can I say? My Muse is the divine Adlibia, patroness of Whimsy.)

Fast Forward to an e-mail received from a fan in New Zealand. He reported that they'd just opened a Barnes & Noble in Wellington, told me he'd bought the aforementioned installment of *Chicks*, and asked if I'd been serious when I said I wanted that personalized photo from Ms. Lawless.

Because, you see, he was a stuntman on *Xena*, and he could get it for me.

Yes, please, thank you, and *WOOT!*

And behold, I was shortly thereafter in possession of that which I had so lightly requested, which just goes to show you that:

A. I loooooove the Internet

B. I should've asked for jewelry

and

C. You really do owe me a drink.

Unless, of course, you managed to say, "I picked the sixth slick *Chicks shtick,*" per the above guidelines, in which case, I owe you a book.

Hey, whaddayaknow? Here it is!

This is the point in the Introduction where you may thank me for not saying it's been a long, strange trip, even though it has. What began for me as a flash of inspiration in the middle of a science fiction convention art show has been with us for nigh unto twenty years. The first eponymous *Chicks in Chainmail* anthology was published back in 1995, as thousands cheered. This means the project is more than old enough to vote, to drive, to register with Selective Service, to marry without editorial consent, and is *nearly* of an age to drink legally.

(Hmmm, again with the drinks? I am beginning to detect a pattern here. On the other hand, since I have been wearing the triple crown of creator, editor, and contributor within the *Chicks in Chainmail* universe for a couple of decades, I'd say that I am entitled to the occasional cup that cheers.)

It delights me no end to reflect upon the longevity and success of the *Chicks in Chainmail* series. I don't know if anyone expected these funny tales of women and armor—in whatever guise—to do so well for so long. Back when it all began, I invoked that tidy little put-down in joke's clothing:

"How many Feminists does it take to screw in a light bulb?"

"*That's not funny!*"

In other words, Feminists can't cope with a joke.

Goodness knows that the Internet and the assorted airwaves have shown us many examples of jokes who couldn't cope with Feminists, but the reverse? Untrue.

You want proof? You're holding it. Twenty years and six anthologies making light of the Grim and Gritty Woman Warrior, with nary a "How *dare* you?" reaching my shell-like (conch) ears.

Maybe things are looking up, civilization-wise. Maybe it's okay to laugh. Maybe laughter is being recognized as one of the best measures of empowerment and security. Maybe most of us are willing to toss aside our Agenda Sticks rather than brandishing them mightily as we leap aboard the Righteous Rage bandwagon *du jour*.

And maybe—oh please, oh please—just maybe enough people are realizing that it's a bad thing when a good cause gets taken over by the ideology equivalent of 'roid rage and becomes a Noble Crusade.

(You remember the Crusades, right? Origin of such Noble actions as the massacres of the Rhineland Jews, Richard the Lionhearted's slaughter of nearly three thousand Muslim prisoners, and the sack of Constantinople, where huge numbers of Christian civilians were slain. Wow. Way to perpetrate full-service, all-embracing *ecumenical* atrocities, people.)

O what a Work-in-Progress we are. But as long as we're not a Work-in-*Regress*, I'm willing to hang on if you are.

I'm also hoping we can share a few laughs along the way.

Editor's Note: As of the writing of this Introduction, I have no idea as to what the cover of this book will look like. Please be aware that such matters are entirely out of my hands, though given the title of this series, I would be very much surprised if it did *not* feature one or more women whose bodies are covered to varying degrees by chainmail, plus a measure of other textiles, fabrics, tanned hides, and/or gewgaws.

If you don't like what you see, smite me not from out of the House of Virtue and Rectitude. Yea, rather do I bid thee unleash thy chastisement where it might do some *real* good, like against those who still stand between women and equal pay, decent healthcare, and the simple, precious right to live *secure* lives.

It doesn't matter if we choose to wear a chainmail miniskirt or a Mother Hubbard when we take on the trolls of this world, as long as the job of troll-slaying gets done. Go smite someone else. I've had a hard day, and I am *this* close to throwing my cat at anyone who gives me yammer about the cover art.

She weighs eighteen pounds. You can't say I didn't warn you.

A Chick Off the Old Block

by Jody Lynn Nye

Jess heard Duchess Caitlin calling from the top of the tower.

"Jessamine! Oh, Jessamine, come and help me!"

The girl sounded as though she was in genuine distress. Jess plumped the two full buckets of water she had been carrying under the nearest bench. Lifting her heavy green woolen skirts in both hands, she took the stone stairs two at a time along the winding spiral stair toward the girl's bower.

"What is it, my lady?" she called.

"Oh, Jessamine, hurry!"

Her mistress was in danger! It must be an intruder! Who would dare to invade the citadel of Kalb De in full daylight?

Jess bounded upward, reaching for the knife she wore upside down against the small of her back, and rushed into the duchess's room. None of the junior maidservants nor any of the pages were in the round, tapestry-lined chamber. Eighteen-year-old Duchess Caitlin, heiress to the grand ducal throne of Kalb De, battled with her enemy alone in the light of the huge, multi-paned window. Jess rushed to come to her aid, then halted, staring.

It looked as though an armored knight was indeed attempting to assail her beautiful young lady, but it was only the ghost—or rather, the shell of one. The girl's long golden hair was tangled in the face piece of a steel helmet, while her slender body was half-encased in odd pieces of metal and leather. She struggled to free herself from both. Jess burst into laughter.

5

"Oh, mistress, what are you doing?" Sheathing her dagger, she hurried to the girl's aid. "Stop fussing and let me help."

Caitlin dropped her hands to her sides. Jess began to unwind the long, golden tresses one at a time from the hinged faceplate.

"Have I not told you time and again, mistress? Plait your hair, then cap, then coif, *then* helm?"

"I remembered the cap only after I tried to put on the helm," Caitlin admitted, her smooth, oval face screwed into the likeness of a wrinkled apple. "Then I couldn't get it off again."

"Small wonder we men- and women-at-arms wear our hair short, isn't it?"

"But you have long hair now," Caitlin said, with a glance at Jess's thick brown braid. "As long as you have served me."

"Only so I won't shame you in court, my lady," Jess said.

Caitlin gave her a fond look. "You could never shame me," she said.

Jessamine had come to be the small duchess's companion, maid of all work, and finally lady-in-waiting entirely by chance. In Kalb De, the second birthday was always Choosing Day, when the heir to the grand ducal throne selected the person who would be his or her faithful friend and confidant for life. Ladies and girls from every honorable family from all over the duchy had come and gathered in the courtyard to attend the noble child's selection. But instead of picking her companion from the bevy of nervous females wearing their jewels and feastday best, Caitlin had pointed to Jess, who had been among the file of soldiers-at-arms standing at attention in the shadow of the gatehouse, awaiting their orders for the day from the mistress-of-arms. Jess could still feel the prickle of shame as the duke ordered her to come and present herself. She was just a country girl who had joined the citadel guard. In contrast to the ladies' finery, she wore a plain work tunic that needed a good wash, under second- or third-hand scale mail sewn to a worn leather tabard. To her astonishment, Caitlin demanded to be picked up and held. Jess had no choice but to comply.

Jess had protested the arrangement as unsuitable to the tiny lady and herself, but the custom had the force of law. Besides, it had been hard to say no when the precious girl had nestled herself into Jess's arms. Jess had cradled Caitlin close, wanting to protect her from that moment on, even more than she had wished to out of duty. She thought the archduke and archduchess would be upset at the choice, blaming Jess for being, oh, who knew, too apparent to the child's eye? But they only smiled. Beside the archduchess, the wizard Uthbridge had offered only a single observation.

"It is as I foretold to you, your grace," he said. "What she needs to learn, only this lass can teach."

Jess had been teased mightily since that day by all her friends and comrades in the guard. She had to shed her comfortable suit of mail for corsetry, skirts, and headgear that was impractical on a good day and downright ridiculous on a windy one. Truth was, she had never felt worthy of the honor, and always felt out of place beside the neatly turned out handmaids and pages who came and went for the lady, and occasionally for her humble self.

Despite her new duties, she kept up her exercises and her expertise at swordplay and hand-to-hand combat. Maintaining her strength and agility made Jess valuable beyond her keep for being able to carry two full pails of scalding water at a time up six flights of steps from the kitchens to Caitlin's bath, even though she had now passed the ancient age of thirty. The youngsters who had occupied the Heir's Tower in the past had become used to cold ablutions. Caitlin always praised and thanked her for her consideration, which made up for some of the loss of camaraderie with her fellow soldiers. Still, Duchess Caitlin admired Jess and clamored to be like her.

Well, why not? Jess had obtained, behind the duke's back and with the mistress-of-arms's attention deliberately turned away, a child's suit of armor and a wooden sword and shield. Cait didn't fit into the clanking breastplate so well any longer, what with her getting taller and growing a figure and all, but she could squeeze into it. Jess also had seen no reason that the girl shouldn't learn a little of swordplay to keep her healthy and fit. The ladies-in-waiting with their many tasks were in better condition, field-wise, than the nobles they served. Many lords and ladies rode out to hunt or to go to war, but those who retired became soft. They could scarcely climb the stairs to their rooms, let alone wield a weapon. Jess helped Caitlin to learn exercises that did not overstrain her maturing limbs. When she outgrew the wooden sword, Cait graduated to the antique weapons that hung on brackets on display all along the spiral staircase leading up to her solar, leaving none outside the tower the wiser. The exercise wasn't as rigorous as learning to be a soldier, but her efforts made Jess proud. If they could have worked openly in the field, the girl could have learned to command any regiment.

"So why put on your armor now?" she asked, holding the helm on her shoulder while she unwound the duchess's hair. Caitlin looked wistful.

"It may be my last chance. My intended, Lord Matew, says in his letters that he is a man of peace. I may rule in court, but he would prefer not to see me attired as for the battlefield. How dull it sounds. I would much rather ride to the horns with my sword swinging in defense of my lands. I hoped I would do that someday. He prefers I let my generals do it."

"Battle is its own kind of dull, my lady," Jess said, pulling the last of the golden strands free. "Lord Matew's people have done well warring only with words and bargains instead of steel. They have prospered in a difficult situation."

"But I know the tedium of court," Caitlin complained. She smoothed her dress of the rarest celestial blue, an odd undergown to wear with chainmail. "I would like some excitement before I am married. I love books and learning and music as much as he does, truly! Ah, well, but I wanted to try on my armor just one more time."

Jess sympathized. In a way, it was an odd match. Kalb De lay in a flat and fertile plain. The lands grew bountiful crops if one so much as whispered the word "seed" to the soil. Because the land was so open, a strong defensive force needed to be maintained. She was proud to have been a recruit since she was old enough to swing a mace. By contrast, mountainous Rocky Ford had to import a lot of the staple foods the country relied upon. It lay just across the wild Ayla Noise River from the Grand Duchy of Kalb De. It was a land with many strange customs that had grown up because of its position at the crossroads between several countries. The capital city lay many miles inland, along a branch of the river flowing down from the sheer Kanka Key Mountains where giant grasshoppers threatened the passes. The ways were heavily guarded, so as to give safe passage to merchants and other travelers.

Matew's parents, Baron and Baroness Ferio, were known as scholars and traders of note. Matew himself was a Doctor of Letters. There had not been a war in their small nation of Rocky Ford for twelve generations, but stirrings along their borders had made them seek out an alliance with a larger and more powerful country. Kalb De would welcome additions to its culture, and offer prosperity to its new province. As a sign of trust, the archduke and archduchess had traveled with their entourage to the Rocky Ford capital to sign the marriage treaty. Lord Matew was traveling in the opposite direction, coming to Kalb De to spend that time with his bride to be, the first time they would meet in person, though they had corresponded by messenger constantly since the match was proposed, seven months back. The mistress-of-arms had been left in charge of the castle, and would guard it well until the archduke and archduchess came home again.

Jess sat Caitlin down at the oval looking glass. It was magical, as were many of the young duchess's possessions. Jess's reflection showed her the right way to braid the girl's hair in the latest fashion. When she faltered, the reflection undid the mirror image Caitlin's hair again and again until Jess saw her mistake and got it right. Caitlin watched for a while, then played with the ivory miniature of Lord Matew in its frame of pearls. He was not the handsomest man ever, Jess thought, with his heavy brow ridge and large jaw, but the deepset blue eyes were drawn with a twinkle that the artist had managed to capture with love as well as skill.

"Won't you rule over all when the time comes?" Jess asked. "It is your choice whether to be a warrior, or a diplomat, or both. That is the truth. He needs to accept who you are."

"I want him to be happy here," Caitlin said, with a kind look that reminded Jess of her noble mother's gentle face. "I will rule, but I want him to be my partner, not my chattel. He must not feel that too much is being forced upon him all at once. It will be a great change for all of us, but more for him than for me. I am not having to move from my home. He is."

"You are wise for your years, mistress," Jess said with a rush of warmth. "Well, let's get you ready to see him."

"Mistress Caitlin?"

They both turned at the sound of Uthbridge's voice. The wizard had grown wand-thin over the years. He could still climb the impossible staircase to his remote tower, but he looked as though a sharp breeze would break him in two.

The two girls rushed to support him and helped him to a chair.

"What wisdom do you bring, lord wizard?" Jess asked.

Uthbridge blinked at her. He had a face like an amiable badger, blunt-nosed and broad-headed. His thick hair and mustache had grayed with time. His hazel-green eyes were as clear as they had been years ago, but he always squinted as though there was a film over them.

"I have been here already," he said, peering around the room.

"Yes, dear wizard, you have." Caitlin was amused. "Often."

"The invasion's been averted, then?" Uthbridge asked. He smiled at Jess. "Well done, my child!"

"What invasion?" Jess asked.

Uthbridge had always been able to foretell the future. The trouble was, as his age advanced, his foresight sped farther into the future so it was virtually of no practical use. Jess regarded him fondly as an eccentric old uncle. But once in a while, he had something true to say.

Uthbridge looked worried. He pulled a tangle of strings and crystal beads from his belt pouch and arranged them over his fingers. He twisted the contraption into one impossible configuration after another. "It can't be the invasion yet, can it? The archduke and the archduchess must defend our gates! Strangers have come within."

"My parents have not gone to war," Caitlin said. "They have gone to the Rocky Ford to negotiate with Lord Matew's parents. Only Matew and his friends are coming here. I am going down to await them for the noonday meal. It will be a feast. You are to join us."

Uthbridge let the cat's cradle drop, his narrow shoulders sagging with relief.

"Ah, yes! The Rocky Ford lands will come under the aegis of Kalb De. You are a wise ruler of your people, my lady."

"Not yet! In time, I will be. I am in no hurry to bid farewell to my parents. So do you mistake my affianced husband for an invader, lord wizard?" Caitlin asked, her blue eyes crinkling with merriment.

"Not he, but one who is as close to him as a second self," Uthbridge said. He drew himself up. "Beware, my lady!"

Jess frowned.

"We are at peace with the lands around us. None have voiced an objection to her ladyship's match."

"But an invasion has happened," Uthbridge said, consulting his strings and crystals. "In fact, it is beginning . . . just about now."

Shouting interrupted them. Jess glanced out the broad window, squinting to see through the rippled panes of glass. Horsemen were approaching at speed, a whole band of them!

"Stay here, my lady. Uthbridge, can you provide protection to defend her?"

The elderly wizard straightened

"Of course! I have brought the necessary elements. Hear me, o spirits!"

His manner might be hazy at other times, but when it came to the practice of magic, he became as sharp as a blade. He snatched forth a handful of items from his belt pouch and threw them into the air, where they hovered like birds. He reached for a jar and shook its powdery contents into his palm. Jess waited to see no more. She flew down the stairs, calling: "To arms! The duchy is in peril! To arms!"

Her cry was not taken up. She heard more shouting and clashing of metal upon metal, but the alarm horn was not sounded. Where were the rest of the guards? She rushed to the guardhouse, where a couple of her fellows lounged against the wall, passing the time.

"Hurry!" she cried. "Invaders approach! Arm yourselves! The wizard has foreseen an incursion against us."

"What?" cried Bainton, a large, handsome man with sandy hair and a big jaw who had recently been promoted to sergeant-at-arms. "Soldiers, prepare!"

Five of Jess's former fellows rushed through the open door and seized polearms and maces hanging from pegs on the wall. Bainton mustered them into a file, waiting for Jess to join them.

She threw open the battered wooden chest with her name carved in the top and began to drag out the pieces of her armor. First the cap, over her hair. Then the felt tunic, to hold the weight of the armor off her shoulders. The Mistress-at-Arms appeared in the door, her tall body blocking out the light.

"What are you doing, Corporal Jess?" she demanded, hands on hips. Her well-polished scalemail was covered by her dress tabard, dyed chestnut brown and embroidered in couched gold with the wheatsheaf emblem of Kalb De. Her long, high-cheekboned face peered out from under her shining helm. Her silvering braids were concealed by the coif. "It is only his lordship of Rocky Ford, come to visit our young lady. The falcon scout spotted the banners miles out. He said his bird identified the lead rider as young Lord Matew."

"What?" Jess asked. She straightened up, a cuirass in one hand and a gauntlet in the other. "Oh!" She slammed them back into the chest. "Oh, when will I stop thinking that Uthbridge knows what he is talking about?"

Bainton's broad shoulders relaxed.

"It's understood, lass. Never you mind."

The mistress-of-arms smiled. "Come and present yourself to greet Lord Matew. Then you may inform the lady of the arrival of her intended."

Jess shrugged out of the long undertunic and cap and put them back with the rest. She took a couple of quick swipes at her braid to tidy it, and brushed down her skirts.

The courtyard was filled with people, most of them kitchen servants who hurried back and forth with armloads of rushes, flowers and beautifully wrought sugar subtleties. Trestle tables were covered and laid out in a U-shape under the sun for the upcoming feast. The smell of roasting meat and baking bread wafted deliciously through the air. How could she have thought there was anything wrong?

She stood in between the double-file of soldiers-at-arms and the servants of the house to watch the party arrive. They all peered toward the broad gravel road that led up the hill toward the citadel gate.

Lord Matew certainly meant to make an impression. Thirty, no, forty soldiers in full armor, even more than remained in the garrison of the castle, rode behind the tall man at their head. Pennants flew from the tips of their swords and from the horns of the heralds that flanked the nobleman. Baggage carts and a covered litter brought up the rear.

For a man of peace and a doctor of letters, Matew certainly held himself on horseback like an expert, thought Jess. His long, lanky body was at utter ease in the saddle of a destrier whose coat was so black it was blue. He wore a shimmering chainmail tunic underneath a sable leather tabard marked with the silver waterfall emblem of Rocky Ford. Both sword and spear were ready at hand. Perhaps he meant to surprise Caitlin and show her he was at home in both worlds.

But something didn't seem right. The shock of hair was darker and the jaw narrower than depicted in the small painting that Caitlin cherished. Heaven knew that Jess had studied it time and again since it had arrived four weeks before. She noticed small differences between the man and the image. It could be that the painter was more skilled at expression than resemblance, if such a thing was possible. Jess herself couldn't draw a circle or a straight line. His expression had no trace of the amiable fellow in the picture. She might even call this man cruelly handsome. She straightened her back. There was deception of some kind here, but what?

The approaching heralds lifted their trumpets to their lips and blew a musical fanfare. The mistress-of-arms drew her sword and held it blade up before her nose.

"Present arms!" she shouted. "Open the gate!"

The creaking portcullis rose. Behind its jagged black teeth, the colorful procession cantered forward, not even slowing as it flowed into the courtyard.

"*Welcome, Lord Matew!*" the crowd cried out.

The black-haired man raised a fist. His contingent of soldiers wheeled their horses and halted facing the guards of Kalb De. He swung out of the saddle.

"Well, a pretty greeting! Where is my lady?"

The mistress-of-arms, as the ranking person remaining in the citadel, stood forward.

"She will appear soon, my lord. I am Captain Leehall. In the name of the Duke and Duchess of Kalb De, I bid you and your people to rest and refresh yourselves. As you see," the mistress-of-arms said, sweeping her arm toward the decorated tables, "your engagement feast is almost prepared."

"But why wait?" the man asked, spreading his arms wide and turning in a circle. "Our parents have already agreed our two lands are to be made one. Let this be our wedding day! I have brought with me a celebrant of the Sphere of Heaven. Come here, priest!"

A stout man dropped the reins of the lead baggage cart and scrambled down. He wore the traditional green robe, but he had none of the rings or a diadem proclaiming him a high member of the church. He was a humble forest priest.

"Shouldn't the Archdruid perform a ceremony between two future heads of state?" Jess asked.

The man spun on his heel, strode toward her, and thrust his face into hers.

"Do you question me, peasant?" he asked. The others gasped. Jess studied him.

"You're not Lord Matew," she said.

"Do you mean my pathetic weakling of a brother?" the man asked. "No! You have surprised the truth out of me just a little early. I am Master Dyved of Rocky Ford, second by minutes to my elder brother." He paced to the covered litter and threw back the cover. Inside was a lady with the same strong jaw, and a slender man who was clearly and truly Lord Matew. Both were trussed like birds for the spit and struggling to get free. Over his gag, Matew glared up at Master Dyved, who grinned at him.

"Here is your Lord Matew. The lady, my Aunt Grace, come to be a companion for the Duchess Caitlin. But she is too old, isn't she? Never mind. The girl can have as many servants as she wants, as my wife!" He pulled a dagger from the sheath at his hip and held it to Matew's throat. "It is a simple matter. I marry the lady, here and now, and my brother lives. Or she refuses, he dies, and I marry her anyhow."

"I cannot allow that," the mistress-of-arms said stoutly, though her pale cheeks showed her shock. "Guards!"

Jess reached for a sword that was not there, but it wouldn't have helped in any case. Master Dyved's soldiers were still on horseback. They lowered spears and rode at the Kalb De fighters. Jess's comrades evaded the spears. They drew their own weapons and charged.

"Kalb De!" Bainton shouted.

They must get out of the way. Jess waved the servants to the shelter of the guardhouse, moving them toward the steps down to the cellars. They used the remaining trestles leaning against the inner wall as shields. The clash of metal on metal made her blood boil to be part of the fight, but she needed to defend the noncombatants. One after another, she pushed the servants down into the cool darkness, keeping an eye on the action.

A muscular woman galloped her horse toward them. She swung out of the saddle. Jess moved to avoid her, but the soldier planted herself at the head of the steps, blocking the way. Jess and the steward hesitated in the face of her sword's sharp metal point.

Across the courtyard, the mistress-of-arms sidled around the bloody scrimmage. Jess saw what was in her mind. She meant to rescue Lord Matew if she could. He was the Heir's intended, and as such was under their protection from the moment he had entered Kalb De. But Master Dyved saw her, too. He turned and crouched into a fighting stance.

Throwing subterfuge away, Captain Leehall charged him, sword high.

"With me, Kalb De!" she cried. The defenders did their best to fend off the invaders, but it was little use. The fight was ugly and brief. The ruffians were heavily armed and fully armored, leaving few points of flesh for the defenders to attack. In a terrifyingly short time, the invaders disarmed most of the soldiers and killed two of them. The mistress-of-arms lay on the courtyard cobbles, bleeding from a shoulder wound. Dyved stood over her, sword at her throat, his eyes alight with triumph.

"I hold this castle. My wizard has stopped your falcon scouts from sending their birds for help. No one will come or go. I will remain here to meet my new in-laws upon their return from my family's pathetic castle." His smile was cruel. "Yes, I think I am going to enjoy myself here." He glared at Jess and the steward. "Bring me the lady! This marriage must take place at once. All this can be over and done with most pleasantly. Let the festivities begin! Bring me my bride!"

Jess grabbed up a spare trestle and swung it, knocking the woman guarding her flying off her feet.

"Never!" she shouted. She ran for the Heir's Tower. "My lady! Lock your door! Invaders! Invaders!"

She hoisted her skirts and hurried upward. She must defend her young charge, even if it took her life!

She had a head start on Master Dyved, but his long legs made it simple to catch up with her. He slashed his sword toward her face. She ducked under the blade. It clashed against the stone wall. She looked around for a weapon. Her own sword still hung on the peg above her armor chest in the guard room. She had nothing but the dagger in the small of her back. She went for it, but the Master smacked her arm with the flat of his blade. The dagger fell from her fingers and went clattering down the stone steps out of sight.

"A shieldmaiden, eh? Not a simple servant?" the Master said, his eyes glowing. "This will be fun."

Jess kept her eyes on Dyved's, judging where the next thrust would go. Above her, one turn of the spiral away, were dozens of swords, shields, spears, and maces that had belonged to heirs of past generations, but she had no weapon at hand. She saw nothing but a broom left behind by one of the scullery servants. Like lightning, she darted out a hand for it, catching Master Dyved's blade just as he tried to cut off her head. She blocked blow after blow, until Dyved chopped the broom handle in half. Her hands sang with the shock of the blow. She dashed the pieces at him, catching him in the side of the face. Blood dripped from the torn corner of his mouth. Jess dashed upward, calling out.

"My lady! Guard yourself! It is an impostor! Lord Matew is his prisoner!"

The girl's voice rang out as clearly as a tocsin. "None shall pass!"

"Oh, I think you're wrong about that," the Master said.

A hand caught Jess's ankle and yanked upward. She fell on her face and slid downward against the wall. The shining boots passed her, going up the stairs three and four at a time.

Bruised, Jess crawled upward, hating the man with every step. She would kill him! He would not have her lady.

"What is this sorcery?" Master Dyved's voice boomed. "Let me in!"

The escutcheon of the eighth archduchess hung on the wall at the third turning. Crossed upon its embossed metal surface were the spears with which the great lady had hunted boars, but stuck through the crest and helm at the top was Her Grace's deadly leaf-bladed sword. Jess pulled herself to her feet and yanked it free. She ran the rest of the way up to Caitlin's door . . .

. . . and stopped a flight below the landing. Spider's webs stretched through the hallway. Master Dyved slashed through the mass without difficulty, though it covered him in draperies of gray. Was this Uthbridge's manner of protecting Caitlin? The old wizard was useless!

Though Jess was trying to move silently, Master Dyved heard her and swung around. The sword met her borrowed weapon and flipped it out of her hands. He pinioned her against the wall with his leather-covered fist.

"Twice disarmed," he said, grinning. "I think that means I win, don't you?"

He shoved her. Jess tripped backwards, but saved herself from falling further, so she had a terrific view as the Master chopped at the last swathe of cobwebs covering the door.

With a deafening boom, the mass of gray ignited. Master Dyved screamed, and beat at his hair and skin to put out the flames. With a mental apology to Uthbridge, Jess picked up the duchess's sword and charged at the Master. Blindly, he raised his sword to counter.

The door opened. The two of them stumbled into the room. Master Dyved fell on the floor beyond the threshold.

A knight in full armor met him, eight feet tall and brandishing a brand of blazing silver. Jess gawked.

"You shall *not* marry me," Caitlin's voice echoed from the cylindrical helmet.

Master Dyved, his hair and eyelashes scorched, scrambled to his feet. His leather gloves were blistered and torn, but he held onto his sword.

"What is this? Matew told me you were a dainty thing. He wouldn't lie about that, would he?"

He slashed at her. Caitlin countered him, swept her sword up in a figure eight, and struck back. He parried the blade easily. He beat her back, one step, two steps, three steps.

He was too good for the girl's limited skill. Jess rushed in to help, sweeping her blade down. She struck his right shoulder. He yelled with pain. Caitlin struck him in the back of the knee. Master Dyved went into a frenzy. He rained blows upon them, one after another. The two women parried each, but with every stroke, the glamor faded away until Caitlin was revealed in ill-fitting student's armor and her wooden sword in her hand. She looked up at Master Dyved in dismay. He grinned ferally.

"That's the girl I'm going to marry!"

"No!" Caitlin cried.

"Courage, my lady! Remember your lessons!" Jess ordered. "Exercise fourteen, now go!"

Caitlin set determination upon her face. The two of them hacked and slashed at their enemy, parrying and riposting, all in perfect unison. The Master was strong and well-trained, but against two fighters, even one small and the other without a link of armor, he was at a disadvantage. Caitlin took an opening to thrust the point of her wooden brand through the chink between arm and chest. Jess enjoyed the man's howl of pain. If it had been a metal sword, it would have been a killing blow. She had never been so proud of Caitlin in her life.

"This is impossible!" Dyved snarled, clutching his side with his free hand. "Matew's fiancée is a wisp of a thing who worships books and music!"

"Not every facet of a jewel can be seen at first glance," Caitlin said fiercely. Jess laughed at the dismay on Master Dyved's face.

"Together, now!" She and Caitlin redoubled their attack. Within minutes, they cornered him against the wide glass window. Jess stepped in, planting the point of her blade against the bottom of his jaw.

"Now, as my lady would no doubt see it, you have four choices," Jess said. "First, you can try to kill us, but you can only attack one at a time. You have only one sword. I promise you that the other one of us will kill you. Second, you can fall out of the window, plummet six storeys, and die. The duke will be upset if you break the glass. It's the nicest window in the castle. Third, you can surrender and live. Duchess Caitlin might even let you attend her wedding. As a guest, of course, not the groom. Or fourth, we will turn you over to the court wizard and let him wrap you in more of his exploding spider webs. That was a mild example to deter your entry, not all of which he is capable. What do you say?" Jess loved the fear that rose in Master Dyved's eyes. Beside her, Uthbridge drew his skinny frame up and brandished his long fingertips. A cloud of gray appeared in the air above them.

Slowly, with hatred now blazing from his eyes, Master Dyved dropped his sword and raised his hands in surrender.

Jess marched him down the stairs with his own sword at his throat. When the soldiers of Rocky Ford saw him, they stopped fighting at once. Sergeant Bainton took charge and rounded them up. Another soldier rushed to free the prisoners in the litter. Lord Matew unfolded his long legs and helped his aunt out of it.

Caitlin approached shyly, conscious of her ill-fitting armor, but with all the dignity of her rank.

"My Lord Matew, I am glad to meet you," she said. "I am Duchess Caitlin. I bid you welcome."

He looked Caitlin up and down, regarding the student's armor with curiosity and concern.

"But what is this?" he asked.

"A part of me that you didn't know," she said.

"She defeated your brother's treachery," Jess said, defending her charge. "She is a shieldmaiden as well as a scholar."

"I hope you are not put off by the truth," Caitlin said. She took off her gauntlets and handed them to Jess. "I would prefer not to live a lie."

"I would always accept truth," Matew said, taking her small hand in his long fingers. "I don't shy away from reality. It's just that the future I want is one of peace."

"We need to enforce safety if we are to have peace," Caitlin said. She looked up at him hopefully. "I will lead by example."

"And I follow," he said. He kissed her fingertips. "I wondered what to give you for a wedding present. Now I know. You need a better fitting suit of armor." The blue eyes twinkled. Jess sighed. This was the man in the picture, well worth falling in love with.

"Come and dine with me," Caitlin said, drawing Matew and his aunt toward the tables. Jess thanked Heaven that they had not been upset during the melee. "We have much to discuss."

"After we rescue my friends," Lord Matew said, his eyes widening with alarm. "My vile brother left them tied up in a copse at this end of the bridge."

"We'll go get them, my lord," said Sergeant Bainton.

"Then I have time to dress for luncheon," Caitlin said. "Jess, will you help me?"

Jess nodded to the other maidservants, who hurried to fall into their wake.

"It's as I said sixteen years ago," Uthbridge whispered to Jess, as she followed Caitlin back toward the stairs. "It's what you taught her that is her most important lesson."

Jess blushed. "Swordplay is nothing, lord wizard."

"Swordplay was not the lesson. Thanks to you, she knows how to defend herself in every way that matters. She will be a wise and confident ruler, and she will also hold her own with her mate. You taught her that. You once thought you were too humble to take your place as her companion, but what you shared has, er, *will* make all the difference."

Jess shot him a puzzled look. He tipped her a wink. Perhaps the old fellow wasn't as far gone as he seemed.

The Girls from the Hood

by Jim C. Hines

"Once upon a time," Stepmama began, "a hunter named Roland made a very poor choice."

The hunter in question rubbed bloodshot eyes and squinted. Empty bottles littered the floor around the cot in his small cabin. One balanced precariously on the belly of a stuffed possum, whose patchy fur suggested it had died of a particularly unpleasant disease. "Who—*what* are you?"

Stepmama's short riding cape was thrown back, exposing the fringed black leather that covered her bosom and left her midriff bare. Matching leather trousers protected her legs, and a skirt of leather and steel provided additional armor for her hips and thighs. A short-bladed sword hung from one hip. Steel studs covered her shoulders and the bracers on her forearms. A blood-red leather helm topped the ensemble.

His attention went next to her tattoos. An image of her first mare, Water Spirit, was inked onto her left bicep. Three horseshoes decorated her right forearm. A blue snake circled her wrist, seeming to cool itself with the small fan gripped in its tail.

"The princess," said Stepmama. "What did you do with her body?"

Roland reached beneath a sweat-stained pillow. Stepmama's hand moved toward her sword, but he pulled out only a mostly empty bottle, yanked the cork, and took a drink. "That'd be a nice costume on someone half your age."

Stepmama let the insult slide past. From the gray sprinkled in his greasy hair to the wrinkles spreading like cracks in the mud through the skin by his eyes, he couldn't have been more than five years her junior.

Roland's cabin was as much a wreck as the man himself. Dead animals crowded the space, preserved in poses ranging from awkward to bizarre. A cross-eyed bear's head with an irregularly shaped bald spot stared from the wall. A fox stood in the corner with one leg cocked. A snake at the foot of the bed coiled in what was presumably supposed to be a threatening pose, but the effect was ruined by the long, stiff tongue lolling from the side of its mouth.

According to her sources, Roland was an excellent hunter. Maybe so, but he was a lousy taxidermist.

Roland frowned. "I know that costume. Didn't the Red Hood Riders used to wear that helm and cape?"

"We still do."

He belched. "We?"

A lumbering figure stepped out of the shadows in the corner, holding a dead raccoon with a lopsided snarl and no tail.

Roland jumped to his feet. "What in the name of Rumplestiltskin's wrinkled balls is that?"

"That's Goldie," Stepmama said.

Goldie grunted, which was about as talkative as she got most days. She was a bear of a woman. Stepmama had once seen her smash a full keg over the head of a handsy barman. Her garb was similar to Stepmama's, but her weapons of choice were the iron chains she wore around her hips and shoulders. The gold-colored padlocks made excellent bludgeons.

Roland reached for Stepmama. Goldie rammed the raccoon's twisted jaws into Roland's face. He brought his hands up to block the dead animal, and Goldie kicked him in the chest. He slammed into the wall and slid down onto a pile of old furs.

"The princess," Stepmama repeated.

"You're really Red Hoods?"

Stepmama simply waited. She had found that silence often worked better than threats.

"I didn't—it was the queen. She ordered me to—"

"Yes, we know." She flicked open her fan and waved it lazily in front of her face, trying to hide her turmoil. If she had gotten word just a few days earlier, they might have saved the girl. As it was, they could at least bring her back for a proper burial . . . where everyone could see what the queen had done. She would deny it, of course, but Roland's testimony should—

"I didn't kill her."

She snapped the fan shut. "You brought her heart back as proof."

"It wasn't hers." He closed his eyes. "I was told to kill her, but she was so beautiful. Skin as white as snow. Lips as red as blood . . ."

"She's fourteen years old!" Stepmama smacked the side of his head with the closed fan. The outer slats were hammered steel, giving it enough weight and strength to make Roland cry out and clutch his head.

"I didn't do nothing," he squeaked. "I killed a boar. Brought its heart back to the queen. She didn't know."

"She's clever. Are you sure?"

Roland paled.

"Let's try this again," said Stepmama. "We can either tie you up and leave you here for the queen, or else you can tell me *exactly* where to find the princess, and we'll let you start running."

Stepmama's girls reacted as she had expected when they learned the princess was alive. Ash looked ready to ride off with her glass sword drawn, mowing down anyone and anything that got between the Red Hoods and the princess. She claimed to have inherited the enchanted blade from the ghost of her mother, and she was ridiculously enthusiastic about using it. Rumor had it she'd gotten glass slippers as well, but they were rather impractical for riding. Or anything else, for that matter.

Legs clapped her hands and grinned. She was the youngest of the four Red Hoods. Her black skin was unmarked, save for a single tattoo of a flounder on the back of her neck. The cut of her scanty armor—steel scale mail instead of the leather the others preferred—left most of it exposed. Legs had never really taken to clothes. She rarely left her horse, Triton, and when she did she walked with a limp, courtesy of the spell that had turned her human.

Regret sank its roots into Stepmama's thoughts. Once, close to a hundred women had worn the red cape and helm. When they rode, the earth itself quaked. As did anyone who crossed them. But that was years ago, before the war with the Wolves had wiped out both gangs. It had taken years for Stepmama to recover enough to begin to rebuild the Red Hoods.

She stomped those memories into the ground like weeds. "She's staying in the guild house of the Dwarf Miners, near the docks. We can . . . Goldie, did you steal that man's weasel?"

Goldie was using a leather tie to secure the animal to the shoulder strap of her armor. The weasel's body curved like an S, and the glass eyes were several sizes too big, giving it a permanently shocked expression. "Bear was too big. Porridge is just right."

"You named it Porridge?" Stepmama rubbed her forehead.

"I'll knit him a little helmet and cape, later."

"What about Roland?" asked Legs. "We should cut open his belly, fill it with stones, sew him back up, and then throw him into the river to drown."

Legs had a rather gruesome sense of justice.

Stepmama shook her head. "He didn't kill the girl, and he told us what we needed to know."

"But—"

"Enough." Stepmama pulled herself into the saddle of her courser, a silver dappled mare named Nana. She and Stepmama had been riding together for seven years now.

Their horses were all well cared for, thanks in no small part to Ash. She had grown up talking to the mice and birds, and claimed to be able to understand them. To this day, Legs insisted Ash should have commanded the birds to peck out the eyes of her stepsisters for the way they had treated her.

It was mid-afternoon when they reached the Miners' guild house, nestled behind a tavern within spitting distance of the sea. Chicken wire covered the windows. The doors were thick oak with a narrow, sliding panel at eye level. There was no sign, just a dwarven axe painted above the door.

Stepmama dismounted and hammered the butt of her fan against the door until the panel slid open. "Tell Doc that Stepmama of the Red Hood Riders wants to talk to him."

Close-set brown eyes narrowed. "The Red Hoods are gone. Are you city guard?"

Stepmama sighed and stepped to one side, letting him get a better look at Goldie, Ash, and Legs. "Do we *look* like the guard?"

The door opened a moment later. Stepmama strode into the guild house like she owned it. She'd been in seedier buildings in her day, but rarely had she seen a gang's guild house so *clean*. The air smelled of pipe smoke, but also fresh fish and lemon. The wooden floors were swept, the walls scrubbed.

The members of the Dwarf Miner gang were neither. They took the name from their founder, an undersized silver miner who had turned to the sea, where he decided smuggling was a safer and more lucrative occupation than crawling through unstable tunnels for twelve hours a day. Safer, that was, until the day he fell overboard and got himself eaten by a whale.

Two men played dice at a nearby table. A trio hunched over their cards at another. Weaving between them, a tray of food in her hand, was the princess.

Snow White was the palest child Stepmama had ever seen. Either the girl had never set foot in the sunlight, or else she suffered from albinism, but how many albinos had hair as black as Stepmama's leathers?

The telltale sound of clinking steel scales made Stepmama sigh. "Leave it on, Legs."

The ex-mermaid groaned. "But we're inside. You said—"

"I said you could make yourself comfortable at home. *Your* home. Not other people's." She offered an apologetic shrug to the Miners. "She's still learning surface customs."

None of the men appeared the slightest bit offended. Disappointed, maybe, but not offended. "How long until Doc returns?" asked Stepmama.

A heavyset man in a sleeveless shirt and leather vest leaned back from the dice table. His beard was a braided brown rope as thick as her arm. "An hour. Maybe two." He wagged eyebrows like overgrown shrubberies. "Any of you girls want to play a game to kill the time?"

Stepmama stepped toward the card table. "Bring me a beer and deal me in."

By the time Doc arrived, Stepmama had taken them for thirty gold, a pearl-handled dagger, and a sack full of Magic Beans, a mild hallucinogen that would have you hearing harps and chasing giants. Legs was enjoying her third helping of fish, with only the occasional complaint about how much better they tasted raw. Goldie was arm-wrestling one of the Miners while Ash cheered her on.

Doc walked straight up to Stepmama and clasped her wrist. She clapped him on the shoulder. "You seem to have done well for yourself."

"Well enough." Doc was an old rider, bowlegged from his time in the saddle, with a long, gray beard and a bare scalp baked brown by the sun. His leather vest struggled to cover his ample gut, but beneath the belly, the man was as meaty as a side of beef. Smelled like one, too. "How much have you won from them so far?"

"Another few minutes, and I'd have this one's trousers."

Doc chuckled and shook his head. "Resurrecting the Red Hoods? You should have gone home, Hase-Hime."

It had been years since anyone used her given name. "It's Stepmama now, and you know better. Would you give up life with the Dwarf Miners? Turn your back on freedom and independence?"

"Freedom's one thing. Risking your hide to rescue a few royal brats is another. Especially in this kingdom."

"You know why we're here," said Stepmama. "How would you like this to go down?"

Ash grinned and moved her hand toward her sword. Goldie stood and stretched. Throughout the guild house, the Miners rose from their chairs and clenched their fists.

"No need for that. Join me for dinner and we'll work out fair terms for the girl." Doc didn't wait for an answer. "Hey, Smiley! Get your hairy arse down to the docks and pick up some fresh scallops."

He scrawled a quick note on a scrap of paper and handed it to one of the Miners. "Smiley's a good scrapper," Doc explained, "but he's got a lousy memory. Too many blows to the head. I once sent him to rough up a sailor who owed us money. He came back with a barrel of pickles and a used bridal gown." He jerked his chin at Legs. "Who's the kid?"

"She's the one who will make it worth your while to give us the princess," said Stepmama. "She has connections under the sea."

"I've heard of her." Doc circled Legs. "Gave it all up for the love of a prince, right? Then once she was transformed and he had what he wanted, he decided he preferred turf to surf."

"Shut your beard hole," Ash snapped.

Stepmama sliced a hand through the air, and Ash fell silent. "What would it be worth to you if the barnacles took a particular liking to your competitors' ships?"

"Tempting," said Doc. "But the boys have gotten rather fond of the young princess."

"You're wasting time," said Ash. "They treat her like a servant, forcing her to cook and clean and who knows what else." Given Ash's history with her stepmother and stepsisters, it was no surprise she'd take this personally. "You know what these men will do to her. How they'll use her. We've all seen it before."

"Hey," said a Miner. "Not all men—"

Ash backfisted him in the nose and continued like he hadn't spoken. "The girl is not a thing to be bargained for."

The bloody-nosed Miner started forward. Ash reached for her sword.

"*Oyamenasai!*" None of Stepmama's girls were fluent in her native tongue. They didn't have to be. The tone translated perfectly.

Drawing steel—or glass, in this case—in another gang's guild house meant war. A brawl was probably inevitable, but if Ash and the Miner could work it out without killing each other—

"Knock it off!" Doc glared at his Miner until the man backed down. "Sorry about that. Grouchy's always been a bit of an ass."

Stepmama frowned. The Miners were known for never walking away from a fight.

"I'm a businessman now," said Doc, as if reading her thoughts. "There's no profit in letting your girl and my man bust each other up. Have a seat. The princess makes a dish with limes and scallops that's to die for. Takes a while to prepare, but it's worth it."

Tension choked the air like smoke. Goldie looked bored, which meant she was about ten seconds away from punching someone. Or setting something on fire. You never really knew with her. Ash was pacing, fists clenched.

The Miners looked as angry at Doc as they did with Ash. They didn't understand why he had interfered either. Stepmama swore silently as the pieces fell into place. "You're stalling."

Doc gave her a too-broad smile. "What are you—"

"That note you gave Smiley. That wasn't a list. You told him to send word to the queen." She flicked four fingers downward, and the other Red Hoods moved into formation.

"Why would he wait until now to tell the queen about the princess?" asked Legs.

"The queen would have paid to get Snow White back." Weariness and disappointment filled her words. "She'll pay more for me."

"Like I said, I'm a businessman," said Doc.

"That's a shame. You used to be a man."

She didn't bother going for the crotch kick. Doc was experienced enough to anticipate that. He shifted his hips to protect his groin the instant she drew back her foot. So she slammed the reinforced toe of her boot into his left shin. He cursed in pain, and *then* she rammed her knee into his stalk and beans.

A golden padlock snapped out to strike another Miner in the forehead. Legs took a punch on the jaw, blocked the follow up, and threw herself bodily onto her attacker.

A fist struck the side of Stepmama's head. She stumbled sideways, arms raised to ward off the follow-up. Nobody had drawn blades yet. She prayed everyone would continue to show restraint, at least long enough to get Snow and the Red Hoods out.

A table flew through the air. That would be Goldie or one of the Miners.

Doc and another of his boys started toward Stepmama. "You knew the risks of coming into *her* kingdom," he said. "Especially wearing those colors. That's a death wish."

So was fighting against these odds. Stepmama ducked another punch, twisted to take a kick on the armor of her hip instead of the gut, and searched for Ash.

There was a loud *clunk*. Doc stiffened, blinked at Stepmama, and toppled forward. The closest Miners paused to see what had happened. Snow White stood behind him, a greasy skillet gripped in both hands. "I'd like to go with you, please," she said timidly.

"Ash!" Stepmama's shout sliced through the chaos. "Call Pumpkin."

Ash wiped her bloody lip on her sleeve and nodded. Moments later, the door smashed inward, and Ash's mare trotted into the guild house.

Doc on the floor and a horse on their side made for much better odds. Stepmama used the confusion to grab Snow and regroup with her girls. "Your boss ratted us out to the queen," she said, hoping to forestall another round. She scowled at Doc's unconscious form. "When he comes to, tell him we took the girl in payment, and we're square."

"Not quite." Ash grinned and whispered under her breath. In response, Pumpkin stepped into the middle of the guild house and proceeded to relieve herself.

Some things never changed, and Ash's warped and often gross sense of humor was one of them.

"Why would the queen want to get her hands on you?" Ash demanded as they rode toward the edge of town. The other girls looked equally upset. Even Snow, who was riding double behind Ash.

Stepmama sighed. They looked so strange with their telltale red hidden away, and a part of her hated having to hide their colors. "Because she used to ride with the Wolves. She and her man were part of the ambush that killed Grandma."

Grandma had founded the Red Hoods to rescue young women and raise hell, not necessarily in that order. But their rivalry with the Wolves had destroyed both gangs.

"That's why you wanted to save me?" asked Snow. "To pay her back?"

"No," Stepmama said firmly. "Pissing off the queen was just the shine on the apple."

"Ugh. Please don't talk to me about applies." Snow grimaced. "If not to slight my mother, why risk your life to rescue a stranger?"

Stepmama cursed at the sight of mounted guards at the end of the street. She urged Nana through an alley that led toward the shipping warehouses. "A long time ago, Grandma rescued me. She gave me the chance to have my own life. But I wasn't there to save hers. That means the only way for me to pay her back is to pay it forward."

Ash scowled. "Why didn't you tell us about the queen?"

"Because you'd run off like a damn fool to attack her in her own castle, and like as not get killed for your trouble," Stepmama snapped.

Ash opened her mouth to respond, paused, and then said, "I suppose that's true enough."

"It was a nice thought," Legs said as another guard cut across the alley ahead of them. "Though I'd have preferred the suicidal attack on the castle to being hunted and killed like crabs in the sand."

Stepmama took a long, slow breath. "This is personal between me and the queen. I'll lead her men away while you take Snow—"

"Nope."

Stepmama turned to Ash. "Are you challenging me?"

"No," said Goldie, before Ash could answer. "We're helping you. The thing about rescuing someone is it can be hard to stop. We don't need to be rescued anymore. Grandma gave you the chance to choose your own life. You did that for us. You don't get to take that choice away now."

It was the most she'd ever heard Goldie say, and Stepmama found herself without an answer.

"After Roland's failure, my mother will have come along to make sure there are no further mistakes," said Snow. "She won't risk herself, though. She'll probably be waiting with her guards outside of town."

"Easier than taking on an entire castle," said Ash.

Legs gave an exaggerated nod. She still had trouble with that gesture. "I say we take her prisoner, lock her feet in shoes of red-hot iron, and force her to dance until she dies."

Snow stared at the former mermaid. "What is *wrong* with you?"

"All right." Stepmama reached down to pull her cape and helm from her saddlebag. If they were going to do this, she'd do it properly dressed, by God. "Let's not keep the queen waiting."

Despite her misgivings, Stepmama found herself enjoying the chase. She and Nana hadn't galloped together like this in a long time. Hooves thundered against the cobblestones, and Stepmama's cape flapped behind her.

"They're herding us like sheep," said Snow, as a group of guards moved to cut them off.

Stepmama guided Nana with her legs.

"Not that lane!" shouted Ash. "It's too narrow. Good place for an ambush."

"I wasn't going for the lane." Stepmama urged Nana into the open doorway of the Golden Goose Tavern. There weren't too many patrons this early in the evening, and she managed to squeeze past the bar, through the kitchen, and out the back door. Goldie had a bit of trouble following, but that was mostly because she stopped to snatch a pastry from the kitchen.

Nana was getting winded. She couldn't keep this up much longer, but they were so close to the edge of town, and once they reached the fields and forest beyond, they could—

"Oh, whaleshit," said Legs. At least ten guards armed with crossbows blocked the road ahead.

"Stick to the plan," said Stepmama.

Legs and Triton galloped ahead, charging the massed guards. They raised their weapons, but before they could shoot, she began to bellow a chantey about a pirate captain with a crooked mast. Not the song Stepmama would have chosen, but it didn't matter. The song of a mermaid had lured many a ship to its doom. It stunned the guards long enough for Legs to break through their line, and then they were wheeling around to chase after her, their orders forgotten.

All but two. In any group of men, there were bound to be a few who weren't interested in the charms of a maiden. Ash shouted to those guards' horses, who promptly bucked their riders to the ground.

They raced past to reach the open farms beyond the edge of town. From here, they might be able to simply outrun the queen and her men. How many times had Stepmama and the Red Hoods escaped the law in her youth?

"I know what you're thinking," said Ash. "But Nana's tired, Snow and I are riding double, and Legs is off who knows where. Also, it's been a long day, and I *really* want to stab someone."

Stepmama nodded. "We finish this."

They found the queen a half-mile up the road, surrounded by roughly a dozen guardsmen. Ash cupped her hands to her mouth and shouted. Birds swooped from the trees in response to peck, scratch, and of course, to poop. Ash had probably been quite explicit about that last bit. Mice, chipmunks, and other rodents scurried out of the weeds to bite exposed ankles and crawl up inviting pant legs.

One guard managed to raise his crossbow. Goldie ripped the stuffed weasel from her shoulder and hurled it into his face. It wasn't much of a missile, but the sight of the unnaturally gaping weasel flying as if to bite off his nose made him cry out and raise his arms.

Stepmama drew her sword, a short, single-edged blade. Nana knocked the struggling guards aside, and Stepmama jumped to the ground to yank open the door of the ornately decorated carriage.

The interior was empty. Stepmama whirled, but it was too late. A

second group of guards emerged from the woods, crossbows raised
and ready. Goldie spun toward the closest, but a bolt punched through
her shoulder, and her chain clinked to the ground.

"If they resist, shoot them, and then shoot their horses." The queen
emerged from the shadows. She patted the hand mirror hanging from
her belt and gave Stepmama a mocking smile. "Mirror, mirror, at my
side. Show me where the Red Hoods ride. You really thought you could
hide your plans from me?"

"Mirror, mirror, made of glass," said Ash. "Shove that thing right up
your—"

Goldie punched her in the shoulder before she could finish. Good
to know her uninjured arm still worked.

The queen was softer than Stepmama remembered. Gone were the
worn, fur-trimmed leathers and metal rivets, replaced by velvet and
silk. Her skin was almost as pale as her daughter's. It was hard to
imagine this pampered royal helping to kill Grandma all those years
ago.

Stepmama dropped her sword.

"The knives too."

She removed both daggers and nodded for the other Red Hoods
to do the same. "What will you do to my girls?"

"Well, they're not true Red Hood Riders, are they? Just children
playing dress-up. But they *did* kidnap my daughter. I could order them
executed, but I may just lock them away until they're too old and
withered to present a threat."

She drew a short sword and walked closer. "You, on the other hand
. . . I remember you."

"Mother, stop!" cried Snow.

Stepmama opened her fan and used it to cool her face. "Is it true
what happened to your man? They say he died breaking into a house.
That he tried to sneak down the chimney and ended up falling into a
pot of boiling water. What an embarrassing death for the leader of the
mutts."

The queen snarled and lunged. Stepmama snapped her fan shut
and stepped into the attack. She jabbed the butt of the fan into the
queen's wrist, then struck the bridge of her nose. As the queen
stumbled backward, Stepmama twisted the sword from her hand and
brought the blade around to press against her throat.

"I wasn't always a Red Hood." Stepmama pulled the blade just enough to start a trickle of blood down the queen's neck. The guards lowered their weapons. "I used to ride with another gang back home. In your language, the name translates to 'Fangirls.'"

"And then what happened?" Legs demanded. She was furious about having missed the excitement.

It was Snow who answered. "Stepmama told me it was my right to decide my mother's fate."

"You should have shoved her into an oven and let her burn," said Legs. "No, wait. Throw her into a tub full of vipers and toads and spiders."

Snow stared.

"Don't worry," said Goldie, who was adjusting the stuffed weasel on her shoulder. Porridge was slightly worse for wear from being used as a weapon. "She's an odd one, but you get used to her."

"Yes." Snow managed a weak smile. "Well, I decided she should be banished. We sent her away in a cargo crate on one of the Dwarf Miners' smuggling ships."

"This was fun." Ash stretched her arms. "I just wish you would have let us go a few rounds with those guards."

"They were only doing their jobs. Besides, what would father say if I let a gang of outlaw riders beat up his men?"

"Oh, I wanted some face-punching time with him, too," said Ash. "How could he let your mother do that to you?"

"He didn't know. And he's been tired and weak for a long time. But without mother and her poisons around, he should recover." Snow grabbed the hand mirror from her belt and studied her reflection. She pushed the thin, red headband higher on her brow. For now, she was only a prospective member of the Red Hoods, but Stepmama had no doubt she would soon earn her helm and cape.

Stepmama looked over her girls. They were still a far cry from the Red Hoods of old, but she imagined Grandma would have given them her blessing.

"Enough chatter. There's a sleeping princess two kingdoms over who was imprisoned behind a hedge of thorns."

"Oh, good." Ash beamed. "I love jailbreaks.

Stepmama squeezed Nana into a gallop. "Let's ride."

Smackdown at Walmart

by Elizabeth A. Vaughan

I decided to take my twelve Sacred Ancient Chinese Warrior-Virgins to Walmart.

Yes, I am aware of the irony.

But how the hell else was I going to get them clothes? They couldn't run around in those colorful silk gowns of theirs, cut tight enough to show every breath, but slit high enough on the sides to show their . . . assets. Not to mention the lack of underwear.

"Well, actually, they could."

That would be Doctor McDougall, who'd patched me up in the ER after I was attacked by ninja rats, and then blew my mundane little world to pieces when he confirmed that magic existed, and that I wasn't losing my mind. McDougall was watching me try to stuff all twelve of the girls into my recently repaired minivan.

Wan agreed with McDougall. "They present an esthetically pleasing appearance in their grace, prowess, and physical form. The clothing is practical and lovely, and allows them the freedom to move when they fight. I do not understand your concerns."

That would be Wan, short for Wan Sui Ye, the talking Chinese mouse that caused me to think I was losing my mind in the first place. His name means "Lord of Ten Thousand Years," a title given only to the Emperor of China.

He hasn't explained his name.

I've not inquired further.

The girls scrambled into the van, squeezing their skinny butts into the seats and giggling amongst themselves, just like normal girls do. It was hard to gauge their ages, but all I really needed to know was "young and nubile."

I fixed Wan with my patented "middle-aged-pre-menopausal-woman" stare. "They are getting proper clothing, and what would you know about the esthetics of human beauty?"

Wan blinked at me from his perch on my shoulder, clearly uncertain of my temper. "It will be as you say," he said. "You are, after all, the Wise One, Bearer of the Scale, chosen of the Emperor Dragon, Lord of the Dragon Kings, Ruler of the Weather and the Waters of the World."

As one, the twelve Sacred Ancient Chinese Warrior-Virgins all paused, placed their palms together, and bowed their heads to me.

I took a deep breath, still uncomfortable that they were sworn to my protection, since I'd been the Wise One for roughly forty-eight hours. Take a piece of advice, for what it's worth. If someone shows you an ancient piece of jewelry, and if that said someone is a talking mouse, and if said jewelry was hidden in the hilt of his magic sword, *don't* reach out and touch it.

Just sayin'.

Dr. McDougall raised one eyebrow at me. "This isn't necessary, Kate. Shop online. It can wait a few days."

"We are going shopping," I said with as much dignity as I could, and closed the sliding door. "You are not helping," I told McDougall as I closed the passenger door and headed to the driver's side. I could hear my two white Westies barking inside the house; no way was I taking them on this little trip.

"This isn't smart," McDougall observed, that one damned handsome eyebrow still arching my way as he followed me around the van. "Your enemies are out there, including—"

"Come with us." I attempted to arch my eyebrow back at him, and failed utterly at my flirtation attempt. It had been far too long, and I just wasn't too sure where I stood with him.

"I would," he said calmly, standing there, his arms crossed, looking all sexy and dignified. "But there is no room in the van. And my shift starts in an hour."

"Coward," I threw out as I settled into my seat. "A powerful sorcerer like yourself, afraid of a tiny lingerie department."

"I share his concerns," Wan said from his perch on my shoulder. He had braced himself by grabbing the hood tie of my windbreaker, his sword strapped to his back. "And his embarrassment."

"Honestly." I gave them both an exasperated look. "I'm going shopping at midnight at Walmart with twelve Sacred Warrior-Virgins and a talking mouse. What could possibly go wrong?"

Walmart was twenty minutes from my house, and the car was utterly silent. The girls all stared wide-eyed out the windows. A few had pinched looks around the eyes, and it hit me that I was an idiot. They'd probably never been in a car before, and here I was pelting down Glendale at forty-five miles an hour.

I cleared my throat and looked at them in the rear-view mirror. All young, with dark eyes and black hair, as if stamped out by a cookie-cutter, or computer-generated *anime*. "So, you all know my name," I said, "but I don't know yours."

They all stared at me a bit blankly, then looked at one another as if seeking permission. One in the far back blurted out something in Chinese, and then looked startled at her own audacity.

"Okay, good. But what does that mean," I asked. "In English."

"Clouds on Moon." The girl sat up straighter. "I am Clouds on Moon."

With that the floodgates opened, and each introduced herself carefully in turn, saying their names in Chinese, then translating. I gave up on the Chinese fairly quickly, and struggled to place faces with names for the future.

"Flying Swallow."

"Morning Orchid."

And so on. There were lots of flowers, including four blossoms: Lotus, Cherry, Almond, and Peach. Glorious Phoenix, who looked like she was about to die of terminal shyness as she mumbled her name. Sun on Snow, Ocean Pearl, Willow on Bank, they continued on in a stream of until—

"Say again?" I asked, as I pulled into the parking lot. "I didn't quite catch—"

"Filially Pious and Incorruptible." The girl spoke defiantly, arms folded across her chest.

I blinked.

"A fine and noble name," Wan said from my shoulder.

"Ah," I said cleverly, and concentrated on finding a parking space.

Which wasn't hard. The place was deserted, with heavy wire shopping carts scattered about like so many lost sheep. I didn't know which entrance was closest to the clothing section, so I picked one and stopped the car in the nearest space to it.

"You can look, but don't touch," I said, gathering my purse. Wan crawled under my collar, where he usually hid when people were about. "And stay with me. Don't wander off."

I was worried about the effect the girls would have on Walmart.

I should have been more worried about the effect Walmart would have on the girls.

There was no greeter in sight, not a surprise considering the hour. I grabbed a cart and hurried them past huge posters announcing the release of the new video game, *Unnatural Disasters*, with a female heroine in metal armor, aiming a huge laser rifle in our direction. I winced at the picture, imagining the chafing that little fantasy piece would involve.

It had taken me six months to kick EVE and WOW to the curb—no way was I buying another addiction. I averted my eyes with the resolution of a reformed sinner. "This way," I said, leading them down the widest aisle.

They clustered next to me like chicks trying to get under my wings. The giggling was gone; now there was just wide-eyed, serious contemplation of their surroundings. They stared at the posters and lights, and bumped into the bargain bins lining the aisle. My Warrior-Virgins suddenly looked uncomfortable, uncertain, and out-of-place.

Clothes first, I thought, heading to the racks of jeans. Pray all the gods they had enough of the same size. It would help if there was a—

"Can I help you?" The rarest of all things appeared from between the racks: an actual Walmart sales associate.

"Crap," I jumped, startled out of my wits by the elderly black woman wearing the traditional blue vest and the nametag that stated she was *Edna*. She stood there, waiting patiently as I caught my breath. Then I remembered what Wan had said to the Wise One: "What is needed will be provided." The trick, of course, was to know the difference between needs and desires.

Apparently, Heaven saw my need.

"These ladies need clothes," I said with a smile before turning to my wards, who were all clustered behind me with looks of stunned astonishment on their faces. Surprised at their reactions, I paused. "What's wrong?"

"She's . . . h-her skin . . ." Cloud stuttered.

"She's black-skinned," one of the girls hissed.

Edna drew in a sharp breath.

They were staring at her like she was a thing, less than human. Mortified, shamed, I lashed out. "Oh my God—you will apologize this instant!" I snapped. "Were all of you raised in a barn?"

Instantly all the girls fell to their knees and kowtowed, their arms outstretched towards us. "No, Wise One," came Glorious Phoenix's voice, muffled by the floor. "We were raised in the Monastery of the Distant Clouds, beyond the influences and corruption of the modern world."

Edna gave me the eye. "For real?"

I smiled weakly. "Exchange students."

"Got your work cut out for you there, that's for sure." She shook her head. "Get 'em up off the floor, and let's get 'em dressed."

We needed two carts for the jeans and tees, enough so that each girl had one to wear and a spare. Glorious Phoenix found one shirt that said *Princess* in sparkling rhinestones, much to my horror.

Edna was truly a miracle, as far as I was concerned. She dealt with the girls kindly, ignored their stares, and did not take offense at their sideways glances and whispers. She even walked with us when we headed toward lingerie, and got me through the worst of that with minimal fuss.

She took a moment to slide up next to me when the girls got distracted. They'd found the D-cup bras, and were holding them up to their own chests and giggling like mad.

"You had the talk with these girls?" Edna asked, pretending to re-arrange the panties display.

"Talk?" I asked absently as I counted out pairs of socks. All white, damn it, I was not spending the rest of my life trying to match socks.

"You know," she kept her voice low. "No glove, no love."

My heart stopped as it hit me. Oh dear God. *Virgins.*

I took the carts and the girls to the pharmacy area, wherein I initiated a very awkward conversation about feminine hygiene products and protection.

Twelve faces flared bright red, and from nowhere twelve pastel-flowered fans were produced to hide behind.

So I threw everything in the cart I thought they'd need, and a couple boxes of condoms. Then we detoured to the fresh fruit section and bought a huge bunch of green bananas.

Demonstration purposes, you understand.

And a large bag of dark chocolate-coated pretzels with kosher sea salt, because I was really not looking forward to the rest of the evening. Virgins, for the love of God.

What the hell—didn't Heaven think sex education was a *need*? The next time that all-powerful, all-knowing Dragon appeared before me, he and I were going to have words.

We got to the checkout. Heaven apparently decided I needed a pimply-faced young man to ring up our purchases. He blushed while scanning the bras and panties, trying not to actually touch them, mind. In between exchanging shy glances with all of the girls.

The girls blushed too, giggling and fluttering their fans and not helping at all, except to get in my way.

I really tried very hard not to roll my eyes at the lot of them.

I got everything unloaded from the carts, praying that the kid would not topple over at the sight of the condoms. Honestly, he did fairly well until he saw the bananas. He couldn't meet my eyes, his face beet red as I swiped my card and held my breath.

"Th-th-that's $6.25," he stammered, and then handed me the receipt.

Yup, that would be Heaven again. Needs, not wants. I made the girls pick up the bags and carry them, all but the bag with the pretzels. The doors slid open as we walked out and I glanced at the receipt. I hadn't been charged for anything except the pretzels.

Apparently Heaven didn't think chocolate was a need.

Nuts to Heaven. Digging through the bag, I brought forth the precious treasure. I needed one for the road.

Surrounded by the girls, loaded down with bags, I headed out into the dark and forlorn parking lot. Storm clouds had gathered; it looked like it was about to rain. I barely gave them a glance as I started handing out the goodies to the girls as we walked. I wasn't sure about the wisdom of introducing them to chocolate and high fructose corn syrup all in one go, but they had to adjust to the real world sometime.

My mini-van sat all alone in the parking lot, somehow looking sad and neglected. I took a pretzel for myself, tucked the candy away in the shopping bag, and started digging for my keys with my free hand.

The warm lump under my collar wiggled. I took a bite, letting the bitter chocolate and salt melt on my tongue as I snapped off a piece for Wan. "It's clear," I said, holding the tidbit up for him. "You'll like—"

"Greetings, fat one," snarled a familiar voice.

The *possum*.

For one long frozen moment, nothing moved. I took in the sight of my nemesis, the scabby old possum with a knobby walking stick, standing on top of my van, his tail lashing back and forth. Surrounding the van was a host of human-sized ninja rats, their faces masked, wearing the traditional black clothing and holding swords.

The small piece of pretzel dropped from my fingers and fell, a long slow tumble to the pavement. Drums started beating, or maybe that was my own frantic heart pounding in my ears.

With a tiny battle-cry, Wan leaped from my shoulder, his sword out and gleaming. At the top of his arc, there was a puff of dust, and Wan stood facing our foes, six feet tall, his own tail lashing back and forth in anger. He looked back over his shoulder at us, the glare of battle-rage in his eyes. "Protect her," he commanded, and turned back before I could utter a word.

With that, time slammed on the gas and everything exploded into action. In an instant, the girls took dramatic defensive positions, their fans acquiring razor edges, their silk gowns whipping about in the growing wind.

Unfortunately, the fans were too much for the shopping bags. The plastic tore open, and for a moment, delicate little panties of various colors floated away on the breeze.

The ninja rats' beady little eyes tracked their flight.

Sword high, Wan charged the enemy. I was torn between sheer breathlessness at his heroism and the absolute stupidity of charging a mass of ninja rats.

"Help him," I shouted.

The girls glanced at me, I swear in unison, gave sharp nods of their heads, and followed Wan in a flurry of silk gowns and steel-edged fans.

The two groups clashed. I stood, stunned, unable to move, clutching my shopping bags as if they would protect me somehow. It was all happening too fast and I watched in terror and fascination.

Weapons sparked off each other, and the fantastical dance began. Swirling pastels against the black and silent ninjas, with their masked faces and pale pink tails. The girls' faces were lovely in their ferocity, eyes gleaming, black hair swirling about them. It was like a ballet, like an awesome scene in a—

A ninja rat swung his sword in a high arc. Blood spurted from Lotus Blossom's arm.

I sucked in a breath as the reality of what was happening hit me.

"Back!" Filially Pious was still at my side. "Back to the store," she demanded. She interposed herself between them and me, pushing me back even as she faced them, two curved swords in her hands.

I pressed my hand to my chest, feeling the necklace, sharp and cold under my clothes. The girls . . . *my* girls . . . they needed . . . protection.

The battle raged on, the ninja rats' eyes gleaming with hate.

The poster flashed before my eyes, *Unnatural Disasters*, and my hand flung out of its own accord, pointing to the nearest shopping cart. I wasn't sure . . . And then I was, as the necklace warmed against my skin.

"Armor!" I cried and the wires of the shopping cart writhed and dissolved into a swirling mass that enveloped Filially Pious. Her dress disappeared, and instead she was encased in the wires, bare skin showing through in ways never thought of by any fantasy artist that I'd ever seen.

She started, blinking, then moved her arms smoothly, weaving her swords before her. With a fierce grin of satisfaction, she ran forward, charging the rats.

"More!" I screamed, and all around the parking lot carts moved and unraveled, seeking out the Warrior-Virgins as they fought. Catching on, each girl leaped for a mass of metal, swirling in mid-air to land lightly on her feet, weapons ready, armor gleaming.

The ninja rats paused, their little beady eyes reflecting fear.

Lightning arced across the sky.

The girls attacked.

The possum still stood on the roof of my van. "The fat one!" it called out. "Seize the fat one! She has—"

Wan leaped atop my van, all six feet of enraged mouse, facing the one-foot-tall possum. "Now, you pay," he growled. "Pay for your threats to my Kate, pay for—"

"No monologues!" I shouted, but it was too late. Ninja rats swarmed up the sides and threw themselves at Wan. One picked up the possum so it was riding his shoulder. The possum's mouth stretched into a smile of jagged teeth as they lashed out at Wan.

"Wan!" I screamed, looking around for something, anything—

There were no more carts. How could there be no more carts? Maybe a cart corral? That—

A scream. Wan was down, a sword to his throat. I didn't have—

A crash of thunder. Lightning. I'd summon lightning.

How hard could it be?

In desperation, still clutching my purse, I raised the hand with the plastic shopping bags still around my wrist. I should've cried out something dramatic, but honestly I just gave a choked cry of fear, and lashed out at the ninja rat on top of Wan.

Electricity filled the night, and the hair on my skin rose in response. There was a sharp smell of ozone, a flash of heat, a loud crackle—

The smell of fried rat hung heavy in the air.

The possum, the ninja rats, Wan—all stared at me like a woman who'd lost her mind.

Oh dear. Metal armor. Swords. I hadn't thought—

The power was building within me, crackling on my skin as my hair rose around my head. I sucked in a breath, knowing somehow that if I didn't discharge it, it would turn on me and burn me to a—

I focused my rage on the possum, and screamed.

The crackles in the air was enough warning. The possum leaped away, landing on another ninja's shoulder. Everyone else on top of the van flung themselves off as the lightning bolt plunged down out of the sky, blinding in its intensity. The image burned into my eyes, leaving me blind.

I swayed, suddenly drained and weak-kneed, as if I'd tried to take a couple flights of stairs.

Okay, maybe just one.

The possum laughed harshly.

My eyes cleared to see my poor mini-van a smoldering wreck, its tires melted and smoking. The girls, each still encased in their shopping-cart armor, were lined up in a defensive crouch before me. Wan was also there, his sword at the ready.

"She does not know!" the possum shrieked as he danced on the ninja rat's shoulder. "Untrained, unknowing, and weakened. *Get her!*"

The ninja rats attacked again, fierce in their determination to cut through the line. Wan cast a desperate glance at me before he met their charge. It was only a matter of time before they did an end-run or flanked the line and got to me. I took a shaky step back, turning for the warm, welcome lights of the store.

A limo pulled up behind me, its back door swinging wide. McDougall was inside, secure within its golden light, his hand extended to me. "Kate," he said, his eyes warm and bright. "Come to me."

The sight was a relief, a vision of safety and shelter. I stumbled forward with my purse and bags, tears forming in my eyes.

"Kate, Kate!" Wan screamed as I reached the limo. *"THAT'S NOT MCDOUGALL!"*

The bony, skeletal hand grabbed my wrist and yanked me inside.

I couldn't breathe; terror closed my throat. The Chinese vampire tumbled me to the floor and straddled me, its mummified face frozen in an eternal grin revealing teeth blackened with age. One hand closed on my throat; the other gestured to the limo door.

He sure as hell wasn't sparkling.

I caught a glimpse of Wan charging toward us as the limo door whipped shut.

Wan slammed into the side. I heard his muffled cries and saw his sword skittering across the glass as he tried desperately to shatter the window.

The vampire leaned in to me, pressing down on my chest with his weight. My vision went gray as his foul breath wafted over me.

"I have so looked forward to this," he whispered as his eyes started to glow.

I closed my eyes and struggled, but my one hand was caught in the shopping bags and it was pointless. The damn monster was bigger, stronger, and more powerful. As I fought to breathe, fought desperately to get free, it occurred to me that in all the stories, movies, and TV series I've ever watched, ever tried to write, the wise one, the old master, usually takes it on the chin. And since I wasn't even close to that, what chance did I have?

The vampire laughed, as if on cue. "Your powers are weak, old woman."

Really? Quoting Vader? I had a hard time believing this—thing— had ever watched *Star Wars*. I opened my mouth to make some snarky reply, but there was no air. Terror ripped through me as I gasped desperately. God, I didn't want to come back more powerful than anyone could possibly imagine, thank you very much.

A knife flashed before my dimming eyes, and I felt the cold edge as the vampire cut through my clothes. It froze as its eyes focused on my chest, but I knew damn well it wasn't lusting after my heaving bosom. Oh, no.

It was staring at the necklace.

Wan was still pounding on the window; I could hear the cries of the girls as they tried to break in. My lungs burned; my vision blurred. I couldn't move, couldn't summon a bit of power.

I was going to die.

I'd never pet my fat white dogs again, never get published, never take a chance on kissing McDougall, never again eat chocolate-covered pretzels—

With *frickin' sea salt!*

Jerking my eyes open, I flailed my free hand around in the bag. The vampire laughed at my struggles and squeezed down harder.

My vision went black as my hand clutched a handful of pretzels. I flung them at its face.

The vampire jerked back, first from the impact of the tiny missiles, but then he screamed in an inhuman pitch as the salt hit his leathery skin. I grabbed another handful, feeling the chocolate melting against my palm, and smashed them into his face. He reared back, and the limo filled with the scent of dark chocolate and sizzling flesh.

He screeched and rolled off me. I drew in a sweet breath and scooted back, dragging my bags with me. Clutching his face, writhing in pain, the reddish glow diminished as the vampire wailed in agony.

I'd like to claim that I screamed in victory at that point, but honestly I shrieked in panic. I started slamming my hand down on the various control panels as I scrabbled to the back of the limo.

The vampire snarled, fixing me with his terrible gaze, his face a mess of chocolate smears and small pits of burnt skin where bones showed through. "You *wangbadan!*" he hissed.

I screamed again and smacked my hand down on what turned out to be the control button for all the windows.

Sacred Ancient Chinese Warrior-Virgins flooded into the space like avenging angels, still dressed in their gleaming shopping-cart armor and looking mad enough to kill a thousand vampires. Wan threw himself through the nearest window, interposing himself between me and the vampire. I cowered behind him on my hands and knees.

"Begone, vile spawn!" Wan shouted.

The vampire lunged at Peach Blossom, but even in the close confines of the limo she dodged and parried with her sword. "Your deaths," he hissed. "All your deaths will strengthen me!"

I let him have it with all the salt at the bottom of the bag.

There was a wild, high shriek of pure rage, and the vampire leapt for the open sunroof and flew into the night, leaving only a trail of melted chocolate drops and sea salt behind.

In the sudden silence, all I could hear was my harsh breathing.

"Kate . . . " Wan leaned over me, sheathing his sword on his back, his worry clear.

I tried to reassure him, but my voice was a rattle in my throat, my neck throbbing with pain.

"We must take her to McDougall. He is a healer," Wan announced.

Oh no, no hospitals, no condescending looks from Dr. "Told Ya So." I tried to struggle up, but only managed to make myself breathless.

The girls clustered around me on the seats, gleaming in their armor. Cherry Blossom eased my head into her lap.

"Her wagon is destroyed," Clouds on Moon glanced out the window. "At least, I do not believe it was designed to work while on fire."

"No indeed," Wan said. "We will take this one. I will operate the vehicle."

I squawked in rough protest.

"I have observed her drive," Wan said. "It does not appear to be difficult, provided a reasonable speed is maintained."

Many hands eased me down to the seat. My vision was going now, but it was sheer exhaustion, not the lack of air.

"How will you navigate?" Filially Pious asked, her voice sharp. She had her doubts. Smart girl.

"There is this device," Wan's voice was growing fainter to my ears. "I believe it is called 'GPS.'"

"And if the spell that enlarges you dissipates?" someone asked, but I didn't hear the response. I gave up, let my eyes close, and sank into a morass of ozone, chocolate, and exhaustion.

Thankfully, consciousness didn't return until I was in the ER cubicle, on a gurney, naked except for a hospital gown, wrapped in warm blankets and feeling no pain.

I was, of course, still wearing the necklace. I could feel the weight of its power, heavy on my skin.

I didn't bother to open my eyes, choosing to float in the darkness a bit longer. I listened to the beeping of the machines, the soft whispers of the girls, and the rustling of cellophane and chewing. For a brief moment, I had a vision of Wan at a vending machine, trying to feed it quarters. It made me smile.

"Kate?" Wan asked. I felt his small weight on my chest as he skittered to my shoulder. I blinked, trying to focus as a warm paw touched my cheek.

"Wan." I smiled at him. He was back to his normal size. The girls were perched around the room, wherever they could find seats, munching health bars and drinking juice, dressed in their jeans and tees.

"Are you hurting?" he asked.

"No," I pulled myself up in the bed a bit. Wan leaped for the controller and raised my head.

"She shouldn't be," Dr. McDougall stood in the doorway to the cubicle, glaring, all "Sexy Stethoscope" with his white coat and broad shoulders.

I crossed my arms over my chest in a purely defensive measure, never mind the lack of a bra, and met him glare for glare.

Wan scrambled to the tray table and stood there, eyeing the two of us, clutching his tail with both paws, a habit he has when he worries.

"So, no permanent injury this time," McDougall said. "But this can't continue, Kate. You need to learn to use whatever powers that medallion has given you."

"No," I said, firmly.

"You need to learn mastery, at the very least," McDougall continued. "Mastery of your emotions, your fear, not to mention some basic defensive moves."

"Oh no," I shook my head, knowing full well where this was going. "If you think for one minute that I am trekking through some swamp with some lizard on my shoulder yelling in my ear, lifting my van from the muck—"

"Your understanding of the forces at your command is weak," McDougall plowed on. "You have no grasp of how to properly wield your power, or control it."

"Wan can teach me," I said.

Wan shot me a worried look, as he grasped his tail. "Honorable Lady—" he started. Wan gets formal when he's upset. "Honorable Lady," he repeated. "While I am learned in history and the ways of magic, I am only a humble guardian, not a wielder of power. The learned Doctor is correct. You need to find a teacher, a wise one to train you in these gifts."

"Oh sure," I growled. "Some Mr. Miyagi to tell me to 'wax on, wax off'?"

"Kate, don't be—" McDougall broke off, looking confused. "Wax?"

"I've watched those training montages in all those movies, thank you very much," I snapped. "And in every one the poor sap with the newfound abilities gets the crap beat out of him as he learns. Thanks, but no thanks."

McDougall had the gall to roll his eyes. "Kate, I am talking about the real world here. You're like a mouse given the keys to a limo who thinks he can drive."

Wan lifted his chin in defiance. "It was a small tree, and planted in the wrong location."

McDougall ignored him. "You have to be trained, and quickly." He saw the same defiance in my face, sighed, and shook his head. "Or you will hurt them," he said gently, gesturing to the girls.

I let my head drop back on the pillows. That got me. "Fine," I said, glumly contemplating the ceiling. "Then train me."

"I can't." McDougall didn't sound all that regretful. "Your powers come from a different source than mine, and I wouldn't—"

Stung by what felt like rejection, I lashed out. "Who's gonna train me then?"

There was a gentle *pop* of displaced air.

"I will," said an ancient, creaky voice.

I jerked my head around to see an old, withered Chinese woman at the foot of my bed, in full formal gown and headdress, arms folded in her sleeves, and looking at me like I was three-day-old cat food.

"I do not know what the Emperor Dragon, Lord of the Dragon Kings, Ruler of the Weather and the Waters of the World was contemplating when he chose a *gweilo*," she said in a tone that made it clear exactly what she thought. "But she will be trained."

"Wan—" I tried to struggle off the gurney.

"Kate—" Wan started to run and launched himself toward me.

The woman clapped her hands twice.

—I stood on the edge of a stone platform, looking down at a classical scene of clouds and mountaintops, a long staircase stretching out below my feet. It was lovely and chilling, mostly because a stiff breeze was blowing up my hospital gown.

Clutching the back together, I turned to see a tall pagoda surrounded by stone walls. In the gateway stood the old lady, surrounded by other elderly women, all glaring at me like I'd offended the very stones I stood on.

My girls were at my feet, once again clad in their silk gowns, now kowtowing toward the women.

"Welcome to the Monastery of the Distant Clouds," the eldest said with a wicked smile on her lips, her eyes gleaming with sharp satisfaction. "Your training will commence immediately."

Oh, no. Who's gonna feed my dogs?

The Mammyth

by Harry Turtledove

The mammyth is out there. Unless, of course, it's not. First there is a mammyth. Then there is no mammyth. Then there is. Unless there isn't.

How do you find a legendary, maybe mythical, creature? You may seek it with thimbles—and seek it with care. You may hunt it with forks and hope. You may threaten its life with a . . . Oh, wait. That's liable to be something else, but there's no need to get snarky about it.

There's a high priest's throne whose panels are supposed to be carved from mammyth ivory. You can see pictures of it in Fallmereyer's famous tome, *Geistkunstgeschichtliche Wissenschaft*. They say you can, anyhow. But you know what they say is worth.

And they also say that somebody went through every single copy of *Geistkunstgeschichtliche Wissenschaft* with a razor and cut out the illo of the mammyth-ivory priestly throne panels, so you can't see it. Some of them say it was Fallmereyer himself. Since *Geistkunstgeschichtliche Wissenschaft* had a print run of nine copies (eleven with a tail wind), it's not impossible. One more time, though, you know what they say it's worth.

There's an Emperor who paraded down the main thoroughfare of his very imperial capital wearing a robe woven from mammyth wool. There's supposed to have been such an Emperor parading down such a thoroughfare in such a robe, at any rate. Such a robe! There's also a nasty little boy who said rude things about the robe the Emperor was or wasn't wearing. Or there's supposed to have been such a little boy who said such rude things. Such a boy!

I could go on. I could go on and on, in fact. After all, I'm getting paid by the word. But we need an Adventure. A Quest! If we don't find one pretty damn soon, you'll go read some other story, and then where will I be? That's right, and without a paddle, too.

So here's Tundra Dawn, seeking the mammyth with all her strength. She wants ivory. She wants wool. She wants glory. She wants to be able to shuck off her chainmail shirt, which is *the* questing fashion accessory this year, but which proves fashion and comfort don't go hand-in-hand, even in jurisdictions where that's legal.

Tundra Dawn isn't alone on her Adventurous Quest. No story's heroine is worth the paper she'll eventually be printed on without sidekicks. Tundra Dawn has a couple of them. Lucky her. She has Cleveland, for instance. No, not Cleveland, the city with the inflammable river. Cleveland, the sidekick. He's fuzzy and blue and excitable and not too bright. But he helps the plot along sometimes. If he feels like it. Which is about as much as you can hope for from a sidekick.

And she has Tremendous Ptarmigan—or sometimes he spells it Ptremendous Tarmigan. TP/PT (he calls himself a translettered avian) is, or may be, worth his weight in drumsticks when it comes to hunting mammyths. In fact, he insists he has one for his best friend. That nobody else has ever seen that mammyth doesn't bother him a bit.

"They're very shy, you know, mammyths," he says. "They don't let just anybody set eyes on them."

"One of them had better let me set eyes on it, and pretty darn quick, too," Tundra Dawn declares. "This here is only a short story. I don't have time to mess around the way I would in a novel, or even a novella."

"Short stories are good things," Cleveland says. "You cannot have a monster at the end of a book if there is no book."

"Maybe there will be a monster at the end of the story," Tundra Dawn says.

"Oh, no! There had better not be! Then it would be a scary story, and it is supposed to be a funny story." Cleveland is better at getting excited over nothing than any other three more or less people you can think of.

"It's a good thing you told 'em the story's supposed to be funny," Tundra Dawn says. "They might not figure it out otherwise."

"Everything will turn out fine." Tremendous Ptarmigan is a great believer in happy endings. He has other annoying characteristics, too, like a high, thin, kinda squeaky voice. But, because he is so Tremendous, he can see a long way. He points ahead. "Looks like we're coming to a town."

"Low bridge! Everybody down!" Cleveland sings out. He knows all kinds of useless things, and commonly turns them loose at the worst possible moment.

There is a bridge over a straight channel of water in front of the canal. Ghosts moan and whuffle their sheets above the eerie canal. Once Tundra Dawn and her sidekicks have got past it, she sees what a big place they've found. "It's not jut a town," she says. "It's a city!"

"It's not just a city," Cleveland exclaims. "It's a metropolis!"

This is not one of the useless things Cleveland knows. There's a sign not far past the bridge: WELCOME TO METROPOLIS! Cleveland isn't wrong all the time—just often enough to be completely undependable.

What, you may well ask, is a metropolis, or even Metropolis, doing in the middle of the tundra? This particular one is kind of sitting there waiting for the adventurers to arrive and get on with things. So they do.

Being a metropolis, Metropolis is the capital of the local kingdom. "What," says a gate guard, in tones of darkest suspicion, "is your purpose in entering our fair city?"

"We're looking for—" Cleveland can open his mouth wide enough to fall right in.

Tundra Dawn stomps on his foot. He yips and does an amazing dance. Tundra Dawn says, "We want to talk to the King, man." She sounds like someone who has wandered into a burger joint with a late-night case of the munchies.

"Right." The gate guard is anything but impressed. He must have heard the routine before. But he stands aside. "Go on in, then. Quickest way to get to the palace is with the subway—the Metro, we call it." His meager chest swells with civic pride.

"Why do you call it that?" Ptremendous Tarmigan isn't the shiniest ornament on the tree, or even on the ptree.

"Beats me." Neither is the gate guard.

There's a Metro station just inside the gate. That's handy. It saves steps, and exposition. A stairway goes down, down, down to the permafrost layer. Tundra Dawn and her sidekicks approach the ticket seller, a short, squat, bearded bloke with a bad case of stocking cap who twitches every so often.

"Who's he?" TP/PT does have that gift for missing the obvious.

"He's the Metrognome," Tundra Dawn explains.

"He certainly ticks like one," Cleveland says.

On getting paid, the Metrognome stylishly turns the turnstile. Tundra Dawn and Cleveland and Tremendous Ptarmigan go on to the subway car. It's pulled by a team of four large, broad-shouldered, metamorphic-looking individuals. "Stop!" One of them holds out an enormous, mineralized paw. "Pay troll!"

"Nobody told us this was a troll road," Tundra Dawn says.

"Is," the troll assures her.

"We already paid the fellow back there!" Cleveland squawks.

"No pay," the troll says, "no go."

"Here." Angrily, Tundra Dawn forks over again. "I still think you're full of schist."

"Complain all you want, meat lady," the troll answers. "Long as you pay, I don't care. I got me a big apatite to feed."

"Meat lady!" The pupils in Tundra Dawn's eyes roll round and round under their clear plastic outsides, she is so mad. Not only is the troll a bigot, he is a stupid bigot. *Must have rocks in his head,* she thinks, which is not altogether tolerant, either. But if he doesn't know foam rubber and terry cloth when he sees them . . . *It's his loss, is what it is,* goes through Tundra Dawn's noodle.

Cleveland, of like construction, is quivering with rage of his own. But quiver is all he does. Even he is not usually foolish enough to piss off a troll. Things that piss kidney stones are better left unpissed. Ptremendous Tarmigan? Even his friends have trouble telling what TP/PT is thinking, or if he is thinking. He is dumb as rocks in his own right, although not constructed of same, and his beaky face ain't what you'd call expressive.

How can foam rubber and terry cloth come to life and have adventures? Because this is a fantasy story, that's how. They could come to life if this were a skiffy story, too, but then I'd have to bore you with a bunch of bullshit explanation. See how lucky you are to miss all that?

The trolls haul the subway car down the long, cold tunnel. People and other forms of allegedly intelligent life get on and off. "Avenue J!" the lead troll bawls, and then, "Lois Lane!" and then, after a while, "Avenue Q!"

"Stop that, Cleveland," Tundra Dawn whispers. "This is a family story."

"I can't help it. I feel like double-clicking," Cleveland whispers back.

They leave Avenue Q behind. Cleveland finally does stop that. After what seems like forever but is really just a long time, the troll roars, "The palace! You wanna play the palace, this is where you get off!"

"I already got off," Cleveland says to no one in particular.

"Someone should beat that troll with a big shtick," Tremendous Ptarmigan says as he and Cleveland and Tundra Dawn get down from the subway car.

No one guards the way out. "Where's the Metrognome here?" Tundra Dawn wonders.

"Probably at the Mets game," Cleveland doesn't quite explain.

Up the stairs they trudge, and themselves in the very heart of Metropolis find. Into the palace they walk. Very palatial it is, yes. Escorted straight to the King they are. Backward run sentences until reels the mind.

If getting escorted straight to the King doesn't prove this is a fantasy story, I don't know what would. In skiffy, you pretend hardest to be realistic when you're most un-. In fantasy, you can roll with it. Sometimes. So roll with it. Please?

The King—his name is Wolcott, which is why he likes getting called King a lot—looks them over. "What are you doing in my throne room?" he asks. This is not the kind of fantasy where everybody, or even anybody, knows everything. It is more the kind of fantasy where nobody knows anything.

You see? It is more realistic than you thought.

"We're hunting the mammyth." This time, Cleveland comes out with it before Tundra Dawn can trample his toes.

"In my throne room?" King Wolcott says. "I don't know everything there is to know about mammyths" (told you so—if he's a reliable narrator) "but I never heard that they were very common in palaces. Isn't that more what the tundra's for?"

Wistfully, Tundra Dawn says, "If they were very common anywhere, we wouldn't have to hunt them so hard."

"Well, why are you hunting them?" the King asks.

"It's a Quest," Cleveland says.

"An Adventure," Ptremendous Tarmigan adds.

"It's a whole 'nother story," Tundra Dawn says. And, since it is, I don't have to tell it here. I can get on with the silly one of which I'm in the middle.

TP/PT raises an arm—a wing—a whatever the hell. "Excuse me, your Kinginess, but where to you keep your big birds' room?"

"Go out there." King Wolcott points to a doorway. "Turn left, then right, then left again. You can't miss it."

He and Tundra Dawn and Cleveland yatter away for the next half-hour. Tundra Dawn presumes that Tremendous Ptarmigan damn well can miss it—damn well has missed it—after all. But when Ptremendous Tarmigan comes back, he does seem relieved. He seems happy, too. TP/PT seems happy most of the time. Tundra Dawn guesses it has a good deal to do with the seeds he eats.

At last, when the spectacle of a muppetoid heroine in chainmail and her clunky sidekicks commences to pall, the King asks, "How can I help you in your quest?" By which he means, *How can I get you the devil out of here?*, but it sounds much nicer the way he says it.

They dicker for a while, which, unlike some of the bits here, is less obscene than it sounds. King Wolcott decides that some horses and some food are a small price to pay for washing these adventurers right outa his hair and sending them on their way. He even throws in a little cash. He watches them ride away into what would be the sunset, only the sun doesn't set on the tundra at this time of year.

And that washes him right outa this story and sends him on his way. Well, almost, because a couple of days later Tremendous Ptarmigan says, "I had a nice chat with the mammyth at the King's palace."

"Is that what took you so long?" Cleveland said. "I thought you fell in."

Tundra Dawn reins in. She sends Ptremendous Tarmigan as exasperated a look as she can manage with eyes from a craft-shop discount table. "Um, you do remember we're searching for a mammyth? Hunting a mammyth, even?" By the hopeless way she says it, she has no confidence that TP/PT ever remembers anything.

But Tremendous Ptarmigan nods brightly. "Oh, sure," he says.

Tundra Dawn holds on to her patience with both hands. With

sidekicks like hers, she has considerable practice. Morosely, she considers it. Then she asks, "Why didn't you tell us that before it was, like, too late to do anything about it?"

"You heard the King," Ptremendous Tarmigan answers. "He said mammyths weren't very common in palaces."

After considering her practice some more, Tundra Dawn says, "They don't need to be very common. There just needs to be one of them, so we can hunt it."

"What did you and this mammyth, if there was a mammyth, talk about?" Cleveland asks. Then he sneezes. Even in tundra summer, baby, it's cold outside.

"Don't snuffle up at me," TP/PT says. "We chatted about all kinds of things. He says to watch out for the one from fit the eighth. I don't know what that means, though."

"The Baker could tell you," Cleveland says.

"What Baker?" asks Tremendous Ptarmigan.

"*The* Baker," Cleveland says. They go on confusing each other, and Tundra Dawn, for some little while.

Then our chain-mailed (but not chain-stored) heroine cocks her head to one side and says, "I hear music."

"But there's no one there." Cleveland comes in right on cue.

"It's, like, a bell," Tundra Dawn says, which is not the next line, but which is, like, what it is.

There may not be anyone there, but Ptremendous Ptarmigan points to motion in the distance. "Look!" he exclaims. "It's a herd of cheeseheads!"

Cheeseheads they are, ambling across the frozen tundra in search of tailgates and other Arcana of the Sacred Pigskin. Instead of by an ordinary bellwether, they, like some other faithful, are led by a lamb. Like an ordinary bellwether, the lamb wears a bell around its neck. Unlike an ordinary bellwether's, the lamb's bell is held on by a pink satin ribbon with a fancy bow.

Tundra Dawn spurs her horse forward, careless for the moment of worries about animal cruelty (what she will do if and when hunting the mammyth segues into killing the mammyth is something she resolutely refuses to dwell on). The horse jumps high over the lamb's bell-bedizened neck. After her touchdown, she waves her sidekicks forward. They too perform the lamb-bow leap.

Cleveland wrinkles his nose. With the kind of nose he has, this isn't easy. With the kind of nose he has, this shouldn't even be possible. But I'm the narrator, and I'm here to tell you he does it. In fact, I repeat myself, slowly: Cleveland . . . wrinkles . . . his . . . nose. Okay? Wrapped your visualizer around it yet? Sweet! Then we'll go on.

"What smells nasty?" Cleveland asked.

"I don't smell anything," Ptremendous Tarmigan says.

"Of course you don't, you translettered avian, you," Cleveland says. "The only avians, translettered or not, with a good sense of smell are vultures."

"Sounds discriminatory to me," TP/PT says. "And elitist. Everyone should be able to smell as good as everyone else."

"If you want to smell good, try taking a bath," Cleveland says. "If you want to smell well, try not being an avian."

Tremendous Ptarmigan gets mad and puffs out his feathers to look, um, ptremendouser. Before the bickering can get really bitchy, Tundra Dawn says, "Boys, boys." She's defused, and defuzzed, these squabbles before. She goes on, "I think you're smelling the cheeseheads, Cleveland. They're Roqueforts."

"Rogue farts?" Cleveland nods. "They sure are!"

"I used to watch *The Roquefort Files* sometimes," the Tarmigan says. "I didn't smell anything bad then."

Tundra Dawn sighs. Good sidekicks are hard to come by. And stinking cheeseheads are a fact of life on the frozen tundra. "Faa-aar-vv!" they bleat mournfully. "Faa-aar-vv!"

"Come on," Tundra Dawn says. "We'll ride away from them. Then we won't smell them so much."

Away they ride. The smell does get . . . not so bad, anyhow. Cleveland keeps complaining about it anyhow. TP/PT keeps complaining about Cleveland's complaining. Instead of resolutely not dwelling on killing the mammyth, Tundra Dawn resolutely doesn't dwell on killing the two of them.

It may be summer on the tundra, but it is the tundra. There is still snow on the ground, at least where the story needs there to be some. In a patch of snow that Tundra Dawn and Cleveland and Tremendous Ptarmigan conveniently happen to ride past, there is a hole as if someone has pushed down with the bottom of a big, round wastebasket. Or it would look like that if big, round wastebaskets came equipped with stubby toes.

"Is that a footprint?" Nothing gets by Cleveland. Nothing gets through to him, but nothing gets by him.

"It is a footprint," TP/PT says. "And do you know what?"

"No. What?" Cleveland says.

"It looks . . . It looks like it could be a mammyth's footprint."

Tundra Dawn rides on to the next convenient patch of snow. "Here is another footprint," she says. "If we follow the mammyth's toes, we will go in the same direction it is going. Pretty soon, we will catch up with it."

"You are so smart, Tundra Dawn! I never would have thought of that," Cleveland says. The good news for Tundra Dawn is that even half-assed sidekicks like hers give you egoboot. The bad news is, she totally believes he never would have thought of it.

They follow the tracks. And they follow the tracks. And they follow the tracks some more. They come to the edge of the cold, cold sea. Walking along the muddy beach are a Walrus and a Carpenter. The Walrus is fat. The Carpenter is skin and bones. In spite of the season, the Walrus and the Carpenter are caroling together.

Tremendous Ptarmigan waves to the pair. "How are you doing, Paul?"

The Walrus waves a flipper back. "Not bad. How about you, Ptremendous?"

"I'm fine. I'm looking for a mammyth right now," the Tarmigan answers. "Oh, and have you seen Dave?"

"Dave? Dave's not here," the Carpenter says quickly.

He's only just begun, but the Walrus interrupts him by pointing with that flipper. "Might be a mammyth over that way. Don't know what else you'd call it," he says.

"C'mon, sidekicks!" Tundra Dawn hollers. "We're heading for the dénouement!"

"For the who?" TP/PT asks as they ride away.

"Not for the who. For the what," Cleveland says.

"For which what?"

"For the end."

They ride up a small rise and down the other side. They ride up another one. Tundra Dawn spots something moving on the far side. "Is that—?" she asks Tremendous Ptarmigan, who may have seen one before. "Could that be—?"

"Yes, I think it's—" Ptremendous starts.

Then they softly and silently vanish away. Tundra Dawn's armor clatters about her, or about where she has been—an epic ending granted a mock-epic heroine. For the mammyth, even if it doesn't quite scan, is a Boojum, you see.

Give a Girl a Sword

by Kerrie L. Hughes

Jessie Ramirez showed her Illinois I.D. to the ticket taker of the Chicago Art Institute. As she put the card back in her pocket, she accidentally dropped her sketchbook and pencils. Sighing deeply, she picked them up and then walked inside.

Her long, dark hair was messy from a sleepless night, and her brown eyes were bloodshot from crying. Her mood was as black as the charcoal staining her fingertips. Battered cargo pants, combat boots, and a black turtleneck sweater that had seen better days made her look every inch the starving art student she was.

Last night Jessie had come home to the apartment she shared with her boyfriend to find him screwing some random girl on their bed. After a three-hour fight, she threw him out. It had been humiliating, stupid, and not entirely out of nowhere, if she were to be honest.

Now, all she wanted to do was retreat to some quiet area in her favorite museum and sketch something until she forgot her troubles. Best therapy in the world, because it was free on Thursdays and she was one paycheck away from going back home to live with her mom. Not something she wanted to do.

Jessie walked around until she saw the armory room. She hadn't been in this wing since it had closed for remodeling, and she'd never really been into weapons and armor, but given her mood, it was butt-kicking 101, and that was downright intoxicating right now.

After a quick search of the room, she located the bench farthest from the noisy hallway and glanced at the nearby displays. Let's see, shiny suit of armor, or ugly bunch of iron swords and daggers? Jessie chose the armor and sat down.

After turning to a fresh page, she leaned forward to read the information card at the base of the suit. *Armor for Field and Tournament, 1560, Germany.* Okay, does that mean field, as in games, or field as in battlefield? She realized she knew nothing about armor and how it was used. Irony at its greatest, given how she had just gotten her heart trampled by someone all her college friends had warned her about.

Ugh, college, another thing she didn't want to think about. She still hadn't decided what major to take, and her two years at the community college were over as of last week. What she really wanted to do was enroll in the Chicago School of Art at the Institute, but living here was expensive, and she needed to find a new roommate. She also needed to find a way to pay for college.

Her mom wanted her to give up art and become a lawyer, so she could take out loans and repay them once she found a job. Jessie liked the idea of being a lawyer and representing people in need, but there wasn't anything creative about it, and she craved creativity.

Still, helping people was kind of a big deal. When her mom had needed help getting a restraining order against Jessie's dad, it had taken far too long. she and her mom had ended up homeless until a women's shelter found them a room. Then it took forever to get the divorce finalized, and they felt helpless until it was over. Jessie ruminated over the possibilities as she sketched the suit of armor.

"Hello. Can you hear me?"

Jessie looked up from her sketch and glanced around, but only saw a few people passing through the room. Probably just someone on a cell phone. She went back to sketching.

"Excuse me young lady, I'm talking to you."

The voice was a bit louder now, possibly female, but definitely coming from behind her. Jessie turned and looked; there was no one there, just a display of Viking short swords and daggers.

"Yes, I'm talking to you. Can you hear me?"

Startled, Jessie stood up and turned around, clutching the sketchpad to her chest. Was she losing her mind?

"Yes, you. The young lady with a sketchpad."

The voice was even louder now, and definitely coming from the Viking display. Was someone behind the case?

"Where are you?" Jessie asked.

"In the case. Come closer, please."

Jessie looked at the case, then up at the security camera in the corner, and finally back around the room, just to be sure.

"If someone's pranking me, I am not amused," she said, perhaps a bit loudly.

The guard across the room looked at her. It seemed like he was about to come over, but he stayed where he was.

The voice continued, "I assure you that I am not pranking you. My name is Vala, and I am the third sword from the left."

Jessie raised an eyebrow, put her sketchbook down on the bench, and edged closer to the case. There were seven swords and three daggers inside, along with a number of informational pictures. She quickly assessed which sword was third from the left and looked at the index card below it.

"'Viking Dagger, 800, Iron.'"

"No. Sorry. My left, your right."

"Okay . . . 'Viking Short Sword, age unknown, Iron and bronze. Gift of the Ericksohn Family.'"

"Yes. That one."

"That can't be you. You look like you're made of steel, and you have gold scrollwork and sapphires on your hilt."

"You see my true form."

"But you look like the other weapon to everyone else?"

"Yes."

Jessie glanced back at the guard, who was chatting with someone. She turned her attention back to the sword. "Are you seriously trying to tell me that a sword is talking to me?"

"Yes. You are potentially one of the Volka."

"Uh . . . what?"

"I believe that you are of the bloodline of Freya's Daughters."

"The Norse Goddess?"

"Yes. Has your mother not told you of your heritage?"

"Look, I don't know what's going on here, but if this is a prank—"

Just then Jessie heard the authoritative steps of the guard approaching and she turned to see him five feet away from her.

"Can I help you with something?" he said with a smile.

"Uh . . . yeah. Is this an interactive display or something?"

"No. It's just a regular armory display."

"He can't hear me, only you can hear me," the voice said.

"Did you hear that?" Jessie asked.

The guard's smile disappeared. "Hear what?"

Jessie sighed. "Never mind, I guess I'm just . . . talking to myself over here."

The guard looked at her like she was addled in the head, but then smiled again. "Just let me know if you need anything," he said and walked away.

"Or maybe the voices in my head," she muttered once she saw him resume his post at the exhibit entrance.

"You don't have to talk very loudly for me to hear you. Even if you whisper, I'll hear you just fine, and once you claim me, you will be able to talk to me in your head."

"Claim you?"

"Yes. As I said, you are descended from the Priestesses of Freya, one of Her Daughters. Although I must admit I have never met a descendant with dark hair and eyes. Your skin reminds me of the Spaniards some of my previous hosts met."

"Excuse me?" Jessie asked, not sure if she should be offended.

"I apologize for not asking earlier, but what is your full name?"

"Jessica Inez Ramirez, but everyone calls me Jessie."

"Are you a Spaniard, Jessie?"

"I'm an American."

"Yes, of course you are—we are in America, after all—but where do your family's ancestors hail from?"

"My father's family is mainly from Spain and France; my mother's family is from the Netherlands. Why do you ask?"

"Well, as I have said, only the Daughters of the Goddess Freya have the ability to hear and speak with me. You do not look like any of my previous hosts, so I am wondering where your connection to the Ericksohn family lies?"

"My grandmother's last name was Erikkson, but she spells it differently from the name on your card. My mother's last name is Engstrom."

"Ah, then the mystery is solved. You are most likely one of the daughters."

Jessie narrowed her eyes and crossed her arms. "Look, this is rather surreal, and I'm not entirely convinced this isn't some elaborate prank. What are you exactly?"

"I am Vala, sword of the Daughters of Freya."

"All that tells me is your name and your religion. I'm going to need more than that."

"I am the sword that the Goddess Freya had her blacksmith forge. Her Priestesses spoke Enchantments as she Herself engraved me with Runic Talismans. Then when she was satisfied with the result, she gave me to the first Daughter of Freya, Thorfinna. Thorfinna passed me to her daughter, Sigrid, then Sigrid passed me to—"

"Stop. This is ridiculous."

"What is ridiculous?"

"That you're a talking sword, and I'm still standing here listening to you."

"I see. Then your mother or grandmother has not told you about me?"

"No, my mother's an office manager, and my grandmother died when I was ten."

It was quiet for a minute and Jessie thought, just perhaps, she had imagined that the sword had been speaking to her. Then the sword sighed, and it sounded like the edge of a blade sliding against a sharpening stone.

"Such is my lot after twelve centuries of life. I was once the hand of my Lady Freya's Will, and now I sit in a museum waiting for one of the Daughters to take me up again and make the world safe for women and children so they . . ." the sword trailed off, but sounded sincere, and the longing in its voice made Jessie's heart ache a little.

"Is it . . . terribly lonely?"

"Yes, a bit. I do have Jürg and Tessa for company though."

"Who are they?"

"Jürg is the suit of armor behind you, and Tessa is a tiara in the next room. I mostly speak to them at night when the crowds are gone."

Jessie looked back at the suit of armor. "He talks, too?"

"His maker, Jürg the Younger, haunts him, so it's not really the armor that's talking, but the spirit that lives inside it. Tessa is enchanted like me, but it's unlikely she will ever find someone to claim her again, as most of her family was murdered by Bolsheviks in 1918."

Jessie must have looked skeptical, because Vala continued without waiting for a reply. "They would introduce themselves, but you wouldn't be able to hear them. Not unless you can hear ghosts, or perhaps are related to the Nickolev family. Are you?"

"Not that I know of. Listen, did you say you defend women and children?"

"Yes. If you take me up and accept the powers I bestow—"

"Powers? What powers?"

"Please stop interrupting me, and do whisper so the guard won't come back over."

"Sorry. I'm getting kinda anxious and freaked out. This is just so weird," Jessie said quietly.

"I understand. It isn't every day that you are told you are Chosen and have a great responsibility to bear."

"No, I suppose not. Right, so . . . what are your powers?"

"I have three powers within me. I can deem the Truth, enact Justice, and bestow Grace."

"And how do you do that?"

"Which one?"

"All three."

The sword paused for a minute before finally answering. "It's complicated."

"That's what cheating boyfriends say on Facebook when they want to hook up with random ho-bags."

"A ho-bag? What is that? Some type of monster?"

"Not exactly, although we do all live in fear of becoming one."

I don't understand, please explain."

"Never mind . . . it's complicated. Look, what do you want from me?"

"I want you to claim me and become a true Daughter of Freya."

"But what does that mean? What would I be doing?"

"Simply put, when a woman or female child is in need, I seek her out and defend her against tyranny and abuse."

"Well, that's sounds pretty cool. What do you do to protect them?"

"It depends on the situation, but usually you geld the rapists and take the heads of the murderers."

Jessie's mouth went dry. She knew gelding was essentially castration. And beheading, that was just barbaric. " . . . What?"

"Geld or behead the guilty, after the Truth has been determined, of course. You would be the hand of Freya and dispense her Justice as you see fit. Unless, of course, you choose to extend your Grace."

"What happens then?"

"You could set someone free if they pay restitution to the woman or child's satisfaction."

"I see."

"You sound unsure. Are there no geldings in this day and age? Surely you behead murderers?"

"Not in America. Besides, I've never even held a sword, and I'd likely get arrested and locked up for life. I could be put to death myself."

"When you hold me, you have all the skills a sword bearer would need. And you would have the protection of a fine suit of armor. Much nicer and lighter than Jürg there."

"Where is this armor?"

"It's contained within me. You call on me, and I instantly sheath you in a layer of mystic armor to protect you from harm."

"That's incredible. Are you heavy to carry? Wait, how can I carry a sword in broad daylight?"

"I'm very light for a sword, and my enchantments make me feel nearly weightless until you need me. The power of Grace can also be used to veil me at your side if you need me to remain hidden."

"That all sounds very cool, but I can't really go around killing men who wrong women. I mean, there'd be dead bodies everywhere. And gelding rapists? Eew, I'd be busy all day and night."

"Are there that many murderers and rapists?

"Yes."

"Well, that could be a problem."

"What about guys who cheat? My ex is a cheater, and he took the TV and computer when I kicked him out last night. They were in his name, but I paid for half."

"I'm not sure what a 'TV' is, but I have seen people bring in things they refer to as computers. I'm not exactly familiar with everything that happens now. I get most of my information from my hosts through the years and from the conversations I overhear when visitors to this museum are near me."

"Well, that explains why you sound like a cross between a Midwestern accent and a French one."

"It probably is the case. Tell me Jessie, is a cheater the same as a cardsharp?"

"No, it's more like . . . an adulterer . . . except we aren't married . . . or engaged. It's someone who has sex with someone other than the person they are in love with, and then lies about it."

"You were living with a man and he had sex with someone else? Then you told him to leave, and he did, but took stuff you shared away with him?"

"Yes. As embarrassing as it is."

"Did he beat you, or perhaps violate you sexually?"

"Uh, no. Pretty sure I would have kicked his ass if he did."

"Well good for you, but I'm sorry, there isn't really anything I can do about that. Though it does seem to me that you are better off without him."

Jessie thought for a minute. A lawyer could certainly use a way to tell who was lying. "You said you could divine the truth? How do you do that? Could I find out who's telling the truth just by carrying you?"

"Yes. I can even do so while veiled."

"And what keeps me from using you to rob a bank or kill someone innocent?"

"Truth prevents that from happening."

"How?"

"I've never had a true Daughter of Freya attempt to use me for anything other than good, so I do not know."

"I see. And do I have to find murderers and rapists? Couldn't I just use you to divine the truth and leave the rest to the authorities?"

"Why ever would you want to do that?"

"It's the way things are done now. It's illegal to physically hurt or kill someone, even if they deserve it. We have a court system for justice and prisons for punishment."

"I am familiar with courts. Several of my previous hosts were magistrates and barristers."

"I'm thinking of going to school to be a lawyer myself."

"A noble cause for a Daughter of Freya. Think of all the good you could do with me to help you."

Jessie thought about the possibilities, knowing the truth could be very powerful, although proving it would be problematic at times. It wasn't as though she could tell anyone she had a magic sword, everyone would think she was crazy. And what about the gelding and executions? "Vala, how do I know you aren't lying to me now?"

"I am a Sword of Truth. I cannot lie to you."

"But how do I know that?"

"Once you take me as your own, you will know I am forthright."

"But then it would be too late for me if you are lying. How do I know you aren't some . . . I don't know, malevolent demon trying to trick me?"

"Do I seem like I am?"

"My ex didn't seem like a jerk when I met him, and he promised to love me forever."

"You seem stronger for the experience, in my humble opinion."

"I probably am, but I don't see how running around with a sword that may or may not compel me to execute murderers will be good for me."

"And geld rapists, dear."

"Yeah, that's even less attractive."

"I don't see why it would be an issue. I have never punished anyone who was innocent. Would you have them running around with impunity?"

"Most of them do now."

"That's because I have been behind glass for nearly one hundred years."

"That might be for the best. You do know that the population of the United States of America alone is well over 300 million, don't you?"

"That doesn't seem possible."

"Well, it's true. I mean, how many people can one sword judge?"

"I don't really know. I've had over 200 hosts in my lifetime, and altogether we delivered thousands of judgments."

"Wow, that's . . . " Jessie wasn't sure what word to use—crazy, perhaps? " . . . impressive."

"Thank you."

"Vala, I don't want to upset you, but I have plans for my life. I want to finish school, have a career, make friends, travel, possibly have kids. I may even want to get married someday . . . and it doesn't sound like I can do that if I choose you."

"But . . . it's your destiny."

"If my destiny is to run around killing and mutilating people, then I don't want it."

Vala sighed. "But it's lonely in here."

"You have Jürg and Tessa to talk to. And you said you can hear what's going on around you."

"It's not the same, I barely learn anything new . . . and it sounds like so much has changed. Please take me with you?"

"No Vala. I can't do that."

Vala started to cry, and it nearly broke Jessie's heart. "I will come visit you, though."

"You will?"

"Not every week, and not for more than thirty minutes or so at a time. I don't want to get kicked out of the museum for talking to exhibits."

"The guard does seem to be looking at us quite a bit."

Jessie looked over her shoulder. He was staring at her, and she suppressed the urge to flip him off.

"I'm going to go before I cause trouble. I'll see you next week."

"Do you promise?"

"Yes. And thank you Vala, you've actually helped me more than you realize."

"Thank you, Jessie. I'm quite flattered."

And with that, Jessie gathered up her things. She still wasn't one-hundred-percent sure that Vala was telling the truth, but she was fairly certain the sword couldn't make her do anything as long as she didn't claim her first.

It also made her think that perhaps she would go to law school. She wouldn't be able to help everyone who needed her, but she could make a difference in some people's lives.

On the other hand, art might be what she needed to maintain a firm grip on sanity. Talking swords? A haunted suit of armor? And a tiara that was probably from the poor doomed head of Anastasia? Maybe she was already crazy? Maybe she should become a museum curator just to make sure objects like those didn't wind up in the wrong hands.

Once Jessie was gone, Jürg spoke up. "That's the fourth one to turn you down, old girl."

"Yes, so sorry, my dear, but at least you are protected and well cared for here," Tessa added.

"Indeed, it is better than when I was lost in the peat bogs for countless years," Vala said. "Still, this one holds promise . . . and she may, in time, change her mind."

"Quite," Jürg agreed.

"Perhaps you should leave out the part about gelding men," Tessa said. "It seems to make them quite uncomfortable."

"Mmm, indeed," Jürg concurred.

"Oh do shut up, both of you," Vala said, putting an end to the discussion.

Bite Me

by Steven Harper Piziks

The zombie woman with her hair in a bun lunged at Dagmar, inasmuch as a zombie could lunge. It was more like a lurch. Or maybe a career. Whatever she was doing, her teeth snapped like a turtle's beak. Dagmar batted her—*it*—aside with the flat of her blade and kept running.

"Eat eat eat," said the zombie in a kindly voice.

"Why didn't you cut it?" panted her brother Ramdane as the zombie lady dropped away behind them.

"And get zombie goo on both of us?" she panted back. "No thanks." One bite or scratch, and it was an eternity of lurch for you, everyone knew that.

One zombie by itself wasn't much trouble. You got some decent distance from it, and then shot flaming arrows at it. *Fwoop* and done. The trouble was, zombies always traveled with friends. Or companions. Or whatever it was zombies had. This one was no exception. Several dozen more tried to lunge—or lurch or career—toward her and Ramdane from the houses and shops lining the village road. Their yellowed teeth snapped with a hundred cold *clicks* that chilled Dagmar to the marrow. So much for finding a kindly innkeeper or friendly baker for the night. Dagmar had even been hoping for a handsome baker's son, though she would have taken strapping, too. Strapping was always good. You knew where you stood with strapping. Instead, they'd gotten a village full of zombies.

Ahead, at the top of a hill near the north end of the village, sat a stone keep. Ramdane ran for it as only a talismonger could run, his talismans bouncing and jingling on his belt. With his curly brown hair, whipcord build, and wide blue eyes, he looked like a terrified scarecrow. Dagmar had a blockier build and straight, ash-blond hair, with the marks and scars that bespoke her profession as a mercenary. A tired mercenary. Beside them trotted Ramdane's familiar, Crystamel. She currently wore the shape of a small, white dog and she looked not at all worried—zombies didn't lunge for animated clay statues, no matter how lifelike.

Zombies horded into the street like a swarm of elderly bees. Groaning and shuddering, they reached for Dagmar and Ramdane as they ran beneath the afternoon sun. The links of Dagmar's armor clinked and jingled. The mail was hot and it chafed, but at the moment, she was enormously grateful she'd put it on this morning. The zombies couldn't bite through it. A warrior's armor protected her while she fought to the death. Or undeath, in this case.

Unfortunately, Ramdane didn't have this particular security blanket. On the other hand, they had puffed more than halfway through town, and the zombies at the other end apparently hadn't gotten the word about the recently arrived free-range lunch, because the street ahead was still clear, even as the street behind them filled with undead townspeople.

"The entire town was zombified?" Ramdane panted. He wasn't in great physical shape—too skinny—and the big sister inside Dagmar filed this away to force him into exercising later—if they lived.

"Looks like." Dagmar grabbed his arm and hauled him forward. "Can't any of your talismans slow them down?"

"I can't concentrate and run," he puffed. "Head for the keep. They might be—"

"Look out!" Crystamel barked, literally.

They had drifted from the center of the road toward one of the houses. From the rooftop dropped a child zombie, a little boy. Dagmar shoved Ramdane aside, but the motion cost her time. The pint-sized zombie landed like a monkey on her back. The smell of bad meat engulfed her. Dagmar snatched at him to fling him away. She grabbed him, and his teeth snapped at her bare hand. She flicked him aside just in time, thank all gods. One bite, and she would be lurching—or careening or whatevering—along with all the others. The boy tumbled aside in a smelly heap.

"Run!" she shouted at Ramdane, because everyone knew that shouting *run* at someone who was already running made them run faster. They fled the village and headed up the hill toward the blocky keep, finally outpacing the zombie villagers.

A chilling laugh floated over the rooftops behind them. Clinging atop a chimney was a tall, thin man in a ragged coat with a tin crown on his head.

"A talismonger and a warrior!" he whooped. "You will both join my horde!"

"Who the heck is that?" Crystamel demanded from ankle height.

Dagmar didn't bother to reply. They reached the blocky keep and pounded on the main gate. The place was too small to have a moat.

"Let us in!" Ramdane shouted. "Zombies!"

A head poked between the gaps in the crenellation above them. "How do we know *you* aren't zombies?"

Dagmar glanced over her shoulder and tried not to panic. The zombie horde was lurching up the road behind them. "Zombies don't demand to be let in."

"It'll take too long to open the gate." The man pointed to the zombies stumbling up the road. "They'll get here first. You understand."

"Oh, for—" Dagmar swore, and drew her sword. The zombies were close enough for the groaning to become audible.

"Don't panic yet." Ramdane felt among the talismans at his belt and came up with a tiny wooden ladder. He held it in both hands and concentrated for a moment. *"Climb,"* he said in a strange, deep voice.

"You'll be mine!" came the awful, chilly voice. The man with the tin crown was in the thick of the zombie horde, with the little boy riding on his shoulders in a ghoulish parody of a piggyback ride.

The zombies were only a few paces away now. The old zombie lady was among them. "Eat!" she cried.

For an awful moment, Dagmar was fourteen years old again, a young warrior at her mother's funeral, looking down at the cold corpse of the woman who had loved her and kissed her good night, and then abruptly wasted away from a heartless disease that ate her from the inside out. The next day, the earl had gifted her with a chainmail shirt, and as the chilly metal settled on her shoulders, she swore to herself that she would spend the rest of her life fighting, to the death, if necessary. It was the warrior's creed: never give in; always fight.

With this in mind, Dagmar waved her sword at the zombies. Crystamel, feeling left out, jumped in front of her and barked.

Ramdane's ladder expanded in his hands. It spun itself into something made of air and light and expanded upward. The man pulled back as the ladder reached the top of the wall and hung there, not quite touching it.

"Come on!" Ramdane scooped up Crystamel and bolted for the rungs.

Dagmar eyed the rungs. "Are you sure—?"

"Climb!" Ramdane was already halfway up. The zombies were within clutching range now. Dagmar sheathed her sword and scampered up the slender rungs after her brother. It was like climbing fog.

And then the thin man with the tin crown threw the boy. He landed on the ladder just below Dagmar, and got his cold hands on her shin above her boot. He bit her, and she felt the pain straight through her leggings. Dagmar kicked out and managed to shove the boy off the ladder. He fell into the horde below, knocking down two zombies who were themselves trying to climb the airy ladder.

"Eat!" screamed the zombie lady.

Don't think, don't scream, she told herself. *Just climb.*

Heart in her mouth, she hurried up the ladder and dove onto the tower. Her leg throbbed. Zombies were making their way up the rungs, but the moment Dagmar was safe, Ramdane tapped the top rung. The ladder unraveled and vanished. Zombies tumbled like rag dolls to the ground.

"You will join me!" called the man with the tin crown. "You will all join my kingdom!"

Dagmar ignored him and slumped behind the crenelated barrier at the top of the tower wall. Crystamel, pushed by instincts she couldn't ignore, stood on her hind legs and put her nose into the guard's crotch.

"Good musk," she said, "with a delicate overlay of fear sweat."

"You're a talismonger," the guard breathed, ignoring Crystamel for the moment.

"Probably handy to have someone like me around," Ramdane said.

"Because you stopped that entire horde single-handedly?" the guard said.

"Little help here," Dagmar put in. Already, she could feel ice crawling up her leg.

"What's—dammit, no!" Ramdane knelt and yanked up her legging, despite Dagmar's accompanying screech of pain. The wound on her calf was already festering, the flesh around it dark and mottled.

"Uh oh." The guard drew his sword. "Lady, in the name of Earl Biddlemeyer, I'm ordering you to jump back over that wall. Right now."

"Not up to it," Dagmar said through clenched teeth.

"I insist," the guard said through equally clenched teeth. "We have forty-five people in this keep; none of them are zombied, and we intend to keep it that way."

"She's not going to— " Ramdane began.

The guard's face went hard, and he pushed Crystamel away from his crotch again.

"Sorry," she muttered. "I can't seem to help it."

"Listen to me," said the guard, "somewhere in that horde down there, my own mother is shambling about because of the zombie king. I had to slam the keep door shut in her face because she wanted to bite me and make me one of them. It was either hide in here or cut her into pieces out there and I— " he paused to take a deep shuddering breath that made his sword arm shake "—I couldn't cut up my own mother, even if that thing down there is nothing but a monster wearing her body."

Dagmar pulled herself upright. "Your mother—a lady about this tall," she held out her hand, "hair in a gray bun, wants you to eat?"

The guard blinked at her. "Yeah . . . although I think you got that last part turned around."

"My mom was like that. I can sympathize," Dagmar said. The guard had fine, black hair, gray eyes, and a jaw you could strike flint on. He was actually quite strapping, now that she looked at him. And, like her, he saw what needing doing and did it, even when it hurt. *Hm . . .*

"Anyway," the guard said, "in this keep, we've got a lot of other people who've gone through the same damn thing who we're trying to keep safe until we can figure out what to do. But, you, lady— " the sword swung around to point at Dagmar's heart "—you I don't know. You I'll slice, so jump."

"You're mi-i-ine," sang out the zombie king below.

"Shut up, Herbert!" the guard yelled back.

Dagmar looked over the battlements at the slithering horde of zombies below. Then she lashed out with her good leg and sent the guard's sword spinning away.

"I'm not hungry for brains yet," she said.

"Look," said Ramdane reasonably, taking his hand away from his belt of talismans, "this isn't over. Did you hear about that gorgon who was turning people to stone a few years back? My sister, Dagmar, and I dealt with her. We can handle a zombie king."

"Right." The guard spat over the edge. "Show the zombie king a mirror and he'll wet himself, I'm sure."

"Just take us to whoever's in charge," Dagmar said.

"That would be me," the strapping guard said. "Earl Biddlemeyer at your service. And keep your dog away from my crotch."

"Nice codpiece," Crystamel said.

Ramdane helped Dagmar up onto the cook's table. The cook would have protested, but she was outside the keep, banging on the gate with meaty fists. The kitchen was otherwise empty— Earl Biddlemeyer had ordered the other survivors to keep their distance in case Dagmar went on a sudden chewing spree. The thought that she herself would soon be joining the filthy, brainless herd of creatures gibbering outside the gate made Dagmar cold and panicky. Here was an enemy you couldn't fight. She wondered if this was how Mom had felt.

Biddlemeyer personally kept guard over both of them with his sword out, even though Dagmar had adeptly demonstrated that she could whap him upside the head whenever she chose. She had to admire him for trying.

"What's going to happen?" Dagmar asked. "How does this work?"

"Zombies come from necromancy, not talismans. No intelligent person touches necromancy because it always gets away from you." Ramdane raked up a fire in a fireplace big enough to toast a small elephant, and poured water into a kettle. Dagmar noticed how the tension made his hands shake, which only made her feel worse. Her brother was a powerful talismonger, and probably the smartest person she knew. If he was scared, they were in real trouble. "Look most people don't know this because we talismongers keep it to ourselves, but zombies aren't really dead—undead. They're just people with a piece of demon inside. We don't talk about it because if we did, people would also start looking funny at a talismonger's familiar—and at talismongers."

"Why?" said Biddlemeyer behind his sword.

"A talismonger's familiar is the opposite of a demon. It's a spirit, but a good one, and it's conjured into a carved talisman instead of a living person. It stays there until the body wears out and we put it into a new one. You could conjure a familiar spirit into a living host, too, but it would eventually push the person's spirit out."

"You never told me any of this," Dagmar said, interested despite herself.

"Like I said, we don't talk about it. Right, Crystamel?"

Crystamel, who was sniffing around the hearth, heard her name and automatically sat up on her hind legs, then plunked back down again with an annoyed look on her face. "Speaking of," she said, "I want a new body. Every time you make me a dog, the stupid canine instincts take over. You think I *like* sticking my nose into people's privates?"

"Bitch, bitch, bitch," Ramdane shot back.

She cocked her head. "Was that supposed to be a pun? Because if it was—"

"Can we get back to the zombies?" interrupted Biddlemeyer. "Two weeks ago, I had a town. Now I have a sort of mobile graveyard, and if there's something I can do about it, I want to hear."

"Sorry." Ramdane poured hot water over Dagmar's wound, and she hissed at the pain, though the heat felt good. "I'm guessing the zombie king started by conjuring a demon into some poor schlub—"

"Did I mention the zombie king is my brother, Herbert, and the first zombie was our mother?" Biddlemeyer said, still gripping his sword.

"—into a lovely lady," Ramdane continued without pausing for breath, "for purposes of revenge or some such, but the demon got hungry, for both power and flesh. It bit someone else and put a piece of itself into that person too, and they bit two more people, and so on and so on. It doesn't take long. Except the zombie king is in something of a pickle himself. If he doesn't keep feeding the demon new victims, it will eventually turn on *him*."

The entire lower half of Dagmar's leg was turning dark, and she was losing sensation in it. "I don't feel much sympathy for him," she snapped. "What can we do?"

"There's no way to get rid of a demon," Ramdane said, his face tight. "That's why no intelligent person touches necromancy."

Dagmar's mouth went dry. The dark flesh was crawling up past her knee, and her fingertips were chilly. "Shit. Maybe I should have jumped after all."

Biddlemeyer drew back his sword. "I'll make it painless."

A dreadful idea came over Dagmar. A awful, terrible, dreadful idea. Just the thought of it made her cold and shaky inside. But it was better than becoming a zombie. She pushed Biddlemeyer's sword away.

"I know how to handle this," she said grimly.

"You do?" Ramdane said.

Dagmar looked down at Crystamel. The dog's ears drooped, and she backed away. "Oh, no," she said. "No, no, no."

"You wanted a new body." Dagmar plucked a heavy frying pan from a hook above the hearth. "Start chanting, little brother."

"Now wait a minute—" Ramdane began.

"No time to debate, Ram." Dagmar raised the pan. Crystamel backed away, but her rump came up against the table leg.

"What's she talking about?" Biddlemeyer asked.

"Now, Dagmar," said Crystamel. "Let's not be—"

Dagmar whacked Crystamel with the frying pan. The dog shattered like a little flowerpot. Ramdane swore and hastily set up a chant under his breath. A silvery mist rose up from the doggy bits. It gathered itself into a featureless silver ball that managed nonetheless to look pretty pissed off. Dagmar glanced nervously around despite her leg, which was now numb to the thigh. This was the point when a talismonger was most vulnerable. The last time Ramdane had done a hasty transfer, an enemy talismonger had captured Crystamel and blackmailed the both of them into going after a gorgon. Fortunately, Biddlemeyer was staring with his mouth open, and didn't seem interested in trying such a thing. She was oddly glad that he looked impressed. *Hm . . .*

Ramdane stepped carefully over to Dagmar with the gleaming ball hovering over one hand and paused his chant. "I can't believe you did that," he said.

She steeled herself. Her armor wouldn't protect her against this. It was like letting in one enemy to fight another. "Just finish it," she said. "You know what to do."

Ramdane released the misty ball. Dagmar inhaled sharply and sucked it in.

A strange heat slithered through Dagmar's body. The warmth met a cold force, and the two clashed hard. She shuddered and fell squirming back onto the table, only vaguely aware that both Biddlemeyer and her brother were trying to hold her steady. She fought, both inside and out, but—

The warmth smashed the cold. The cold gave a little yelp and squashed down into near nothing, though Dagmar could still feel it, small and resentful, like a frog tossed off its lily pad. Dagmar slumped against the hard wood of the table. The zombie demon was still there inside her, but powerless.

"*You went too far, Dagmar,*" said Crystamel inside her head. "*Now you've got about ten minutes to live.*"

"Yow!" Dagmar jerked upright, spilling both Biddlemeyer and Ramdane away. "No one said you'd be talking!"

"What's going on?" Biddlemeyer picked himself off the floor.

Ramdane did likewise. "It's my familiar. Crystamel's spirit will push Dagmar's out in a few minutes if we don't do something. But if we take Crystamel out, the zombie demon will just take over again, so we're booted either way. You only made it worse, Dagmar."

"No," Dagmar said, steeling herself a second time. "Now we move to phase two."

"Phase two?" Ramdane echoed. "When did we enter phase one?"

Dagmar flexed her leg. No pain, no cold. The wound had shrunk, too. Good. Except she was still dead in a few minutes if she didn't get a move on. Why did these things always come with a time limit? Gods, she was tired of all this.

"Don't worry, Lady Dagmar. We won't let your spirit get . . . pushed out," Biddlemeyer said stoutly. "You're too fine a—you're a very good— that is—" he halted, a little flushed. "I mean, my brother has hurt too many people, and we won't let anyone else come to harm. Especially you."

Hm . . . Dagmar hopped, clinking, off the table and gave Biddlemeyer a sideways glance. A lot of men liked women who knew their way around a sword, and he was certainly strapping. But no. She had signed on to be a warrior, and warriors fought. To the death.

Inside her, Crystamel darted about like a mixture of grease and lightning. It made her sick, but with it also came a strange sensation, like she was steadily filling with light, and she might explode at any moment.

"Come on," she said. "We don't have much time."

She towed a bewildered Ramdane out of the kitchen and into the main courtyard, with Biddlemeyer coming behind. Clumps of frightened-looking village survivors scattered to get out of their way in a strange reversal of the zombie horde outside the gates.

"If Crystamel is the reverse of the zombie demon," she explained as they went, "then I can share Crystamel's spirit with the zombies, right? Her spirit will spread and push the demon out, and it'll cure all the victims." *Right?* she added mentally.

"Oh. Er . . . possibly," Crystamel replied. *"Except . . ."*

Except what?

"Except I don't know what'll happen in the end. The demon has to go somewhere, you know."

Does that matter at this stage?

"Cure everyone?" Biddlemeyer gasped. "Even my mother?"

"If I'm right, yes."

Hope crossed Biddlemeyer's handsome face like sunlight. "Lady, if you truly cure everyone, you can name your price. You can name two."

"Don't give her that kind of opening," Ramdane warned.

Hm. They were climbing the stairs to the top of the wall again. The zombies were still below, with the zombie king in the back. All the zombies, perhaps two hundred of them, were beating at the gate, and it was creaking a little. Eventually, they would break through, and the other villagers, reluctant to kill their own family members, would fall victim to the horde.

"What does Herbert want, anyway?" Dagmar said. The slick light inside was growing stronger, and it was hard to concentrate.

"He's a good talismonger, but a bad earl," Biddlemeyer replied. "I offered to make him captain of the guard, but I think he'd rather rule over zombies than live under his own brother. Trouble is, he might get his way and spread all this to the entire kingdom—or the world."

The little boy who had bitten her pounded at the gate below. His fists were bleeding. Herbert the zombie king laughed. "Give up, Jack! I promise you won't feel a thing!"

"Button it, Herbert!" Biddlemeyer yelled back.

Crystamel stirred. The pulsing light inside grew stronger still, and Dagmar set her mouth. "Can you get me down there?"

Ramdane pulled a bit of string from his talisman belt, blew on it, and tossed it over the edge. The string hung in the air, then lengthened and thickened into a hawser. "How are you going to get Crystamel's spirit into the zombies?" he asked.

"The same way they got the demon into me." Before she could think overmuch about it, Dagmar jumped over the edge, grabbed the rope, and slid down.

The zombies saw her coming and reached up for her with their chilly hands. Most of them were covered with nasty sores, and the stench of rotten flesh hung on the air. Dagmar slid straight toward the morass. If this didn't work, she was going to need a whole lot of mint tea for her breath. Assuming she lived. But warriors fought to the—

"I knew you'd come back," cooed the zombie king. "With you on my side, pretty warrior, we'll take the keep and I'll rule the country forever."

"Eat, eat, eat," groaned his mother.

Dagmar didn't reply. She simply dropped into the middle of the zombie horde like a swimmer dropping into the world's nastiest swimming hole. The hawser above her vanished. The zombies clumped around her. They grabbed her arms and gnawed on her mail, but were unable to penetrate the links. The armor held.

Dagmar took a deep breath—the smell made her promptly regret it—grabbed the nearest zombie, and bit it on the arm. Her teeth sank into the soft flesh, easily breaking the skin. Dagmar's stomach threatened to come up and have a look around, but she fought it back down and ran her tongue over the wound, giving it a good dose of spit before shoving the zombie away.

The zombie stumbled, but had no other reaction.

Uh oh, said Crystamel.

Other zombies were still pulling at her, gnawing at her and breaking teeth on her armor. They apparently hadn't twigged to the idea of going for her knees like the little boy. Dagmar grabbed another zombie.

"I love that you're so aggressive," giggled Herbert. "I'll make you my captain."

Dagmar bit the zombie's peach-soft flesh and shoved it away. Still no reaction.

"I'm not getting in," Crystamel reported. *"And your spirit is losing ground."*

She was right. Dagmar felt the interior light pulsing stronger and stronger, a star that was going to explode any moment. Grimly, she drew her sword. At least she would die like a warrior, defending her brother and earl Bidd—and those in the keep. More zombies closed in.

And then she knew. Crystamel had it at the same moment.

"I'm the opposite *of them,"* she said in Dagmar's head. *"If you want to share my spirit, you can't bite them. They have to—"*

No! Dagmar thought. But her sword was motionless in her hand.

"You did it once. You can do it again."

This is different. More zombies were chewing on Dagmar now, still foiled by the chain mail. *A warrior fights to the death!*

"Sometimes a warrior has to stop fighting," Crystamel said.

Dagmar looked up. Ramdane seemed far away at the top of the keep, but she could see the frightened look on his face. Biddlemeyer looked equally concerned. She remembered her mother—and Biddlemeyer's. She couldn't save her mother, but she could save his. If she stopped fighting. Like a warrior.

"Eat, eat eat," said the mother zombie. The light pulsed so strong inside her, she felt like she was about to burst.

It was the hardest thing she had ever done, there in a crowd of zombies, to drop her sword and shout, "Ramdane! Get this mail off me!"

"What?" he shouted back. "Why?"

"Just do it! Now!"

He threw something from his belt at her—she didn't see what—and in a flash of green light, her chainmail unraveled like bad knitting. The zombies fell back as wire coiled at her feet with a bouncy, springy sound. Dagmar spread her arms, standing vulnerable among the undead.

"Bite me!" she said.

For a heart-stopping moment, the zombies paused. Then they clustered around her again, grabbed her arms, and bit.

Dagmar forced herself to let them. Oh, it hurt. It was like being stung by a thousand wasps, stabbed with a dozen daggers. She cried out, but with each bite, she felt a little of Crystamel's light leave her, and the pressure eased. Each zombie that drew blood dropped away, squirming on the ground before the gate. And each one . . . changed. The festering wounds healed, the smell faded, the skin lost its pallor. From each one fled a small shadow that raced back to Herbert the zombie king. He staggered, and his tin crown went crooked on his head.

"What are you doing?" he screeched. "What are—?"

The shadow around him grew stronger, fed by the ones fleeing Crystamel's light. With each bite, each stab of pain, Dagmar felt more and more of the light leave her. The baker staggered, then stood upright, fully himself. The little boy bit her, then rose up, healthy and new. The last zombie was the mother zombie. Dagmar offered her an arm.

"Eat," Dagmar said. Biddlemeyer's mother bit, then staggered back. The sores and blackened flesh cured themselves. She looked around herself in wonder while the crowd of cured people cheered and embraced one another in sheer joy.

"No!" screamed the zombie king. "I'm the earl! I'm the king! I'm—"

The shadow surrounding him took on a deep and powerful blackness. Something stirred inside it, something black and hideous, the sort of the thing that might hide under the bed in a torture chamber. It swirled around the zombie king in a dreadful cloud. His face went pale and wetness stained his crotch. Inside Dagmar's head, Crystamel made a sniffing sound.

"*You failed,*" the darkness said. "*You failed Me!*"

"No!" shouted Herbert in desperation. "I just need more time!"

But the dark cloud, filled with red eyes and scarlet claws, enveloped the zombie king. There was a rushing sound and a *whump* and a blast of wind. Dagmar shielded her eyes. When she brought her hands down again, the zombie king was gone. His tin crown spun a lonely circle on the ground.

"Eat," said Biddlemeyer's mother. "Eat, eat!"

"Thank you, I think I will." From her vantage point as guest of honor, Dagmar plucked more roasted turkey from the platter and surveyed the great hall. The entire town was there, feasting in celebration. Musicians played, food made the rounds, people laughed and danced. Biddlemeyer sat next to her, the kindly, generous earl. On the other side of him, also in a guest of honor position, sat Ramdane. Crystamel, now in the body of a plump tortoiseshell cat, perched on the arm of his chair. She didn't need to eat, but in the manner required of felines, shamelessly demanded a steady stream of turkey from Ramdane anyway.

I could get used to this, Dagmar thought, casting an eye toward the strapping, handsome Earl Biddlemeyer—Jack—who cast an equally interested eye back at her. She didn't feel so tired when he looked at her. Maybe it was time to give up the wandering sword and sorcery thing, settle down with a husband and talismongers. Maybe her story was coming to a close.

Jack raised his glass. "A toast," he called, and the room quieted. "To the skilled and beautiful, Dagmar, who saved our town!"

"Hear, hear!" cried the room.

"I did help a little, you know," Ramdane said while everyone drank.

Jack leaned toward Dagmar, who found herself flushing. "There's a lot of room in the keep," he said. "And I hear we could use a new captain of the guard. If you were willing to . . . stay?"

"You know," Ramdane said wickedly, "*I* hear a town to the southwest is having trouble with a vampire. Maybe we should . . . leave?"

Without taking her eyes off Jack, Dagmar dumped her ale into Ramdane's lap. "Bite me," she said.

Dark Pixii

❧

by Wen Spencer

She never thought she would be Magical Girl Dark Pixii ever again.

When she put her cosplay outfits into storage, she thought she was done with that part of her life. Since she could no longer be combat medic Lieutenant Valentina Loveworth, all she had left was pieces of who she used to be.

She pulled on the pieces of the costume armor, trying on her civilian life again. Everything was a little snug, but that was due to the bandages protecting the still-delicate scar tissue. She'd picked the costume because it was the only one that covered all the damage to her body. Last thing on was a fake eye patch to cover the very real and necessary dressing on her left eye.

After pulling the black wig into place, she inspected the result in the mirror. Magical Girl Dark Pixii stared back. All that was missing was the huge chip on her thermoplastic pauldron. She'd had a chip on her shoulder long before she joined the Navy; she'd been the shortest kid in her school (including all the grades below her) and the only one with a black belt in jujutsu. She'd lost the chip when she lost her eye.

"One weekend. You can say anything you damn well please." She promised her reflection. "But try not to kill anyone."

She'd forgotten what a pain it was to get the black wings through doors. The elevator tried to eat the tip of her impossibly massive sword, Dork Buster.

She eyed the sword darkly. "Someone was clearly compensating."

The elevator stopped with a *ding*, the doors slid open, and eight giggling girls spilled into the car with her. They were dressed as the assembled cast of some anime she didn't recognize, each wearing a different color wig. They all had animal ear headbands and horsetails. Some had strap on wings and others had unicornlike horns. It was like being caught into a sudden stampede of mythical horses.

Pixii might have been a decade older than the girls, and wounded in combat, but they were all four to eight inches taller than her. They were fifteen and sixteen, true innocents, judging by their nervous laughter. None of the cosplay costumes were entirely decent, a fact that was just now dawning on them.

"I told you they'd be shorter once I hemmed everything." The unicorn seamstress was in a snug white mini dress with three blue diamonds riding her left hip. The costume fit like a kid glove but came to mid-thigh, making it the longest dress among the girls.

"Can you see my panties?" The yellow pegasus had on a diaphanous baby-doll top that matched her wings and ears. It really wasn't long enough to qualify as a "dress." She turned beet red as everyone tilted their heads slightly and studied her panties, which matched her pink wig and long tail. She slapped her hand down on the hem of the dress, but it didn't help much.

"Nope, can't see them," the other pegasus with rainbow wings lied.

"There's only girls here." The only one of the herd decently dressed was the girl with a cowboy hat. She was wearing boots, blue jeans, and a plaid shirt tied at her waist. "No need to kick up a fuss."

"Chibi, I told you to wear your bikini bottoms," a quiet voice said from the back of elevator. Pixii was too short to see the speaker.

"I didn't bring a swimsuit!" Chibi cried.

The girls exchanged worried looks.

"Do you have shorts?" asked the only girl with both a unicorn horn and wings.

"No!" Chibi pranced slightly in distress. "All I have is my school uniform, and Inkling is wearing that!"

"Just tell people you're wearing bikini bottoms." A girl in an even skimpier pink outfit lifted up her skirt to show off what might have been the bottom of a bathing suit. "It's not like anyone could tell one from the other."

The red deepened in shade. "I would know."

"It's not like they're thongs," a unicorn with a mint and white wig said. "Or are they?" The unicorn flipped up the pegasus' tail and the back of the yellow skirt.

"Lyra!" Chibi grabbed the edge of her hem and moved as far away from her friend as the elevator allowed.

"Your tail covers you in the back, sugar," the cowgirl noted. "At least, it usually does."

"What am I going to do?" This was a near-panicked wail.

Did the girls not have an adult riding herd on them?

"There are booths selling cosplay outfits in the dealer's room," Pixii said. "The hair, wings, and ears are the main part of the costume . . . "

"She has to be yellow!" all the girls cried.

"There might be someone selling skirts or shorts," Pixii continued. "Anything white or black will work, it just needs to cover her panties."

"What do I do until then?" Chibi wailed.

Pixii doubted the skimpy dress would matter that much during the block-long walk to the convention center, but she was no longer fifteen. What part of her modesty that had survived boot camp was stripped by her first deployment.

A hand reached through the crowd, plucked a big, leather-bound book from the winged unicorn, and handed it to the distressed pegasus. "Hold this in front of your panties."

The book managed to be in place just as the elevator dinged, announcing their arrival in the lobby. The girls spilled out, laughing.

In the back, the voice of reason was apparently Inkling. Her borrowed Catholic school uniform passed as cosplay. Her deep gold hair had been ironed and put up into impossible pigtails to heighten the illusion that the normal street clothes were actually a costume. She leaned in the back corner of the elevator, writing in a notebook with a retractable ballpoint pen. There was something about her, though, that made her seem luminous in the small confines of the elevator.

Pixii stood in the doorway, staring, feeling like the breath had been kicked out her until the elevator started to complain about being held open. *Danger, Lieutenant Loveworth, danger, jailbait off the starboard bow.*

"You coming?" Pixii asked.

The girl seemed lost in her writing.

"Hey!" Pixii stepped forward and tapped her on the wrist. "Inkling? Are you coming?"

Inkling dragged herself out of her writing and blinked at Pixii in surprise. She had stunningly blue eyes that were too old for her face. "What?" She clicked the ballpoint pen nervously.

"Are you getting off?" Pixii jerked her head toward the lobby.

Still clicking her ballpoint, Inkling stepped off the elevator. "I don't know why, but I didn't expect it to be this—this surreal."

Shinigami Rem from *Death Note*, two shrine maidens, and a samurai brushed past them, pouring off the second elevator car that opened beside them.

"First anime convention?" Pixii asked.

Inkling gave a tiny nod. "First of a lot of things." She scanned the lobby, looking for someone.

"They headed for the convention center." Pixii pointed in the direction the other girls had galloped off toward.

She looked back at Pixii. "Are you alone?"

"Yeah."

Inkling held out a hand. "Come on. You can hang out with us."

Pixii stared down at the hand. *You know you really want to.*

The puberty Easter bunny had not been kind to Pixii. She was four foot ten, boy flat, and had the voice of a first grader. Inkling was mistaking her for a kid wandering around all alone. "I might look twelve, but I'm really older than you are."

Inkling twiddled her fingers at her. "Please? I really want someone to talk to that isn't obsessing about ponies."

Pixii laughed with surprise and relief. "So they are cosplaying equines." She took the offered hand. It was warm and soft and welcoming. After six years of drowning in testosterone, it was a healing touch. "I wasn't sure, I don't know the show they're doing."

For some reason this triggered a blush. "They're actually cosplaying this angst-ridden fanfic *loosely* based on the show. It's a story about a girl that sees a ghost . . . and . . . well . . . by the end all the characters are dead."

Been there. Done that. Got the T-shirt. Not that she ever talked to people about it. She'd learned early in life that telling people about the weird stuff only she could see was very bad thing to do.

Instead, she said, "I'm doing Magical Girl Dark Pixii, which is a totally original character, so I can't criticize."

They caught up with the others and moved as a herd to the steel and glass Baltimore Convention Center. Even in the sea of cosplayers, the girls drew notice, although all but Inkling seemed oblivious to it. They were thoughtlessly free with one another in a way that was innocent and yet provocative. Add in young, athletic, and skimpily dressed and Pixii found herself subtly blocking men with Dork Buster as they moved through the crowds.

By the time they hit the convention center, Pixii had pieced together that the eight girls all lived at different private schools for girls of very rich and powerful families in the Beltway area. They were the ultimate in sheltered innocents. Most of them had never actually met before; their friendship was based on an online message board for fan fiction. The older sister of the skirt flipper had gotten them a hotel room, and then vanished with a boyfriend. The missing sister, however, was the only adult who actually knew that they were in Baltimore, and not where they were supposed to be. Pixii didn't count herself because she had no clue who the girls really were since they were using a mix of character and screen names. Lyra was a character from the story, but Chibi used ChibiX on the forum.

In the lobby they fended off several requests for photos of all the ponies together.

"You didn't want to be a pony?" Pixii asked Inkling.

"I didn't want photographic evidence that I was here plastered all over the Internet."

They made their way to the dealer's room as a united front. The massive room was packed to the brim with dealers of everything imaginable related to Japanese culture in general and anime in particular. Testament to the range of items, the first booth had Japanese snacks and in the far corner, there was a towering samurai statue. All the bright treasures on display quickly peeled away girls with squeals of "Look!" and "Oh my God!" and "Oh so cute!" Before they'd reached the end of the first aisle, only Pixii and Inkling remained with an increasingly nervous ChibiX.

"Where are the people that sell costumes?" Chibi whimpered.

"There's probably at least a dozen here, don't worry." Pixii couldn't see over the heads of the people around them. She bounced up, was surprised to see a second samurai statue ahead of them just beyond a dealer selling Goth Lolita outfits. Pain lanced through her when she landed.

"Note to self," she whimpered, "don't do that again."

"You okay?" Chibi asked.

"Yeah, there's a cosplay dealer by the statue." Pixii pointed the direction.

"What statue?" Chibi bounced too, attracting lots of attention as she forgot to keep the book in place.

"Stop. Stop. Stop. Stop." Inkling used her own body to shield her from the stares at the girl's groin.

"The statue just like . . . " The one in the far corner was gone. "Oh, donkey balls!"

Pixii really wished weird spooky shit would stick to places like abandoned houses and graveyards. She could possibly avoid it if it didn't keep showing up at places like shopping malls and convention centers. It was her experience, though, that the things that showed up in very public areas were harmless. Usually.

She wasn't sure what she would do if it were dangerous. Whack it in the shins with Dork Buster? If she was going to pick a fight with a twenty-foot-tall statue, she wanted something more than a foam sword. Most of her life she'd studied everything she could find on the occult, from ninjutsu mediation rituals to college classes on world religions. Over and over again, she was told: it is believed. Nowhere could she find: it has been proven. Legends. Lore. Folktales. Whispers in the dark around campfires.

She wanted an occult equivalent of an assault rifle, not "throw salt and pray."

"Oh!" Chibi squeaked, making Pixii jump. "Clothes!"

The girls headed toward the statue, oblivious to it.

Pixii trailed behind them, trying to keep her one good eye on both the girls and the statue. She got the distinct impression that the giant stone samurai was tracking them through the crowd but it could be her natural paranoia kicking in.

Chibi made squeaky noises as the girls flipped through the various outfits. "No. No. No. Oh, Inkling!" Inkling held up pink three-layer lace bloomers that were a perfect match to Chibi's hair. "That's perfect!"

Chibi found the price tag and read the amount. "Oh! I know I don't have the much cash." She started digging in a small purse that looked like a white rabbit. "I'll have to use my—oh, where is it? Where's my credit card?" She gave a long distressed whimper. "Oh, no, no, no! Don't tell me I left it on my desk after I ordered the *doujinshi* on Thursday!"

"It's okay." Inking clicked her ballpoint nervously. "If everyone chips in three dollars, we can cover it. Team Banzai Go! Right?"

"Oh, Inkling! If you give me three dollars, you won't be able to get anything for yourself."

"You picked me up and Lyra is letting me crash in the hotel room. Being here with friends is all I really need. That's the whole thing with Team Banzai: we take care of each other."

Pixii swallowed, filled with sudden envy. She missed the gentleness of female friendship. "Here." She dug out her wallet and found a twenty and a five. "I'll cover it. You can pay me back later."

It earned her a squeal and an enthusiastic hug from Chibi.

In the back of the booth, the dealer had created a makeshift changing room out of panels of *yukata* fabric. Chibi disappeared into it to pull on the bloomers without giving the nearby boys a free show.

Movement warned Pixii that someone was on her left. She spun around, bringing up Dork Buster. "Back off!"

A surprisingly tall Japanese man stood in front of her, dressed in an elegant, dark kimono. His white hair and the lines on his face suggested he was old, but there was no hint of weakness in his powerful build. He looked down at her with surprise.

She started to relax when she realized that she couldn't have seen movement out of her blind eye. She took at step back, tightening her hold on Dork Buster. The massive statue was gone. From his *geta* sandals to topknot hairstyle, the man looked very much like a samurai. Off-balance, she stammered out, "What—what do you want?"

"I need a shrine maiden." He had a low, rumbling voice.

None of the weird things that Pixii encountered had ever spoke to her before. They screamed and whispered and muttered, but never to her. They were like homeless mad men standing on the corner, screaming insanity. She just happened to be sole witness to the discussion they were having with the universe.

But it really seemed like the man—the thing—had answered her question.

"Seriously?" she asked. "Do I look like a shrine maiden to you?"

He considered her a moment. "You can see me."

She gasped and took another step backwards, crowding into the racks of lace and silk. "What are you?"

"I am a god. I am Yamauchi Kami. There seems to be many shrine maidens here, but none of them seem to be able to see me."

He meant all the girls doing cosplay as shrine maidens. They were easy to spot with their bright red billowy trousers and crisp white kimono jackets. There were at least three in sight range; all Caucasian.

"You're—You're a Japanese god?"

"I am *kunitsukami*, or a god born in the land you know as Japan."

The individual sentences made more sense than the normal ranting of the boogeymen Pixii had stumbled across earlier in her life, but put all together, it didn't make a lick of sense. "What are you doing in Baltimore?"

"I am seeking something, but I am not here. Not completely. I have merely sent a seed of myself across the ocean to this land to find something that was lost."

Still wasn't making complete sense.

"Seems like a long way to go for a shrine maiden," Pixii said. "Don't you have a passel of them in Japan?"

"A shrine maiden is not what I came to find, but what I need at this moment. Are you one?"

The classic advice was if someone asked if you were a god, you said yes. Shrine maiden? This was not a position she thought she would find herself in, but of late, nothing was how she thought her life would turn out. She'd joined the military to prove that, despite her size, she could hold her own against anything. Time had taught her that "anything" was too broad a definition.

It seemed, though, that the safe answer was the honest one. "No." But then her rampant paranoia got the best of her. "Why do you need one?"

"The *shintai* I'm using to travel the world is with a collection of other artifacts. One was a very dangerous *yokai* sealed within an urn. This morning, the urn was broken and the *yokai* released."

"A *yokai* is a monster?"

"You would term it as such. It is a being that is not like humans or animals. It exists as a spirit that can take a form and manipulate the world about them."

"Like a ghost?"

Yamauchi frowned at the question. "The two are nothing alike. It is more like a carnivorous plant than a ghost."

"Carnivorous? It eats people?"

"Those it traps within its hold, yes."

"If you're a god, why don't you seal it back up?"

"I am not here." The god pointed at his sandaled feet. "You have those little things that you hold in your hand and people who are not there talk out of them? What appears before you is like the voice that comes from . . . " He tapped his palm. "Those—those—talking things."

He meant a cell phone—or at least—she thought he did.

"And you're speaking English instead of Japanese . . . because?"

"The language I speak is not Japanese, but that of gods. You can understand it just the same as you can see an image that you recognize as a being. No one else can hear or see me."

Right. Luckily, the Dark Pixii costume had a headset that could be mistaken for a Bluetooth device. She pressed a hand to it, pretending to listen to some real human conversation. "And how do I know you're a god and not this monster trying to lure me into a trap?" At least at an anime convention, this was a totally reasonable discussion to be having. If anyone asked, she could be claim that she was taking part in one of the many LARP games currently running.

He reached out, making her flinch back and raise Dork Buster. "If you allow me, I can prove myself."

"Don't touch me," she growled. She couldn't back up any further.

"Very well."

Pain flared in her left eye like it was on fire.

Note to self: don't ask gods to prove themselves!

She tore off the eye patch and peeled up the bandage. What did he do to her? She looked at the dealer's full-length mirror. Her left eye seemed perfect. Too perfect. That morning the pupil had been a smear of darkness across the iris. She slapped her hand to her right eye. She looked out her left eye and saw perfectly. Giddy terror went looping through her. "Oh! Oh! Oh fudge!"

He *was* a god. So, there probably was a monster. And he wanted her to deal with it. Because no one else could.

Pixii looked around with her newly healed eye. Almost everyone in sight was a child, some as young as eleven. She breathed out a curse.

"Chibi?" Inking called loudly. "Chibi? Are you okay?"

Pixii turned, her breath catching in her chest.

Inkling stood next to the jury-rigged fitting room. She pulled an inch of the fabric door aside to peer in. "Chi? Where are you?" She reached up and undid the clip.

"Inking!" Pixii caught hold of her and pulled her back even as the cloth dropped open. For a moment, Pixii saw a glistening cavern, like a giant throat, and then it was simply a tiny, yard-wide fabric booth.

"What the hell?" Inkling glanced down at Pixii and then scanned the area, completely ignoring Yamauchi. "Where'd she go?"

Pixii pulled Inkling away from the changing booth. "What happened to her?" Pixii asked Yamauchi.

"I don't know." Inkling clicked her ballpoint pen nervously. "I didn't see her come out."

"She's been taken," Yamauchi stated.

"What?" Pixii cried.

"I wasn't paying attention," Inkling answered the question first. "I was writing."

"The *yokai* uses enclosed spaces to trap its victims within a maze. Once inside, its victim cannot escape. They wander deeper and deeper in, until they come to the killing chamber, where they are devoured."

"How do we kill it?" Pixii asked.

Inkling gave her a startled, confused look.

"Sorry." Pixii pressed her hand to her earpiece. "I'm LARPing. Why don't you see if Chibi looped back to show the bloomers to the others?"

Sent toward safety—hopefully—Inkling started back toward the entrance.

"By its nature, I cannot reach the *yokai*," Yamauchi explained. "Nor do I have the power to kill it here, in this place. A shrine maiden must enter its trap and seal it with an *ofuda*."

"A what? What-a *fuda*?"

"*Ofuda*. A paper talisman that acts as a *shintai* that allows part of my essence to seal the *yokai*."

"Oh, one of those." She'd watched enough anime to know what he was describing, but didn't know enough Japanese to know the word for it. "You have one of these here?"

"You will have to make one."

"Make?" She would have asked if he was kidding, except she knew the answer was no. She'd done calligraphy in the past for cosplay props, but creating a magical holy artifact? And make it good enough that she could use it against a monster? "Are you sure there's not a real shrine maiden around here somewhere?"

Luckily they were standing in the middle of all things Japanese. They found a calligraphy set two aisles down. It had four brushes, an ink stone, and a traditional sumi ink stick.

Pixii scanned the table. "I don't know how to make ink. I've always used bottled stuff."

"I will teach you," Yamauchi pointed at a package labeled: *mitsumatagami washi*. "This is the paper you will need."

"I'm getting it!" Along with all of the paper, she bought a Hello Kitty flashlight, the largest backpack that she could find, and a hardwood bo staff. She had a medical kit and her survival knife back at her room.

They also paused at the dealer selling the one-foot-tall samurai statue that housed Yamauchi and bought that, too. The man wanted a thousand dollars for it, but Pixii didn't want to risk someone buying it and carrying it away. At least it was museum-quality work and worth the amount.

"You've made this?" Pixii hefted the statue, marveling at the fine details. "But you can't make the *ofuda*?"

"I made my *shintai* in my own realm where I can fully manifest. Most of my spirit is still there, in my own realm. This holds only a small part of my essence. It could not hold all of my power; it would shatter to dust."

Her fingertips were all stained black by the time they returned to the dealer's room with the talismans. It should read: It bothered her, as her fingers felt like they had after she was wounded, when the blood on her hands dried.

She wished there was time to wash them; she rubbed her fingers together in a vain attempt to clean them. "We have to hurry; that thing has Chibi."

"You must be on your guard." Yamauchi's wooden sandals made no noise as they hurried down the aisle. "All humans are aware of the spirit world to some degree. Only a rare few are impervious to it. The more aware you are, the safer, because you can keep up your guard. The *yokai* will slowly strip away your thoughts and desires. You must hold tight to you."

"Okay." She tapped where she had the talisman carefully tucked inside her breastplate. "I just slap one of these on it, and it will be sealed?"

"Yes. Once it is sealed, you will return to safety."

She stepped into the small fabric booth and used the binder clip to fasten the cloth door. For a moment she stood in dim enclosure, listening to the roar of human voices just beyond.

Then she was someplace dark and silent.

She fumbled the flashlight. She stood in a tunnel, the pale smooth walls reflecting the light. The impression of a throat remained. The air was warm and moist. The smell of carrion wafted in a breeze that came and went, like breathing. The silence, after the roar of humanity, took her breath away.

She stood there, panting. She listened to her own loud, ragged breath until she realized she'd lost track of time. "This isn't frigging Lamaze class here." What was she doing here? "I've got to find Chibi. Chibi!" The silence ate her shout and that annoyed her. "Chibi!"

Pixii started forward. "Keep hold of yourself? I'm running around with a pair of fairy wings on. What part of that seems like I know who the fuck I am anymore? I'm twenty-five years old, damn it, not fourteen. I don't even know why I'm at this con; I can't find myself by going back to what I was before."

It occurred to her that with her eye healed, she could go back to duty. Of course, explaining it would be difficult. "'Yes, yes, its fine now because a Japanese god—touring the world like the traveling gnome—healed it.' That would go over so well."

Who was she without the massive chip on her shoulder? What did she want now that proving herself was no longer feasible, or even sane? What did she do with the rest of her life?

"Chibi!" Pixii shouted again because didn't really want to deal with those questions. She'd been racing through life at a hundred miles per hour. Combat medic. Two deployments into war zones. College classes while she was stateside. Then *boom*; one IED exploded too close to her, and she's at a dead stop. She didn't even know in what direction to go if and when she got started back up. "What I want is to find—find—"

She was standing, trying to remember, when Chibi came bouncing down the passageway. Singing. "*Stamp on the ground, jump, jump, jump, jump, moving all around, tap tap it down.*" She stopped to blink at Pixii in surprise. "Oh, hi! Isn't this cool?"

"*Cool?*" Pixii had been sure she would only find the girl's half-eaten body. The word exploded out of her.

"Um." The girl flinched back. "In a scary, creepy kind of way? It's just that cool, weird things happen to other people all the time. I live the most boring life in existence. I've always, always wanted some kind of superpower or something strange to happen to me, and now it has!"

Pixii stared at her for a moment. Was Chibi one of the rare people impervious to spirits? Was that why nothing odd never happened to the girl?

They found the killing chamber. It was vast cavern that glowed eerily. Water pooled around the blood-red pith in the center. Mist drifted through the room. It was almost beautiful. At the edge, though, were bones, picked clean and bleached to stark white.

"Oh, awesome!" Chibi breathed.

Pixii sighed, pressing a hand to her forehead. A dozen dead people within reach and the teenager thought it was cool. At least she wasn't hysterical with fear. The question remained: how deep was the seemingly shallow liquid? And how corrosive it was since it seemed to be operating as stomach acid.

"Pixii?" Chibi shook her by the arm, startling her.

"What?" Pixii had her knife out before she realized it was Chibi.

"Are you okay?" Chibi pushed the knife tip to one side with her finger. "You've been standing there staring at it for like ten minutes."

"I have?"

Chibi nodded.

Spacing out would be bad while deep in the acid. She put away her flashlight and took out the talismans she'd made.

Chibi squealed, making her jump again. "*Ofuda!* Oh! Oh! Oh! I want to do one!"

Pixii shook her head. "You're staying here where it's safe."

"Oh please! When am I ever going to get to use an *ofuda* against a monster again?"

"Hopefully never."

"How do you know that this spot is any safer than staying right beside you? What if when you use the *ofuda*, you go someplace else and I get left here?"

Both totally valid points.

"Okay." Pixii handed her one of the slips of paper.

Chibi squealed and hugged Pixii quick and hard. "Team Banzai Go!" She pumped her fist in the air.

Pixii braced herself and took a tentative step out into the water. It was surprisingly warm. Bones rocked in the waves put out by their passage, clicking together quietly.

Chibi caught hold of Pixii's arm with a slight whimper. "Okay, want to go home now."

Four steps in and it was up to Pixii's knees. She stopped, peering across the murky waters to the distant gleaming pith. There would be no way to keep the talisman dry if they had to swim to the center. The next step was deeper yet.

"Shit, shit, shit, shit." Pixii paused again. "How are we going to get across without getting the talisman wet?"

"We could try performing *Kuji-Goshin-Ho*."

"What?"

"You know. *Rin. Pyou. Tou . . .*" Chibi stuttered to a stop when she realized Pixii was staring at her. "You don't know it?" *Akuryō Taisan!* Evil spirits begone!"

The *kuji* was chanting nine words of power while making the associated hand gestures. While the meanings changed from religion to religion, it was a cornerstone ritual of Asian beliefs.

"I know it." Pixii had actually begged her ninja-crazy jujutsu sensei to teach her the *kuji* along with some other more esoteric ninjutsu skills. Her sensei had spent hours tirelessly beating the correct form into Pixii. Explaining not only the finger positions and the mind thought behind it, but thousands of other hard won truths.

"Falling down does not make you weak, it makes you sore. Not getting back up means you're weak."

Words that drove Pixii all through boot camp and both

deployments. Truths Pixii believed because her sensei was a small woman holding her own in a man's world.

"Pixii." Chibi tugged at her elbow. "You're zoning again."

"Sorry." Pixii took a deep breath. They had a half-dozen talismans. They could waste one or two trying crazy shit. If nothing else, the monster seemed not to be affecting Chibi. "Here, take one."

"Awesome!" Chibi took it, struck a drama pose. "*Rin, pyo, to, sha, kai, jin, retsu, zai, zen! Akuryō taisan!*" The girl waved the talisman furiously and then flung it. It fluttered down into the water. "Did it work? It didn't seem to work. Do you think it worked?"

Chibi obviously only knew what she'd seen on anime.

"No, it didn't work. Let me try." Pixii tucked the talisman back into her breastplate. She took a deep, cleansing breath and corrected her form. *Clear your mind; focus your chi.*

She pressed her hands together into the first position. *Seal of the thunderbolt.* "*Rin.*" She shifted her hands into the second position. *Seal of the greater thunderbolt.* "*Hyo.*" *Seal of the outer lion.* "*To.*" *Seal of the inner lion.* "*Sha.*" Hands together, fingers interlocked, the tips on the outside. *Seal of the outer bonds.* "*Kai.*" Fingertips on the inside. *Seal of the inner bonds.* "*Jin.*" Seventh position. *Seal of the wisdom fist.* "*Retsu.*" Spread fingers, thumbs and index touching. *Seal of the ring of the sun.* "*Zai.*" Right hand overlapping left fist. *Seal of the hidden form.* "*Zen.*"

She felt potential crawl over her skin like static electricity, raising the hairs on her arms. She pulled out the talisman and held it up. "*Akuryō taisan!*"

The strip of paper jerked out of her fingers and leapt across the distance to slap tightly against the blood-red pith.

And they were suddenly standing in a boy's restroom, a half-dozen teenage boys shouting in surprise.

"It worked! It worked! That was so awesome!" Chibi flung herself at Pixii, nearly knocking her over. "You were awesome!"

Pixii dragged her from the bathroom. "You were great, too."

Chibi deflated. "No, I sucked, like normal. I should have known; I always fail."

And Pixii knew then what she wanted to do with her life. She wanted to be a teacher. She smacked Chibi in the back of the head like her sensei used to when she said something stupid. "Failing is part of learning. If you're not failing, then you're not trying. You did great;

you kept your head and you kept me focused. I couldn't done it without you."

"Yeah, we were a great team." Chibi grinned and fist pumped. "Team Banzai Go!"

A Warrior Looks at 40

by Julia S. Mandala

I was losing faith in the power of my boobs.

As a young woman, when my cleavage had blossomed into fullness, I discovered that my breasts had the power to bend men to my will or render them drooling idiots. At the very least, my charms blanked men's minds long enough to give me an advantage. As magic powers went, mine proved pretty useful for a journeyman-at-best sell-sword.

But as the first blush of my youth faded—okay, the second blush of my youth—my breasts seemed to have a tiny bit less magic than before.

I first noticed a difference when I returned to the city of Callum, where I'd trained as a mercenary in Lord Barlin's company, years ago. I entered my favorite haunt, the Randy Rogue Tavern, accompanied by my black cat, Saber. I wore a fox-fur cape over my brass bra and chainmail. It was frosty outside, and I didn't want my nipples to freeze to the metal. Plus, it allowed for a more dramatic revelation of my glory.

I sauntered to the crowded bar and set down my shield, which my mercenary friends had dubbed Nosehammer for reasons which escape me. When I whipped off my cape, a dangling fox tail struck a hapless teenage lad in the face as he took a swig. Beer spilled down his chin, drawing laughter from his friends.

In the past, when such mishaps occurred, a flash of my bosom garnered instant forgiveness—and drooling.

"Watch what you're doing, ya hag," the lad snapped.

My cheeks heated. *Hag?* His friends guffawed again—but this time at me!

Saber jumped onto the bar stool and hissed at the lot of them. I picked up my shield and "accidentally" slammed the rim into the little snot's nose. Blood spurted in a satisfying stream. Okay, perhaps I *do* recall how the shield earned its name.

I turned back to the bar. The bartender stood a few feet down, washing mugs with a rag of suspect cleanliness. I waited for my cleavage to penetrate his consciousness—such as it was.

He kept washing.

"Ahem," I said.

Nothing.

I pressed my arms against the sides of my breasts to deepen my cleavage and leaned forward to give him a better view.

Nothing.

A middle-aged man next to me whistled, and then said, "If she's not getting served, none of us have a chance."

I felt better—until I considered his age relative to the boy who called me hag. I glanced down at my breasts, plumped up by the brass cups. In the soft lamp light, they looked the same as ever to me.

Sighing, I turned to my cat, with whom I shared a magical link. *<Saber, do I look . . . mature?>*

The cat licked his paw. Saber is nothing if not discreet. His non-answer made me scowl.

Then I remembered that scowling would cause lines around my mouth. I forced a smile. Who cared what some wet-behind-the-ears *boy* thought? He probably couldn't even see straight in the state he was in.

How he'd gotten drunk was a mystery, since apparently no one could get a bloody drink in this bar.

A hand planted itself on my mail-clad buttocks. "Keara, my girl," a familiar voice said. "It's been an age!"

I turned slowly to let my breasts make a grand entrance. "Trystan!"

Trystan—handsome and athletic—was good for a fun tumble whenever I came to Callum. By the glassy sheen in his blue eyes, I could tell he'd had a few pints.

Saber's ears flattened. *<You're better off with your cat.>*

<Oh, Saber, it's just for fun. No offense, but there are some things a girl needs that she can't get from her cat.>

<When he behaves like an ass, don't come yowling to me. See you in the morning.> Saber jumped off the stool, flicked his tail, and sauntered to a corner near the fireplace.

Trystan didn't even try to charm me, just went straight to a proposition. But considering how the evening had gone—and the fact that *I couldn't get a bloody drink*—I didn't make him woo me before letting him take me to his room.

Trystan's performance seemed a little less . . . satisfying than the last time we'd tussled. Perhaps it was the beer. Or his age. Such things happened.

Sunlight streaming through the window woke me. As soon as I stood, Trystan stirred. His muscles rippled under his skin as he stretched and yawned. When his gaze fell on me, nude and bathed in golden light, his eyelids, half-closed by sleep, flew open wide. Ah, I still had it.

"Gods, *what* was I drinking last night?" he muttered, putting a hand over his eyes.

I winced. But maybe I was being overly sensitive. It wasn't *always* about me. I sat beside him and ran a finger down his chest. "Want to try again?" I asked in my most seductive purr.

"Can't. I . . . have to . . . do something."

I huffed. He couldn't even bother to come up with a good lie.

While I sat in stunned dejection, Trystan set a record getting his clothes on. "Look, Keara, this has been fun and all, but I . . . I really shouldn't have been with you. I have a girl—one of Lord Barlin's mercenaries, Furi."

"'*Furi-with-an-I*'? Is she even potty-trained?"

He lifted a shoulder and turned toward the door. "She's twenty-two."

I snorted. Twenty-two. About the age I'd been when I'd met Trystan—and Furi had been four. Apparently, his taste in women hadn't changed—including his age preference.

"Uh, take your time getting out of here," he said. "Good to see you again."

I grabbed Nosehammer, intending to smack away his pitying

expression, but Trystan wisely hustled out the door, closing it behind him.

I glanced down at my forty-year-old body in the harsh daylight. I looked hot . . . didn't I? Faint wrinkles marred the skin on my breasts. Without the support of the brass cups, they didn't stand as pert as they used to. Unlike on Trystan's still-perfect body, a pad of fat had insinuated itself over the muscles on my mid-section.

It wasn't fair! Why did men get to retain their looks so much longer than women? Women warriors already had to work harder and achieve greater to get the same recognition as our male counterparts.

As I finished fastening my brass bra, a scratching at the door told me Saber had arrived. I let him in.

<And so?>

<Don't ask.> Such was my anguish, however, that I couldn't contain my misery. *<He thinks I look* old! *He only slept with me because he was drunk.>*

Saber head-butted my calf. *<Who cares what he thinks?>*

<I care! If he thinks that, probably other men think that too. Did you hear what that boy in the bar called me? Hag!>

<Looks can't last forever—unless you're a cat.>

<But what am I, without my looks?>

Saber smirked. I realize cats can't help it—their faces come with a permanent smirk. But it rubbed me the wrong way.

<You could work to be a better swordswoman, instead of relying on your breasts for distraction,> he suggested. *<You've been lucky to fight easily distracted men—or women like you who rely on their looks rather than skill. Or you could take the money you've saved and start a business. You've a good mind for ledgers, when you care to use it.>*

The money I'd saved . . . *<That's it! I'll find a wizard to restore my powers.>*

Saber huffed. *<It's like talking to a stone wall.>*

Feeling better now that I had a plan, I scritched along Saber's back. His butt raised of its own accord. *<Come on, Saber. It'll be an adventure.>*

We traveled by horse, Saber riding in a basket fixed behind my saddle, to the Wizard Alphonse's tower, deep in the Canyons of Doom. No doubt, he'd named them that to discourage visitors. The canyons were really quite lovely in the winter, dusted with snow, trees glazed in ice.

When Alphonse opened the door of his tower, his eyes widened in alarm. "No refunds! I warned you that you didn't really want to know what that animal is thinking."

"I'm not here about my mind link with Saber," I said. "It's something of a more delicate nature."

He glanced at my mid-section, exposed by a gap in my cape. "Aren't you a bit old to be having a baby?"

"*What*?" I shrieked, my voice rising several octaves. Icicles shattered and ice chips rained down on us. "I am *not* pregnant."

The wizard didn't even have the decency to blush. "You may want to lay off the sweets then."

Nosehammer smashed into his face before I even realized what I was doing.

Our next stop took us to the Caverns of the Damned. I was starting to believe that wizards were just antisocial.

The wizard who resided in said caverns looked puzzled by my request for more pert and youthful bosoms. "You look good, for a woman your age."

As I wiped his blood off Nosehammer, I said, "Here's a tip. There's no good way to use the phrase 'for a woman your age.'"

We journeyed on to the Maggoty Marsh. The young wizard who lived in a hollow tree listened patiently to my tale, until I reached the part about my age.

"You're only forty?" he interrupted, astonished. "I was about to offer you a senior discount."

I'm pretty sure no one will ever find his body.

Saber and I headed through the Valley of the Shadow of Auditors to the Plains of Really Bad Luck. Judging by that name, I already feared this wizard lacked panache.

A wizened old man opened the door to a one-room sod house. He invited Saber and me inside.

"Ah, I rarely receive visits from beautiful young women," he said as we sat at his rickety kitchen table.

I waited, my recent experience making me expect his next words to wipe out the compliment.

Instead, he asked, "What brings you here, my dear?"

I explained about my waning powers.

The old wizard nodded sympathetically. "Yes, my dear. I fear it only gets worse from here."

"But you can fix it, right?" I said, desperation tinging my voice.

"Do you think I would look like this"—he swept a gnarled hand down the length of his stooped body—"if I had magic that could restore youth?"

I suppose I should have realized that when I first saw him.

And so we traveled to the Abysmal Abyss. My spirits were sagging worse than my breasts, and Saber complained constantly about the travel, the lack of good food, and the folly of middle-aged women— after which he judiciously jumped out of shield-strike range.

The wizard whose tower lay at the bottom of the abyss looked promising—young, but not so young as to be inexperienced, and handsome to boot. He listened to my tale of woe, and then said, "I have something that will restore your youth. Take this magic cream and rub it all over your body—good gods, not right here! I learned the secret from some alchemists in Sweedland."

Hope bloomed in my heart. "How soon should I see results?"

"In four to six weeks."

I paid him a hefty sum of gold, but it would be worth it to look like my old—er, young—self again.

At first, I convinced myself that the cream was working, but in four to six weeks, I returned, full of righteous fury, to the Abysmal Abyss and pounded my shield against his door.

The wizard leaned out of a window two stories up. "No refunds!"

"You charlatan!" I shouted, throwing my weight against the wooden door. "I'll chop you into stew meat if you don't open this door and return my gold!"

"Calm down and I'll let you in," he said in a reasonable tone.

Since the door had bruised my shoulder, but showed no sign of opening under my assault, I took several deep breaths. "Very well. I'm calm."

"You're not just saying that?"

"No, no," I said, assessing. "I actually have calmed down." Once he let me inside, if I didn't like what he had to say, I could always fly into a rage again.

After the click of a bolt being drawn back, the door opened. The wizard, a wary look on his face, led me to his workroom. "I think the cream is working—"

My shield struck with lightning quickness. When the wizard came to, I said, "I want my gold."

"I don't have it," he said, his words muffled by the rag he held to his bleeding nose. As I raised Nosehammer again, he cringed and hastily added, "*But* I have an elixir that I *guarantee* will work."

Such was my desperation, I decided to hear him out.

"Take this oil—" He rummaged around on a shelf and retrieved a shiny gold bottle.

"What kind of oil?" I asked, intrigued and mesmerized by the shining gold. Something about the packaging just made it seem . . . trustworthy.

"Oil of snake," he said. "It cures almost everything, returns the pep to your step and gives your skin a youthful, golden glow."

My steps *had* been feeling somewhat less peppy in recent days and my skin looked pasty. He held the bottle close enough for me to see a runic label that read: *New and Improved!* and another which said: *Twenty-five percent more elixir than in the four-dram bottle!*

<*You can't seriously be considering giving this fraud more money,*> Saber thought.

<*But what if this is it—the elixir that can actually restore my breasts to their former glory?*>

<*Don't be a dupe,*> Saber said.

"How do you know this works?" I asked.

The wizard gave me a charming smile, which was no small feat, considering the blood smeared across his nose and chin. "How old would you say I am?"

I cocked my head and studied him. "Twenty-five?"

"I'm fifty," he said.

<*And I'm really a handsome prince, turned into a cat,*> Saber thought.

I stared down at Saber in surprise. <*Really?*>

<*No! Honestly, woman, you're making me reevaluate my estimation of your intelligence. Am I supposed to bear the burden of being both the beauty and the brains of our partnership?*>

<*I'm just . . . desperate.*>

<*And he knows it.*>

<But what if . . .> I couldn't escape the niggling fear that I'd be turning down something that would give me what I wanted.

"So why didn't you give me this oil in the first place?" I asked.

"It's *very* expensive," the wizard said, holding the bottle just out of reach. "And it's so powerful, I didn't think you needed it yet. This oil has been tested on dozens of women in Franz."

Oooh. Women in Franz were renowned for their youthful beauty—and armpit hair. And the packaging was just so . . . shiny.

"I'll give you a discount," the wizard said, "since the cream didn't work as well as hoped."

I reached for my money pouch. "How much?"

Four to six weeks later, the gold color had flaked off the bottle, my skin had turned orange, and my breasts looked depressingly the same. Saber and I returned to the Abysmal Abyss, a portable battering ram in tow. When the wizard's door lay in splinters, I charged up the stairs and stormed into his workroom.

"Wait! Wait!" he said, cowering.

"I want my money back." I stepped toward him, Nosehammer cocked back for a strike.

"But I have another remedy, newly arrived from Grease. Just take this wonder pill, then swing a dead cat over your head under the new moon—"

Saber flattened his ears, sank into a crouch, then launched himself, claws out, at the wizard's face. The wizard shrieked as the cat dug long furrows into his cheeks. Saber dropped lightly to the floor and started licking the blood off his paws.

<Thanks,> I thought to the cat. *<I'm tired of cleaning blood off my shield.>*

I ransacked the place until I found where the wizard stashed his gold. After reclaiming what I'd paid him, plus a little extra for travel expenses and the battering ram, Saber and I headed for the last wizard on my list.

Sunlight dappled the Mysterious Meadow. Smoke rose from the chimney of a cozy-looking thatched cottage. A plump woman with gray-streaked brown hair opened the door. She wore a loose linen dress that looked oh-so-much-more-comfortable than my brass bra and mail. I'd never worried about comfort before—my looks being far more important to me—but just then, not being chafed and pinched by my clothes sounded heavenly.

"I am the wizard Cyrene. Welcome," the woman said, her kind blue eyes looking me over. She extracted my shield from my grasp. "Let's just leave this out here, shall we?"

It was like she knew me.

Cyrene led me to a homey kitchen and settled me at a table covered with a lace cloth. "Now, what's troubling you, dearie?"

As I spilled out my sad tale, she poured me a cup of hot tea, got Saber a saucer of cream and set a generous hunk of cake in front of me. My mouth watered. I'd given up all sweets for weeks, yet the pad of fat remained plastered over my abdomen. I really shouldn't . . .

As I ravaged the cake like a hyena on a dead gazelle, Cyrene hummed thoughtfully. "It's so hard to adjust to life's changes, isn't it? But there's no cheating nature, *except*"—her gaze darted around, as though making sure we were alone—"for this special potion I brew for Princess Tarien and her friends. She wrote this letter praising it."

Princess Tarien was my age, yet still looked twenty-something. I stared at the page. Yes! There was the royal seal.

"So this really works?" I asked over a mouthful of cake.

Cyrene smacked me upside the head. "No! Of course it doesn't work! Princess Tarien gets a piece of the profits for saying it does. She comes from a lineage of youthful-looking people. Plus, she puts her makeup on with a trowel."

My ear stung, but not as much as my pride. How could I be so gullible—again? "Isn't it against your interest to tell me this?"

"I don't mind swindling rich, vain noblewomen," Cyrene said, "but I can't bring myself to take advantage of someone who had to work for her money. I think about such things more, now that I'm closer to dying." She chuckled.

"How can you laugh about this?"

"I laugh so I won't cry." Cyrene patted my hand. "I'm sorry to say, dearie, that you *can't* defeat nature. But getting older isn't all that bad."

"Really?" I asked through tear-blurred eyes.

She smacked me again. "No! It stinks. Your back bows, you get hot flashes, your hair thins, your skin thins, your bones thin. And yet, your middle gets fat."

I groaned and laid my face in my hands.

"There are little compensations, though," Cyrene said. "I used to wear a getup like yours in my youth when I traveled with a band of mercenaries. I can't say I miss freezing my tits off—or having to starve myself to keep the padding off my exposed midriff. And don't get me started about going into combat in high-heeled boots. I *still* have corns."

"But what about . . . men?" I asked. "Who's going to look twice at a frumpy, dumpy, middle-aged hag?" I flushed. "No offense."

Cyrene waved away my insult and tsked. "What do you want a man for? They're so high-maintenance—only concerned with their own needs, acting like taking out the trash makes them even with you for doing the cooking, cleaning, and laundry. It seems to me you have a perfectly fine cat. You're better off with him."

Saber purred and rubbed against Cyrene's leg. She scratched behind his ears.

"But what will I do now?" I asked. "I've always relied on my breasts to give me an edge."

"Life is like a book," Cyrene said. "It's time to start a new chapter. Think of it as an adventure."

"And that'll make me feel better about getting older?" I asked.

Smack! "No! But you can't wallow in self-pity. At your age, no one will put up with your moods the way they did when you were young and beautiful."

I sighed. "You're right. I need to start anew, maybe open a shop. But what should I sell?"

"You could sell my youth potion," Cyrene said, her blue eyes glittering. "I've been thinking about franchising."

"But you said it didn't work."

"It moisturizes the skin, which reduces the *appearance* of fine lines and wrinkles," Cyrene said. "If we stick to that claim, those rich biddies will expand on that in their own minds."

I perked up. "I could also get other women to sell it and give me a percentage. In turn, I would give you a percentage."

"Ooh, I like that." Cyrene nodded thoughtfully. "We could create a competition—whoever sells the most gets a prize. I bet I could get Princess Tarien to give a new carriage to the winner."

"It should be pink," I said, "so everyone will know it's owned by one of our representatives."

"Brilliant."

Saber purred in agreement.

"And maybe one day," I said, feeling hopeful again, "someone will come up with a potion that works—"

Smack. "Stop it!"

I sighed. "I guess you're right."

But it *could* happen. Couldn't it?

Roll Model

by Esther Friesner

"Who does a man have to turn into a frog before he gets a loaf of raisin bread around here?" The cloaked, gray-bearded figure strode through the doorway of the Happy Yum-Yum Fun-Time Bakery and dropped the bulky sack he was carrying. It made a dreadful clank and clatter. A trickle of deep purple liquid seeped through the burlap, staining the oak boards and sending up numerous threads of azure steam.

"*Pick that up!*" From a round table near the bakeshop counter, five women scowled condemnation at the man who had dumped his unknown burden willy-nilly, heedless of the harm it was wreaking. A sixth, waiting on the five with a teacup-and-pastry-laden tray in hand, looked pained by their outburst.

"Please don't get upset, ladies," the waitwench said, a slight tremor in her voice. "I can scrub that." She was a lovely creature with a piquant face made utterly stunning by large, long-lashed, golden-brown eyes and a mouth that imperiously demanded its lawful tribute in kisses.

"Hush, Tazadei," one of the five seated women snapped. "It doesn't matter if you *can* do such a chore when you shouldn't have to."

"It's not like I've got much else to do," Tazadei replied. Thick cascades of wavy auburn hair tumbled over her shoulders, mocking the headcloth that tried and failed to confine those wayward locks.

"Tell me about it," another of the women grumbled.

"You've already done plenty, Tazadei," a third at the table said in the chilliest of tones. "*Again.*" She appeared to be considerably plumper than the others, though it was difficult to discern much about the figures of any of the women present. They were all clothed from neck to ankles in shapeless dresses that made them look like bales of fabric awaiting the tailor's attention.

Tazadei was the sole exception. Like the seated women, she wore an all-too-ample dress—beige fustian, in her case—but at the moment, she was also clad for work in an apron that revealed her slim, embraceable waistline. The guilty garment likewise gave several broad hints as to the voluptuous curves above and below its snugly tied strings. The visitor stared at her.

"Men with beards shouldn't drool," the plump woman muttered.

"I was *not* drooling," the aged caller harrumphed as he hastily dabbed the telltale moisture from his whiskers. "I was, er, was—"

"—sweating from your lips?" a fourth woman asked archly.

Her companions laughed. "Good one, Donya!" someone called out.

"Drooling, lip-sweating, who gives a pilchard's pickle?" Donya went on. "He should be busy cleaning up after himself." She jerked her chin at the still-spreading purple stain and added: "I'm sure he's going to be *very* glad to do it." Her hand vanished into the folds of her skirt and suddenly an exquisite dagger glittered on the tabletop. "And soon." There was a brief rustle of over-abundant cloth and the first dagger was joined by an array of three more.

The only person at the table who was not participating in the great revelation of lethal cutlery was the plump one. Indeed, her expression had gone from hostile to harried almost as fast as the other four had whisked out their blades. "Ladies, please, I don't want any trouble from the authorities," she said, making calming motions with her flour-flecked hands. "Perhaps we *should* let Tazadei take care of the mess. It's the least she can do, after she ruined your refreshments."

"Oh yes, please let me see to this!" Tazadei exclaimed. She set her tray down on the shop counter and rushed to fetch a rag. When she bent over to pick up the graybeard's burlap sack, the enshrouding purpose of her too-voluminous gown was utterly defeated in the face of the truth: There was not enough fabric in all of the realm to conceal the fact that Tazadei's dazzling derriere could enslave millions.

"My dear girl—Tazadei, is it? Call me Gyrfahl, please, and *do* let me get that for you." The aged caller hurried forward to stay Tazadei's hand. A chorus of barking laughs went up from the seated women.

"Every . . . single . . . time," one of them said, pounding the table with a fist to emphasize each word. "She gets them to bow before her every single time, and how? By bowing before *them*!"

"'Before' with the power of 'behind,' Naleesa," the lady to her left said with a sarcastic curl of her lips. "And don't tell me *you* never used a bit of your natural charms to get out of tight spots. We all did. I remember the time I'd been disarmed by the evil elfin minions of Corusco, the Dark Oracle. They took my sword, my shield, my spear, my throwing knives, my—"

"Story now, shopping list later, Pej," Naleesa said, elbowing her companion in a friendly manner.

"Anyway, there I was, down to my bare chainmail, about to be led to the oubliettes, when I pretended to twist my ankle." She grinned. "It's amazing how gracefully one can manage to show off a bit of bosom during an 'accidental' fall. And how much more one can show as your captors help you get back on your feet. You should have seen their faces! Randy little squirrel-thumpers, the lot of them."

"Lucky you, going after a fiend with elfin minions," Donya grumped. "Everyone knows it's all they can do to keep their pixie dust in their pants. It's a different story when you've got to fight ogres, believe me! The only cleavage that affects those oafs is when your blade splits their skulls." She sighed. "Good times."

Pej dismissed Donya's cavil with a wave of her dagger. "The point is, I used Tazadei's tactics to my advantage, and I was out of the Dark Oracle's dungeon before dinnertime, carrying his severed head back to King Lungwort."

"Not much of an oracle if he didn't see *that* coming," Gyrfahl remarked from the floor where he was helping Tazadei clean purple stains out of the planks. "If you were commissioned to dispatch a seer who failed to foretell his own beheading, I'm surprised old Lungwort paid you for your labors on that loophole alone. He always was a tightfist."

"What do you know of King Lungwort, granddad?" Pej demanded.

"Aside from the fact that he was worth a thousand of his miserable, murk-minded daughter, Queen Kadua," Naleesa added.

There was a general murmur of agreement from everyone, save only for Tazadei, who was still busy scrubbing, and the plump woman, who looked ready to squirm her way under the table, down through the bakeshop's foundation, and six feet into the earth.

"Stop it, stop it, *stop it*!" she cried. "For goodness' sake, Naleesa, don't I have enough to contend with, struggling to earn a living out of this pathetic business when my baby sister keeps ruining every second batch of my wares?"

At this, Tazadei rose and faced the plump woman. "It's not my fault, Jilletta," she said in a sorrowful voice. "At least, I hope it's not. I don't know why losing my temper makes the loaves and cakes bake so—so thoroughly."

"'Thoroughly'?" Jilletta echoed. She pushed away from the table and strode to where Tazadei had left her tray. She picked up one of the pastries and hurled it to the floor with great force. A fountain of splinters gushed up on impact. "We sell scones, not stones! And as for *this* man—" She gestured to where the cloaked visitor still crouched with a cleaning rag in his wizened hand "—this *potential customer*? He wants bread, but what can we offer him, thanks to you? Boulders! If he paid me good coin for one of this morning's loaves, the poor old thing would break every tooth left in his head. I wouldn't be surprised if he hauled us before the queen's sheriff demanding reparations, after. I can't afford that kind of trouble. Gods witness, if anything goes wrong with the batch of bread that's in the ovens right now, I can't even afford to buy more flour!"

Tazadei's limpid eyes grew even more luminous with tears. "Maybe I should go away," she said. "I wouldn't be your problem anymore, and maybe I could find a job in my old line of work outside of Queen Kadua's realm."

"Don't bet on it," said Pej. "Her chuckleheaded Majesty rules more than this land alone. It might not be direct rule, but it's just as effective: She told every sovereign within a twelve-days' dragon-flight that if they failed to honor her Decree of Decency, their merchants couldn't trade anywhere within her borders. Why do you think *we're* still here?" She indicated everyone at the table save Jilletta. "We can't afford to travel far enough to escape her influence; not unless we turn to brigandage to feed ourselves on the road."

The bearded man gave her a quizzical look. "What's this Decree of Decency thing?"

The women all stared at him as though his ears had sprouted salmon.

"Are you joking us?" the tallest of the dagger-wielders demanded.

"Because I left my sense of humor in my other dress." She aimed the point of her weapon at him in a significant way. "And I don't *have* another dress."

"Hey, take it easy on the old fella, Vendra," Pej said. "Maybe he's sincerely ignorant." She squatted beside the visitor and in a voice reserved for children and the cognitively undersupplied asked, "You *really* don't know about the Decree of Decency? Where've you been living for the last five years, granddad? Under a rock?"

"Actually, in a dire tower built from the blackened bones of my enemies," came the cool reply. "Please, do continue to address me in that disrespectful manner. I've been thinking about tacking on a sunroom."

As he spoke, the very air around him began pulsing with power. The sack he'd dropped ceased leaking arcane purple fluid and commenced vibrating so rapidly that it became a clattering blur. A minor whirlwind dashed into the bakeshop, lifted the bag, and twirled it aloft until it began casting its contents in every direction. As they hit the ground and bounced to a halt against the walls, it was possible to identify most of them as pieces of plate armor, though some were plainly bones, and at least one was a badly charred and stove-in skull of elfin provenance.

Pej, Donya, Vendra and Naleesa looked grim, but held their ground and their weapons with equal firmness. Not so Jilletta and Tazadei, who flung themselves into one another's arms and trembled.

"Woman, know to whom you speak!" the whitebeard thundered. "I am Gyrfahl the Formidable, Master Wizard, Keeper of the Abysmal Keep!"

"Keeper of the Keep?" Donya laughed. "That's certainly an abysmal load of redundancy."

"Sounds more like Gyrfahl the Gasbag to me," Vendra remarked.

"Who's your good-looking friend?" Pej asked, jerking her thumb at the skull, now oozing more purple fluid onto the bakeshop floor. "He's more impressive than you."

Naleesa simply yawned.

"Why, you gaggle of insignificant little—!" Gyrfahl's face turned vermillion with rage. "Do you *want* to die? Because I can arrange that."

"Try it," said the four ladies in chorus.

Master Gyrfahl gave them an appraising look. "You're rather . . . brave," he said slowly. "For girls."

It was only his decades'-long morning ritual of:
1. Brush teeth
2. Comb hair
3. Don all-purpose shielding spell

That saved him from the four simultaneously flung daggers. The blades hit his protective enchantment and were instantly deflected into the bakeshop ceiling. Naleesa, Pej, Donya and Vendra howled battle cries and, against all common sense, would have launched themselves at him barehanded if Tazadei hadn't leaped in front of the wizard.

"Oh *please* don't, ladies," she begged, raising her hands. "It's useless. Look what became of your knives! I don't want that to happen to you."

Her words took effect. The angry quartet subsided. Muttering curses and canards as to the wizard's most intimate anatomy, they stomped back to their chairs.

Tazadei then turned to Master Gyrfahl. "Shame on you," she said.

"*They* insulted *me*," the wizard protested.

"But you're older. You should know better."

"I simply asked an honest question. I didn't expect a flock of dowdy females to draw steel over it. What are they, a bunch of warrior woman wannabes? Ugh, these fan clubs get out of hand at the least possible—" Abruptly he became aware of the weighty silence that had fallen over the Happy Yum-Yum Fun-Time Bakery, and of the sour glares aimed his way. "Oh, *now* what did I say?" he exclaimed, exasperated.

Jilletta, the baker, clasped her hands before her and lowered her eyes. "M—Master Gyrfahl, these women are not—are not—"

"We *are* warriors, you old goat!" Pej declared.

"Or we *were*, until Queen Kadua shoved the Decree of Decency down our throats," Vendra said. She struck a pose familiar to anyone who'd ever seen a schoolchild recite a lesson and in a sardonic sing-song intoned: "'Let it be known throughout our realm that for the moral improvement and spiritual fortification of our people, from this day on no unaffiliated or freelance female fighter of any sort shall pursue so perilous a profession unless wearing *plate* armor that completely covers her most vulnerable vitals. From knees to navel and from navel to neck, all must be securely encased and concealed. We do this out of the great love and respect we bear our dear sisters, for we greatly regret that the heedless wearing of skimpy chainmail would mean their deaths.'"

"That seems like a benevolent decree," Master Gyrfahl said with only a touch of uncertainty coloring his words. "Queen Kadua just wants you to be properly protected in battle."

"Queen Kadua doesn't want us in battle *at all*," Donya corrected him sharply. "The loathly sow knows we can't haul ourselves around while shingled in thick steel. One misstep and we'd look like a bunch of upended turtles!"

"We don't wear those teensy chainmail outfits to flaunt our bodies," Pej put in.

"No?" The wizard's brows rose.

Pej shook her head emphatically. "Only according to idiots and Queen Kadua. But I repeat myself. Even *she* didn't believe that load of wyvern droppings until the day her beloved Prince Fantod dumped her for Walzi Trollslayer."

"Why does that name sound so familiar?" Master Gyrfahl muttered.

"Walzi was one of us," Vendra said. "She wore chainmail scanties because they're *practical* garb, not prince-bait."

"Practical for *women* warriors," Donya specified. "They'd look ridiculous on a man, and it'd be silly *and* painful if the lower garment caught on his—"

"The point is—" Vendra cut in hastily, her cheeks aflame. "The point is that *we* can move nimbly in such outfits. Sometimes being able to out-dance your enemy is half the victory."

"Sure, chainmail fripperies don't offer a lot of protection," Naleesa admitted. "So what? Every girl who chooses our career is aware of that, and such knowledge inspires us to become supremely good with weaponry. Nowhere to hide *our* hides." She indicated the shards of armor that had tumbled out of the wizard's sack. "That's more than I can say happened to whoever used to inhabit *that* pile of scrap iron."

"Oh, and that bit in the Decree about how wearing chainmail would mean our deaths?" Donya said. "That's because the penalty for failing to conform to Kadua's bureaucratic bullying is *punishable* by death! Did you ever hear of anything so—?"

"The Adventure of Walzi Trollslayer and the Crag of Uncounted and Accursed Returns!" Master Gyrfhal shouted, smacking his forehead so loudly it made all the women jump. "*That's* where I heard the name."

His hand dove into the folds of his robe and extracted a small, rather worn scroll, which he unfurled with a flourish. It was sloppily lettered and rather smudged, but the illustration was a thing of beauty: A detailed sketch of a splendidly bellicose young woman wearing the very sort of scanty chainmail that had sent Queen Kadua into a tizzy of aggressive priggery. A suitably slaughtered pile of moldering revenants—the "returns" of the title—lay dismembered at her feet and her stern gaze transfixed the beholder with an "All right, who's next?" challenge.

There was something familiar about the triumphant swordmaiden.

"You!" Master Gyrfahl exclaimed, jabbing one scrawny finger at Tazadei. "That's you, isn't it?" He waggled the scroll insistently.

Tazadei gave an almost imperceptible nod, but her sister was more forthcoming. "Of course it's her," Jilletta said crisply. "Her, back in the good old days, P.C." An inquiring look from the wizard caused her to add, "Pre-Crackdown. The Happy Yum-Yum Fun-Time Bakery's always been a skin-of-the-teeth concern. After all, it's not the only bakeshop in town, but with Tazadei's income as a limner's model, we were always comfortable."

"Scribes and artists were constantly outbidding one another to use her image for illustrating tales of women warriors' exploits," Donya said, then grinned. "Including mine."

"Not just yours," Naleesa said. "We all wanted Tazadei to represent us."

"But why?" the wizard asked.

"Because *her* image on a scroll sells more copies and the scribes give us a cut of the profits." Her face fell. "I should say *sold* and *gave*, huh?"

Master Gyrfahl looked at his scroll wistfully, then turned his gaze to the original. "I will admit, my dear, this tale of high adventure did much to ease my solitude in the Abysmal Keep, but I drew even more solace from contemplating the accompanying picture. By the seven bearded stoats of Stet, goddess of divine defiance, what man wouldn't sell his birthright to purchase a single night with your—"

"My *what*?" Tazadei's eyes suddenly flashed sparks of green fire and a dangerously sharp note crept into her heretofore dulcet voice.

The wizard said, "—scrolls?" at the same moment that Jilletta cried, "Tazadei! Temper! No!"

Both utterances came too late. There was a great rumbling from beyond the bakeshop's rear wall and then a BOOM! so mighty it sent everyone sprawling.

"Well, that's it," Jilletta said with an air of resignation. "We're through." She stood in the yard behind the bakery and regarded the wreckage of what had been two free-standing ovens. Their conical shapes now resembled volcanoes that had recently blown their tops. Ashes drifted out of the smoke-streaked sky, though the lingering scent of fresh-baked bread mocked the devastation.

"I'm sorry, Jilletta." Tazadei wrung her hands. "I shouldn't have reacted like that, but you know how much I hate it when people presume I'm a hedge-honey just because of the way I dress for work."

"*Used* to dress when you *had* work," said Naleesa, who seemed to have a grim dedication to accurate verb forms.

"What happened here?" The wizard stared at the backyard laid waste.

"What happens every time my sister gets angry enough," Jilletta replied. "And the only thing that does make her *that* angry is when someone salts the wound of her lost employment. At first her flare-ups only made the bread bake a tad crustier. Then it singed. Then it turned stone-solid in the oven. This is the first time she blew up the ovens themselves."

"I made a joke about Queen Kadua this morning, just before you showed up," Pej told the wizard. "It set her off and *pow!* No scones."

"Why does this *happen*?" Tazadei moaned. "I don't have any magical powers, I wasn't cursed in the cradle by a wicked fairy, and I've never angered a witch."

Master Gyrfahl pondered matters, then addressed the lissome limner's model. "My dear, take comfort: I can help. Now that I know more about the situation, I believe your troubles stem from a simple bit of contributory sorcerous seepage."

"A what?" Tazadei looked like a kitten confronted by its first firefly.

"Limners and talemongers are like witch's familiars, vessels of magic-by-association. They pick up a bit of the enchantment woven through every heroic exploit that they ever, er, exploit. You worked with them for so long that you became touched in turn by their arcane powers."

"Hey! No one touched me with *anything*. I'm a professional!" Tazadei said hotly. This was a literal phenomenon, for as her temper rose, so did the ambient temperature.

Master Gyrfahl felt the heat and nodded with satisfaction. "There it is, just as I said: a scrap of sorcery you picked up from your employers, unaware. It's taken the form of a defensive spell, turning likely materials hard as armor when it senses a rise in your belligerence."

"Huh?"

"When you feel like you want to smack someone, magic wrecks the bread," he explained. "And in this case, the ovens. They could not contain the power of your enchantment."

"Oh, *you*!" Tazadei blushed and giggled.

Master Gyrfahl didn't bother trying to dissuade the lovely girl from her misinterpretation of his words. Instead he said: "If you'd like, I can disenchant you—"

"Just like a man," Vendra muttered.

"—as soon as I return." He turned on his heel and headed back into the bakeshop, only to find his way suddenly barred by Jilletta and the four warrior women.

"Where do you think you're going?" the baker demanded.

"Breakfast," the wizard said dryly. "I'm bringing bad news to the palace, and I refuse to do that on an empty stomach."

"No you don't," Pej said, folding her arms. "You said you can fix Tazadei's problem. You're staying put until you do."

"We'll fetch you a meal from the nearest cookshop. The queen's not home now anyway. She's on a royal progress. She can wait for her bad news," Vendra declared.

"Queen Kadua *is* the bad news," the wizard countered.

He was not amused by the guffaws and exclamations of "*I'll* say she is!" from the chainmail-deprived champions. "Oh, grow up! I'm carrying word that will bring war, destruction and chaos to this entire realm. *So* glad you think that's a laughing matter!"

"All you're carrying is a sack full of scrap metal and bones," said Donya.

"Which *used* to be the famed elfin warrior, Sir Inesmus the Undefeated!" Master Gyrfahl shouted. And before the women could make the obvious remark about the inaptness of that hero's epithet, he added, "Know now that a fiery-breathed dragon of uncommon size and viciousness awoke from his sleep of centuries with a parlous appetite. He emerged from his lair in the Mountains of Ibid, intercepted and devoured most of that royal progress you mention, and carried off the queen a fortnight ago. A lone survivor reached the palace under cover of night and informed the council, who promptly sent out word to every intrepid and discreet warrior they could find. I learned all this when Sir Inesmus stopped at the Abysmal Keep en route to rescuing your queen. He was the only one who thought it would help to have a wizard on his side."

"Not so much, huh?" said Donya.

Master Gyrfahl gave her a poisonous look. "This dragon is half-fire elemental. I've never set my magic against the like. I couldn't even get close to the beast, and when Sir Inesmus did—Well, you saw the results. That plate armor works better than an oven if you want to bake a hero. And he wasn't the first extra-crispy corpse outside the monster's lair—"

"Wait, wait, wait." Naleesa raised her hands. "If the Royal Fathead was captured by a dragon, how come no one around here's heard about it? This is the royal capitol, after all!"

"Because the council's been keeping it quiet, partly to avoid panic, but mostly to keep the situation secret. If the rulers of neighboring kingdoms hear Kadua's as good as dead, they'll pounce on this realm like dogs on a dead gopher. They'll fight your people and each other so viciously that there'll be nothing left of your land but crumbs amid the ashes!"

"Too bad the crumbs won't come from Tazadei's little baking 'accidents," Pej muttered bitterly. "Our conquerors would break their teeth."

"Looks like we've got no choice." Naleesa sighed. "We'll have to kill the dragon and save the cow—I mean, the queen."

"Dressed like *this*?" Vendra held up a fistful of her copious skirt.

"Well, we can't do it wearing plate armor," Donya said. "Not unless we want to end up like Sir Inesmus."

"If we wear chainmail, we'll end up dead anyway," Pej said. "Remember the Decree of Decency! Do you want to wager your life on Kadua being grateful enough to grant us a royal pardon, or even a royal variance once we've saved her spotty skin?"

"If we do nothing, war will come and innocents will perish."

"Hey, I'm a mercenary! Who's going to pay for this?"

"I had to pawn my chainmail to survive."

"I put on some weight, with all this enforced retirement, so I don't know if I can still fit into—"

"How big is this dragon?"

"How do we know he hasn't eaten Kadua already?"

"Naaaahhhh, when a dragon's got heartburn, you *hear* about it."

"Some things even a monster can't stomach."

"Good one!"

"Yeah, maybe I could get work as a freelance jester, do a little tour, hit all the major taverns—"

"Has anyone seen my sister?" Jilletta's question cut through the swordswomen's back-and-forth. Everyone looked around the yard but Tazadei wasn't there. Neither was Master Gyrfahl.

All they found when they went back into the bakeshop was a note in the wizard's spidery hand that read: *Tazadei had an idea. Off to save the day. Back soon.*

And it came to pass that Tazadei and her wizardly companion *were* back soon, relatively speaking. Not soon enough to slap anyone unable to credit the former limner's model with the ability to *have* an idea (beauty coupled with brains was too razor-edged a pill for lesser folk to swallow) but soon enough to prevent the lowering war.

They returned to the capitol in triumph with a somewhat singed and thoroughly contrite Queen Kadua. The rescued lady sailed into the palace, summoned her council, called for the royal executioner, and applied the skills of the latter to the necks of the former in the market square without delay.

As the bards and broadsheet-sellers later told the tale, it seemed that the council had not kept the queen's captivity a secret for purely political reasons. Rather, the lone messenger who informed them of Kadua's plight also said that the dragon—being a dragon—wanted gold, jewels, and plenty of both as his price for releasing the queen. It should have been a short and simple business transaction. However, the council members knew that upon her release, their sovereign would claim a portion of *their* wealth to make up for the deficit her ransom inflicted on the queen's own coffers.

Tax the *rich*? That wouldn't do. The messenger was quietly put out of the way, and the council carried on as already described. The results were not what they'd envisioned.

Their epic public beheading was small turnips next to the spectacle of Tazadei, standing with Master Gyrfahl in places of honor at the queen's side. The three of them were in plain sight on a platform just beyond the splash zone of the scaffold. Tazadei was still clad in the armor that had allowed her to defeat the dragon, and it drew a flood of comments from the crowd.

"What *is* that?" one nearsighted citizen demanded. "It looks like plate, but it's not shiny and it looks—" he squinted "—brown?"

"That's because it's bread," said Jilletta. "My baby sister charmed a bushel of dough from the Crullers 'n' Things bakeshop, carted it off to the dragon's cave, had that wizard's magic shape it into greaves and breastplate and helmet and who knows what-all on her naked—*Stop drooling!*—body. Then she shouted at the monster to surrender the queen."

"Did he?"

Jilletta scowled. "Are you daft? Of course not! He laughed at her. And do you want to guess how *that* made her feel?"

The man had never cared for loaded questions. They reminded him too much of post-tavern confrontations with his late wife. "Errrrrrr . . . mad?"

"Oh yes." Now the baker smiled grimly. "*Very* mad. Mad enough to fry an egg on her forehead. Mad enough to boil water at a touch. Mad enough to bake bread dough into armor so impermeable it rendered her proof against the worst flames even a fire elemental-dragon mutt could douse her with. And when that creature tried to destroy her with a snap of his mighty jaws, do you know what happened?"

"Uhhhh, ummm, that is—gotta go!" The man dashed away.

"The dragon broke his teeth, that's what!" Jilletta hollered after him. "And that was when my sister drew her sword and—"

"—killed the dragon?" An eager, ink-blotted stripling popped up at Jilletta's elbow. He held a stubby bit of sharpened charcoal in one hand, a tatter of paper in the other. She could smell the reek of *starving scribe* emanating from his lanky body in waves.

"Kill him with what?" she snapped. "She picked up her blade from the charred remains of one of the dragon's victims. The monster's fire made it so brittle that one flick of a hummingbird's tongue would have shattered it."

"Then how—?"

Jilletta made an impatient sound. *I've had to tell this story a thousand times since Tazadei's return. I'll be so glad once the talemongers get the word out. I just hope they publish before I perish.*

She took a deep breath. "Tazadei didn't have to do more than strike one of those ridiculous poses from her days as a scroll model. No real fighter would see such posturing as a threat, but dragons can be as foolish as people: One look at her, one realization that his own means of attack were either lost or useless against her, and the beast took wing. The end."

"Ooooooh, that's perfect! Or it will be, once I've fixed it." The scrawny lad set to his work with glee. His quill flew as if it were still attached to the goose that grew it. In his haste, her described the crust-clad heroine as *Our kingdom's doughty darling*, but a slip of the nib rendered Tazadei *Our kingdom's* doughy *darling*.

In the mansions of the gods, in the midst of feeding her stoats the hearts of those who would sacrifice a good story on the altar of her brother Snit, god of nitpickery, the lady Stet smiled.

Second Hand Hero

By Jean Rabe

The sweater had a scattering of fuzzy little knobs on the shoulders and at the waist, evidence of wear by its previous owner. Teri figured she could draw those through with a crochet hook or shave them off with a gadget an elderly aunt had given her a few birthdays ago. Make it look practically new. It was a rosy pink, sized a very generous medium, and it would go with practically anything in her closet. Teri considered it a steal at two bucks.

"Perfect," she pronounced. "I'll take it." She sat her purse on the counter and rummaged inside for her wallet. "Those things, too." She nodded at a neat pile that included a macramé belt studded at odd intervals with polished wood beads, a purple scarf with paisley swirls, three pairs of carefully folded slacks she'd have to hem, and a chalky turquoise fob hanging from a thin suede cord.

"Very vintage," the clerk pointed at the necklace. "Shabby-chic. Didn't think anyone was gonna ever buy it."

"Well . . . I like it." To emphasize that, Teri plucked off the price tag, handed it to the clerk, and put the necklace on. "See?"

"See? Hard not to see it," the clerk said flatly. "That'll be it? Anything else?"

"That'll be it," Teri said.

"Fifteen even," the clerk pronounced after reading all the tags. She chomped on a wad of gum and yawned.

"Oh . . . my. What's that?" Teri's gaze focused on a rack behind the counter, clothes that recently had come in on consignment, and hadn't yet been priced and put out for display.

"A bikini," the clerk replied, chomping her gum harder. "Chainmail." She retrieved it and dangled it distastefully in front of Teri, as if holding a dead rat by the tail. The scant chainmail top was hooked to the hanger proper, but the bottom was tied on with ribbons. The links shimmered like Christmas tinsel under the fluorescent lights. "Came in about an hour ago." She looked Teri up and down.

Teri considered herself short at 5'2", but the clerk was a few inches shorter—and about sixty or seventy pounds lighter.

"Want to try it on?" the clerk taunted.

The links shimmered brighter.

"It would never fit."

"Yeah, you're right." The clerk turned to hang it back up.

"Wait a minute." Teri *knew* it wouldn't fit, and even if it did, she'd never wear a bikini, let alone one that looked like it had been made out of pop tabs linked together, a piece of sexist kitsch left over from a costume party. Still . . .

"Hand it over." She owned one swimsuit—*swim dress*, she mentally corrected, according to the description in the Lane Bryant catalog— and she hadn't put it on in three years because it didn't go with her cottage cheese thighs. She hadn't been invited to a Halloween party since sophomore year in college a dozen years ago . . . where she maybe would've worn something like a chainmail bikini after downing a half-dozen beers followed by Jell-O shot chasers.

"Sure thing, lady." The clerk thrust out the hanger, the links glittering even more fiercely.

Teri's stubby fingers wrapped around the handle. It felt heavy, well . . . duh! . . . it was made of metal. "I'll just be a minute."

She slipped into the dressing room and sagged onto the bench. "What the hell was I thinking?" she whispered. "I wasn't—thinking." But she'd been insulted by the clerk's "Yeah, you're right" comment, and the up-and-down ogling she'd been given. "I'm not that . . . fat."

Teri looked in the dingy mirror, at the fold of belly flesh that was hidden by her blouse and which sagged over her belt so only half the buckle showed. She was on the wrong side of thirty for something like this, and if not fat, she was plump. God, that five-letter word made her sound like a Butterball turkey. And she was a turkey, to be rattled so easily by the clerk—who must be new, because she hadn't seen her before. Teri was a regular at Second Hand's Shop—and at the Salvation Army and St. Vincent DePaul stores—where she somehow always managed to find things to fit both her and her meager budget. Rattled her enough to come into the dressing room with a bikini—chainmail, no less—that wouldn't fit her, and even if it did, would be as uncomfortable as all get out.

And she'd have no place to wear it.

Except to maybe a comic book convention, and she hadn't picked up a comic book in ages.

"What the hell was I thinking? I don't have time for this." And she didn't—she was on company time.

Teri figured she'd been in here just long enough to have tried on the bikini. She'd tell the clerk it wasn't her style, which it certainly wasn't . . . and which the clerk would certainly agree with. Still . . . she eased off the bench and undressed, reached for the bikini. Good lord, what was she thinking?

"I'm not thinking."

But she tried it on.

And it fit.

"Dear God."

The fold of skin that had lopped over her belt was gone. The cottage cheese thighs . . . it was as if they'd been airbrushed out by a Photoshop artist. The skin under her chin was tight. She looked a little pasty. Okay, a lot pasty, and the loafers didn't go well. But she thought she could give Red Sonja a run for her Hyborian currency.

"Damn. I'm . . . friggin' gorgeous!"

Red Sonja? Well, not quite—there was the too-pale complexion, but . . .

"Double damn."

How was it possible, that years and stretch marks and flab could just . . . just . . . vanish? Magic . . . The chainmail was magic. It had to be. She'd seen the *Lord of the Rings* movies, watched Bilbo put on a chainmail shirt made of mithril. *Magic.*

The chainmail bikini was magic . . . even though magic couldn't possibly exist in Milwaukee, Wisconsin.

Moments later, Teri added the chainmail bikini to her pile on the counter. She didn't care what it cost; she'd take out a loan to buy it.

"Doesn't have a price tag. But I want it."

The clerk raised both eyebrows, the pierced one with the hoop in it seeming a little off-kilter.

"I said, I'll take it, the bikini. How much?"

"That'll be twenty-eight even," the clerk repeated. "It was just fifteen until you added the bikini. Even second-hand, I gotta charge you thirteen for the chainmail."

"I've only got a twenty. Wouldn't you know it? I hate to write a check, but . . . " But she had to have the magic bikini.

"Make the check out to Second Hand's."

Teri dropped the wallet back in her purse and reached for her checkbook, scribbled in the amount and signed it, and passed the check over with a flourish. She drummed her fingers against the counter while the clerk bagged her treasures and then picked up the check.

"El-eff-tear-ia," The clerk slowly sounded it out, studying the check.

"I go by Teri."

"Elefteria," the clerk repeated with confidence. "Elefteria Murphy. That's an interesting name. I need to see a driver's license, Elefteria."

"The check's only for twenty-eight—"

"Gotta see the license, Elefteria. Interesting name."

Interesting. Teri rummaged for her wallet again and tugged out her driver's license. Not "that's a pretty name" or "charming." "Interesting." It's what people usually said about her name—when they said anything at all.

"Elefteria." The clerk chomped her gum.

"It's Greek, though I'm not. Irish, mostly." Teri put her wallet and checkbook back. "It means freedom." She reached for the bag.

"Interesting." The clerk gave her an insincere smile.

"Interesting," Teri parroted when she was on the sidewalk and heading for her car, the worn soles of her loafers slapping rhythmically against the pebbled cement and her coat drawn tight to cut the early November chill. She'd parked across the street from the thrift shop, right in front of Turkish Delights, the restaurant she'd eaten lunch at a scant half-hour ago. A cold appetizer of *yalanci dolma*—vine leaves stuffed with pine nuts and onions and rice, topped with black currants—had been followed with *akdeniz levrek izgara*, chargrilled Mediterranean sea bass. She could still taste the fish and saffron.

The meal would have set her back at least what she'd paid for her finds at the thrift shop, but the newspaper had footed the bill. It always footed the bill when they sent her out to review a restaurant. She'd wanted to try the *Narince* from the Black Sea, a white wine that the waiter had told her was both crisp and acidic. Instead she had opted for a third cup of Turkish coffee, and the jittery caffeine rush hung with her—even after the sojourn up and down the second-hand aisles of the shop on Old World Third Street.

There were a few other shops here Teri would have liked to browse, an old bookstore in particular. Deciding she could spare a few more minutes, she headed toward the ten-foot-long sign that spelled BOOKS, and then stopped abruptly, the hair on the back of her neck itching. She stared into a big glass window of a sandwich shop, not looking inside, but wanting to see what was reflected behind her; she had the feeling someone was watching her or tagging along. Although she didn't spot anyone either suspicious or familiar, the odd sensation was enough to end her shopping trip. Besides, she again reminded herself, she was on "company time," and trying to live within the strict budget dictated by her recent car repair bill. So she headed back to the paper to write her review.

That didn't take long.

The article was brief and to the point:

The food has an attitude, she wrote. *Generous portions are artfully presented on linen-draped tables accented with fresh flowers. Spicy aromas waft out of a kitchen that bustles with activity beginning at 11 a.m. The condiments are imported from Istanbul, where the owners were born. The lunch choices are intriguing and numerous, the flavors strong and earthy and providing a welcome heat that is lasting, but not oppressive. From the appetizer to the salad to the main course, I found it alluringly delicious, though a little on the pricey side.*

She went on to describe the décor, provide a brief history of the place, and compliment the courteous waitstaff. Then she gave the piece a quick once-over, corrected a few typos, and hit *send* to whisk it off to the lifestyle editor's desk. It was one of the more favorable reviews she'd written in the past few weeks; her palate was not easily impressed. Besides, she was in a good mood. Maybe the magic bikini tucked away in the trunk of her car had lifted her spirits.

Teri leaned back and cracked her knuckles, a habit her mother and past roommates had never managed to break her of. She glanced around the newsroom.

Tuesday late afternoon, it bustled with activity. The *Journal* was a morning paper, but it had an online edition that was constantly updated, and stories were produced throughout the day. Fingers clattered across keyboards. Reporters talked on telephones—their heads crooked against receivers jammed between their ears and shoulders—postures that required regular chiropractic adjustments.

On the surface, the place looked big and shiny, clean and modern. The desks were all metal and glass, the bright overhead lights reflecting off computer monitors as well as the big windows and the every-third-night polished tile floor. But Teri saw its dark heart: the grime that had gathered for decades in all the little cracks, and the streaked, eggshell-colored walls that had been stained from years of cigarette smoke—before smoking had been relegated to the sidewalk. The smell of pine air fresheners strategically placed here and there could not cover the musty odor of newsprint or the various scents of lunches left too long uneaten and strewn across desk blotters.

"Hey, Cookie!"

Teri let out a hissing breath when she spotted the lifestyle editor headed her way.

"Hey, Bob," she answered.

Bob looked like he belonged in the sports department—shirtsleeves pushed up past his elbows, collar frayed, tie crooked, middle-age spread, hair a tad greasy with a hunk of it splayed over the top of what would otherwise be a bald pate. In fact, he had been a sports reporter-turned sports editor, or so Teri had heard—"back in the day" when Milwaukee had two newspapers, and he worked for the one that had folded.

"Just sent you my restaurant review, Bob."

He gave her a lopsided grin and thrust his hands against his hips. He leaned forward, reminding Teri of one of those little plastic pot-bellied drinking-birds that dunked their beaks in colored water at various bars around the city.

"Yeah, Cookie. I saw it pop up on my screen. I'll get to it in a bit. I'm sure it'll be fine." He paused, as if waiting for her to say something else.

Teri tapped her fingers on the edge of her desk. She didn't like Bob. And she certainly didn't like the nickname he'd given her. Bob had a nickname for all of his reporters. Sometimes he called her Smart Cookie, when he was especially pleased with a review, or Sugar Cookie when he needed a favor. Usually it was just Cookie—his designation for his food reporter.

"Say, Sugar Cookie—"

Teri groaned. "I've got plans tonight, Bob."

"Cancel 'em."

"Can't." She wanted to try on the bikini again.

"Did you do something different with your hair? New style? More color? Flattering?"

She didn't have a reply to that; it wasn't like Bob to compliment her. No doubt he was buttering her up in an effort to get her to cave in.

He rocked back on his heels and straightened. "Museum's fund raiser is at seven."

"That's Bernice's story, and—"

"And she called in sick. Gotta be covered. The fund raiser's basically a big dinner, so—"

"You figured it was right up my proverbial alley, huh?" Teri closed her eyes. "I said I've got plans, Bob. Really." She kept thinking about the second-hand chainmail.

"And I said you'll just have to cancel 'em." He thrust two doughy fingers into his shirt pocket and pulled out a pair of tickets, then dropped his gaze to her waist. "You losing weight, Cookie? You look nice today."

"Not going. Plans." Again she thought about the magic bikini.

"Who are you to turn down a free meal, Sugar Cookie?" He waved the tickets in front of her face until she took them. "And if it's a date you've got, just invite him along." He looked around the newsroom, eyes resting briefly on the finance reporter. "A good, free meal, something he won't have to spring for. It's supposedly gonna be catered by some fancy German place, not Mader's, but something along that line. You can make it easy on yourself and write it up just like a restaurant review, but make sure you throw in something about the speakers and how much money the museum pulled in. Maybe a few lines about what folks were wearing. Hey, do you got something halfway decent to wear to the gig?"

A chainmail bikini? Teri swallowed hard. "Bob, I—"

"Nah, I'm sure you got something. A dress would be good."

"Bob, I—" She was going to broach this subject with him later in the week, but now seemed like a good time. "I'm putting in for the opening in city-side."

Bob raised a thick eyebrow.

"The opening on the police beat, Bob. It's been posted for a few days."

His face drew forward until it looked pinched, like he'd bit down on a sour ball.

"It's hard news. I want hard news. I told you that when you hired me." Teri squared her shoulders and forged ahead. "Not that I haven't enjoyed this past year, but—"

"I'll give you a recommendation for the police beat, if that's what you want, Cookie." Bob's face softened a little. "Don't want to lose you, though. And, no offense, but I don't think I'll lose you just yet to city-side. Mack's looking for a cop reporter with some experience. He's not looking for someone who can report on the jail cafeteria."

You bastard, Teri thought. *I'll land that damn police beat just to get out of your department and out from under your ugly thumb.*

"You might have a good time at the museum tonight." He whirled on his heels and made a course toward the men's room. Halfway there, he stopped and glanced over his shoulder. "Oh, and I'll need that museum piece for the morning edition, Sugar Cookie. So get it in by midnight."

Teri clenched her fist, wrinkling the tickets. "A police reporter with experience," she growled. "Well, how the hell do you get experience?" She thumped her elbows on the desk. She caught several reporters looking at her, and after a moment they all looked away—save one— Lang Stewart at the financial desk. She held up the tickets, fanning them so he could see there were two, and then she gave him a sad smile.

"Free meal. Wanna join me?" she asked.

Four hours later, Lang sat to her right in the museum rotunda, which served as the event's dining room. He was in a blue suit a few shades darker than Teri's peasant silk dress. She'd managed to put her long, black hair in an "updo" in an attempt to look a little glamorous— for Lang, not for the assignment. Teri noticed that most of the guests were dressed in somber shades, some of the perfectly coiffed women in flouncy taffeta skirts better suited for nights at the orchestra or opera than a museum fundraiser. They had pearl necklaces and glittering diamond earrings that dangled to their shoulders. Teri was still wearing the necklace she'd picked up at the thrift store, finding the turquoise oddly yet pleasantly warm against the hollow of her neck. She'd managed to find some black and silver earrings in her jewelry box that, while they didn't match the necklace, didn't clash with it either.

Under it all, she wore the chainmail bikini. She'd tried it on again when she went to her apartment, the magic in the links seeming to smooth out even more imperfections in her short frame. It wasn't uncomfortable, it didn't feel heavy, and for some reason she looked downright svelte under the shimmering metal. She simply liked it—no, loved it, was admittedly obsessed by it—and decided to keep it on. Hell, maybe she'd even sleep in it.

"Doesn't look German," Lang said, staring at his plate. He dropped his left hand beneath the table and brushed Teri's leg. He hesitantly picked up his fork with his right. "You're looking good tonight. Seriously good. You been working out? And your face . . . you're glowing."

"It's not German. It's French. Mediterranean pasta."

He idly stirred it, separating the asparagus and olives and wrinkling his nose when he came to the mushrooms. After a moment, he speared a piece of tomato and firmly rested his hand on Teri's knee.

She grew warm at the contact, and conjured up an image of Bob splayed out under the museum's dinosaur skeleton, a sugar cookie stuffed in his mouth.

"It's instead of salad, this pasta." Teri tried it and found it acceptable, but not wonderful. "The main course, according to the program, will be Shrimp Crêpe Florentine with green beans almandine and garlic mashed potatoes."

"I'd rather go out for pizza and beer," he whispered. "Let's go out for beer and pizza tomorrow night, Teri. And after this . . . we could go back to my place. I've got a widescreen TV." He gave her knee a gentle squeeze, then swallowed the tomato and speared another one. His fingers drifted higher. "You really are looking sweet, toned, like you've been hitting the gym, and—"

"Sorry, Lang. I have to go back to the paper and write this up." She scooted farther away.

Lang abruptly brought his hand back up to the table. He sighed and stared at his plate.

The sounds of soft conversations and glasses clinking took over, and Teri nibbled at the pasta.

She took another forkful and held the mushroom on her tongue, letting its flavor seep in. Then she took out her notebook as the first speaker came to the podium. Teri stared at her hands—the fingers were thin, the nails long, manicured and polished; they glittered all silvery, like Bilbo's magic mithril shirt.

She'd had a nice time, but she was a tad pissed about it. Lang hadn't shown any interest in her before this evening—but shed some weight because of her chainmail underwear, give herself an updo, and . . . why couldn't he have been a little friendlier *before* her thrifty Second Hand's renovation?

It was 10:55 when Teri drove back to the paper, parking under a lamppost on the street between the *Journal* offices and a hotel under construction. She would've parked in the paper's lot, but the attendant at the gate was nowhere to be seen, and so she couldn't get in. *Probably taking a break or making the rounds,* she thought. The hairs on the back of her neck itched again, and she glanced around. No one out on the street. She dismissed the odd feeling, ducked under the gate, and wove her way through the cars scattered in the lot, mentally going over options for her lead on the fundraising piece and finding the words coming slow because she was preoccupied . . . alternately brooding about Lang and wishing foul things upon Bob.

She didn't see the creature across the street skulking in the shadows of the half-finished hotel. She didn't know that it had ventured into this very lot several minutes ago and grabbed the parking lot attendant, dragging him back to the construction site, where it devoured most of him.

But she did see the beast a few minutes after midnight, while leaving after writing her story, and fumbling with her keys at her car door. The hairs on the back of her neck were at attention.

"What the hell is that?" She stared across the street, trying to squint through the shadows.

It looked like a cross between a toad and a wolf, about the size of the latter, thickset around the middle, and wildly hairy in places. The glow of the streetlights reflected in its red eyes, and showed its hide to be a mottled gray-green that seemed to draw in the darkness. When it crept closer, she smelled it, reeking of mold and spoiled things, the odor so strong Teri gagged as she tried to jam the wrong key in the lock.

"Diseased dog. Open damn damn damn. Please open." The paper had just run a story about a delivery man attacked by a group of big mongrels on the city's north side.

The creature scuttled to the middle of the street, cocking its head to watch as she dropped her keys and uttered a string of curses. It raised a bulbous lip, revealing a double row of jagged teeth covered with yellowish slime. Drool spilled down, sizzling like acid on the pavement in front of its clawed feet.

Teri crouched, feeling for her keys, looking over her shoulder at the thing, which she decided wasn't a dog after all. Then she screamed as it threw back its head, howled shrilly, and sprang toward her.

Her fingers closed on the keys and she stood, tingling all over—from fear, and more than that.

The beast's leg muscles bunched and it leaped—and in that instant, when Teri was so close to death, she came truly alive.

The car key extended, the head becoming a hilt that fit snugly in her hand, the ridges, teeth, and notches melting and stretching as the shaft turned into an elegant saber. Without even thinking, Teri performed a perfect advance-lunge, the point of the sword stabbing into the monster's belly. It jumped back in surprise and growled, more acidic spittle dripping onto the pavement. There was a pattern to its growling as it paced furiously in front of her, scratching furrows in the concrete . . . Wait, was that—language! She could *understand* it?

"Curse upon you, World Guardian! You cannot keep my kind from overrunning this realm! I shall tear you apart, drink your blood, pick my teeth with your sword, and send your pieces to the Seven Hells!"

"This is insane. I must be on *America's Funniest Videos*." But Teri knew otherwise. She performed a *balestra*, a fencing maneuver she previously hadn't known even existed. Jumping forward, she lunged, changed the rhythm of her footwork and slashed down, biting deep into what amounted to the creature's sloping shoulder.

It howled again, the sound so shrill it cracked the glass of the streetlights and shattered her car windows.

"Oh, hell! Now how much is *that* repair bill gonna run?" Fuming, Teri employed a composed attack, incorporating a feint while the beast swept in with its claws, slicing through her blue silk peasant dress. The dress fell in tatters, revealing the chainmail bikini. "I shop at thrift stores, for the love of God! I can't afford any more car repairs!"

The beast slashed again, and this time she was certain its claws had connected, but her skin was somehow unmarked.

"Curse on you, World Guardian!" the monster raged. It belched a cloud of noxious gas at her, the hot steam doing nothing more than making her curls go limp against her forehead. The beast's breath had, however, melted some of the paint on her car's rear fender.

"Curse on me? On me? I'm a friggin' food reporter! I'm no World Guardian!" Well, she wouldn't be a World Guardian any longer when she got home and took off the magic chainmail bikini. "And I'm not made of money, either! Stop wrecking my car!"

The beast's claws dug a deeper rut in the pavement as it opened its maw wide and leaped again. She chose a *compound-riposte* maneuver, two feints this time, a disengage, a variety of clear tempo beats, and found that she was quite effectively slicing tic tack toe grids on its warty hide. Deep purple blood bubbled and hissed and added to the creature's already awful stench.

"World Guardian—"

"I. Said. I'm. No. World. Guardian! I'm Elefteria Murphy. Food reporter for—"

"You may defeat me, World Guardian, but others of my kind will come." The beast belched again, its horrid breath curling the back bumper and disintegrating a rear tire with a *pop*! "Destined to fight you, they will crawl up from the darkest depths and—"

"Leave. My. Car. Alone!" Teri wasn't sure she'd ever felt such righteous anger before; it dwarfed her ire at Bob calling her Sugar Cookie, and Lang grabbing her knee. It fueled her swings as she came full-bore at the creature. The tact was called a *forward recovery*— somehow she knew that, too. It consisted of a lunge, pulling her back leg up into an *en garde* position, gaining ground on her demonic opponent, and then surprising him with an *in quartata* evasive action, turning a quarter to the side before attacking with a series of rapid slashes that turned him into so much hamburger.

Teri stared at the pile of disgusting remains. The purplish blood continued to ooze and bubble, flowing to stop just short of what remained of her car.

Invigorated by the battle, unable to change the flat tire, and armed now with a sword rather than a car key, Teri walked back to her apartment.

She slew three more of the foul, warty creatures along the way.

Wednesday morning found her outside Second Hand's Shop, waiting for it to open.

Her reflection in the window was impressive. While she hadn't gotten any taller, Teri now carried herself as if she were a giant. Shoulders back, chin up, eyes fiercely sparkling, jaw firmly set. Her pasty complexion was a memory; her skin was ruddy, as if she spent a great deal of time outdoors. There were muscles in her arms, and she felt more confident than ever.

The chainmail bikini was in the bag, the bits of demon gore cleaned off with a tablespoon of Comet and some serious scrubbing.

Teri liked the way she looked—and felt and had shamelessly liked the feel of the bikini against her flawless tanned skin. But obviously she didn't need to be wearing the bikini to look like this. And, besides, she didn't like fighting monsters or having the responsibility of being the World Guardian.

"I want to return this," she almost reluctantly told the clerk as the door opened. It was the same short gum-chomping woman from yesterday.

"Didn't fit after all, eh?"

"No place to wear it, actually. What was I thinking?"

"Maybe you weren't—" the clerk said almost too softly to hear, "—thinking." Slightly louder: "Really, who'd wear a chainmail bikini anyway?"

Teri bristled and pulled the bikini out of the bag. The links glimmered merrily under the fluorescent light.

"And it's not the chainmail, you realize," the clerk said.

Teri raised an eyebrow.

"That's not the magic. No magic in the chainmail."

"Beg your pardon?" Teri didn't know what else to say.

"I said, it's not the magic that turned you into the World Guardian."

"World Guardian? I'm not the World Guardian. I'm a food reporter . . . no, I'm going to be a police reporter. Bob's not stopping me."

"Nothing can stop the World Guardian, huh?"

"World Guardian. Now how the hell would you know—"

The clerk grinned, and her eyes turned so dark Teri couldn't make out the pupils. "It's that tacky turquoise fob you bought, that's the magic." She pointed an impossibly long finger at the necklace that rested warmly against Teri's skin. "Vintage. Shabby-chic. The piece I didn't think anyone would ever buy. The talisman that summons the long-dormant World Guardian back to the realm. *That's* the magic. You awakened the magic when you put it on. The World Guardian is in you now. *Is* you."

Teri tried to take off the necklace and found that it had adhered to her.

"Told you it wasn't the chainmail." The clerk ran her fingers over the shiny links. "So . . . do you want your thirteen dollars back all in ones?"

Teri's mouth fell open like a goldfish. "I'm stuck?"

"Yeah, that's what I said. You're stuck with the World Guardian role . . . until something manages to kill you and the talisman finds its way back here. That's how it works, Elefteria. Interesting name. You said it means freedom, right?"

"Stuck." Teri spit the word out like it was a piece of rotten *yalanci dolma.*

"Yeah, stuck. Freedom. Appropriate name, I guess. Now you can fight to keep the world—or at least Milwaukee—free. Do you want that all in ones?"

Teri reached for the bikini. "Never mind. I'll keep it." And maybe she'd find a cape to go along with it. A red one.

The Second Hand's Shop hero needed something appropriate to wear.

Burying Treasure

by Alex Shvartsman

The wizard rode a cart full of gold into the village.

The wooden cartwheels creaked, protesting the enormous weight of coins and miscellaneous trinkets that filled the cart to the point of almost overflowing. The coins shifted and jingled as the horse pulled the cart forward on an uneven road, their sweet sound summoning gawkers much faster than any magic could have.

"Now that's something you don't see every day," Hurlee said to her twin sister as the two of them watched the cart make its way down the road.

Burlee grunted assent, the straw she was chewing on teetering at the edge of her lip, and then got up and headed over for a closer look.

"Careful," said Hurlee. "Anyone flaunting such riches is either very dangerous or dangerously stupid. Or both."

Burlee turned back for a moment, straightened the iron-studded jacket of her old military uniform, and nodded at Hurlee, who was wearing the same outfit. "When did that ever stop us?"

Hurlee reached toward her sister, wanting to hold her back, but thought better of it. She lowered her hand and reluctantly followed Burlee instead.

The cart came to a stop. The entire village gathered to see what the wizard would do next. A pile of coins, jewelry, and small trinkets glimmered in the sun, awing the onlookers. A small gargoyle rested atop the treasure. It glared at the villagers, making sure no one got any ideas.

Hurlee hung back, close enough to observe, but far enough to quietly retreat in case there was trouble.

"I need a pair of guides," declared the wizard. "Young people who know the nearby woods. A gold coin is offered in payment."

There was no shortage of volunteers. Villagers jostled each other for a chance at earning the princely sum.

Burlee pushed and shoved her way to the front of the crowd. And although Hurlee was still conflicted, she followed right along.

"What do you seek in the woods, Sir Wizard?" asked one of the village elders.

"A place to bury this treasure," said the wizard. His gargoyle purred loudly and shifted to find a more comfortable spot. It cuddled up to a jewel-encrusted chalice.

"Why would you do such a thing?" asked Burlee, devouring the gold with her eyes.

"The Emperor decrees it," said the wizard, "to help the economy."

The villagers murmured. "I thought them dragonses liked to hoard treasure," said Olaf. A tall, lanky youth, he made up for what could be generously described as below-average wit with excess enthusiasm.

"Quiet, fool." An elder glared at Olaf. "Don't disrespect the Emperor in front of our esteemed guest."

"Indeed," said the wizard. "His Majesty is long-lived, and his complexion is, perhaps, a little scaly, but vicious rumors of dragon blood in his lineage are falsehoods told by anarchists and malcontents. You would do well to discourage such talk."

"Won't happen again," said the elder.

"The Emperor plans ahead," said the placated wizard. "Word of the treasure will spread. Knights and adventurers from other lands will come to seek it. They'll spend coin in taverns and inns, patronize blacksmiths and apothecaries. They'll pay a special tax levied on all seekers. This is called tourism."

Hurlee was well-familiar with the Emperor's eccentricities. The new ruler had signed a peace treaty with the orcs, inconveniently interrupting the conflict that had been successfully ongoing for over a hundred years.

Hurlee and Burlee had enlisted and were just finishing their training when the Emperor had cut down the size of the army. They were sent back home with nothing to show for their effort but a pair of hand-me-down oxhide uniforms. Thousands of young men and women who counted on the war for their employment were now back in their villages, struggling to adjust to this new peace, and to find work. Still, dumping gold into the ground like some storybook pirate was highly unusual, even for the Dragon Emperor.

"You," the wizard turned to Olaf. "Do you know these woods well?"

Olaf nodded enthusiastically.

"You're hired." The wizard scanned the crowd for another recruit.

Hurlee thought that the wizard wasn't particularly discriminating. Drawing his attention might be enough to be picked. She wasn't thrilled about getting involved in this crazy scheme, but there was no other work to be had in the village that didn't involve tending the fields, and she and her sister needed the money.

"Won't the adventurers stop coming once the treasure is found?" Hurlee asked.

"That's why I need guides. The treasure must be hidden so well, it'll take decades to find."

"My sister and I know the best hiding spots," said Hurlee. "Our father was a famed hunter. He showed us places so remote even the wild beasts would have a difficult time finding them."

Hurlee stood still, praying that none of the other villagers would speak up and tell the wizard that their father was actually a cabbage farmer. But others knew better than to incur the ire of the sisters.

The wizard sized them up. "Twins, eh?"

"Idontical," said Olaf.

"Don't you mean *identical*?" asked the wizard.

Olaf scratched his head. "I mean, I don't know how to tell them apart."

The wizard chuckled. "I'll hire the two of you for the price of one. Do we have a deal?"

The wizard and his three guides wandered in the forest all day, looking for a perfect spot.

Despite their exaggerated claims, Hurlee and Burlee did know the land very well. They'd spent their entire childhood exploring the nearby groves, picking mushrooms and berries, and snaring an occasional hare.

The three young villagers shared the secrets of their forest with the wizard. They followed deer paths to small clearings, far away from where any people might tread. They pointed out holes created by generations of woodpeckers, deep enough to conceal a purse of coins. They showed him uprooted trees with tangled roots that formed perfect hiding places for a larger cache. The wizard rejected them all, and urged his poor horse ever deeper into the woods.

It was slow going. The wizard's cart did not navigate easily through the wild growth of the forest. The gold pile jingled precariously each time a wheel hit a protruding tree root. On several occasions the wizard was forced to unharness the horse and levitate the cart over a particularly rough patch of terrain. Hurlee watched in awe. This was real magic, far more impressive than the healing salves and love potions brewed by the local hags.

As they walked, Burlee passed the time planning on how to spend the gold they'd been promised.

"We should buy new clothes," she said. "I'm sick of wearing this ratty uniform. I want to wear green again."

"Green does not flatter your skin tone," said Hurlee. "And besides, we should invest the money into something more practical. We could buy a horse. That way we could try for jobs guarding nobles' carriages and merchant caravans."

"I'm going to buy a goat," said Olaf. "It's cheaper than a horse, and I'll get all the milk and wool for free."

Having not found a satisfactory location by nightfall, they were forced to set up a makeshift camp under the open sky. Burlee started a fire and the four of them shared an evening meal.

"I still don't understand," Hurlee said, exploiting the chance to chat up the wizard. "Can't the Emperor make better use of his gold than to leave it lying around in some ditch? You know, hire more soldiers, pave the roads, that sort of thing?"

"His Imperial Majesty has thought of everything." The wizard poured himself some wine from a large flagon he produced from the back of the cart. He did not offer any to his companions. "Since the gold will be hidden, rather than spent or lost, the exchequer will issue paper money backed by its value."

"Coins made out of paper?" Burlee snorted. "That's a wild thought. They'd be ruined by the first rain. Besides, paper isn't worth very much."

"The value of the paper money is guaranteed by the Emperor," explained the wizard. "So each note will be worth exactly as much as a gold coin. It's a novel concept and it may take some time for people in the countryside to get used to, but we're already having some success introducing the new currency in the capital."

"City folks might be too stupid to tell paper from gold, but we ain't," said Olaf. "You best plan on paying us with the real deal."

The wizard promised that they'd be paid with actual coins, and didn't seem interested in any further conversation.

That night, Olaf tried to steal some of the treasure.

Hurlee had known this would happen. She could tell from the way Olaf kept glancing at the cart, his face alight with greed. So, when the fire went out and everyone settled in for the night, Hurlee willed herself to remain awake.

Both Burlee and the wizard were fast asleep, exhausted by the day's journey. Even the wizard's horse was snoring lightly. Hurlee pretended to be asleep, but instead watched out of the corner of her eye as Olaf got up, checked to make sure his companions weren't alert, and crept toward the cart.

The gargoyle was curled up atop a gilded plate, covering its face with a winged paw. Asleep it looked like a big, gray cat. Very quietly, Olaf reached into the cart and palmed a large nugget. The gargoyle was up immediately, hissing and screaming and clawing at Olaf with its sharp talons. Olaf dropped the nugget and staggered back, clutching at the shallow, bleeding cuts along the length of his right arm. The gargoyle perched at the edge of the cart and hissed at Olaf until the wizard, roused by the noise, waved it off.

"You're lucky Maynard didn't rip off your face," the wizard told Olaf. "Go clean yourself up. Next time you try to steal, or interrupt my sleep, I'll turn you into something unpleasant."

Olaf skulked off toward the nearby stream. Hurlee finally allowed sleep to claim her.

By the late following afternoon Hurlee feared they'd be spending yet another night in the forest. But to her great relief, the wizard found what he decreed to be a perfect hiding place, far from where any hunters or gatherers might roam.

The wizard produced a pair of shovels from the bottom of the cart and instructed his guides to dig a hole. He rested in the shade while Olaf, Hurlee, and Burlee worked, sweated, and cursed.

"Look at us," said Burlee, "reduced to digging around in the dirt. If we wanted to do this sort of filthy work, we could have remained on Father's farm."

"It's paid work," said Hurlee. "It's not perfect, but we need the money to see us through until we can find something better."

"There is nothing better," Burlee said bitterly as she drove her shovel deep into the moist earth. "We might as well get used to handling a shovel, because there's no room for our skill set in this weird new age of peace treaties and paper money."

"You can't give up hope," said Hurlee. "We're young, and we're smart. We'll adjust."

"Your problem is, you're too picky," said Olaf. "Shovelin' is good work, when you can get it." He put his back into it to underscore the point.

"Shut up, Olaf," said Burlee. She turned to her sister. "Take the shovel. It's your turn to dig."

When the hole was deep enough, the wizard placed a few handfuls of gold into a sack and lowered it to the bottom. He then motioned for the others to begin refilling the hole.

"That's it?" asked Burlee, eyeing the lion's share of the treasure that remained on the cart.

"Our empire is vast," said the wizard. "Hiding smaller amounts of treasure across the land will serve the Emperor's plans better than a single large trove."

Covering the hole with freshly dug earth was easier work than digging. Afterward, the wizard made Olaf collect some leaves and twigs to cover up the recently disturbed patch of ground.

Halfway back to the village, the wizard stopped the cart. "Now that the treasure is hidden, I must remove your memories of its location with a spell. Then you'll be paid."

Hurlee had expected something like this to happen. After all, burying treasure would be pointless if one left behind three greedy and highly motivated locals who knew exactly where to look. If anything, Hurlee was relieved that the wizard hadn't planned on a more severe and permanent solution to this problem.

"This won't hurt very much," the wizard promised. He beckoned Olaf to him.

The wizard touched Olaf's forehead and recited a spell that he said would drain away the memories of the past few days. Olaf lumbered off like a drunk, looking like he just got hit in the head with a rake. He appeared to be stupefied by the experience, but with Olaf it was rather difficult to tell.

Burlee was up next. Hurlee watched her sister step forward, and an inkling of a plan began to formulate in her mind. Burlee was right; they couldn't just wait around and hope for their circumstances to improve. She saw an opportunity, and she was going to act on it.

While the wizard was reciting his spell for the second time, Hurlee touched Olaf's shoulder and pointed at the cart.

"Look. Gold," Hurlee whispered.

Olaf's eyes grew wide as he discovered the treasure. Without the memory of Maynard to restrain him, Olaf stumbled toward the cart. The gargoyle hissed in warning, baring its teeth at the hapless villager. And while the wizard, who had just finished enchanting Burlee, was distracted by the commotion, Hurlee traded places with her twin sister.

Hurlee counted on the wizard not being able to tell the two of them apart. Their army uniforms hadn't helped the sisters land the cushy bodyguard or sentry jobs they'd hoped for in the past, but in this one instance, the matching garments might help them secure their future.

Having made certain that the treasure was safe from Olaf, and Olaf was safe from the gargoyle, the wizard turned his attention back to the sisters. He gently nudged Hurlee, who was standing in front of him with as blank an expression on her face as she could muster, out of the way, and grabbed Burlee.

Hurlee watched as the wizard zapped her poor sister with another forgetting spell. She wondered if Burlee would lose a few extra days' worth of memory, or just forget their forest adventures that much more thoroughly. Either way, she reckoned it was well worth keeping the memory of where the treasure was. Even the small portion of the cart's riches that the wizard had left behind was enough to set them up for life.

The wizard let his guides rest for a few minutes, until they regained their senses. Their old memories of the forest were unaffected and so they had no trouble finding the way back to the village. There, the wizard paid them, just like he promised. He was even kind enough to let the other villagers know that the guides' memories had been erased. That way no one would think of trying to force the treasure's location out of them.

Hurlee waited for over a day, to make sure the wizard was gone and not coming back, before she shared the secret with her sister. Burlee was so excited by the news that she didn't even grumble too much about being made into the lightning rod for the wizard's forgetting spell. The twins immediately decided that such information was best kept away from Olaf. So it was just the two of them sneaking out of the village to claim the treasure.

They traveled back to the site, dug up the still-fresh earth, and retrieved the sack. But when they opened it, there was no gold at all. The sack was filled with rocks.

Burlee examined one of the rocks and tossed it aside. "That treacherous wizard must've enchanted these rocks to look like treasure, and kept the real gold for himself," she said.

"For his purposes, the rumor of hidden treasure is as good as the real thing," reasoned out Hurlee. "This way, the Emperor can keep his riches and still get adventurers to come searching for them."

Frustrated, Burlee kicked some dirt back into the hole. "But then, why bury the rocks in the first place?"

Hurlee mulled it over. "The old warlock must've suspected that some of our memories might eventually return. If so, he couldn't risk not going through with the charade."

"What a cheat!" Burlee continued to rile herself up. "We should go back home and let everybody know the truth. Screw up his convoluted plan. That'll show him!"

"No," said Hurlee, after thinking hard for a while. "No, we shouldn't. I have a better idea."

Hurlee picked up a shovel and began to fill the hole again. "Let people think that the treasure is buried somewhere in these woods," she said as she worked. "We aren't supposed to remember exactly where, but we're the local guides, and we're the ones who showed the wizard all the likely hiding spots. This information will be worth something, once the adventurers come."

Burlee was beginning to understand, annoyance and

disappointment draining from her face as she listened to Hurlee's plan. "The Emperor wants these treasure hunts to help spur the local economy? Well, we're part of the local economy, too. There's no reason why we can't cash in."

"It won't be long until the adventurers show up," said Hurlee. "There will be no shortage of demand for guides, then."

"There must also be other ways to profit from this," said Burlee. "Let's get some parchment and start drawing maps. Two . . . No, three silver coins for a genuine treasure map sounds about right."

"That's the spirit, sister," Hurlee clapped Burlee on her leather-clad shoulder. "Who needs the dangers of the orc wars, or the tedium of sentry duty? We're getting into the tourism trade."

Calling the Mom Squad

by Sarah A. Hoyt

Fighting dragons is nothing to removing gum from a three-year-old's hair, and it doesn't hold a candle to keeping a three-year-old and a six-year-old amused during a snow day in Colorado, with all the roads closed and the schools closed, too. I should know. I've done all of it.

The alarm came at the worst possible time. It always does, of course. If there is one thing you can count on, it's that life will happen exactly like a sitcom, with difficulty piled on difficulty and situations going for the most ridiculous laugh line.

It was a snow day. I was home. Mind you, I was usually home. I worked as a freelance translator, which was a way of staying with the kids, and being there when they came home from school, and generally being a housewife as well as a breadwinner. Not the main breadwinner, but translation—scientific, multilingual—did bring in a good amount, even if it was irregular. And it afforded me time and cover for my other activities.

My world-saving activities.

There were six of us in Colorado Springs. We called ourselves The Mom Squad. All of us had kids. Only one of us had a day job away from home. And she'd been involved in the original fiasco that had caused our group to come into existence. I mean she'd been one of the scientists. The only female.

Look, I've nothing against men. Heaven love them, they're no worse than women, but they're . . . different. One of the ways in which they seem to be different is that they're better able to concentrate on tasks or details, to the exclusion of the big picture.

This is an advantage in some ways, but also a problem that afflicts scientists with peculiar intensity. If they're pursuing the millionth digit of pi, or better rocket fuel, or a way to open a portal into another dimension, that's *all* they're pursuing, and they're not likely to realize the consequences of their discovery. So, if they starved while calculating pie to the one-millionth digit, they just did, and if the rocket fuel would poison the crops in half the world, it didn't matter, provided it could still power rockets. And if portals into other dimensions allow creatures to come through that could lay waste to humanity, or at least seriously wreck a half-dozen cities, well, that wasn't their business. They'd been tasked with opening a portal to another dimension, and that's what they'd done.

So, five of us women had had husbands who worked at Cheyenne Mountain, back when it was an active missile silo and a center of research. And Alicia had worked there herself. As had her ex-husband. She'd been unable to convince him, or any of the rest of the team, that it was a very bad idea to do what they'd been tasked with doing. But after the incident of the lizard people, she had become a whistle blower. Which had caused her marriage to implode, but had kept the world safe from lizard beings from the dungeon dimension.

Or at least we had kept the world safe from lizard beings from the dungeon dimension after we'd been caught in a battle with them.

After that, we'd saved the world from other things, too. Since the five of us had been pitchforked into that first battle, we'd formed The Mom Squad. No one knew except the three men who'd also been involved in that battle. And none of them were any of our husbands.

Which was the problem, when the alarm sounded. You see, my husband, Wayne, was also home for the snow day. After Cheyenne had closed, he'd found a job in a local research facility. But the facility was closed for the day, and, what was worse, Wayne was sitting in the living room sofa, hacking and coughing, as he suffered through a massive cold.

When the alarm sounded, he said, "Honey, I think the washer is done."

Thank heavens he didn't actually have the slightest idea what the washer alarm sounded like. I put down the ice cube I'd been applying to the wad of gum in my son Tim's hair. I shot a dirty look at my daughter, Jennie, who was coloring a princess book at the kitchen table. I had an idea that the gum hadn't so much drifted onto Tim's white-blond hair as it had been carefully applied there. And if I had to cut his hair to remove it, he was going to be mostly bald. But if there's one thing most mothers learn about early, it's the perfidy of angelic-looking little girls.

And I didn't have time to deal with her, right then. Instead, I edged around her, past the family room, where Wayne was blowing his nose loudly, and into the laundry room, just to the left of the basement door. The alarm was there, but it wasn't coming from the washer. Instead, it emitted—sharp whistle and red lights and all—from a panel behind the cat box. Because no matter if the cat box caught fire, no one else in the house would go near it.

I shoved the catbox away with my foot, then tapped a rhythmic code into the wall behind it. The weird light stopped shining behind what appeared to be perfectly normal wallboard, and the whistle cut off.

"Anne?" a voice said from the ceiling. I jumped about three feet, straight up, then leapt to the door and closed it. Hell and damnation. I had to learn to carry the headphones with me. I could pretend it was music or something.

I locked the door to the laundry room and spoke to the ceiling, "Yes?"

"There's a breakthrough in sector twenty-four," the voice said. I knew the voice. It was Bill, the oldest of the scientists who'd been there for the lizard people battle. He was now supposedly retired, which gave him free time to keep a scan on the mountain. His wife thought he only went there out of nostalgia, and to make sure no one stole anything.

I realized I'd said a swear word after I said it. "I can't," I said. "The kids are both home, and so is Wayne. Our neighborhood hasn't been plowed. I can't say I'm going to the store, and I couldn't leave him alone with the kids anyway."

There was a short silence. Then Bill sighed. "If he's working from home—"

"That's just it," I said. "He isn't." Normally when Wayne worked from home, he worked from a desk in the spare bedroom and was safely deaf and mute to everything and everyone around him. "Even if he were, it would be difficult to leave him with both kids, but he's home sick, and he's in the family room. He'll notice if I'm gone. I can't tell him I'm going to the store, or working in the garden. And he's in no state to look after the kids. Can't you call Alicia?"

"Uh. No. She had a car accident and is stuck out on the road from Woodland Park, waiting for triple A to pick her up."

"Lucy?"

"She has a cold. And she has her in-laws visiting." He added in a tone that gave me the impression he was ticking people off on his fingers and counting, "Jill is in the hospital with pneumonia, Paula has her neighbor's kids over and she can't leave, Mary's having an issue with her armor and we really can't send her out there without it. The mechanics aren't in the shop, and she couldn't take it to the shop to repair, anyway, because the roads are a mess. I'm afraid it's down to you."

I swore again. Sometimes it's a relief to be able to do it without the kids around. "But I can't," I said. "What am I supposed to do with the kids?"

"Your son, Tom?"

"Tim."

"Right, Tim. He's what, two?"

"Three! I was pregnant with him when—"

"Yes," he said. The man was notably squeamish about the frog-things battle a few years ago. That had been a terrible one. Maybe it was the poisonous blood. Or perhaps the holes they had eaten into the floor. "Well. He's not so small anymore. You can probably sit him and his sister in front of cartoons or something, right?"

I remembered that Bill and his wife had never had children. I started to say it was impossible, but if all the others were more incapacitated than I was . . . Oh, sure, I could tell Bill to fight whatever it was himself, but not only was he over seventy and a scientist who'd never fought anything more dangerous than a recalcitrant computer, but he also didn't have the armor. Had never had it made. He'd already been too old for this when we'd fought the lizard people.

"What about Mike?" I asked. "Or Al?"

"Mike is in Hawaii, on his honeymoon," Bill said, in a deeply disapproving tone. "And Al . . ."

"Yes?"

"Hospital. His wife is giving birth. Look, it really is only you. You have to stop this dragon. There's no other way. We're containing him for now, sort of, behind the doors of sector twenty-three, but he's denting them pretty good, and, sooner or later, he's going to come right through. Do you want a dragon eating his way through Colorado Springs? Or setting buildings on fire? I mean, the only good thing about the last dragon breakthrough is that it was in summer when fires—"

"Dragon," I said. It wasn't a swear word, but it might as well have been. I thought we'd seen the last of the things.

"Dragon," he said.

And that was the problem. There are breakthroughs from the dungeon dimensions you can explain, and breakthroughs you can't. Take the lizard people. Ah ah, rubber masks. Or take the time that we'd been invaded by a bunch of alien creatures who had studied our culture but not . . . well enough. They'd thought the way to blend in with humans was to dress like Waldo, since no one could ever spot him. We'd started the story that there had been a *Where's Waldo?* fan convention in town. Implausible, of course, but people bought it. UFOs, and even pink blob monsters could be explained away. But dragons?

Dragons look very much like dragons. And they couldn't be a human in disguise. Not unless the human happened to be fifteen feet tall, have wings, and emit jets of flame from his mouth. In which case he would look uncommonly like a dragon.

Dragon. No, I had to go fight the dragon. But how?

Even as I thought it out, I had a sort of sketch of a plan. I'd have to take Tim, of course. No two ways about it. Not only was that boy capable of getting in endless amounts of trouble all by himself, but he was also a constant temptation to his older sister, who—if she had him on hand—would find new and more creative ways to torture him and get him in trouble.

If he wasn't left in the house, I could leave Jennie behind. Provided enough crayons, coloring books, and the promise of a box of comic books, she could behave for an hour or so on her own. It ought to be enough.

"Right," I said. "On my way."

I could practically hear Bill sigh with relief on the other side of our connection.

One of the advantages of Wayne thinking he's dying every time he catches a cold is that he's less than observant. Had he not been so worried about how feverish he was, and the fact that he kept coughing, he might have noticed how long I'd spent in the laundry room with the door closed.

He certainly would have noticed when I came out, held a whispered conversation with my daughter, which consisted of my offering to buy her her weight in *Pretty Princess* comics if she would just stay at the kitchen table and color while I went and fixed something in the basement. And had Wayne been his normal self, he would almost surely have realized that it was a very odd thing for me to run towards the basement door with Tim on my hip, saying, "I'm going down to see if the pipes are freezing." After all, while various strange implements have been used to thaw pipes throughout history, I don't think anyone has ever tried rubbing a little boy on them.

But Wayne was so out of it, all he did was say, "Dab's fine," and cough into a tissue.

I opened the door to the basement, locked it behind me hoping he didn't try it and find it locked and wonder who had installed a lock on that door and why, and ran fast down the cement steps.

"Weeeeee," my son said. "Run."

"Yeah, fun run," I said, and rushed towards an inconspicuous portion of what looked like unfinished wallboard. I punched a code in just the right place, by memory. The wall slid aside, and Tim said, "Shiny!"

It was. You see, in this space, I kept my armor. It was power armor and had been designed especially for me, right after the incident at Cheyenne Mountain when the lizard people came through, and the nine of us had fought them, and Bill had closed the portal.

It made me as strong as . . . well, much stronger than the average male, and it also kept me from being too easily injured. Though I had the scars to show that it was terrible at protecting people from cuts inflicted by the teeth of creatures that were made of stuff harder than diamond. Stuff that didn't exist on Earth. This is one reason why I hated dragons.

As for what the armor looked like? Well, it looked like a full suit of shining chainmail. Fitted. Clinging. Don't judge me. If I'm going into battle, I'm going to look hot doing it.

In mid-change, I thought of what hot might mean and shuddered. Then I realized that Tim had—somehow—managed to punch the code in the wall that opened the other door. The one that displayed my horse. My black horse made of the sort of ceramic they used on the outside of space vehicles, with the laser eyes and the array of weapons built into it. It activated as the door slid away, and the eyes came to glowing red light, while the hooves struck sparks from the cement floor.

I scooped Tim up just before he ran under the hooves screaming, "Horsie!"

"Yes," I told him. "Nice horsie." And as I spoke, I put my foot in the right indentation, by dint of long practice, and threw my leg over, sitting astride the robot horse—which was about as comfortable as riding a flower pot. And possibly half as safe.

I knew what the guys had said about devising the robot horse as our main form of conveyance in these battles. They said, after all, the portals to other dimensions often remained open, which meant we might be seen by people on the other side. Human people. And while human civilizations might or might not have tanks or other vehicles, almost all human civilizations had at least had some portion of their history when they rode horses.

This seemed rather specious to me. There were human civilizations here on Earth that had never ridden anything. I suspected the real reason for the guys to have designed a robot horse was because they could. And because it was cool. Which was about par for the course. But right then and there, I wished my conveyance had been an Abrams tank. Though, of course, with dragons, that might simply have made me a ready to heat meal.

The robot horse reared, and I managed to stay on by grabbing its ear with one hand, while wrapping the other around Tim. With my third hand—All right, I realized I didn't have one, as I tried to use it, and, instead, I let go of the ear, tightened the grip of my thighs on the horse's middle, and punched the abort sequence into the set of buttons that Tim had been playing with. Whoever had thought of putting the buttons for the horse on the back of his neck was going to spend eternity in a very hot place. For that matter, why in heck did the horse have buttons? Exposed and easy to manipulate buttons?

"Horsie stand," Tim said, and reached a chubby hand for the buttons again. I slapped it away. He wailed.

"I'm sorry," I said, "but the horse is mommy's. You must let mommy—"

His wail reached fire-siren levels. Any minute now, my husband was going to break through the basement door, with an extinguisher in his hands. I fancied I could already hear him pounding on it.

"Shhh," I said, and reached in the pouch to the side of the horse for a candy bar—what, like you never needed a power snack while battling evil?!—and thrust it at Tim. The shriek cut off and he said, "S'occulate" which had also been his first word, because some things are genetic.

I took the opportunity of his being busy—and increasingly stickier—with the candy bar to attach him to the waist belt of my armor. And then I punched a code into the horse that turned it around, and another code that was answered by the portal in the wall.

Yes, yes. Portals can be useful. The point, of course, is not to overdo it. And also not to make them span more than say thirty miles, and to make sure they stay in the same universe. They'd learned enough by the time they'd established this one, to know how not to get in trouble. The ones in Cheyenne Mountain, though . . .

This portal opened straight from my basement to the closed areas of Cheyenne Mountain. The areas where no one was allowed. Except Bill. And Mike. And Al. And the six of us. Because someone had to make sure that the breakthroughs—which I'm still convinced were the inspiration for a well-known science fiction series—that plagued the mountain, resulting from a portal we simply didn't have the technology to close, didn't spill out into Colorado Springs. And the world at large.

The portal opened in a flash of light, and I crossed through in the twenty seconds before it closed again.

The horse was running down a marble-paved hallway that looked like any government office. Bill's voice came from the ceiling. "About damn time." I didn't answer, because I tried not to swear in front of the kids. Also, because I was busy pulling my lance from the holster across the horse's chest.

It's not really a lance, of course. It's some sort of vibration weapon with a laser-tip, and one of the few things we'd found effective against dragons the last time they'd attacked.

I held it in one hand while holding on to the horse's neck with my other hand—I really had to get the guys to put some sort of safety belt or a saddle on this thing—while running full tilt at the door of sector twenty-four.

Bill was supposed to open it before the horse and the toddler and I careened into it. This was the theory, at any rate, but it didn't get tested, because before we got there, the dragon came through it instead. Two paws full of claws, a roaring mouth, a head that looked like a cross between an iguana and a particularly ugly bulldog, and the disposition of a train at full steam. The noise of a train at full steam, too.

I aimed the laser at its eyes to blind it, then, before it could recover, slipped the blade into its mouth and engaged the vibration. And found that my son was no longer tied to my middle, but—somehow—on the floor next to the dragon. This was what is technically known as a miracle. There was no possible way he could have untied himself, much less any way he could have got down from the robot horse. But, as every mother knows, toddler boys have a magic all their own.

I made the sound best transcribed as *"ARRRRRGH"*, let go of the lance, and jumped down from the horse. The dragon pulled the lance out of its mouth, focused its eyes on my son, and said, "Slurg," which was probably dragon for "snack."

My son lifted chocolate-stained hands to the dragon, and said, "Doggie."

The dragon opened its mouth as it started to rear up. I looked in horror at the huge, inflated, fire-producing tonsils. My hands had gone to my pouch for a weapon, but the only thing I had was another chocolate bar, and I didn't think chocolate killed dragons. In about minus twenty seconds, Tim and I were going to be statistics. Crispy, crispy, well-done statistics.

And all my weapons were on the horse, which was still standing, as I'd left it, because, well, until someone punched the buttons, it wasn't going to do anything at all.

To reach it, I'd need—Too long.

I heard the characteristic intake of air, and the hiss that preceded a dragon's flaming. And then the hack-cough of the dragon flame starting.

"Eat fire retardant, smoke breath," said a voice I knew all too well. As a shot of white foam went past me, I turned around to see Jennie standing there, aiming the fire extinguisher.

"Jennie!" I said. But I'd recovered enough of my wits to get to the horse. You have to use a vibrating blade to kill the dragons, because anywhere you hit them, unless you slip it between two scales and use a vibration frequency that disables their neurons, won't have any effect but make them lash out.

Unless, of course, the dragon's mouth happens to be wide open, and the dragon is too confused by a stream of fire extinguisher hitting its tonsils to fight back. In which case, you can reach into the arms pouch of your horse and retrieve the grenade, which the designers of your armament put in there just in case.

I removed the pin, counted to five, and flung the grenade right at the dragon, hoping he didn't have the hiccups and upchuck it. But even as I was hoping, I was scooping Tim with one arm, scooping Jennie in the other while I jumped, and jumping as far away as possible from the dragon, behind the horse.

We landed with the kids sort of under me, and I leaned over them as I continued the count, *Nine, Ten,*—

Maybe the grenade was defective, maybe—

There was a sound like "hick" followed by a sound like "*paff,*" and then there was light.

No, I mean it literally. There was light, and sound, and something wet hit the back of my head. Okay, a lot of stuff hit, and it sounded like rain all around, and it smelled like . . . someone had burned really old shoe leather.

I opened one eye. There was dragon all over. Minced dragon. In really small pieces. Greenish and pink bits of it decorated the ceiling, dripped down the wall, and made a pattern on the marble floor.

"Yuck," Jennie said. She wrinkled her nose. "Yuck. Dragon guts."

Tim had a handful of something green and wobbly in one chubby chocolate-stained fist. I pulled it away before he could put it in his mouth, and he started his fire alarm scream again.

I picked him up, looked in my pouch, grabbed the candy bar and gave it to him, cutting off the sound.

Jennie, drops of what she would doubtless call "yuck" running down her blond hair, and a pink shred of dragon dashingly adorning her brow frowned at me, "Dad says you shouldn't bribe him with chocolate, because—"

"I know," I said. "But I couldn't have him crying. Bill," I called towards the ceiling. "Bill!"

"Yeah. What happened?"

"Grenade," I said. "I blew up the dragon. Can you make sure the sector is secure and then open the portal back to my basement?" I looked behind me. "Oh, yeah, and put in a requisition for a new horse. With a safety belt or a saddle. Or both."

I started walking towards the place my portal home would be.

"I heard Tim cry," Jennie said. "And I figured you were going on an adventure. So I jimmied the basement door open."

"Have you done that often?" I asked. I was so tired that all this seemed like a very distant concern.

"Not often," she said. She sighed. "Just, you know, the other times you went, that I was home. I wanted to know what you did! But I never . . . I never came after you. Only I couldn't believe," she said, her voice sharpening, "that you'd take Tim and not me."

"I *thought* I could trust you to behave for an hour."

She made a sound like a snort. "If I hadn't come—" she said, and then suddenly stopped, and stopped walking too, and looked at me with shocked eyes, as if she'd just realized that if she hadn't come none of us would be going home.

I said quickly, "I know, I know. And I'm grateful. But it's too dangerous for you to—"

And then I stopped because there, in the hallway, just before the place our portal home should open, Bill stood.

He's of medium height and wears his salt-and-pepper hair in a military cut. And he looked not at all amused. "Anne, may I ask—"

"Take your daughter to work day," I said.

He opened his mouth, closed it.

I sighed and told him the truth, the whole truth, and the parts of the truth that were guaranteed to piss him off. It couldn't be helped.

He sighed. "What if your son talks?"

"What, if he says I was fighting a *dragon*? Who's going to believe him?"

Bill opened his mouth, closed it, then turned to Jennie. "And what about this young lady?"

"I'm not going to say anything," she said. "I've known for months, and I haven't said anything. Besides, no one would believe me. I just want—"

"Yes?"

"A set of armor like mom's."

"I see," Bill said. "Fine. We'll get you one."

I'd have to have a talk later, and explain to him he really would have to because Jennie never forgets. There are breeds of elephants that are jealous of her memory when it comes to things she was promised.

But right then I was so tired I couldn't talk. I held one kid up on my hip, and gave my hand to the other as we crossed the portal to the basement that contained nothing more threatening than a furnace and a water heater.

In a just world, Wayne would have been asleep on the sofa, or even have made his way to the bed upstairs, as we emerged from the basement, tired, bruised and covered in dragon yuck.

But the world isn't just and whoever is writing my life has a sense of humor. A bad one. After all we had to go through the family room to the bathroom, where we could get cleaned up and change clothes.

My clothes were fairly clean, because the armor had taken the worst of it and I'd, of course, taken off the armor and put it in its secret storage space, pending clean up. The kids, on the other hand, were covered in dragon.

"Good lord," Wayne said, as he sat up on the sofa and forgot to blow his nose on the tissue he was holding. "What happened to you?"

"Mommy fought the dragon," Tim said, helpfully. "An' Jennie hit it with fire 'stinguisher, and mom fed it a bomb. And it 'sploded."

"It was one of the pipes," I said.

"It broke all over us," Jennie put in. "But we've fixed it."

"What? All three of you?"

"No," I said. "Just me. The kids just got in the way."

I was aware of a look of betrayal from my daughter, but it served her right because, unless I were much mistaken, she was going to insist on going on calls with me from now on.

I dragged her by the hand into the bathroom before she had a chance to say anything else, filled the bathtub with bubbles and tossed both kids in it. At this point I was going to have to shave Tim's head to get rid of the gum. I looked in the mirror. There was a bit of dragon on my eyebrow, and another bit on my cheek.

It could have been much worse.

"Mommy 'sploded the dragon!" Tim said.

"With help from me!" Jennie said.

I made a face at my dragon-yuck-adorned reflection. It could be much worse.

And doubtless, it would be.

Rabid Weasels

by Robin Wayne Bailey

It was just an ordinary winter night at the Rampant Rooster Tavern, where lords and ladies from the upper tiers of society mingled shoulder to shoulder with the roughest, dirtiest, low-life scum the city had to offer. Expensive silks brushed against tanners' leather and flea-infested rags, and nobody cared. The walls fairly shook with bawdy laughter and ribald conversations as the noblemen lined up their conquests and the prostitutes anticipated their coins.

Sherri served up two more foaming mugs of beer to the Northern barbarian in the fur loincloth and heavy cloak who had wandered in for the first time tonight. His fingertips brushed hers as he reached to claim the vessels, and she felt an electric jolt. Her eyes widened slightly, and her lips parted. His entire body rippled with sun-bronzed muscle. The barbarian smiled at her, and Sherri allowed herself a brief fantasy that ended when he turned away and passed the extra beer to a slim young sailor from the docks. The two clinked glasses, and then clapped arms around each other's waists as they drifted toward a dark corner beyond the blazing fireplace.

Sherri sighed, but there was little time to curse her luck. Her customers demanded constant attention. Lord Pompey pounded his hammy fist on the bar and beckoned toward his empty mug while the Lady Gravelot, out for a night on the town without her husband, nibbled on his ear and carelessly splashed her own beverage on another man's boots.

A high-pitched shriek erupted from the center of the tavern. One of the prostitutes, known in the streets as "Sweet Tansy," beat frantically at her colorful skirts. Her face flushed with shock and surprise, and she screamed a second time. A moment later, a bearded dwarf crawled from beneath her legs with a broad grin on his face and his fist clutched tight.

"It's the Mother of all Cockroaches!" he cried, opening two of his fingers to show off his prize. The pinched cockroach arched its chitinous back, waved its legs, and hissed.

Sweet Tansy stared at the gigantic insect. Her red face turned white, and she fainted into the arms of a moneylender, who stood behind her. "Now this is a lucky piece of change," he laughed. Taking advantage, he pressed his mouth against her painted lips

"Be careful," a sailor shouted from the other side of the tavern. "She'll give you a bug!"

Then, without warning, the boards of the tavern's old roof shattered. Amid a cascade of straw thatching, splintered boards and snow, a fat city guardsman crashed to the floor.

Pompey stared with an arched eyebrow and his drink at his lips. "Nice red shirts the guards are wearing these days," he commented. "But God's engines! We're damned lucky that one didn't land on somebody."

Sherri pushed Pompey aside as she came around the bar. "I'm sure he's touched by your concern," she said with an eye toward the hole in her roof. The dwarf hurried to her side, and the two of them bent down over the guard as her other guests clustered around grinning and drinking as if the guard's unusual arrival was just another bit of entertainment. "Is he alive?" Sherri asked the dwarf.

The dwarf bent down to listen for a heartbeat as he fingered the guard's purse. He looked up at Sherri and nodded. "Do you want to see my roach?" he asked, holding the bug under her nose."

Before she could answer, the guard suddenly regained consciousness. Legs and arms flailing, his face pale and bloodless, he cried out. "Weasels! Rabid weasels! They're attacking the city! Run for your lives!"

Sweet Tansy suddenly woke up in the moneylender's arms. "Weasels?" she asked.

"Rabid weasels," the moneylender answered, unconcerned. Then he kissed Sweet Tansy again without objection.

Sherri, still bent over the fallen guard, called out. "Help me get this man up," she said, pulling a nearby chair over. To the dwarf she said, "Get him a drink, Bud, and be quick about it."

Before he could obey, the tavern's front door flew off its hinges. A squad of booted soldiers charged inside. Sherri shot to her feet and glared at the red-shirted captain. "Can't you use a door handle like all the rest of these people!" Her poor tavern was going to need major reconstruction.

The mustachioed captain sneered as he gazed hot-eyed around the room. "I'm looking for the red-tressed, sword-slinging she-devil called *Beer-Sheba,* who is reported to be seen sometimes around this dubious establishment." He glanced toward the hole in the roof. "And I hereby levy a fine of one hundred copper *klarks* for conducting business in a structurally unsafe building."

Bud held out his roach toward the captain, and the roach hissed.

"The bug is a good judge of character," the barbarian laughed, his arm still around the sailor.

The captain turned as red as his shirt. "Kill him!" he ordered his men with a snap of his fingers. Then he snapped his fingers at Bud. "Then kill that one and his little bug, too." He shot another look around the room. Then, with three more snaps, he drew his sword. "Oh, just kill everybody!"

The fallen guardsman still on the floor flailed again. "Rabid weasels!" he cried. Sherri put her foot on his chest. For a fine winter night, things were not going well at all. If word spread around town about this kind of excitement, it could triple her business, and the Rampant Rooster really couldn't handle the overflow.

Throughout the tavern, steel suddenly glittered. Even Sweet Tansy produced a blade as her customers prepared to square off with the captain and his guards. Sherri knew she had to act. "Wait, wait, wait!" she appealed as she moved to the center of the room. "Can't we all just get along? I've been to the mountain, and I have a dream . . . "

Lord Pompey put on a look of boredom and waved his hand. "Whatever," he said.

Sherri frowned at the pompously plump nobleman as she held a staying hand toward the captain. "Well what about *free beer for everybody!*"

The crowd surged past her, even the captain's men, as they pushed up against the bar where the dwarf, perched upon a stool, began to set up mugs as fast as his short arms could draw the brews. Sherri leaned toward the captain and whispered in a deepening voice, "If you really want to find the legendary warrior, the Queen of Steel, and the Scourge of Patriarchies Everywhere, then gird up your shriveled loins and be in the alley in ten minutes." She put out a surreptitious hand and brushed her palm over his crotch. "A piece of advice as well. If I were you, I'd forget about the fine of one hundred *klarks*."

Suddenly nervous, he blinked. "What fine?"

Sherri put her nose right up against the captain's, staring into his eyes, controlling him now as a snake-charmer would a snake. "Fine," she answered.

A scream sounded in the street beyond the shattered door, and a barely glimpsed body went flying past. Lady Gravelot, turning pale, set down her beverage and covered her white diaphanous gown with a heavy cloak as she edged toward the tavern's back door with Lord Pompey in tow.

The captain of the guard fell back a step. "Did you hear that snarl?" he said. "Rabid weasels! They're running amok!"

Except for the scream and the drunken muttering throughout the room, Sherri heard nothing, no snarling or any other animal noises, but she couldn't deny that a man had dropped through her roof and another had just flown past her door. Her green eyes narrowed to slits. "The alley," she reminded the captain. "Ten minutes." Then, she called to the dwarf, "Bud, a last drink for everybody, then close it down!

Sherri pressed through the crowd to a staircase that led to upper rooms. The Rampant Rooster had been a brothel before she bought it and converted the upstairs for her own use. As she climbed the stairs, she glanced back and noted that her customers were already beginning to slink away, aware that something strange was happening. Or maybe the hole in the roof was just putting a chill on their good spirits. It certainly chilled hers.

At least her bedroom with its own fireplace was warm. Sherri began shedding her skirts and throwing them upon the bed. In her undergarments, she crossed the room and opened an old chest. As she did so, Bud walked into the bedroom. "Does this mean we're saddling up, boss?" he said

Sherri nodded as she bent over and, deliberately giving him a view of her shapely rump, reached into the chest. "I assume you're coming," she called over her shoulder. "Shouldn't you go get ready?"

Bud stared. "I'm ready!" he assured her. "I'm ready!" Then, he rolled his tongue back up and shook himself as if breaking free from a spell. "Oh, you mean armor and weapons and stuff. Sure! I'll be right back!"

Sherri straightened as she watched him depart. She'd known him for a lot of years and trusted him with her life. It was cruel to tease him, but sometimes a woman just had to practice her skills. Even a swordswoman.

Reaching into the chest again, Sherri pulled out a gleaming bikini made of leather and chainmail. It shimmered in the fireplace glow as she held it up. Every link seemed to contain the memory of an adventure, and the gentle jangling spoke to her like an old friend.

Beer-Sheba! She had thought to give up that identity with all its weight and legend. *Beer-Sheba the warrior! The pirate! The hero! Red Beer-Sheba!* It had been exciting for a while, but legends had a way of wearing one down. She had changed her name to Sherri and bought a tavern. Maybe she had been a fool to think the simple life would ever be enough, because here she was, climbing into armor again at the invitation of a mere captain and the preposterous threat of *rabid weasels*! She couldn't even say those stupid words aloud without laughing. What fool had concocted them?

Still, she slipped into her armor, such as it was, and pulled out doeskin boots that laced up to her knees. Next, she put on a narrow belt with a sheathed dagger, and then a weightier belt with an immense sword, no dainty blade, but a real man's weapon, long and thick and broad. Finally, she drew from the chest a cloak of leather and fur and threw it around her shoulders. She tossed back her long red hair.

Bud dashed back into the room without announcing himself, and Sherri turned. The dwarf stopped on the bedroom threshold so suddenly that he nearly fell, but he caught himself and stared for a long moment. Then he swallowed with a noisy gulp. "You've still got it, Sherri," he said.

"Beer-Sheba," she reminded him.

He glanced past the fireplace toward the shuttered window. "Yeah, well, in this snowstorm, it's going to be *Brrrrr!-Sheba*! It's really coming down out there, but at least all the customers have gone home. Even the guards left."

Sherri—*Beer-Sheba*, she reminded herself—reached into the chest one last time for a pair of metal-scaled arm-guards, which she slipped onto her forearms. Then, she gently closed the chest. "The captain is waiting in the alley," she told the dwarf. "And the snow will make it easy to track the . . . " She hesitated, and then laughed. She still couldn't bring herself to say it—*rabid weasels*!

Bud crossed the room to stare into the fire. He wore armor, too, a chainmail shirt that reached to his knees with sleeves that extended to his wrists. He wore no blades, neither sword nor dagger. His strange religion didn't allow edged weapons. Instead, he wore a belt from which depended a dozen fire-tempered, heavy glass beer mugs. Another follower of the faith might have opted for a mace or hammer, but those were not the choices of Bud the Wiser.

Beer-Sheba unlatched the wooden shutters. Her window looked out upon the alley behind the tavern. Leaning outward into the wild snow flurry, she spied the silhouetted form of the captain of the guard. With a hand on her sword, she threw one leg over the windowsill.

"Are we going to jump?" Bud asked with a frown.

Beer-Sheba grinned. "Do you want to live forever?"

"Well, sort of, yeah," Bud shot back. "The tavern's empty. We could use the door."

"What door?" she grinned. "The captain kicked it in." With that, she jumped outward into the darkness, her armor lightly jingling, cloak fluttering, red hair flying. With agile grace she plummeted to land like a cat on her feet in white drift. Bud followed a moment later, falling with the grace of a cow. He landed face down and rose sputtering, yet somehow with dignity intact.

Beer-Sheba gathered her cloak about herself and extended a hand to Bud. Her poor dwarf companion stood trapped shoulder-deep in snow. As she tugged and pulled him forward, a shrill scream issued from the mouth of the alley. Instinctively, she spun about, releasing Bud, allowing him to slide back into his snowy hole, as she whipped out her blade and ran toward the street to find the captain of the guard stretched out, his throat and stomach ripped open.

"I saw them!" Bud cried as he struggled through the drift. "Rabid weasels! I only got a glimpse, but I saw them! They were giants!"

Beer-Sheba glared at her companion. "How could you possibly see them with a face full of snow and the drift over your head?" She bent over the captain's body. No tracks showed in the snow around him. Beer-Sheba moved into the empty street. The wind howled and the snow swirled; the Rampant Rooster's sign creaked on its chains as it swung back and forth above her head. Nothing else stirred, no person crept about, no dog or cat prowled for scraps. Yet clearly something was afoot.

If Beer-Sheba shivered, the cold was not the cause.

She crept toward the broken door of her tavern. Light from the fireplace inside seeped out upon the snow, staining it with shifting shades of orange and yellow and red. In that glow, she observed the footprints of her customers, already filling with snowfall and nearly invisible. With Bud close behind, she moved up the street.

"Something's there!" Bud whispered, pointing into a narrow alley between a warehouse and a stable. He clutched a beer mug in his hand, a sure sign that he was nervous and ready for action. The dwarf was deadly with a beer mug. Beer-Sheba peered, and then spied something softly fluttering in the wind. With sword held ready, she moved toward it only to find the crouching form of Lady Gravelot.

Lady Gravelot looked up, her eyes bright with terror. "He's dead!" she cried, pointing farther down the alley. "He's dead! He tried to kiss me, and then it happened!"

Beer-Sheba recognized hysteria and dealt Lady Gravelot a sharp slap across the face. "Stop it!" she ordered. "What happened?"

Lady Gravelot sniffed. "Lord Pompey! He tried to kiss me! Then suddenly, he was flying around in the air like some animal was shaking him, and blood was flying everywhere! And guts and veins and . . . and whatever! It was awful! Look at my white diaphanous gown!"

More hysteria. Beer-Sheba slapped Gravelot again. "But what killed him? Surely you saw something—some animal or some creature?"

Bud waded through the snow toward the far end of the alley. He made a retching noise and then called back over his shoulder. "It's Pompey, all right. There's no head left or much else by which to recognize him, but I know the foppish clothing. Something made a right mess of him."

"Rabid weasels!" Lady Gravelot cried. Beer-Sheba drew back to slap the hysteria out of her again, but Gravelot put up a hand. "No, honestly! That's what he kept screaming! It's like he was seeing something I couldn't see. *But there was nothing there!*"

"Well, he couldn't have done that to himself," Bud grumbled as he returned to Beer-Sheba's side.

"I'm not so sure," Beer-Sheba muttered. She helped Lady Gravelot up. "We'll see you safely home, but any explanations to your husband are strictly your affair. He might wonder about all the blood."

Gravelot said nothing as she tried hastily to wipe her hands, but she followed Beer-Sheba and Bud from the alley into the street. In short time, they passed through the town's rough wooden gate and past the small cluster of homes and shops just outside the walls. All the homes were dark. Here and there, a chewed and shredded body lay along the path. Beer-Sheba watched the doors and windows. She could feel the townspeople cowering behind them, barely daring to peek out.

"Always a man," Beer-Sheba noted. She turned toward Gravelot. "Why weren't you eaten, too, I wonder?"

Lady Gravelot clutched her throat. "Too sweet?" she suggested.

Bud snorted. "Old meat is more likely." Then he stopped in his tracks.

Beer-Sheba stopped, too. Close ahead, the walled estate of Lord and Lady Gravelot stood framed against a background of distant gray mountains. "What is it, Bud?"

"I hear them," the dwarf whispered, his eyes widening, his bearded face coloring with fear. "Clawing and gnawing! Rabid weasels!"

Beer-Sheba listened. All she heard were snowflakes falling on the crisp ground and the frightened, raspy breathing of her companions. But then, a high-pitched shriek came from behind the walls of the Gravelot estate. A chorus of screams followed that. The manor gates flung open, and a member of the household guard rushed out to collapse in the snow. Beer-Sheba rushed forward to find the man's back slashed open, his spine nearly severed. With his last breath, he raised a hand and gasped, "Rabid weasels!"

Lady Gravelot also screamed. "My beloved husband! My Hugo!"

Beer-Sheba scowled. Gravelot wouldn't be offering any explanations to her beloved husband tonight or any night. She ran through the gates and through the open manor doors, finding dead servants and guards everywhere.

"Don't you have any maids?" Beer-Sheba inquired. It couldn't be a coincidence that all the victims were men.

"What kind of fool do you think I am?" Gravelot snapped indignantly. "I never hire women. I wouldn't trust my husband with them!"

Beer-Sheba rolled her eyes and hugged her cloak more closely around her for warmth. The manor's main hall was a gory scene of death and destruction with splattered walls and blood-slick floors. Gravelot had quite a cleanup job ahead. "Now that your husband isn't an issue, you might want to rethink that," she said.

The Lady Gravelot sprang to a staircase. "I don't know that Hugo is dead yet!" she shouted. "He can't be dead! I love him!" With that, she gathered her gown and bounded up the stairs to the upper levels.

"Shall we follow her?" the dwarf inquired.

Beer-Sheba shook her head. "I can't think of a reason why. We walked her home—that was all I promised." She headed for the door. "I want to search a little further up the road."

As they passed back into the snowy night, Beer-Sheba heard a long wail behind them. The sound echoed through the manor and followed them into the road. For a moment, she felt a twinge of sympathy for Lady Gravelot. It couldn't be easy to lose a Hugo.

"You said you heard them," Beer-Sheba said to Bud.

Bud nodded. "A monstrous sound! My very scrotum shriveled up in fear." He glanced from side to side as they walked, dark eyes searching, and a beer mug ready in each hand. Beer-Sheba had fought many a battle with Bud at her side, but she'd never seen him so wary and anxious.

Not far outside of town, they arrived at a bridge over a frozen creek. There were no footprints at all in the snow. If any of her customers had passed this way, the snowfall had long since covered their tracks. Beer-Sheba paused long enough to gaze toward the looming mountains and back at the Gravelot estate. Some feeling—not a rabid weasel!—gnawed in the back of her mind. She felt that she was being watched.

Frowning, she stepped onto the bridge. With a loud howl, a snow-troll leaped up from the frozen creek to block her path. Its pale skin and white hair camouflaged it in the snowfall, yet Beer-Sheba saw it raise a massive fist to strike her down. As she raised her blade, Bud flashed heroically past her and slammed his fire-hardened glass mugs down upon the creature's bare toes. The snow-troll roared in pain and swept the dwarf aside to turn toward Beer-Sheba again.

Beer-Sheba swept the folds of her cloak back, revealing her chainmailed bikini-clad body in all its shapely glory. The troll hesitated. "Huh?" it grunted as it looked closer. It was all the hesitation Beer-Sheba needed. She slammed a booted foot into its trollish groin. The creature doubled over in pained surprise. Beer-Sheba swung her blade in a glimmering arc and blood showered the snowy bridge as the troll's head flopped over the edge and into the frozen dark.

Bud stood back as the troll fell dead. "He just got mugged," Bud said.

"Cut down in his prime," Beer-Sheba added. "And that's the advantage of a chainmail bikini. They fall for it every time." She wiped her blade and sheathed it.

The dwarf nudged the far larger troll with a boot. "Think this is what got the others? It's practically invisible in this kind of a storm. That might explain why so few people saw it."

Beer-Sheba pursed her lips thoughtfully, and then pointed to the ground. "This thing leaves footprints," she observed. "Very big footprints. And it wasn't exactly silent when it attacked us."

She moved forward, jumping the troll's body and crossing the bridge with an energy and eagerness that surprised her. The cold wind blew against her face and swept through her hair, but she barely noticed.

"You're enjoying this, aren't you?" Bud observed with a wry grin.

Beer-Sheba let go a deep sigh and admitted, "I haven't felt this alive since we braved the dreaded labyrinths of Sefwah and fought the Flame Wars."

"Those were good days and good times," Bud acknowledged. "I've been thinking we're not cut out to be tavern-owners. Not that you don't make a fine barmaid."

"I've had the same thought, myself." She trudged forward through the snow, her thoughts churning. Did she really miss the adventure, the constant danger, the impossible perils piled one upon the next? She couldn't deny just how quickly she had shed her barmaid's identity to take up once again the mantle of Beer-Sheba, and without even the promise of recompense! "Oh, my gods!" she muttered. "I'm working for free!" She glanced behind at Bud for reassurance. "Does that make me a bad mercenary?"

Bud wasn't listening. The dwarf stood some paces back, staring back toward the way they had come. "I hear them!" he whispered fearfully when she called his name again. "They're chasing us!"

Beer-Sheba stared back along the road, toward the bridge and the field beyond, back toward the Gravelot estate, now invisible in the distance. She saw nothing at all. "What are you talking about?" she demanded. "There's nothing there! Nothing's following us!" Yet, Bud's fear proved contagious. Beer-Sheba drew her sword and clutched Bud's shoulder.

Then, in the instant her bare hand made contact with the dwarf, she saw. "*Rabid weasels!*"

Her heart pounded and her breath caught in her throat. Terrible chittering and gnawing rodents racing to overtake them. And so big! Giants in the field! Soon they would be over the bridge and the frozen creek! Beer-Sheba could almost smell their rabid stench! Dropping her sword, she cowered behind poor Bud.

In that moment, her hand slipped from his shoulder. The rabid weasels vanished. "What the . . . !" she exclaimed as she reclaimed her sword and leaped to her feet again. As far as she could see, no rabid weasels, no trolls, no threat of any kind.

She touched Bud once again on the top of his head, and there they were in their entire slavering monstrosity. She jerked her hand away at once. Beer-Sheba thought hard, and then sheathed her sword. "Bud!" she said. "Bud, do you trust me?"

The dwarf licked his lips and wiped a hand over his ice-crusted beard. "I think so," he rasped. "Yes! Yes, of course I trust you!"

Beer-Sheba put both her hands on her companion's head. Immediately, she saw the weasels and felt the same chilling grip of terror. "Then look at them, Bud. Look long and hard, and don't turn your eyes away. Don't flinch! Just look!"

"I—I can't!" he cried.

"Do it, Bud! Trust me!" Beer-Sheba gripped his head and forced him to look. At first, he tried to break away, but she held him fast. Bud shivered, but he stopped fighting and looked as directed. The weasels were nearly upon them. Beer-Sheba could hear their claws on the snow, hear their gnashing teeth, and feel their cold spittle upon her skin. Yet, she didn't flinch, didn't give in to the fear. She stared through Bud, and he stared with her.

They both saw another shape take form, an intangible face floating in the sheets of snowfall above the rabid weasels, guiding them—commanding them.

"There's nothing there, Bud," Beer-Sheba whispered in Bud's ear. "It's a spell—an illusion. There's nothing there!"

Breaking contact with Bud, Beer-Sheba rose to stand, and Bud also got shakily to his feet. With a loud, angry roar, he flung first one mug and then the other in the direction of the non-existent rabid weasels. "Did you see?" Beer-Sheba asked quietly.

Bud scowled. "I saw!"

They took off through the snow back the way they had come. Beer-Sheba outpaced her dwarf companion, yet she knew he would have her back when it mattered. Back across the bridge she ran, leaping the corpse of the snow-troll, charging back across the field and up to the gates of the Gravelot estate.

The Lady Gravelot waited in the doorway, dark eyes glimmering, hair blowing wildly.

Beer-Sheba drew her sword. "I suspected you were a lot of things," she shouted, "but *witch* wasn't one of them."

"You have no idea what I am!" Lady Gravelot called back, her face a mask of raw anger. "Or what I can do!"

Beer-Sheba advanced. Gravelot had much to answer for. "Your *rabid weasels* won't work anymore. They're not real! They never were anything more than constructs of your own tortured mind!"

"I have other spells!" Gravelot answered. She made a sweeping gesture. Some glittering substance scattered from her palm and fell upon the snow.

Beer-Sheba smirked. She had seen this bit of magic before performed with dragon's teeth or wizard dust or whatever. She raised her sword and prepared for an army of skeletons to rise up in her path. It was a tired and unexciting spell.

The snow before her shook and shivered, but what rose up to oppose her were not skeletons. They were marionettes. Marionettes with swords and shields and strings that extended up into the gray, snowy sky. "You've got to be kidding me," Beer-Sheba said.

A beer mug sailed past her head to smash against the painted face of the nearest marionette. The construct stumbled and collapsed, and its strings cascaded down upon it. It thrashed in the tangle until Beer-Sheba cut off its head.

On the manor's threshold, Lady Gravelot extended her arms and made motions with her fingers. Two more marionettes charged Beer-Sheba. As one swung its sword at her head, she ducked and cut its wooden legs into kindling. The other smashed into her with its shield, knocking her over, but Bud intervened, expertly shattering the marionette's knees with his mugs.

Beer-Sheba leaped to her feet again. With Bud fighting at her side, they made short work of the arcane puppet display. The Lady Gravelot screamed in frustration. "I'm not done!" she shouted.

"Yes, you are," Beer-Sheba answered. Picking up one of Bud's mugs, she flung the vessel with unerring accuracy, knocking the witch cold. The Lady Gravelot collapsed like one of her own marionettes.

All around, the broken constructs faded and vanished. The snow continued to fall, and the night became still and quiet. "Why do you think she did it?" Bud asked as he tilted back his head and caught a snowflake on his tongue.

"Who knows," Beer-Sheba answered with a shrug. "For some people, evil is its own reward, even if it's a banal kind of evil." She sheathed her sword, scooped up a handful of snow and flung it at Bud. "Maybe she did it to cover up the murder of her husband."

Bud looked thoughtful. "She might have gotten away with it, too, if a barmaid hadn't interfered. What should we do with her?"

Beer-Sheba let go a sigh. "Not much you can do with that kind," she answered. "For now, we'll bind her and carry her upstairs. Leave her lying beside her husband. She'll have her Hugo for company."

Following Bud's example, Beer-Sheba tilted her head back and caught a snowflake on her tongue. She loved the snowflakes. They were each so special.

A Girl's Home Is Her Rent-Controlled Castle

by Laura Resnick

I nearly became the ravenous Sewer Beast's tasty *entrecôte* dinner one chilly night because I was trying to spice up my sex life with Bryce.

Which isn't to say that Bryce was into beasts. He might have been into a threesome (though I kind of doubt it, since he was pretty fastidious), but he'd definitely have wanted the third party to be human.

I just mean that I would never have encountered the infernal horror of that sewer-dwelling monster intent on devouring human flesh if I had not, earlier in the evening, followed through on a desperate plan to rekindle Bryce's passion for me. He'd been distant and distracted lately, hadn't touched me in weeks, and I really wanted to rescue our relationship and bring back the spark.

He was the kind of guy I'd always thought a girl like me couldn't get. A handsome, charming, twenty-six-year-old graduate of Yale Law School, Bryce came from a well-to-do old Connecticut family. We met about six months before my encounter with the Sewer Beast, back when I had a brief temp assignment at his office. He was a junior associate at a prestigious law firm that represented oil magnates, hedge fund managers, and famous athletes who sometimes made bad choices that couldn't necessarily be proved beyond a reasonable doubt. I could tell my first day there that other women at the firm were interested in him, and that was certainly no surprise. What did surprise me was that he asked me out to dinner at the end of my two-week assignment there. And then he called me a few days after our first date to ask me out again.

I was living with my mom in New Jersey, office temping by day and taking classes at night. It was my sixth consecutive year of trying to get a college degree without accruing any debt. So after Bryce and I became a steady couple, which happened fast, I started keeping some of my stuff at his apartment, since the commute to my mom's place was more than an hour each way on public transportation. And after only a couple of months together, Bryce asked me to move in with him.

Thanks to some personal connections, he had a rent-controlled apartment on Manhattan's Upper East Side. It was a really nice place, too, not some falling-apart, mold-infested rattrap with the shower in the kitchen. The apartment was a large, sunny one-bedroom in a clean, quiet building on a nice block. It was the kind of place that the average, law-abiding New Yorker would cheerfully have murdered him to get their hands on, especially if they knew how low the rent was. I'd loved that place ever since the first time Bryce brought me there. (To be honest, the sex that first night wasn't good enough to distract me from admiring the polished hardwood floors, spotless bathroom grout, and new stainless steel oven.)

Bryce didn't want me to help with the rent after I moved in. He insisted on covering it by himself. I felt a little weird about being there without paying my way, but Bryce had a good salary, and the rent was amazingly low. We agreed that what would be fair would be for me to take over the household chores. So that's how I contributed.

Living in the city meant I could sign up for an additional night class, since I wasn't spending so much time and money on that commute to Jersey any more. I was finally getting close to completing my degree, and I was eager to reach the finish line. And when I wasn't at work or in class, I cleaned the apartment, did the laundry, ironed Bryce's shirts, took his suits to the dry cleaner, and shopped for groceries. I painted the bedroom and living room to get him to stop complaining about how drab they looked. I learned to cook gluten-free meals, since he thought he might be allergic, or at least have a sensitivity. And I caught up on my studying when Bryce went up to Connecticut on the weekends to play golf and visit his parents.

But after a few months, I realized that with both of us being so busy, we were growing apart instead of closer even though we were living together. That really worried me. This was the most serious relationship I'd had with a guy, and I wanted it to work.

So I asked to go with him to Connecticut the next weekend. But Bryce explained that those visits were "guy time" and "family stuff," and a girlfriend tagging along for the weekend would just be bored. Then I tried to convince him to stay home one weekend so we could do something together, but he got grumpy and accused me of being too possessive.

I thought about dropping one of my classes, though it was too late in the term for me to get a refund, so we could have one guaranteed night together each week.

But when I suggested it, he said, "I wish you were more serious about getting your degree, Cathy."

"I *am* serious, but—"

"Anyhow, I'm usually at work when you're in class. There's a lot of pressure on me! Come on, Cath. I don't need *you* pressuring me to guarantee I can be available to you every Wednesday night just because you want an excuse to quit your class."

That stung so much I dropped the subject.

But I still felt we were drifting apart, so I thought maybe reviving our sex life would set things right. Although I'm no expert, it seemed to me that our physical relations were pretty infrequent for a young couple who'd only been together a few months. So maybe that was the problem. I was certainly available to him, but maybe that wasn't enough. Perhaps Bryce needed to feel encouraged, desired, *wanted* in bed. I needed to show him that I was hot for him.

After my initial overtures met with distractedly negative responses (he was tired, he wasn't in the mood, he had to pack for the weekend), I got more creative. When he came home from Connecticut that Sunday, I was lounging on the bed (in what I hoped was a seductive pose) in a filmy negligee I'd splurged on while he was away, with an open bottle of wine on the nightstand in our candlelit bedroom.

Bryce stormed into the room, turned on the lights, and complained bitterly to me for the next twenty minutes about his weekend. An incompetent caddy had ruined his golf game, a colicky newborn nephew had repeatedly disrupted the family dinner at his parents' house, and the traffic coming back into the city was murder. Then he decided to take a shower—after warning me that candles were dangerous and asking me not to use them again in the apartment.

By the time he came out of the bathroom, I was wearing a flannel robe instead of my new negligee, and I didn't think he noticed the difference. He had a late supper of gluten-free lasagna and fell asleep in front of the TV.

I was pretty discouraged by now, but I'm no quitter. I was in a *relationship,* we were making a *home* together, and I was not going to let this gradually fall apart just because I didn't try hard enough. Fearing that I was in danger of becoming little more to Bryce than a live-in housekeeper, I decided to go for broke.

One of the unexpected things I'd discovered about him while living together was that this handsome Ivy League lawyer from a genteel family had a secret, intense, and feebly-denied thing for babes in brass bras. No, not strippers or show girls. I mean fantasy heroines.

Bryce owned all six seasons of *Xena: Warrior Princess* on DVD, and the screen saver on his personal laptop was a collection of sultry photos of the warrior princess in her skimpy black leather costume and bronze breastplate. He had bookmarked various YouTube clips from an old movie called *Conan the Barbarian* (which had apparently starred a muscle-bound California governor), all of which segments featured a lithe woman warrior dressed in armor much too tiny to interfere with her skilled sword-wielding. One of his most treasured possessions was a poster of someone called Princess Leia wearing a brass bikini while fighting bad guys in *Return of the Jedi* (another oldie). He owned a big collection of *Red Sonja* comics ("the She-Devil With A Sword"), and he had a lifelong crush on Wonder Woman.

So maybe the reason he'd rejected (or just ignored) me on Sunday wasn't, as I thought at the time, that he'd been overwhelmed by stress. Maybe he hadn't responded to me, wearing my lacy negligee and posed invitingly in a candlelit bedroom, because that image didn't represent his dream date. *His* fantasy involved a sexy warrior woman who would sweep him off his feet.

Okay, I could do that.

I mean, no, I couldn't slay half an evil emperor's army with my amazing sword skills. But I could certainly rent a skimpy warrior princess outfit at a costume shop and do some role-playing with my boyfriend. Dressing up for sex games was a little outside my experience (okay, *completely* outside), but I didn't have a problem with it. And if fulfilling Bryce's erotic fantasies would bring us closer together, then it was worth the effort—and worth whatever discomfort I might experience in a chainmail bra.

As luck would have it, the opportunity to enthrall Bryce by playing his lusty lady warrior occurred only a few days later.

My temp assignment at the time was at a data-processing company, and as I was leaving work that day, planning to get a quick bite to eat before heading to my evening class, I received a text message that changed my plans. My professor was stuck at an airport, all flights delayed until further notice, and so class was canceled.

I was just about to phone Bryce and suggest we do something together that evening, if he wasn't stuck at the office, when I suddenly realized *what* we could do together. And I wanted it to be a surprise.

I put away my phone and started walking in the direction of a costume shop I'd seen a few blocks away. When I got there, finding the right outfit was easier than I had expected (so maybe a *lot* of girls' boyfriends have the same fantasy). I was able to choose from a wide selection of brass bras and chainmail teddies they had in stock.

The outfit I settled on was not exactly *me,* but it was fun to wear, and I looked more natural in it than I'd expected. It had a tight metal bodice (not the most comfortable thing in the world), a chainmail loincloth, and thigh-high boots with faux-fur trim. It came with a dainty, little silver-horned helmet that was just darling, and there was even a big sword. The sword was just for show, and it was no sharper than a spoon; but it was sturdy and heavy, and it looked wicked scary.

I couldn't wait for Bryce to see me in *this.*

Since this outfit was tricky to get into, I decided not to change back into my street clothes. It would spoil the surprise (and kill the mood) if, before ravishing Bryce, I had to go lock myself in the bathroom to spend fifteen minutes putting everything on, and then ask him to help me fasten the clasps that I couldn't reach.

After paying the rental fee and signing the paperwork (I guaranteed I wouldn't misuse the sword and agreed to forfeit my deposit if I damaged the outfit), I donned my raincoat, which covered me from neck to shins, and headed for the subway.

Upon reaching my stop, the walk from the subway to our apartment was chilly, since my chainmail loincloth wasn't practical for a brisk autumn evening in New York, but I was too excited to care. When I got to our building, I bumped into Mr. Dalrymple, our landlord, who lived on the ground floor. He was a tall, plump, older gentleman with a face like a basset hound. He wore baggy wool sweaters with little holes in them, loved gardening in his window boxes, and was always very polite. Maybe because he was English.

"Ah, good evening, Miss McConnell," he said as I entered the building. A slight frown creased his lived-in face. "Hmm, this is a surprise."

Feeling self-conscious about bumping into someone I knew while dressed the way I was, even though my coat covered the costume, I mumbled a greeting as I ducked past him and headed for the stairs.

"Aren't you usually at your class now?" he asked as I started climbing to the second floor, where we lived.

"Canceled," I called down, feeling embarrassed as the chainmail loincloth clinked and jangled.

"Oh, dear," I heard him say.

I got to the top of the stairs, headed down the hall to our door, and put my key in the lock with a feeling of relief. I entered the apartment, closed the door, and called, "Bryce?"

I heard a sound in the bedroom. So I removed my coat quickly, hung it up, and then pulled my little silver-horned headdress out of my daypack and put it on.

I called Bryce's name again as I knelt to pull the sword out of its carrying case. I wanted him to get the full effect of his warrior queen in the very first glance.

I heard him grunt and then he called, "Huh? What . . . *Cathy?*"

I struck a pose and tried to adopt an attitude to go with the outfit. "That's Catherine the Manslayer to you!"

"*Huh?* Um . . . Wait a minute! I'll be right out," he called.

I realized that since the bedroom was where I wanted this scene to end up anyhow, it made more sense for me to go in there than to stand around posing in the living room.

"No, *you* wait," I said, embracing my role. "Stay in the bedroom, where you can best serve my pleasure."

Oozing savage sword-wielding woman attitude, I stalked across the room in my tight metal bodice, thigh-hugging boots, and swinging chainmail.

I entered the bedroom, big sword pointed straight ahead of me, and said sternly, "*I* give the orders around here—"

A pretty blond woman was sitting in our rumpled bed, clutching the sheets to her chest. She appeared to be naked. Also startled. Very, very startled.

Beside the bed, Bryce was frantically pulling on his trousers. He'd obviously been naked a nanosecond ago.

I froze and stared at them.

They froze and stared back at me.

My mind went blank. I couldn't think of what to say. I just stood there staring, still pointing my sword at the naked woman in my bed.

Then Bryce said, "Cathy? What are you wearing?"

"What? Um, oh . . . God." I was mortified. I lowered the sword. "Oh, my *God.*"

"That's not yours, is it?" He finished pulling on his pants while staring at me. "I mean, I've never seen it before."

"What's going on?" I asked stupidly. I suppose I was hoping, having just been air-dropped into the humiliating end of my relationship without any warning, that there was some explanation other than the obvious one.

"Nothing!" Bryce said. "Nothing's going on. We were just, um . . . um . . . working late." He took a breath. "Have you met Janice before?"

"Janice?" I said blankly.

"Maybe not," Bryce said. "I think she joined the firm after you were there."

"Who *is* this?" the woman asked Bryce.

"You're . . . working?" I said incredulously. "Naked?"

"It's not what you think," said Bryce.

"What is it, then?" Tears clouded my vision. "Bryce, what are you *doing?*"

"Oh, my God, it's *her,* isn't it?" the other woman said slowly. "I knew it! I *knew* you were lying! But . . . what's she doing here?"

"I live here!" I snapped at her.

"You *live* here?"

"Yes!"

Janice said to Bryce, "She's not the girl you've been fucking in Connecticut?"

"No!" he said.

"You've got a girl in Connecticut?" I cried.

"No!" he said.

"Of course he does," said Janice. "Do you honestly think he goes up there every weekend to see his parents?"

"You've been going up there every weekend to cheat on me?" I asked Bryce, wounded anew.

"No," said Janice, "he's been going up there to cheat on *me*."

"Would you let it go?" Bryce said to her. "It was just that one time, and I told you already—she means nothing to me."

"What?" I said.

"It was more than once," Janice insisted coldly.

"Is she telling the truth?" I asked Bryce.

"It was just a guy thing, Cathy," he said. "Men have needs."

"What?" I said.

Janice gestured to me, which caused the sheet to slip a little. "So who is the, uh, warrior princess?"

"I'm his girlfriend!"

"I'm his girlfriend."

"I live here!" I flung out my sword arm in a gesture that encompassed the room—and hit a lamp that crashed noisily to the floor.

"Whoa! Take it easy!" Bryce exclaimed.

"You live here?" Janice said shrilly. "You *live* with him?"

"Let's all take a deep breath and try to calm down," said Bryce.

"She *lives* with you?"

"The closet's full of my clothes," I pointed out testily. "My cosmetics are in the bathroom. How did you *not* notice before now that a woman lives with him?"

"This is the first time I've ever been here," she said. "We always go to my place."

"Oh." Of course. Bryce knew I'd soon notice something if he fooled around with her in the room where I slept every night.

"But now I know why he never spends the night at my place," Janice said bitterly. "And why he's never brought me here before."

I wondered why he'd brought her here *this* time. Even though he couldn't have known I'd come home early tonight, it seemed reckless. Feeling the wound deepen, I supposed he'd stopped even caring if I found out about her.

"You bastard." Janice threw aside the sheet and headed for the chair in the corner, where she started putting on her clothes with rough, clumsy movements, fuming with anger. "When we started dating, you didn't think it might be worth mentioning to me that you *live* with someone?"

"It's really just a roommate arrangement," he told her. "Cathy's a student. I let her live here rent-free in exchange for cooking and housekeeping."

"You *what?*" I blurted.

"This place is rent-controlled," Bryce said to Janice. "So I can afford to be a little kind."

"*Kind?*" I repeated.

Janice paused for a moment, looking at him as she considered this explanation. "Where does she sleep?"

"Uh . . ."

"Here!" I hit the bed with my sword, making them both flinch. "It's a one-bedroom apartment. Or didn't you have time to notice?"

"And there's only one bed." Her gaze met mine. "Got it." She turned her back on Bryce and continued dressing.

"Okay, yeah, she sleeps here," Bryce said to her posterior, "but it's not what you think. We hardly ever have sex."

"That's the first true thing you've said so far," I said in disgust. "And now I know *why* we haven't had sex in weeks. With a girlfriend at the law firm and another one in Connecticut—"

"She's not my girlfriend. It's just a sex thing."

Janice whirled around. "What?"

"Not you," he said. "The one in Connecticut."

"Oh." She continued dressing.

"With such a busy love life," I said, "it's perfectly understandable that you had no time or energy for sex with the girlfriend who *lives* with you!"

"Look, if you'd just try to see this from my perspective, Cath, you'd underst—"

"Your perspective?" I hit our bed with the sword again, mostly so I wouldn't hit Bryce with it and wind up going to prison. "Are you kidding me?"

"And I thought he was self-centered *before* this," Janice said with a shake of her head.

"Do you know, I painted this whole damn apartment for him," I told her.

"Oh, don't exaggerate," said Bryce. "You didn't do the bathroom, Cath, even though I *asked* you to—"

"*I* loaned him my car for two weekends," Janice told me. "Before I realized he was going up to Connecticut to pork some other woman, not to visit his dear old mother."

"I learned to cook gluten-free for him!"

"I wrote his last two briefs for him and let him take the credit!"

"I do his laundry and ironing," I grumbled. "The jerk."

Janice finished dressing and picked up her purse. "Do me a favor, Bryce, and lose my phone number."

"Wait!" he said. "You can't leave!"

"Watch me."

He grabbed her arm. "No, Janice. I mean, you *can't* leave."

"Of course I can." She shook off his grip. "One foot goes in front of the other, and—"

"*Mwwwwwwaaaaarrrrrr!*"

We all froze as a hideously menacing roar soared up through the floorboards of the apartment. I'd never heard anything like it. I was too startled to breathe, let alone speak.

Janice put a hand over her heart. "What was *that?*"

"It's um . . . the plumbing," said Bryce.

"The plumbing?" I shook my head. "It's never made a noise like *that* before."

"First time for everything," said Bryce. "This could be serious. Let's go downstairs and take a look at it, Janice. Come on."

"What? I don't know anything about plumbing," she said.

"It's a good time to learn," said Bryce. "DIY is the fashion these days. I'll teach you."

"But you don't know anything about plumbing," I said.

He ignored me, took Janice's arm, and started dragging her from the room. Since she wanted to leave anyhow, she went with him. And since I didn't want to be alone in the apartment after hearing that scary noise, I trailed after them.

I followed them out the door and down the hall. Only when we were halfway down the stairs did I realize I was still dressed (or barely dressed) as Catherine the Manslayer. I was about to turn around and go back upstairs when we heard that noise again. Louder and closer now.

"*MwwwwaaaAAAARRR!*"

Janice gave a little screech. "What the hell *is* that?"

"It doesn't sound like plumbing," I said with certainty.

Janice struggled against the tight grip Bryce had on her arm. "Let me go! You're hurting me."

"Sorry, Janice, you *can't* go," he said.

My grip tightened on my sword, and I suddenly felt glad I had it with me. Bryce was behaving strangely. I didn't know why he had a death-grip on Janice's arm and wouldn't let her leave, but it was becoming clear that it wasn't because he hoped to salvage their relationship. He was dragging her roughly behind him as he trotted down the steps, and when she again demanded to be released, he dismissively told her to shut up. And that *noise,* that menacing roar we'd heard . . .

"What was that sound, Bryce?" I demanded, following the pair of them down to the ground floor.

"Bad pipes!" chirped an elegant voice as I reached the bottom of the stairs. I turned and saw Mr. Dalrymple hovering by the basement door. "The plumbing in these old buildings is a scandal, I'm afraid."

"That noise is *not* plumbing," I insisted as Janice struggled in earnest and Bryce concentrated on subduing her. "What's going on here?"

"My, my, that is an *impressive* ensemble you're wearing, Miss McConnell." Frank appreciation of my appearance warmed Mr. Dalrymple's saggy face. "Dare we hope you've come to slay the *fwa'qa'rhen?*"

"The what?"

"Ah." He smiled. "You may know him instead by his *nom de guerre,* the Sewer Beast."

"The *what?*"

He looked at Bryce. "So you haven't told *either* of them?"

"Told us what?" I demanded.

Bryce continued struggling with Janice, trying to drag her toward the basement door, as he answered the older man. "Things got complicated. After I decided not to use Cathy and found someone else,

I realized that she probably couldn't be told anyhow, because she'd kick up a stink. You know what women are like."

"Use me for what?" I asked.

"You seemed like the perfect choice. So eager to please. Only one relative, and she'd probably believe whatever I told her. But then you were so handy to have around, I started rethinking the whole plan. You're a great cook, after all. You press my shirts just right. The bathroom still needs painting . . . "

"The *bathroom?* I'm *handy?* Eager to *please?*" I stopped sputtering long enough to focus on something else he'd said. "Perfect choice for *what?*"

Bryce said, "So I found a replacement for you."

Janice stopped struggling long enough to say, "A *replacement?* Did I hear right? That's what I am to you?"

He covered her mouth with his hand and said to me, "And you weren't supposed to *be* here tonight. What are you even doing here?"

"I *live* here."

He looked at Mr. Dalrymple. "You see what I mean? *Women.*"

"Fascinating as these explanations are, dear boy, we really must hasten," said Mr. Dalrymple. "The Beast shall lose its tenuous hold on patience any moment now."

"What the hell is going on?" I pointed my sword at Bryce, then at Mr. Dalrymple, and then at Bryce again. "What are you two up to?"

"Preserving our home, my dear Miss McConnell. Protecting our castle, if you will," said Mr. Dalrymple. "I'm afraid that real estate in Manhattan is a very dark and brutal realm."

"What are you talking about?"

"Don't be naïve, Cath." Bryce wrapped his arm around Janice's throat and pressed on her windpipe. "Do you think great apartments in rent-controlled buildings on desirable blocks just grow on trees?"

"Bryce," I said sharply as Janice struggled for air, "stop that! Stop it right now or—or—or I'll use this sword. I swear I will!"

Janice gurgled, her face turning red, and made a gesture urging me to attack him.

"I am afraid the Sewer Beast must be pacified, Miss McConnell," Mr. Dalrymple said sadly. "A deal with dark powers, you might say. Indeed, you'd have to say it, as there really is no other terminology that accurately—"

"Get to the point!" I snapped.

"It is the price that I and my chosen tenants pay for our domain, for our tenure in this humble urban castle, if you will."

"What tenure? What domain? What are you *saying?*"

English people. Honestly.

"It's the price for this building," shouted Bryce, trying to make Janice hold still. She was gasping, struggling, and kicking. "The thing we have to do to have a great apartment at a low rent on the Upper East Side!"

"*What* is the thing you have to do?"

"Once every ten years," said Mr. Dalrymple, "we must offer a human sacrifice to the Sewer Beast."

I stared at him. "You're making that up."

He shook his head. "Indeed not. I swear on my honor as a gentleman. We retain our rights to this blessed and cursed domain by entering the bowels of the cellar once every ten years to present a human sacrifice to the Sewer Beast—that grisly manifestation of the fearsome powers who oversee such matters in New York City."

My jaw hung open and my sword arm wavered. "Seriously?"

"By tradition, the duty always falls to the newest tenant of the building." Mr. Dalrymple nodded toward Bryce. "So you can understand why I have to be very choosy about my tenants."

I looked at Bryce. "You started dating me . . . you asked me to *move in* with you . . . so you could feed me to some subterranean monster?"

Realizing the full implication of the word "replacement" now, Janice threw her whole body weight against Bryce, knocking him back against the wall as she fought for her freedom.

"You *bastard,*" I said. "My mom was right about you all along!"

Gasping for air as he wrestled with Janice, he protested, "Your mom likes me!"

I snorted. "You're a fool as well as a philanderer and a murderer."

"I'm not a murderer," Bryce insisted, clearly offended. "It's just going to be this one little sacrifice, for the sake of my great apartment—an apartment you love, too, Cathy! And that's it. It's not like I'm going to make a *regular thing* of killing people." When Janice bit him, he added, "Ouch!"

I was about to explain to him that one murder was all it took to make him a murderer, but the Beast roared again, emphasizing that this discussion wasn't theoretical.

"MMWWWWAAAAAR!"

"That sounded really close!" I said.

Mr. Dalrymple nodded. "The creature is here. It's time."

He opened the door for Bryce, whose arms were full of a furiously fighting female. Bryce dragged Janice into the doorway, ignoring me as I followed in fear and confusion, randomly ordering him to let her go, leave her be, drop her right *now*.

A terrible, unearthly red glow rose from the depths of the building, along with a thick cloud of yellow smoke that stank of sewage and sulfur. The stench filled the stairwell and floated into the hall. I reflexively covered my nose while Bryce paused at the top of the steps.

"Sorry, Janice. This isn't personal. It's just something that's got to be done."

Janice was shaking her head, begging for her life and rocking all her weight frantically away from Bryce, trying to break his hold on her.

His face was cold and determined. I realized he was really going to do it. He was going to murder her right in front of me—all so he could keep his rent-controlled apartment.

Which *I* had painted and cleaned and tended for him!

"No!" Well, *I* was Catherine, warrior princess, and I would not let him do this. "Unhand her!"

I leaped forward and slashed at Bryce with my trusty fake sword. He flinched in surprise—which loosened his hold on Janice. She broke free and ran down the hall, screaming, then disappeared through the front door and out into the street. Bryce sprang into action and tried to run after her, but I jumped into his path, kicked him, and pushed him back.

"Okay, fine. If that's the way you really want it, Cath, so be it," he said grimly. "It'll have to be you."

As he loomed over me, his expression foreboding and his arms outstretched, I realized he meant to sacrifice *me* now. He would really do it! He'd feed me to that *thing* down there. He'd kill me to keep his apartment.

"Bryce, no!"

"You should have let me use her, Cathy." He shook his head. "Your mistake."

As his hands shot out to grab me, I reflexively raised my fist and pounded my sword pommel into his face. Bryce cried out in surprise and pain, his nose gushing blood. He staggered backward into the hellish stairwell where he lost his footing, screamed, and fell headlong down the steps.

"Bryce!" I stumbled forward and tried to go after him, but a billow of thick, odorous smoke and a wall of fire flooded the space, forcing me back. "Bryce!"

I heard a terrible scream—the last sound Bryce ever made—and then some grotesque chomping and slurping. This was followed by a burp and a satisfied sigh.

I realized I was on my knees, staring helplessly into the stairwell. I was also shaking like a leaf, breathing like I'd just run a mile at top speed, and weeping.

As the horrifying sounds of the Beast below us began retreating into the distance and the stinking smoke started to clear, Mr. Dalrymple closed the basement door and helped me to my feet. I leaned heavily against him, my knees trembling and my stomach churning.

"Thank you, Catherine," he said quietly. "You have saved this building for another ten years."

"Oh, my God," I said, feeling the full weight of his words. "I killed Bryce."

"Or, to look at it another way," said the old gentleman, "you saved the life of that young woman, as well as your own. Someone was destined to die here tonight. You just ensured that the person who met the jaws of the Sewer Beast was, shall we say, the one who deserved it."

I had saved Janice. And, yes, myself. I shuddered as I realized again that Bryce had tried to murder me. Then I said bitterly to Dalrymple, "But what makes you so sure that *you* aren't the person who deserves that fate?"

He chuckled. "Because I am not a person, my dear Catherine. Not anymore. Not for a very long time, in fact. But that is a story for another day. Suffice it for now to say that the Beast does not consume my kind and would reject me as a sacrificial offering."

"Well, that's convenient, isn't it?" I stared numbly at him.

"Yes, it is, rather," he agreed. "And speaking of conveniences . . . I realize that you are upset at the moment, and I don't wish to appear insensitive . . . but may I point out that in satisfying the Beast's demands, you have just secured for yourself a well-maintained rent-controlled apartment in an excellent neighborhood? Your young man no longer has any need of his lease, after all, and I find you a most acceptable tenant."

I gazed incredulously for a long moment at this courteous and chillingly ruthless old man . . . and then I decided to accept his offer. After all, *I* was the one who'd been maintaining that apartment so well.

And now that I knew the true cost of the lease, I had approximately nine years, eleven months, and twenty-nine days to think of a better way than *this* of renewing the deal next time around.

... And Your Enemies Closer

by Lee Martindale

The wagering began within seconds of Horatia entering the commander's pavilion. By the time she left it, nearly every person in the encampment had coin in play.

Horatia was well known among her comrades, who had long ago dubbed her "The Heroic" for both her skill in battle and her impressive physical dimensions. Her attitude on the subject of mages was equally well known. And the fact that there was a mage with the commander when Horatia was summoned spread faster than the wagering.

"Horatia, this is Maran Cav Rowan," the commander said as he motioned the warrior into a seat. "She's replacing Asaria Katri, who decided—just after you left for Forgecroft, as it happens—that the battlefield was not the best environment for her ... ah ... talents. Maran here has an impressive resume. Served in the recent Gelgould Border campaign, and before that, contracted to Morbano's Mercenaries."

The warrior glanced sideways at the blond woman in the other seat. "Meaning no disrespect, Commander, but wouldn't it mean more to hear how impressive she is from someone who actually served with her?"

"No disrespect taken, Horatia," said Maran, smiling.

"I meant no disrespect to the commander," Horatia snarled.

"Horatia has good reason to be wary, Maran," the commander conceded after a sharp look toward Horatia. "Asaria caused her considerable inconvenience before her departure—"

"—as in nearly getting me killed—"

"—and I'm inclined to be tolerant of her attitude." He glanced at Horatia again. "To a point." He waited until Horatia had nodded that she understood.

"Now, as to why you're both here," he continued. "A mission has come up for which the two of you are uniquely suited. We have reports, confirmed, that a mage-built weapon—a rather nasty piece of work from the sound of it—was being transported to those who commissioned it when raiders waylaid the caravan. Reports, also confirmed, say it's being held in a small town called Sevry, near the Keldaough border. The raiders plan to sell it to the highest bidder which, in all likelihood, will be the duke whose forces we're currently engaging. A weapon with the powers ascribed to this one deployed against us would make for a very bad day."

"One of these days," Horatia muttered, "someone with the clout to make them stick will come up with rules of war that outlaw mages and mage weapons. Wars should be fought with honest steel in the hands of flesh-and-blood fighters."

"Unfortunately, that day has not come." The commander turned to the other woman. "Maran, I've been told what a mage has built, a mage can destroy. Is this true?"

"It is."

"And I'd rather have it done before we end up having to face it. Hence your part of the task."

"Of course," the woman agreed.

"Obviously, sending you out alone through hostile territory and into the middle of a pack of raiders with incentive to protect a valuable prize is out of the question. You'll need a fighter with you. Horatia, that will be you."

The woman warrior opened her mouth, but before she could protest, Maran beat her to it. "Commander, I mean no insult to either your judgement or this . . . lady's . . . abilities. But shouldn't I have more than one guard, and . . . well . . . someone who isn't a . . . ah . . . someone who is . . . male?"

"Horatia is one of my best," the commander said quickly, recognizing the portent of Horatia's clenched teeth, "and you can be assured that she will protect you as well or better than anyone under my command. And, as it happens, the fact she *is* a woman works into a plan with decent odds of success. In addition to being where the raiders call home, Sevry is the site of a shrine to one or another of the regional goddesses, and it appears to be a busy one. Our scouts report seeing priestesses traveling in and out of town almost daily. They always travel in pairs, without guards, and they always wear voluminous robes that cover them completely. It's against their religion to see anything of one of these priestesses but her eyes. Apparently, people go to great lengths to avoid looking at them at all."

"That could give us something of an advantage," Horatia mused. "Commander, when you say those robes are voluminous . . . "

"The scouts describe them as looking like walking tents. One of these priestesses on horseback, and you can hardly see the horse. More than roomy enough for you to be fully armed and armored beneath it without anything showing."

"It might work, at that," the warrior decided.

"Good. Maran, any questions?"

"Do we know what this device looks like? How big it is?" the mage asked.

"Unfortunately, no. Is that a problem?"

Maran smiled engagingly. "None at all. I will be able to identify it by its energy. Depending on the effectiveness of its shielding, it may even be possible to pick that up from a distance as a means of locating it."

"Good. Your orders are to get in, find the thing, render it permanently impotent, and leave before anyone realizes their prize is now a worthless piece of junk." He picked up a small rolled map and handed it to Horatia. "This shows the route to Sevry and the last known positions of our opposition's encampments. The quartermaster will have supplies, equipment, horses, and those robes ready for you in the morning. You'll ride out at first light. And, Horatia?"

"Yes, Commander?"

"I'll want the name of the armorer you got your new armor from. He does good work. Dismissed."

The first wagers were won and lost when both women came out of the commander's pavilion still alive.

To any spies or casual observers, the two figures on the road looked just like any other pair of Priestesses of Piltha. Certainly, the one riding in front was quite a bit larger and rounder than most they might have seen before, but beyond that there was nothing about them that warranted undue attention.

The women rode in silence. Horatia's eyes moved constantly in a steady sweep of the surroundings, alert for any indication that they were not alone. Maran's eyes were—much of the time—closed, boredom and the swaying of her horse having considerable soporific effects. Two days in a row, they halted mid-morning to rest and water the horses, then again at mid-day to eat a light meal of dried meat and travel bread, at mid-afternoon, and near dusk to make a sparse camp. Through it all, except for occasional instructions from Horatia, not a word passed between them. For Maran, it was an entirely new experience.

By mid-afternoon of the third day, she'd had enough. "Are we going to pass the entire journey without talking?"

Horatia sighed heavily and mumbled, "Apparently not." A bit more loudly, she asked, "Is there something we need to discuss, spellslinger?"

"That word, for one thing," Maran replied, pulling even with Horatio. "I have a name, and yet you insist on calling me by that pejorative term. Spellslinger." She spat the word as if it were an unripe fig.

"Where I come from, you only call your kin, your friends, and your swordmates by their names. And you are none of those to me."

"But that word demeans both me and my calling. It's . . ." Maran groped for further condemnation to level against it. "It's nothing but the basest slang."

Horatia chuckled. "You're likely too highborn to have heard the basest of slang for your kind. 'Spellslinger' is downright polite compared to it."

"It's uncivil and uncollegial," Maran lectured. "And it's an insult!"

Horatia shrugged. "It's also an accurate description of what you lot do."

A look of frustration crossed Maran's features. Having someone fail to immediately apologize and modify their behavior or language when she labeled it as she had was another new experience. The thought crossed Maran's mind that Horatia might be uneducated or feeble-witted. She decided to explain it in more colloquial, more personal terms. "Wouldn't you be insulted if I continuously referred to you as an ugly cow?"

"Not particularly," came the immediate reply. "I've been called all manner of female animal in my life. Doesn't make me one of whatever they're calling me."

"Wouldn't you feel demeaned?"

"No."

"Damaged?

Horatia laughed. "By words? Swords do damage. Spearpoints getting past my shield do damage. Getting whacked by a mace could split my skull. Words are just sounds in the air. The only power they have over me is what I'm willing to give them."

"Oh, for . . . " Maran pulled her horse to a halt and waited for Horatia to rein in. When the warrior kept moving, the mage sighed and nudged her horse to follow.

Near mid-morning on the fourth day, Horatia heard Maran ask, "Why do you dislike me?"

Without looking back or altering her horse's pace, Horatia replied, "Is there some reason I'm not aware of that would cause me to like you?"

"Why do you dislike mages, then?"

"Because I haven't met one yet who could be trusted."

"How dare you insult me again!" Maran shrieked as her horse came even with Horatia's.

"Two things," said Horatia, conversationally. "First, if you don't want to hear an answer you will take as insulting, don't ask me a question about what I think of mages. Second, stop screeching. I'm fairly sure the priestesses we're supposed to be don't scream like *bann seighe*, so anyone who might be watching us at the moment might start to wonder who we really are. Not something we want to have happening just now."

The mage took several long, slow breaths. "Very well. Asaria is a friend, and she told me what happened during that battle. Terribly unfortunate, but surely you can't believe she was deliberately attacking you, can you? Accidents do happen, even to the best of us."

"And Asaria didn't even remotely approach being the best of your ilk." Horatia turned her head and studied the woman riding beside her. "Accidents do, indeed, happen. And while I was angry at the time—suddenly finding myself in the midst of battle with only my skin, my skivvies, and a sword between me and enemy blades tends to have that effect—she made it right. With a little persuading from the commander, but I don't hold even that against her. No, what added fuel to my opinion that mages can't be trusted was not her deed, but her words after. The mistake was clearly hers, but she claimed it was caused by mistakes made by others . . . every other she could think of to lay blame on. *Not* an accident, but a deliberate act of lying to protect her own ass. Anyone who does that has no honor, and a person who lacks honor is not someone to be trusted."

Maran was quiet, clearly thinking about what she'd been told. "But she is only one mage."

"She's also not the first spellslinger I've dealt with. There have been many, and every one of them has caused me grief of one kind or another."

"So you assume I'm going to, as well."

Horatia regarded the woman riding beside her. "Right up until the point you prove to me that you won't."

Entering Sevry, even at dusk, proved to be even easier than Horatia expected. The two guards on the road leading into the cluster of buildings bowed deeply and waved them through with eyes dutifully focused on the ground. The women easily found the stables they'd been told to seek out and the liveryman who was in the commander's pay. "I don't know for a fact that what you seek is there," he told them, "but Ander and his men took to hanging out at the Caltrop about the time I got word to keep an eye out for that missing weapon. They're real keen on keeping everybody out of the hallway that leads to the storage room in the back. And one of 'em always seems to be hanging out in the alley by the back door to the place. Worth checking out, I'll warrant."

Horatia drew a small purse, heavy with coin, from under her robes. "Commander sends his regards," she said, handing it to the liveryman. "Food and water for our mounts, but keep them saddled for the time being. We'll either need them immediately if we're successful, or come back and ask about lodgings if we're not."

Darkness, and the apparent reluctance of the town's inhabitants to be out on the narrow streets after its fall, aided the women in making it into the alley. Under cover of even darker shadows, they threw off their robes, rolled them into tight bundles, and stashed them atop a curtain wall before moving forward. As they'd been told to expect, there was a guard, if one could call a man leaning against the wall next to a door and casting a desultory glance up and down the alley between long, deep pulls from the tankard in his hand a guard.

Horatio reached for a throwing dagger in her boot, only to feel Maran's hand on her arm. "*Let me*," the mage mouthed. Her hands started making patterns in the air, her lips moved in silent chant, and a double-handful of seconds later, the man's legs gave way and he slid down the wall. Horatia dragged the body away from the door and into the shadows before opening the door slightly and peaking in. She motioned for Maran to follow, and in very short order, they were in the storeroom.

Horatia leaned down and whispered into Maran's ear. "What did you do to him?"

"I froze his heart," the mage whispered back.

"Is the weapon here?"

Maran paused for a second, her eyes unfocused, and then she nodded. "Oh, yes. It is here."

"Good," Horatia said as she unsheathed her sword and turned toward the door. "I'll stand guard. You find it and pull its magical fangs."

"Magecraft isn't magic. It's . . . " Maran caught sight of the glare being directed at her, turned, and began moving around the loot piled in the room.

Minutes ticked by, with Horatia getting more impatient with each one. She had just turned, with the intent of finding Maran and impressing on her the need for a speedy conclusion, when the room erupted in a brilliant flash of light and just as quickly went back to darkness. Maran reached her side to find her blinking rapidly, trying to shake off having nearly been blinded. "A warning would have been nice," she snarled quietly. "You found it? It's done?"

"Yes and yes. The spell that gave it power has been removed without altering its appearance. Only another mage will be able to tell it is not the same as when it was brought here."

"Good. Now let's get out of here."

They retrieved their robes, donned them, and returned to the stables without seeing anyone except the liveryman, who was waiting for them. Horatia handed the him another small sack of coin, thanked him, and the two women rode out of town without an alarm being raised.

Even as Horatia maintained the same level of vigilance on the journey back to camp as she had on the ride out, part of her mind worked on numerous small oddities and inconsistencies. Most of them had to do with changes in Maran's demeanor. On the ride to Sevry, there was the usual arrogance Horatia was accustomed to from mages. Since leaving the town, that had been joined by a touch of smugness. There was also the matter of a new habit she seemed to have acquired. Periodically, her hand would go to her chest, just below her neck, as if checking that something still hung there under her robes.

A day and a half out from camp, the numerous small oddities and inconsistencies gelled into a strong suspicion.

"Maran, you never told me what the weapon looked like."

"Didn't I? Well, we *were* a bit occupied with getting out of there undetected," Maran answered cheerfully. "It was disguised to look like a rather elaborate funeral urn. I can only imagine someone thought that a form less likely to be examined. Silly of them, really." One of her hands lifted off the reins and touched the usual spot.

"And you are absolutely sure it was dead after that big flash?"

Maran smiled indulgently. "Just as I told you, completely quiet. Not the slightest whiff or trace of power after the flash. I would think that, by now, you'd believe me."

Horatia chuckled. "I do. I have no doubt the urn was dead when we left the storeroom.

Maran looked vaguely surprised, and then smiled broadly. "You trust me!"

"About as far as I can throw my horse." Horatia smiled at the look of shock that spread across Maran's face. "You found the weapon, something small enough to hang around your neck. You decided to keep it instead of following orders and decided that lying to me was the best way to convince me to get you back to camp in one piece. What I can't figure out is why you want the thing. Personal gain?"

"Are you even *capable* of not being insulting?" Maran snarled. "I serve a higher calling than mere greed." She was silent for a long while, and then said, almost pleading, "At least let me explain. Perhaps we can come to some kind of arrangement once you understand."

Horatia pretended not to hear the muttered "if a stupid sow like you is even capable of understanding."

"Very well, explain it to me."

Maran looked surprised, then eager. "I had every intention of destroying it if we found it. And then we did, and . . . I had never seen anything so beautiful in my life. The elegance of the equations involved, the intricate balancing of energies, the artistry involved in the layering of power. The crime would have been in destroying such a masterpiece."

"And here I thought we were talking about a weapon that was probably going to used against us, not m'lady's newest necklace."

Maran saw her opening and took it. "But don't you see? Now it's a weapon in *our* hands. I'm sure the commander only ordered me to destroy it because he expected it to be something too big to carry away. If he'd known what it was, he'd have ordered us to do what I'm doing, bringing it back to him so it can be used to force a surrender. We're bringing him back a prize. We're bringing him back the means to victory. Surely it won't be considered disobeying orders if the results are so much better than what they would have been if we'd done what we were told."

"The ends granting justification to the means?"

"Precisely," Maran replied quickly, her tone confident that she had convinced Horatia to her way of thinking. "And just think of what that will mean for you personally. Think of the ways their gratitude will be expressed. Wordfame! Power! Status! Riches! A command of your own, if you want it, or the wherewithal to retire to an estate and never have to fight again!"

"It's more likely that I'll get twenty lashes and be left for dead in the middle of the next available nowhere for having let you get that thing past me this long."

"But you don't know that."

"True," Horatia conceded. "At least I don't know it for a certainty. The odds are, however, deeply in favor of that particular outcome."

"There's another alternative," Maran suggested after a time. "Instead of taking the weapon back to the commander, we can take it to the Elder Mages of my order. You would undoubtedly be rewarded even more generously than you might by the commander, and without even the most remote possibility of being punished."

Horatia appeared to consider the idea. "And you? Would you likewise be rewarded?"

"Most assuredly. For securing something of this magnitude, and for bringing it to my Elders, there would, without question, be significant rank bestowed." She smiled at the thought. "Yes, that's what we should do. It is but an additional day's ride from here."

"Thereby adding the crime of desertion to that of disobeying orders. Maran, you make Asaria and every other spellslinger I've had the misfortune to know look like paragons of virtue. We will, you and I, be going back to the commander and handing over the weapon. I'm willing to take whatever punishment he deems fit to administer."

Maran regarded Horatia through narrowed eyes. "I will not."

"And I don't care."

"You are a fool, Horatia."

"Most likely."

"Still and all, I am sorry."

"For . . . ?"

"Even though you've been rude, dismissive, and seemingly intent on insulting me at every turn, I had really started to like you." Maran raised her hands and began to move them in an intricate pattern. "I'm sorry that you've made it necessary for me to do to you what I did to that guard in the—"

Horatia's fist connected solidly with Maran's jaw, sending her out of the saddle and onto the road in an unconscious, cloth-covered heap. The warrior, a satisfied smile on her lips, dismounted and went to where Maran lay. By the gods, that felt good! She flipped the woman onto her back, tore lengths of cloth from the hem of the mage's robe, and twisted them into sturdy ropes. In short order, the weapon—a small medallion tucked into a leather bag on a long neck cord—had been transferred to Horatia's neck, and Maran had, by virtue of a gag in her mouth and the binding of her hands, arms, and legs, been rendered harmless.

Horatia threw Maran across her saddle and tied her to it as if she were a sack of grain. It wouldn't be the most comfortable of positions for the next day or so, but Horatia was of a mind that the mage had earned a certain level of discomfort. She might give some thought to letting her ride, bound and gagged, at some point after she regained consciousness, but then again . . .

As Horatia drew closer to the camp, she wondered how the wagering pools would translate the manner of the women's return into the winning and losing of bets. Just before their departure, the return of both women alive had been drawing long odds. But those who'd bet on Horatia being the mage's undoing would certainly have a valid argument.

Lucky for Horatia that she had coin riding on both outcomes.

Knot and the Dragon

by P.C. Hodgell

"Doesn't Auntie Maude look good in black?" said Stepmother Marta, plopping dollops of porridge half into the children's bowls, half onto the tabletop. "She should wear it more often."

Knot glowered up at her through shaggy bangs which, somehow, never would hang straight. "She only had one husband, and now he's dead."

"Hush!" said Marta in her special voice. "He's gone to a better place."

"What, underground in a box?"

Her two stepsisters dropped their spoons and, squealing, stuffed their fingers into their ears.

"Now see what you've done! Why don't you take a walk?"

"In the rain?"

"It's nice and soft today. Really, Knot, you must learn how to see things properly."

Knot abandoned her breakfast—it was crunchy with charred bits anyway—and left the house. The rain had stopped. The cobblestoned street steamed in the growing warmth of a summer day.

She had never liked her stepmother, even less so since her father had died, but she didn't dwell on that. It was simply part of her twelve-year-old life. Somehow, she saw such facts differently than anyone else in her village, who always found something good to say about everything.

"Really," Auntie Maude had said at her father's funeral, loud enough for Knot to overhear, "that girl needs a mother more than a father. How fortunate that he drowned and she didn't."

Maude was Marta's older sister. Father had come from a distant village. He had never quite fit in here either.

Two women gossiped in the shelter of a doorway as Knot trudged past.

"There goes that peculiar child," one said to the other. "Isn't it a good thing, for their mother's sake, that her own daughters are both so pretty?"

Knot hunched her shoulders. She was not only red-haired, but stocky and sun-burned, with hands roughened from getting into trouble. At least, that was what Marta called it. Knot thought of it as learning things.

The miller and the butcher passed her, one carrying a leaking sack of flour, the other a haunch of beef around which flies swarmed.

"I hear the dragon passed through Lyle last night," said the first.

"I'm sorry to hear that," said the second, "but, of course, it will never come here."

Knot snorted. Everyone in Little Sotting was so smug. Dragons usually stayed to the north, close to their mountain aeries, but occasionally one flew south in search of a particular tidbit. Surely somebody would notice, sooner or later, that the dragon in question was getting closer and closer, day by day.

And then, abruptly, someone did notice. A boy ran down the street toward her, waving his arms and shouting, "It's in the high field!"

People piled out of their houses to stare. Sure enough, something big and red was snuffling through the wheat. It raised a scaly head, peered down at them, and snorted a puff of fire. Heat danced over the field. The wheat began to burn.

"How can this be?" neighbor asked neighbor in shocked disbelief. "We've never done anything wrong! Quite the opposite. Who is to blame for this?"

"Maybe it's that witch who moved into the forest cottage," said the baker, wringing fat, greasy hands. "I hear she came from one of the burnt villages. Maybe it followed her here."

"Or maybe it's after one of us," said Marta.

Knot turned to find her stepmother standing behind her, her

stepsisters peering around her skirts, all three of them staring at her in horror.

"We should give it a present," said the mayor, also looking at Knot. "Surely then it will see that we are good people and it will leave us alone."

"Of course you will be happy to do your fellow citizens such a service," said Marta to Knot. "Come back in a half-hour, there's a dear." Then she scurried off with her neighbors to gather wood for a ceremonial platform.

Knot went the opposite way, out of town and into the forest. As a small child, she had played in the deserted cottage, but it looked much different now than it had then. For one thing, the chimney was on upside down, leaking smoke from its base. For another, a blazing fireplace replaced the front door. And the kitchen was spread out under an oak tree.

"Drat," said the witch as she climbed out a window in a flurry of patched skirts.

She was younger than Knot had expected, about Marta's age, with gray-streaked auburn hair and green eyes. She also had a pleasant if somewhat bemused face, as if she had left a pot on the fire, but couldn't remember where.

Hens clustered about her feet, squeaking. They had the heads of dormice. Some scratched the ground, but couldn't seem to figure out what to do next. A large white pig with a red cow-lick charged around the corner and scattered them.

"Alix, don't!" the witch called after him. "Oh, I'll never get them to settle down! When one does lay an egg, the others try to eat it."

"I need help," said Knot, "or the dragon is going to eat me."

The witch clutched at her tangled hair. "The dragon! It's found us!"

"I don't understand," said Knot.

The witch sat down on the outdoor hearth, as if her legs had given way under her. "In the mountains where we come from," she said breathlessly, "there are lots of dragons, of all sizes. One came to our village looking for redheads like you. Like me. Like my son. We taste especially sweet, I suppose, or maybe spicy. Anyway, to save my boy, I tried a transformation spell. There was an explosion. When the dust cleared, there was the dragon, looking dazed, and my son, looking like that."

"The pig is your son?"

"Yes. Oh, the trouble I had with him at first, the trees I had to lure him out of! He thought he could fly, you see. Fortunately, he's always liked my cooking." She drew a handful of biscuits out of her pocket. They looked as hard as river rocks. "Alix, come here! We have to flee! Again!"

Knot thought about asking for similar protection, but was afraid she would be turned permanently into something nasty. A two-headed calf, perhaps.

"Before you go," she said, "can you show me a way to defend myself?" Her father had told her tales of knights errant. She had found their chivalry silly, but the fights had interested her. "Armor would be nice. And a weapon."

The witch considered this. "From what I hear, you always tell the truth. Maybe I can twist that so that whatever you say comes true, as long as you believe in it."

There was something wrong with this line of thought, but Knot couldn't immediately figure out what. Besides, she was running out of time.

The witch jumped up and led her to the kitchen where a pot was indeed boiling, over cold coals.

"Now, what here might be used as armor?" she asked Knot. "Oh, and by the way, call me Magda."

Knot looked around. It was hard not to see everything for exactly what it was. She supposed that this job called for imagination, something she had never had much of, but so much around here seemed to be what it wasn't.

She emptied the pot, which turned out to be quite cool despite the boiling water it had contained. "I suppose this could be a helmet."

When she put it on her head, at first it tipped over her eyes and its handle stuck straight up behind, but jiggling made it fit better.

"Good," said Magda. "Now try this."

She handed Knot a metal scrub-board. As Knot held it up to her flat chest, the witch secured it around the back with some clothesline. It gave a reassuring sound when thumped, and the pleats rippled.

After that, it got easier. Bread pans formed arm and leg guards, an apron the skirt, oven gloves gauntlets. It was a bit unnerving to feel the wind up her bare backside, but Knot forgot about that when a kitchen knife became a short sword and a meat tenderizer a mace.

"There," said Magda, handing her a shield made out of a bread board.

And none too soon: Shouts and screams came from the direction of the village. Smoke billowed up over the trees.

"Ooinnk!" trumpeted the pig, and he launched himself off the cottage roof. He did not so much fly as fall flat on his snout with a loud, "Oouff!" As Magda hurried to his rescue, Knot stomped back through the forest toward the village.

The first thing she saw was the dragon standing in the middle of the high street, his head swaying back and forth at the level of the first story windows. He was clad in almost translucent red scales, with white ones on his neck, throat, and belly. Wings folded close to his shoulders. His long, scaly tail twitched from curb to curb, almost absentmindedly destroying facades. Behind him, the half-finished platform writhed in flames.

The door of the village's grandest house was flung open and the mayor popped out, followed by his family and a stream of citizens from the upper street. They rushed across the cobbles, almost under the dragon's nose, into the opposite house. That door slammed shut behind them, and hands yanked closed the shutters. If they weren't in sight, they apparently felt that they weren't in danger.

The dragon stuck his head into the mayor's house, his snuffles echoing throughout its halls. Heat radiated off his scales and they rattled as he breathed. Knot tried to imagine him as small and fat, but such wishful thinking didn't go far with a dragon. The knights in her father's stories had looked for a vulnerable spot—a missing scale or a bare patch. The skin where his leg met his body looked thinner than elsewhere. Knot poked it with her sword. The dragon gave a surprised snort that blew out the house's windows and launched an array of chimney pots. The sword clattered to the ground, becoming a kitchen knife again. Knot scrambled out of the way as the dragon backed into the street.

The dragon's stomach rumbled and he burped, incinerating her wooden shield. She looked through the flames into enormous, oddly familiar green eyes. When she stepped away from him, walking backwards, he followed. She turned and trotted out of town, leaving a trail of pots and pans behind her. Knot heard the dragon launch himself into the air with a mighty *whoosh*. She cringed, expecting his pounce. None came. She burst into the witch's clearing where Magda was frantically piling household gear into a small cart while the pig fretted in the shafts.

"What happened?" she asked Knot breathlessly.

A shadow fell across them. The caged hens and the pig shrieked. With a huge thump and a blast of wind, the dragon landed on the cottage, which collapsed.

"Quick," said Knot. "Recite the transformation spell."

The witch gave her a wild look, and then stammered it out.

There was a vast inrush of air, followed by an explosion as it expanded again.

Knot blinked dust out of her eyes.

Magda and a boy Knot's age were embracing before the ruins of the cottage.

"I looked for you everywhere, mother," the boy said, half-laughing, half-crying. "Why did you keep running away?"

In the cart's shafts, not a pig but a small, red, porcine dragon was bouncing up and down, its stubby wings a blur.

"I don't understand," said the witch.

"Mother, don't you see? You turned the dragon into a pig and me into a dragon. How did you guess?" he asked Knot.

Knot shrugged. "You weren't really trying to hurt anyone, and you have your mother's green eyes. Besides, when has one of her spells ever gone right?"

"This one did," said Magda proudly. "You believed Alix was the dragon, and so he was."

This still didn't sound quite right to Knot, but she shrugged again, accepting it.

The pig-dragon squealed and bounced higher, jerking up the shafts and spilling caged hens off the back. The witch gave him a biscuit, whereupon he settled down and ate it.

"Yes, he's got a temper," she said fondly, scratching him behind the ears, "but by now I think we understand each other."

Shouts came from the direction of the village. The villagers had apparently gotten back their courage, which had transformed into outrage.

"How dare you attack the nicest people in the world?" boomed the mayor. "Have you no shame?"

"Witch, monster!" others cried.

"Take me with you," Knot said to Magda.

The witch hesitated, frowning. "Child, are you sure?"

"Knot!" That was Marta's voice, rising shrill over the approaching uproar. "Ungrateful girl, after all that I did for you!"

"I see what you mean," said Magda.

Meanwhile, Alix had piled the caged hens back into the cart. They set off, the pig-dragon following the witch, snuffling for treats, Alix and Knot pushing from behind.

"Next time," said Knot as they left the clearing, "I want to be the dragon."

The Rules of the Game: A Poker Boy Story

by Dean Wesley Smith

As Poker Boy, the superhero, I get some really strange jobs. And I work with my share of strange people, including my girlfriend and sidekick, Patty Ledgerwood, aka Front Desk Girl, who can make time slow, and calm even the most angry hotel customer. She has other superpowers I'm still discovering, thankfully. Keeps life very interesting, since she's a few hundred years older than I am, at least.

But right now, walking toward me down the center of the left lanes of Las Vegas Boulevard, was about as strange a person as I have seen outside a comic book convention. She had on a skimpy golden bikini that showed a lot of very attractive and very white skin. She carried a big, golden shield that matched her suit. The shield looked damn heavy unless it was a fake, which I doubted.

A huge broadsword with a large, wrapped, dark-brown handle dangled from one hip, swaying back and forth with her walking motion, yet somehow not ever swinging around and tripping her.

The July day was already hot, almost record hot for Las Vegas, and that's saying something. And it was projected to get hotter. I could feel the heat baking everything, and I would have wagered that even the palm trees were shouting "uncle."

I was pretty certain my New Balance running shoes were about to melt on the pavement. And to make matters worse, I had on my superhero costume: a fedora-like hat and a black leather coat.

Standing in the middle of a hot street, in over one-hundred-and-twenty-degree dry desert heat, in the middle of the summer, in a leather jacket was just stupid.

No other word for it. Stupid.

I had had no intention of leaving air conditioning today, but somehow my tingling warning power had told me trouble was below. I looked down from my floating and very comfortably cool office at the big, wide boulevard in front of the MGM Grand and watched an almost-naked woman with the big shield and sword walking up the middle of the street.

Not unusual for Vegas. I would wager any amount of money that she was not the first near-naked person to walk up that boulevard.

Maybe not even this week.

But then one driver got too close as he tried to go past her. She waved an arm and smashed the car aside like a fly.

Wow, that took some real power.

The car ended up on the sidewalk, luckily not hitting any pedestrians.

It was too hot for any sane person to walk anywhere outside, so the sidewalks weren't as full as normal.

I teleported to a spot in the middle of the road in front of her while shouting for my boss, Stan, the God of Poker, to join me. Patty was still working, and I didn't have time to get any of the rest of the team.

The near-naked woman just kept striding toward me as Stan appeared on my right.

"Wow, a hot one," Stan said.

"The day or the woman?" I asked.

Stan was dressed as he was always dressed: in tan slacks, a button-down sweater, and loafers. We must have looked really goofy out there in the middle of Las Vegas Boulevard—a guy in a leather coat and another guy in a sweater on one of the hottest days of the year.

Yeah, one superhero and one god to your rescue, assuming we don't pass out from heatstroke first.

"Who's that?" I asked Stan as he stared at the woman marching toward us.

He said nothing, which honestly scared me more than the weather.

I could feel the heat burning up through my shoes, yet the woman had no shoes on at all, and didn't seem to even notice.

There was no doubt in my mind that we were facing a powerful god of some sort, one clearly with a bolt loose.

The woman got closer, and I could see she was stunningly beautiful. She was about my own six-foot height, with strong, wide shoulders. Her dark eyes seemed to radiate power. She had perfect skin and didn't seem to be sweating at all.

But I had no doubt that in short order she was going to be very sunburned. Her long, flowing, blonde hair didn't cover much, and that golden bikini of hers just flat covered almost nothing.

It was sort of an afterthought as far as clothing went, a tiny step from being naked.

A very tiny step.

The cars behind her were keeping their distance as she walked forward; this was the first time I had ever seen a Las Vegas driver doing anything smart.

When she got about thirty steps away from us, a transformation started. From seemingly nowhere in her bikini bottom, scales that looked like thick metal flowed out. I had no idea from where, since there just wasn't much left unexposed under that golden cloth. The scales formed a full suit of armor around her, covering her head and face last.

Better for not getting a sunburn, but not good for heatstroke. And I thought I was silly wearing a leather coat. Wearing metal under this kind of sun in this heat would be like putting yourself in a big baking pan, and then in a hot oven.

Very soon, we were going to be smelling sizzling bikini woman, unless she had something really, really powerful going on inside that armor.

Fifteen paces away from us, she stopped and drew her sword, the shiny blade reflecting the sunlight like she was holding onto a long, razor-sharp mirror.

It didn't seem threatening in any manner, and none of my warning senses went off. Drawing the sword and holding it up toward us seemed more like a greeting instead.

What kind of greeting, I had no idea.

She had to be damn strong to hold that sword like that in her right hand, carry the armor that covered every inch of her skin, and hold a very, very heavy-looking shield in her other hand. I was amazed she just didn't sink into the hot pavement.

That was when Stan took the three of us out of time, freezing all movement around us.

I had the same power of stepping between a moment of time, or what I called freezing time. But being between a moment in time sure didn't cool anything down in the slightest. It just made sure that no one else saw what was about to happen.

"Bow," Stan whispered to me.

The God of Poker bowed, and I followed his example.

The woman in the armor bowed slightly, but I didn't hear any clanking or clinking. Then the armor retreated into the nether regions under her tiny bikini bottom, and she put the sword back into whatever was holding it to her thin hip.

If she had a boyfriend or lover, I hoped the poor person knew enough to watch out for that armor during amorous times.

"Great to see you again, Stan," the woman said, her voice clear and powerful. She then looked at me, nailing me to the concrete with those intense brown eyes. "You must be Poker Boy. I have heard so much about you and your team."

"I am," I said, bowing slightly again. I always figured that with a god I didn't know, it was better to bow a little extra than not enough.

She nodded back to me for my courteousness, and then looked at Stan. "Mom around?"

Mom? I almost blurted out.

But somehow I kept my mouth completely shut, which I must admit, is unusual for me. Patty would be happy with me when she heard.

"Let's head up to Poker Boy's office and out of this heat," Stan said. "Have Madge get us something cool to drink. Your mom will meet us there. I know she'll be happy to see you."

"Will she?" the woman asked, smiling slightly.

A moment later, the three of us stood in my office high in the clear, hot air over the MGM Grand Hotel and Casino.

My office was nothing more than an invisible floating glass cube a thousand feet in the air. In the center of it was a replica of a diner booth on a checkered tile floor. The booth was patterned after one taken from The Diner, a sixties replica place in the downtown area of Las Vegas.

The booth had a scarred tabletop and red vinyl seats. There were also about five chairs that often got pulled up to the end of the booth when we needed to meet with more than six.

Stripping off my leather jacket and hat so that the cool air could reach me, I tossed both on a chair near the booth. Wow, did that feel good. Not so sure how much longer I could have been out in the heat dressed like that.

Stan's sweater vanished as well, leaving him in only a short-sleeved dress shirt.

Our guest kept her shield in her hand and, luckily for all of us, didn't shed any more of the slight wisps of golden cloth she had on.

She looked at the view of the city for a moment, then at the booth. "Feels like old home week."

Again I kept my mouth shut, but at that moment Madge appeared from The Diner. She was a superhero in the food and beverage world, and kept us in milkshakes and fries and lunches every day. She was part of my team and seemed to know everyone, which had come in handy more than once on missions.

She was a large woman who always wore the same waitress uniform and dirty apron. Although Madge had grown out of the waitress uniform a few sizes back, she still wore it.

"Well, look who the cat dragged in," she said. Then she frowned at the bikini and sword and shield. "Halloween isn't for another three months. What's with the costume?"

"Long story," the woman said.

"They always are," Madge said shaking her head. "Vanilla shake, like the old days?"

The woman smiled. "I would love that. And a glass of water."

At that moment Laverne, Lady Luck herself, appeared in my office. She had on her usual black business suit, and her hair was pulled back tight. Stan had been wrong. If this was one of Lady Luck's four daughters, she wasn't happy to see her in the slightest.

I had met two of of Lady Luck's four daughters before. One was married to one of my team members, and had joined my team. She was also a superhero in the food and beverage industry and sometimes went by The Queen of Spades, but she didn't much like the name.

The other daughter, the Queen of Hearts, we had rescued from the city of the Titans.

So this one was either diamonds or clubs, and I was betting on the Queen of Clubs.

"Nice outfit," Lady Luck said.

Stan and I moved over to the booth and slid in to get out of the way, leaving Lady Luck facing her daughter.

"You know why I wear the shield and the sword, Mom," she said. "We talked about that years ago, remember?"

"I know," Lady Luck said. "And I'm proud of what you are doing."

That seemed to take the daughter back slightly, and she didn't say anything.

"You didn't think I wouldn't be following your adventures, did you?" Lady Luck said. "After all, I am your mother."

The woman smiled at that. Then I saw something I never thought I would ever see: Lady Luck being hugged by an almost-naked woman with a big sword and shield.

After the hug, Lady Luck turned to me. "Poker Boy, I would like you to meet my daughter, Andarta, the Queen of Clubs."

I nodded. "A pleasure to meet you."

Andarta turned to talk with her mother for a moment, whispering near a far edge of the office while I tried to figure out where I knew the name.

Stan looked at me, smiling. "Figure it out yet?"

At that moment I did. "Andarta was a goddess of war."

Stan nodded.

"Not was," Andarta said. "I still am a goddess of war, although not the original Andarta. Mom named me well."

She moved over to stand in front of the booth next to her mother. I made sure I looked up into her eyes instead of at the wispy parts of the golden cloth at eye level from where I sat in the booth.

"She fights the great Orcus and the remains of his evil army to keep them from coming into this realm," Lady Luck said, clear pride showing in her voice. "Our world is much better because of the battles she wages every night."

"Thank you," Andarta said, smiling at her mother again.

It was really nice to see a family-bonding moment between the most powerful woman on the planet and her daughter, a god, but I had a hunch that a homecoming and summer picnic weren't why Andarta was here.

And that hunch had my stomach twisting. Last thing I wanted was me and my team to be involved in some centuries-old ongoing war, no matter how right the fight.

So I decided to just tackle the topic head on. "I assume you came looking for me and my team for a reason. Correct?"

She nodded and my stomach twisted up even tighter.

"I am told that you have a way of asking the right question at the right time," she said.

"Along with a bunch of stupid ones, yes," I said. "But I do manage to hit a smart one just because I ask so many. Odds of getting one right are in my favor."

She smiled and beside her Lady Luck just nodded, which I wasn't sure how to take.

"I need you to put that skill into play," she said, "with a situation I face in the war."

Now my stomach stopped twisting and just flat cramped up. "I know nothing about war."

"Not true," Stan said beside me. "You are a poker player, and maybe the best in the world. At its base, poker is simply a war waged in a mostly civilized manner, with set rules and stakes."

"People are seldom killed," I agreed.

"I do not need you or your team to join the fight," Andarta said. "I have come for tactical advice to help us finally end this war after centuries of bloodshed."

I glanced at Stan and he nodded. So I looked back at Andarta. "I'll be glad to try to ask a bunch of really stupid questions to find the right question for your problem."

She laughed. "No wonder my old friend Patty loves you so much."

I rocked back in the booth at that one. Patty and Andarta were friends? Exactly how old was my girlfriend? One of these days I really needed to pin her down on that.

"Show him the situation," Lady Luck said.

Andarta nodded and suddenly that armor came snaking out of that bikini cloth and quickly covered her from head to toe.

Then she said, "We will return."

And I found myself standing beside her on a hilltop.

The sky overhead was dark, with swirling clouds that looked

damned threatening. The hill we stood on was rounded and just bare ground that stretched in all directions. Not a tree or bush of blade of grass to be seen.

"This is our battlefield," she said, her voice clear through her armor. "Orcus and his remaining masses are in that direction in this large cavern." Her shield arm pointed off to my right. I could see nothing through the dim light.

I was just stunned to find myself inside a cavern. Must be very, very large to have swirling clouds. I sure couldn't see any walls.

"My troops are on the other side of the hill."

She pointed with her free hand to my left. Again, they were so far off I could see nothing. This was a very, very large place.

"Every night, the two forces meet on this hill to fight. Then, as the sun rises, we retreat with our dead and wounded to sleep, eat, and prepare for the next night's battle."

Wow, what a totally depressing place. It just made me shudder. "How long has this fight been going on here?"

"Over six centuries," she said. "I only joined the fight, much to my mother's disgust, about fifty years ago. I now lead my troops, and we are winning most nightly battles. But I want to find a way to end this forever."

"Six centuries?" I asked, stunned.

I looked around at the bleak hill and tried to see the two camps in the distance. They were both too far away.

She said nothing, so I knew it was up to me to come up with something really stupid to say. "Why do you always meet here on this hill?"

"For the same reason you always play poker at a poker table," she said. "This is our table, our field of battle."

"Wow, who made up that silly rule?" I asked.

"It was in place far before my time," she said.

"Maybe it's time you start questioning that and a few other rules," I said.

"Maybe," she said.

But I could tell she was not convinced. And something more was nagging at me, that little power I had that sort of dinged in my head when there was a thought about ready to come out of the oven and I needed to be ready to catch it with oven mitts.

Suddenly the image of poker chips and stacks of money filled my mind.

"Beside the nightly life and death battle that is part of your play here, what is the ultimate prize for the winner?" I asked,

"If we win, Orcus and his slime are beaten and remain here forever."

"And if he wins?"

"He and his dark minions pour out into the world to spread their evil." She said like it was a pat speech she gave to the unbelievers to get them to join up and fight. For all I knew, it was.

"So if this is a cavern, where is the exit to the outside world from here?" I asked.

Suddenly, every warning bell in my head went off, alerting me that I was in extreme danger. The warning was so strong that I wanted to drop to the ground and crawl away. My heart was racing, but I saw nothing dangerous around us.

She looked at me for the longest moment, and then suddenly raised her shield like she was going to hit me.

Instead, I heard a *clang*, and an arrow bounced off her shield and stuck in the dirt at my feet. It had dark green feathers and quivered there in the ground, about as much as I was quivering at that very moment.

"They have seen us here, so I will show what you ask."

We vanished from that hill. Now granted, I'm a superhero, but I think honestly that's the first time I have been shot at with anything. I use my wits and poker skills and superpowers to save the world. Never real weapons.

And now I understood why. Having come that close to being another casualty on that barren battlefield, I was shaking like a leaf in a high wind trying to escape the tree it was connected to. And let me tell you, that's some shaking.

Suddenly, we were standing in a very thick forest growing up to the bottom of a cliff face. And there really was a rock staircase that led up through a crack in the wall.

"That leads to the real world," she said. "It is how both sides bring in food, water, and weapons. We cannot remain here long because today is their day to use the staircase."

"You alternate days to get supplies?" I asked, shocked and finally not shaking so much. "Another ancient rule, I bet."

She again nodded. "To maintain the battle, we must have supplies."

"I've seen enough," I said.

The next moment, we were back in my office high, over Las Vegas. And never in my life was I so glad to see clear blue sky and a Southwest Airline plane turning for a landing at the airport.

Madge was there with a milkshake for me, and one for Andarta.

As we arrived, Andarta's armor retreated back once again into her bikini. I had no idea where, or why she would even think of wearing a bikini in that horrid place, but that giant cavern sure explained her lack of suntan.

"Thank you for saving my life," I said.

"You were in no danger," she said. "I saw the arrow coming from a great distance."

"Well, thank you anyway," I said, sitting across from Stan and taking a sip of my vanilla milkshake, letting the coolness and sweet flavor calm me down some.

Stan raised one eyebrow to let me know I was going to have to tell that story later.

I sure wished Patty was here right now to touch me and calm me down even more. I didn't think what I was about to say was going to make either a goddess of war or her mother, Lady Luck, very happy.

Andarta sipped on her milkshake and stood facing the booth, her shield in one hand. After saving my life with it, I was starting to see why she never set that big, heavy thing down. Had to be tough to take a bath or shower with it, though.

"So, do you have any suggestions for how Andarta could finish this long war?" Lady Luck asked.

I took one more sip of the cold, vanilla shake, and then moved it into the center of the table before turning to look up into the eyes of the war goddess and her mother.

"I need to understand the rules of the game before I can help. And why they were put into place."

Lady Luck nodded. "Before Andarta was born, Orcus and his troops controlled a large part of many areas here in the real world. But every day they retreated to that deep chamber you saw. It was their lands, their farms, their world."

"They lived off of what they could in that underground cavern?"

"Very much so," Lady Luck said. "With numbers fifty times what they have now."

"So, what happened?" I asked.

"After we won the war with the Titans and the death of the giants, we turned our attention to Orcus and his kind. They had sided with the Titans."

"And you drove them back into their own cavern," I said, nodding.

"Yes," Lady Luck said. "And the battle fought to a stalemate on that hill."

I looked at the war goddess with her big sword and shield and hidden bikini armor and just shook my head. I had no idea why she had come to me for advice, but I had a hunch her mother had had something to do with it. It was one thing to let your daughter go fight in a war for a few hundred years, yet another to actually try to convince her to stop fighting and come home.

"You have a suggestion, Poker Boy?" Lady Luck asked me.

"I do," I said.

I looked directly up into Andarta's dark eyes. "You said your battlefield is similar to a poker table, and it has its rules."

She nodded.

"And rules have been set to allow both sides to continue living, and the battle to continue being waged?"

Again she nodded, so I went on.

"And you are now ahead in this fight, am I correct?"

"Yes, very much so," she said. "Which is why I am here: to try to figure out an end game to finally stop this war."

"A valid goal," I said. I took another deep breath, wishing Patty was beside me with her special, calming touch.

"In a poker game," I said, "the key is to leave the table, the field of battle, when your ahead in the game."

Andarta frowned, which was not something you wanted to see from a goddess of war. But I pushed on.

"When it comes down to it, you and Orcus are basically playing a two-person game," I said. "In poker, we call that a heads-up game. And when one player leaves the table, the game is over."

"Are you suggesting that we surrender?" Andarta asked, her eyes now flashing with anger.

For a moment, I thought I could hear her armor rattling

somewhere in those wisps of cloth, wanting to come out and beat me to a pulp.

"I am not suggesting any such thing," I said, staring right back into her eyes. "You are a great warrior as I am a great poker player. Surrender is not a term we understand."

"Then what are you suggesting?" she asked.

"Fight one more battle, one more night," I said, "then declare a victory because you have cut down their forces to a place where they are no longer a threat to the real world, and have driven them back into a corner of their own land."

"Then what?" she asked.

Beside Andarta, Lady Luck smiled slightly and nodded for me to go on.

"When both of your forces return to your camps for the day," I said, "you pack up all your forces and head for the staircase and the real world, leaving them some food and supplies so they won't starve until they can start growing their own food."

"And at the top of the staircase," she said nodding, now lost in her own thoughts, "we block it and put guards on it, enough to repel any attempt to escape."

"Exactly," I said. "A good warrior, like you on the battlefield, and me at a poker table, must know when to walk away a winner. And from what I saw, you are clearly the winner."

"And sometimes, letting the enemy live to understand they have been beaten is the best victory," she said.

I nodded to that.

She stared at me, and then said, "Thank you for showing me such an obvious and simple and elegant solution. I never would have seen it."

"You are welcome," I said.

She turned to her mother and nodded. "I'll be home shortly."

With that she vanished, taking her armor, sword, shield, and tiny golden bikini with her.

I grabbed my milkshake and took a long sip, just long enough to calm my shaking nerves but not long enough to give myself an ice cream headache.

"Thank you once again, Poker Boy," Lady Luck said.

I smiled at her. "How did you set that up?"

She laughed and Stan, the God of Poker, laughed as well, something I seldom saw him do.

"I just got word to her in a few different ways," Lady Luck said, "making sure it didn't come from me, that you were an expert in figuring out simple solutions to very complex problems that others cannot always see."

"So, in other words," I said, "if you, as her mother had suggested she just call it a victory and leave, she never would have listened."

"Exactly," Lady Luck said, smiling. "You know how it is with moms and their warrior daughters."

I honestly didn't, but I just nodded. She thanked me again and left, leaving only Stan and me in my office.

"Awful place, isn't it?" Stan asked.

"Horrid," I said. "But one thing I don't understand."

Stan motioned that I should ask him.

"In that dark, nasty place, why does she wear a skimpy bikini?"

"That's all she has ever wanted to wear since she was born," Stan said.

"Seriously?" I asked.

Stan nodded. "Never seen her in real clothes, ever."

"So tell me, where does she hide that armor?"

Stan smiled and shook his head. "You really need to ask? Kid, you need to really talk to that girlfriend of yours about the secrets of women."

"She hides it there?" I asked, stunned. "Seriously?"

Now he laughed. "I honestly don't know. But it is sure fun to see you get shocked by something and drop that poker face."

With that, Stan vanished, his laugh echoing behind him.

I just shook my head and sipped on my milkshake, alone once again in my own office.

Patty was never going to believe that I met a goddess of war and her old friend and stopped a centuries-old conflict while she was at work.

Not a typical day for a professional poker superhero.

I sipped my milkshake. Patty wouldn't be off work for another two hours. For a moment, I wondered where in Las Vegas I might get Patty one of those thin, gold bikinis. Then I quickly dismissed that idea as just about as dumb as they came.

So instead, with one more sip of my vanilla milkshake, I jumped to a spot near the MGM poker room, in a dead camera area, and went to see if I could get a seat on a poker battlefield.

Luckily, the only armor I needed there was a good poker face.

Beginner's Luck

by Linda L. Donahue

Maybe it was the ale talking, but I couldn't lose. All I needed was a twelve or higher. The bones rattled in my cupped palms. Hopping on one foot, I tossed them onto the table, just past my overturned cards— a jackal, the nine of axes, and a priestess of daggers. The eight-sided dice bounced twice before landing with a pair of threes. Six. My shoulders sagged as I stared at the pot containing the money I'd saved for a breastplate—one that could accommodate my double-Ds. The chainmail I currently wore squished me something fierce.

Marni, a warrior I'd just met in the Cock and Bull Tavern, likewise stared at the pot. Her milky blue eyes glazed over as a tear formed. Boy, she was so happy she was crying.

I heaved a sigh. Another six months wearing the same, tight-fitting mail. It was like armorers made everything for twig-figured gals, just because that was the popular look at court. "You won it fair and square."

Marni wiped the tear. Then her eyes widened. "Wait. You were on your left foot."

"So what?"

"Kirsta, that means you won." The words rattled off her tongue. "By standing on your left foot, the score is doubled. You got twelve!"

"Really?"

"Why would I lie?" Marni swept her hands over the pot then over her dwindling stack of coins. "One more hand like that and you'll clean me out."

231

"If you want to quit—"

"And lose my last chance at winning back my gold?" Marni shook her head, her black hair shorn short.

"It's my deal." I shuffled the worn cards then dealt us each three, face up. In front of me lay a two of hawks, a priest of daggers, and another jackal. Man, I kept getting jackals.

Marni pushed another frothy ale towards me. "You know the rules."

A drink for every four-legged card—jackals, wild dogs, bears, they all counted. At least this time Marni had two dogs.

I squinted. "Is a pair good?"

"No," Marni answered quickly, "because they're dogs."

I chugged my tenth drink of the evening. In truth, I had lost count after nine, so every ale after was the tenth. Marni swallowed her two like a man dying of thirst. Then the alcohol hit me. My vision blurred around the edges, but more alarmingly, it swam and doubled in the middle.

Next came the bets. Leaving the pot untouched, I said, "I'm in."

Marni drummed her fingers on the table. "I can't match that with gold . . . but I can't afford to lose either." She unhooked the sword from her belt and reluctantly laid it on the table. "This is easily worth the pot. It's a magic sword."

"Magic?" I scoffed then burped. "Who needs magic to win a fight?" I pulled it from the scabbard. Good edge. Slight curvature. Well-balanced. Fine point. "Accepted."

"I'll toss first." Marni flicked the dice on the table. A seven and an eight. Good roll. But Marni only scowled. "Curse those dog cards." At my confused stare—at least I guessed I looked confused—she explained, "Dogs like to dig. So I get the bottom numbers instead. A one and two."

I jumped up to stand on one leg.

"Not this time. You don't have a priestess card."

So I tossed the dice with as much deftness as my numb fingers could manage. Double ones.

"You get another turn. Because of the two of hawks. Hawks are good cards."

Frowning, I said, "Weren't you penalized five points because you had the seven of hawks?"

"Seven's an unlucky number."

I shrugged. Marni knew the rules. I was just having beginner's luck. My second toss came up a four and six.

"You win again! Unbelievable! Are you sure you've never played this game before?"

"Never even heard of it before."

"I'm out." Marni scraped her last few coins into her leather purse then shoved it in her wide belt. "I lost a lot, but it was worth it to play with such a fine player."

"Who knew I was good at Binfizz?" Gingerly, I fingered the edge of the ornately carved, wooden scabbard. "What's this sword do anyway?"

"Er." Marni bit her lip. "It . . . well . . . it sorta has protection magic." She wobbled as she shoved the blade across the table. Before leaving, she laid a hand on my shoulder. "Good luck, Kirsta."

I hooked the sword on my belt and didn't think about it the rest of the night—mostly because the night was an alcoholic blur that faded into sleep around dawn.

I woke to the early hours of late afternoon and stale hay. I lay in the stables, underneath my horse. Buckwheat snorted, spraying my face with misty horse-snot. I'd woken to worse . . . sadly. Such was the lot of a warrior-for-hire.

Hire. I should've been in Hellhole by now. Don't let the name fool you—I've heard it had become a nice place since the ladies' drive for renovations. Oddly, it was becoming the "in spot" to retire.

My thoughts briefly strayed to my sister's twins and their unfortunate siege on the local prince's fortress. A long story that ended with my going to Hellhole to retrieve the prince's prized poodle, which was being held for ransom. *Poodle rescue.* I'd captured a gang of cutthroats terrorizing a town, rescued not one but four princesses, killed seven ogres, and brought Stinky, the three-eyed were-skunk, to justice. Soon I could add "poodle rescuer" to my resume.

I paid the stable master and rode off at a steady gait, just beneath a gallop. Any faster and the local constable would give me a citation— or worse, impound my horse. Outside of town, I gave Buckwheat his head. We had a lot of dreary open space to cross, broken only by an even drearier forest.

Every tree appeared half-dead, drooping with dried, bare branches. Even the undergrowth struggled to live, producing gray-green leaves.

The lack of vitality wasn't caused by drought. I slowed my horse, my gaze suddenly wary. This sort of withering disease resulted from troll habitation—not the bridge variety but a distant cousin that more resembled ugly ogres . . . as opposed to the non-existent pretty ogres.

Luckily, trolls were easy to spot.

About dusk I spotted the telltale shock of vivid hair standing straight up a good four or five feet. Then I heard the heavy stomping and husky breathing. The troll broke through a bit of dying spruce, its bright orange hair snagging bits of the dried-up tree. Spotting me with big, round, popping-out eyes, it rushed me, its pot-bellied, androgynous (and naked) body jiggling as it ran.

I jumped to the ground, standing between the troll and my chestnut steed. The troll let out a blood-curdling giggle—the high-pitched sort that only little girls usually managed.

I drew my new sword. No better time to try a little protection magic than against a life-sucking, smooching troll. A literal kiss of death. Accepted belief held that trolls only wanted to love everyone and everything. Unfortunately they sucked too hard. From the looks, trolls had been loving on every tree and shrub. Even a few large rocks looked kinda pasty.

"Back off," I cried, brandishing the sword. It felt nice in my hand, perfectly balanced, almost weightless.

"Me kiss the pretty man!" it said in its childlike voice.

Man? With my generous endowments? Granted, I wore my hair short. Long hair was just something the other guy could grab.

"I said, 'Back off,'" I repeated, not wanting to hurt it. Trolls weren't mean or vicious. But they were deadly and dangerous, like an overly friendly viper—or a ten-year-old with a catapult.

The troll swung its stubby arms, reaching to pull me into a hug. I jumped aside, swinging my sword.

I heard a tiny scream, and then my sword vanished. I stared at my gloved hands, my fingers springing open as if to prove they no longer held the magic weapon.

"What the . . .?" I stumbled sideways from surprise.

The troll's four-fingered hands clubbed the air before me.

Buckwheat stomped nervously and shook his head, tossing his golden-red mane.

"Ooh, pretty horsie." The troll veered right. "Horsie wanna kissy?"

I reached for my old sword. As my fingers closed on air, my gaze locked on its hilt sticking up on the far side of my saddle. "Crap."

Buckwheat shied, his tail whipping so hard it stunned a surprised butterfly. He turned a half-circle, presenting the butt of his argument to the troll. But now the sword was closer.

I lunged for my sword.

Buckwheat hunched forward a little, and then kicked. His shod hooves connected squarely with the troll's rounded gut, sending the monster flying. It landed on its bulbous butt, rubbing its belly.

"Horsie give me boo-boo!" It wailed.

I pulled my old sword, shouting, "I'll give you worse if you don't beat it!"

The troll rolled over, and scrambled to its feet, mooning me as it ran off into the darkening woods.

I took a step and kicked something. In what remained of the light, I saw a faint glint on metal. My new sword. Lying right where I'd dropped it.

Snatching it from the dirt, I grumbled, "Some protection magic."

"It protected me," said a tiny voice.

Squinting hard, I studied the rounded pommel. The smith had fashioned it into a head—a tiny person's head, a very worried-looking head.

"Did you just talk?"

"If it wasn't your horse, it was me," the sword said. "But who ever heard of a talking horse?"

"I did once . . . but it was really Duke Edward who'd pissed off a sorcerer." I raised the pommel head so we could stare eye-to-eye. "Why did you vanish like that? I could've been killed."

The sword winced. "I got scared."

"Why? You can't suck the life out of metal." If I could've, I would've throttled the sword.

"Metal rusts. And rust itches."

I couldn't argue that. Still, my grip around the hilt tightened and I gave it a little shake. "You're a *sword* for crying out loud. You're supposed to fight monsters. It's why you were made."

"Who says I wanted to be a sword?" The tiny voice almost crooned as it sighed. "I wanted to be a crown, shiny and golden with bright gemstones. I love emeralds. They're such a pretty green."

"Crowns are made of gold. You're steel." Even as I said it, I felt ridiculous for arguing with a sword.

"A good alchemist could change me."

"A good alchemist," I muttered under my breath. Louder, I said, "Could he also give you a backbone? Do you always vanish in the middle of a fight?"

"I didn't vanish. I turned invisible. Then you dropped me."

I replayed the sequence of events. It could've happened that way. With my gloves on, I couldn't *feel* the hilt. And the sword was practically weightless.

"You still haven't apologized," the sword said.

"Me apologize?"

"*You* dropped *me*."

"I thought *you* vanished on me. Oh, never mind." I shoved the sword, perhaps a tad forcefully, into its scabbard. "Will you always turn invisible when I need you?"

"I'm here to talk anytime."

"Terrific. Just what I need."

Actually, what I needed was a secure place to set camp. Traversing unfamiliar woods in the dark was foolish enough, but to do so with trolls about fell into the stupid category. And frankly, after the drinking binge yesterday, I could use some sleep. My head pounded—although I couldn't say whether it'd been pounding all day or just after my "magic" sword's vanishing act.

Glaring at the sword's tiny black eyes, I said, "Can I count on you to scream if a troll approaches while I'm asleep?"

"At the top of my lungs."

I dug a small hole and positioned the sword like a post to serve as sentry. Amazingly, I managed to sleep undisturbed. I woke to the sword whistling a rendition of "The One-Eyed Wench Stole My Heart, Then My Horse."

While I ate the last of my dried provisions, the sword said, "You've never asked my name—which is a little rude, don't you think?"

"You have a name?" The dried pears tasted like stale paste.

"All magic swords do."

"Fine, what's your name?"

"It's Thomas."

"Thomas? I thought swords had names like Slasher, Bloodthorn, or Sting—not to be confused with the wandering troubadour."

In a miffed tone, the sword said, "Well, my name is Thomas."

"I'm Kirsta, by the way, seeing as *you* never asked either."

"*You* should've introduced yourself to me. *I'm* the sword."

"You aren't much of sword if I can't use you." I tossed away the last couple bites of dried pear—or maybe paste. "A sword is supposed to slash, cut, and pierce the enemy. It's not supposed to scream like a little girl and run away."

"I can't run. You dropped me. Some warrior you are."

"So I dropped you. I didn't see you." I cocked my head and squinted hard at the cowardly blade. Thoughtfully, I drawled, "But you were still there. Just invisible."

"If it helps, I didn't want to be there. I would've rather traded places with your other sword."

I managed not to snipe that I would've preferred that too. Yet the longer I considered the situation, the more the possibilities grew. An invisible sword could be useful. The enemy wouldn't see it coming. Of course, I wouldn't see it going. Maybe I could learn to sense where it was.

"Sword—Thomas—can you turn invisible when you want or only when you're scared?"

"I *want* to turn invisible when I'm scared."

"Can you at least try to be useful?" I snapped.

The sword vanished.

"Really? That scared you?" An exasperated gasp escaped my lungs.

"No." Yet its voice quavered. "I was just showing you." Thomas reappeared, still stuck in the hole.

I scrambled to my feet and plucked the sword so swiftly from its scabbard that the scabbard remained embedded in the ground. "Let's try something. Turn invisible."

"Is this a trick? Are you going to throw me away when you think I'm not looking? Because you can't get rid of a magic sword that easily. You can't give me away either. Or sell me. I can only be transferred though inheritance or as payment on a debt of honor."

"Such as a gambling debt," I finished, fighting the urge to smack my forehead. Considering I held a sword, that would've hurt. "Don't worry. I have other plans for you. Now turn invisible."

An instant later, I stared at my clenched fist, seeing nothing, but feeling the slight weight of the smooth hilt. I hefted my hand a couple of times to reassure myself Thomas was there. Then I sought a target.

Some dead branches stuck out of a nearby bush. Feeling foolish, I raised my hand then slashed downward. The row of branches split down the middle.

"I have an excellent edge," Thomas said from nowhere.

"I would expect so, since I doubt it's ever been used."

For about an hour, I trained with the invisible sword until I felt fairly confident I knew where the edge and point were. Remembering I had a deadline, I sheathed Thomas, struck camp, then set out for Hellhole.

By mid-afternoon, Hellhole loomed on the horizon like a toad squatting on an eclair. Towering over the town dotted with brightly painted roofs, like candy confetti, stood a rickety tower, home of the Mad Moffett gang. They weren't crazy-mad, just always in a bad humor. And Prince Duryea had pissed them off. So they kidnapped his beloved poodle, Prince. Yeah, the prince had named the dog after himself.

I approached the tower with the careless appearance of a tourist. I rode right past the gate guards, waving as if they were supposed to know me. I even tossed a casual, "How's Bruce today?" Bruce was the leader of the Moffett gang.

Scrunching his forehead, a guard answered, "In his usual snit." In their confusion, the guards let me pass. Or maybe they thought killing a trespasser would brighten Bruce's day.

Oh, well. Getting *into* the bad guy's tower was always easy. It was getting out that killed many a hero.

As soon as I entered the fortress's grounds, I recognized the layout. The keep was a standard design of Home and Castle Depot, from their budget line. Assuming the poodle was locked in the playroom—this floor plan didn't come with a dungeon—it'd be in the second room on the right.

Without a hitch, I found the room unlocked. Why lock it? Dogs couldn't open doors. I stooped and patted my knees. "Here, Prince."

I don't know why, but I expected a standard poodle—something with some teeth that looked like a man's dog . . . sort of. Instead a miniature poodle, dyed pink and purple (the royal colors) and wearing an emerald-studded collar with a tiny ermine cloak pranced towards me. I scooped it into my arms and turned around.

Bruce filled the far end of the corridor, wielding a two-headed axe. He wore an eye patch and one gold hoop earring. Tattoos covered his arms, bulging from his sleeveless, leather jerkin. A thick chain with a jeweled coat-of-arms pendant hung around his muscular neck. And he'd tied his stringy blond hair back in a ratlike ponytail. To top it off, a dozen honorable mention and participation ribbons hung from his baldric.

"I trust the award ribbons aren't for your wardrobe," I sniped. Realizing that could be taken two ways, I added, "Your get-up doesn't deserve last place." I scowled; that, too, could be misinterpreted for a compliment. My wit was definitely dull. Hopefully my swordplay would be sharper.

Bruce squinted his one eye. "Is that some kind of crack about my looks?"

"I'll give you credit for almost being sharper than I'd figured. You should've *known* it was a crack."

He swung the axe over his shoulder. "Put . . . the . . . poodle . . . down."

"Were you pausing because you were trying to think of the right words, or did you think that gave them emphasis?" Nevertheless I released the dog and drew Thomas.

"Prepare to die, thief!"

"The dog's not yours. Therefore it's not stealing."

"Unless you've brought the ransom, you're not leaving here alive with the mutt."

At that, Prince barked.

"I think he objects to being called a mutt—especially by the likes of you." I widened my stance. Considering Bruce's bulk, even blocking a blow would take considerable strength and balance.

Bruce let out a frustrated scream.

"Run out of words already?" As he charged, I shouted, "Now, Thomas!"

"Now what?" the sword asked.

"Do your trick!" Bruce was nearly upon us. I swung the sword upward, certain it would see Bruce and the axe and get scared.

Suddenly, Bruce's axe disintegrated. The metal head rusted until it dissolved, and the wooden handle turned to dust. Bruce skidded to a stop so close I could smell the excessive amount of aftershave on him—something between woodsy and old farts. He stared at his empty hands for a second then lunged for my neck.

I tried not to show my surprise—but later I would definitely have questions for my *magic* sword.

With a flick of my wrist, Thomas whipped between us, his point gleaming. Now would be an inopportune time for the sword to vanish. Gritting my teeth, I smiled and said quietly, "Don't you dare disappear."

"I won't go anywhere," Bruce said. "How'd you do that?"

"You just remember that I *can* do that." I bent slightly and called Prince. The poodle jumped into my waiting arm like a carnival dog. "Now, I'll take Prince and be gone."

"Sure, sure," Bruce said.

"And you'll forget the ransom," I added.

"Forgotten. But it's not fair."

"How's it not fair when crime doesn't pay?" I regretted the question as soon as it danced off my tongue.

"Prince Duryea should've let me ride in the royal procession last month."

"Why?" I couldn't stop the stupid questions from coming.

"Because I'm his thrice-removed second cousin-in-law."

I rolled my eyes. "Assuming you have some connection to the royal line, who wants to ride in the processional anyway? People just throw rotten eggs at you. Be glad you weren't included."

While that didn't mollify Bruce, he let me leave the fortress unmolested. Once Buckwheat had carried Prince and myself to the forest's edge, I stopped to finally spit out the questions burning on my tongue.

Pulling Thomas from its scabbard, I stared into its beady black eyes. "What was that back there?"

"You said to do my trick."

"I figured you'd go invisible."

"That's just a nervous habit. My trick is turning something really old really fast."

"But how?"

"I *am* a *magic* sword. I can affect time in a small area—make it move fast or slow or even reverse itself."

"How come you never told me?"

"You never asked," Thomas said.

"I'm asking now. Can you do anything else?"

The crossbar on the hilt shrugged. "I can always point north."

"I still don't understand why you didn't turn invisible when you saw Bruce. Didn't he scare you?"

"No. I *am* a sword, you know."

"You were afraid of the troll."

"I'm . . . afraid of monsters," Thomas said sheepishly.

"You're quite the gem." I eyed Prince's gem-encrusted collar. "I believe you said you liked emeralds." At the pommel-head's nod, I grinned. "I think we can fit you with a few." Prince Duryea could consider the donation part of his payment—or I could just blame Bruce for the missing stones.

One Touch of Hippolyta

by Laura Frankos

Assistant Curator should have been a title worthy of respect, especially for a young woman barely out of grad school.

Except the institution in question was the Hiram U. Rowbotham-Finch Museum in Graustarkton, Massachusetts, and Elena Jimenez wasn't so much curator as flunky. She didn't even feel she'd gotten the job honestly—her great-aunt Tilly had helped Adele "Bandicoot" Rowbotham-Finch run a girls' school in the fifties.

Not that Elena wasn't qualified. She had a degree in Greek history, she'd interned at the Getty Villa, sweated at Turkish digs, and most critically, had been obsessed with weapons since she could tell a *gladius* from a *pilum*. The bulk of the HURFM's collection was arms and armor, with other odd antiquities. The rest was just . . . odd.

When she was hired, her best friend, Ian Sherwood, came to congratulate her. He croggled at the entry hall, which was cluttered with medieval German suits of armor; display cases (swords, axes, preserved ferns, tear catchers); a whatnot crowded with fern-festooned ceramics; a sarcophagus; and a stuffed crocodile. Ian stared in disbelief. The croc's glass eyes glared back. "What is this, a Victorian garage sale?"

"You're not far off," Elena said. "And this is the normal stuff." Ian gave a theatrical shudder. "It all started with Maud's bad case of *pteridomania.*"

"Is that catching?"

243

"Only if you're into ferns, real and representational. Maud and her hubby Ned got rich selling opium in China; she spent it on ferns, he bought Ming vases. Their sons inherited the collecting gene. Typical Victorian adventurers, Hiram and Ezekiel roamed the world for treasures and trash. Hiram, a.k.a. Bulldog, specialized in arms. He moved the clan here after a fistfight with Richard Burton—*not* the actor!—over the provenance of a Burgundian axe-head. Brother Zeke, known as Batty, collected everything from fossils to porn."

"Seriously?"

"Could I make that up? He liked bearded ladies. Their children and grandchildren collected, too. The holdings 'jest growed,' like Topsy. It all needs to be cataloged, even the porn. Brace yourself."

The next room contained stuffed guinea pigs staged in tableaux (a riverside picnic, a soccer game between Scunthorpe and Hull City). Ian shuffled slowly around, muttering, "No, no, no . . . " before stopping dead. "Tell me that is not a guinea pig *Importance of Being Earnest*."

"Yup. See Oscar Wilde in the box seat?"

"Aggh. I'm going to have nightmares."

"Cheer up, the next room's only beetles and beer steins."

After the tour, she took Ian to her office (formerly Bulldog's), where he gratefully accepted a beer. "Sweetie, I was thrilled when you got hired in my town. But how is this a museum? The layout, the decor! My set designer, Gene, could do better—and his aesthetics suck! At least organize it: bugs here, implements of death there."

"Nope." Elena shoved aside snuff boxes and mustache spoons to set down her bottle. "Ever hear of Isabella Stewart Gardner? She was a pal of Bulldog's. She kept her art collection in her house, and her will states that *nothing* can be altered. Bulldog and Family did likewise. Nothing downstairs can be rearranged. My job is sorting the junk upstairs. Honestly, they should have been named Rowbotham-*Magpie*, not Finch."

"Horrific taxidermy aside, are you happy here?"

Elena fiddled with an Assyrian bone dagger. "I like bringing order to chaos, and this is Chaos Central. But it's lonely—visitors are rare. I find myself talking to the statues."

Ian drained his bottle. "As long as they don't answer. And your boss?"

"Ugh. Solitude is better. Willard Pomeroy is an officious twit who specializes in interrupting my work. Thank goodness Bandicoot keeps him in line."

But now Bandi had been gone for nine months, and Pomeroy was even more obnoxious. The clan no longer had any direct descendants, but as distant cousin, he acted like the place was his. He sidled in late one day as she was sorting Hittite arms in the main workroom. Ziegfeld the cat, a gray tabby from Ian to keep down the mice, promptly fled.

"Ah! Roman legions?" Without asking, Pomeroy picked up Elena's laptop. "Oh. Hittites. That stuff's not valuable, is it?"

Elena was sitting cross-legged, chunks of bronze laid on sheets around her. "As I've said before, I'm *not* an appraiser. I'm just working through each bloody box."

Pomeroy smoothed his thin, dark mustache, looking hurt. "My dear, I'm merely thinking of this institution's future. A juicy discovery would help us economically and in the community at large. Now, get me a coffee and a donut, and we'll finish the newsletter."

Pomeroy retreated to his office, once Batty's. He had jettisoned every old thing in it except creepy artwork entirely made of butterfly wings. Muttering darkly, Elena fetched his snack and spent ninety minutes wrangling over text that should have taken fifteen. Pomeroy left, chortling, "Nothing like a good day's work!" Elena stomped back to the Hittites.

She stayed late, determined to finish. *It's not like there's anything going on in my life.* It was ten when she reached the last piece. Disintegrating burlap wrapping revealed an iron short sword. A slip of yellowed paper fluttered to the ground. In faded ink, she made out Bulldog's firm hand: *Pontus, 1872.*

"Huh." She studied the other items. "One of these things is not like the others. Maybe a Persian *akinakes*?" She took some notes. "Hey, Ziggy, Pontus was the land of the Amazons. Maybe it's Hippolyta's."

Ziegfeld washed his paws, unconcerned with Amazon queens. Elena smiled. "Hippolyta" was one of Bulldog's better finds, a largely intact bronze. Its right leg was lost, but the left clearly showed trousers. The face was a blob with empty eye sockets, but Elena loved it for that single trousered leg, which predated other depictions of Amazons in pants. Pomeroy, however, didn't like its staring eyes, and demanded that Elena cover it.

Thinking about the statue, Elena got a silly idea. Ian, who taught high school drama, once told her about a musical called *One Touch of Venus*. Mary Martin starred as a statue of Venus that came to life when a dweeby guy slipped a ring on its finger.

"Come on, Ziggy. Let's arm Hippolyta for battle." *It's not entirely ridiculous; the statue clearly once held a weapon, now a mere bronze sliver, separated from the body.* Elena ran back to her office and removed the draping. "Hello, Hippolyta!" Ziggy watched with interest as she snipped twine and slid the weapon into the statue's right hand. "I'll secure it for the photo. Then we'll have dinner, okay?"

The tabby didn't answer. He puffed up his tail and skedaddled. Simultaneously, Elena saw the statue's fingers close over the hilt. The room glowed with a bluish light not from any compact fluorescent bulb.

Thump! Somebody slammed Elena into a case of Inuit bolas. Cold metal pressed against her neck.

"Do. Not. Move," said a husky, accented voice.

"Eep!" Elena squeaked. The pressure eased. Her assailant stepped back—a helmeted woman, about five-foot-five, in trousers and tunic, a semi-crescent shield slung over her back. Apparently judging a pudgy academic as no threat, she lowered her weapon. Behind her, the statue's pedestal was empty, save the sliver of the original bronze sword.

"What does 'eep' mean?" the Amazon asked.

"Uh . . . an expression of surprise," Elena said. *This can't be happening!* "I am surprised. You . . . shouldn't be here."

"You are right. My spirit was at rest in the cliffs above the Green River, then Hiram Rowbotham-Finch dug up that cursed statue! Damn Naudar's skillful hands!"

"Wait, what?"

"And stop calling me Hippolyta! That name is sacred in my tribe. I am Harmothoe."

"'Sharp nail,'" Elena translated.

"Even so." Harmothoe raised the *akinakes*. "Had I been a weaver, I would still sleep peacefully."

Elena sank into her desk chair. "So many questions! Where to start? You've been aware of your surroundings since Bulldog excavated the statue?"

"Correct. He already had my sword in his camp. It roused my spirit." Harmothoe paced in front of shelves of self-pouring teapots and boomerangs. "I have listened to his family's chatter ever since."

"You . . . changed when I put your sword in your hand." Elena hesitated. "If you set it down, will you change back?"

Harmothoe studied her weapon—intact, without a speck of rust. "If I do, have you the courage to repeat your action? I dislike the prospect of returning to mute metal."

"Certainly."

Harmothoe snorted. "Nothing certain about it. I have listened to you, too, for months. You lack a warrior's heart."

Ouch! What has she heard? "I swear I will. Uh, by my mother's ghost."

That oath got Harmothoe's approval. She set the sword on the desk. Her hand remained on the hilt (now beautifully inlaid with gold and pearl) for a moment, then withdrew.

Nothing happened.

Both women exhaled. Harmothoe shoved the sword in her scabbard. "Evidently, I need not hold it, though it feels better here. Now! I believe you promised Ziegfeld dinner. I am ravenous."

I'm eating pizza with an Amazon, Elena thought. She looked at the armored woman seated across from her in the kitchen, happily devouring a slice with pepperoni. "I'll need help getting you out of here. Mr. Pomeroy is *not* going to believe all this."

"Pomeroy! That petty fool. Why do you cower when he comes in the office?"

Elena didn't answer, but got out her cell phone. "Ian! Yes, it's late, but I've got an emergency at work. I need a spare t-shirt and your dressmaker's dummy. Don't argue, just get over here."

Harmothoe smiled. "Better! That was a commander's voice."

While they waited for Ian, Harmothoe explored the kitchen. The microwave perplexed her, but the oven, fridge, and pantry were fascinating. "So much metal for *food storage*!" She held up a can of pineapple with wonder.

But canned food was nothing compared to Ian's truck. When it puttered up to the back entrance, Elena opened the door. Harmothoe gaped as Ian climbed out.

Ian stared back, stroking his wispy beard. "Sooooo. Are we staging *The Trojan Women*?"

Awe gave way to anger. "My ancestors fell on the fields of Troy! Do not mock them!"

"O-kay. I'll just get the stuff." Ian carried the dummy inside, his eyes demanding an explanation—*pronto.*

"You remember *One Touch of Venus*?" Elena asked.

Her friend bristled. "You do classical history; I do musical theatre history."

"Well, Harmothoe appeared when I stuck a sword in the fist of our Amazon statue. It's *not* a joke." She explained what they knew of Harmothoe's background.

Ian blinked, then found his voice. "Right. She needs the t-shirt because that get-up is *seriously* old-school, but why the dummy?"

Elena pointed upstairs. "So Pomeroy won't notice the statue-sized hole in my office."

"Ah," said Ian and Harmothoe. Warrior and director exchanged looks. Finally, Harmothoe said, "You remind me of a Greek sailor I met in Colchis."

"Sweetheart, you have no idea." Ian laughed. "Let's go."

They draped the dummy; Elena nodded with satisfaction. "Although Pomeroy's not likely to peek. It always creeped him out."

"But you admired it," Harmothoe said. "You even spoke to it. Yet you meekly covered it for him."

"He's my boss!"

"It's *your* office!"

Ian held up a hand. "Ladies, please! This isn't helping. We have to think about Harmothoe. What does the modern Amazon do? What's her—"

"I'll smack you if you say, 'What's her motivation?'" Elena picked up a lethal Brazilian *macaná.*

"What's her next step?" Ian finished smoothly.

"I have much to learn," Harmothoe said. "Then, perhaps, I can return to Amaseia."

This isn't easy, Elena thought. "It's . . . gone. Hundreds of years of Romans and Byzantines and Turks."

The warrior bit her lip. "Of course. I am alone."

Ian threw out his arms and sang, "'You'll never walk alone!' Sorry, it's automatic. But we'll help you."

Elena began pacing, complications piling up in her mind. "Ian. What do you know about illegal immigration?"

"I know somebody, but it might get pricey."

Neither of us has money. "Call him tomorrow. Harmothoe, change into this so you don't attract attention, and we'll go to my place." She tossed her the shirt, advertising Ian's production of *Gypsy*, and waved at the bathroom. But Harmothoe was either too intrigued by screenprinting or simply unconcerned about privacy. She stripped on the spot, handing gear (scabbard excepted) to Elena. *So much for the myth of Amazons mutilating themselves to pull bows more easily.* Harmothoe's bosom was intact, though pale scars marked her body.

They headed downstairs. Elena set the alarm as they left the mansion. *Good thing there's no video. How would we explain two going in, three coming out?* "Ian, thanks for everything."

"Of course." His hug felt wonderfully reassuring.

The ride to the dodgy part of Graustarkton overwhelmed Harmothoe. They drove in silence. Elena parked in her spot and noticed with dismay her nasty neighbor, Igor, lurking by the stairwell. Igor's harassment never went beyond talk, but he made Elena terribly nervous. He'd done time for theft—who knew what else he could do?

"Hey, *Doctor* Jimenez, who's yer friend? Hey, Doc! Hey! Izzat a sword? Hey, come on! Where's some love for Igor?" He blocked the stairwell, legs spread, arms crossed.

"Ignore him," Elena whispered. "We'll use the other stairs."

But Harmothoe approached the punk. "I have traveled far, and wish to rest. Stand aside."

"Gonna make me? Nice tits, but a big mouth!" He leered.

Harmothoe smiled sweetly . . .

. . . and Igor was suddenly crumpled on the concrete with a bloody nose. "Bitch! I'm callin' the cops!"

Elena thought quickly and gambled—successfully. "I'll tell Manny you stole his stash last week." Swearing, Igor skulked off. Big as he was, Manny was even bigger and had a fierce temper.

Elena dashed up the stairs, keys in her hand. "That was bad," she said, fumbling with the lock. "Now he'll be after me."

"I do not think so." Harmothoe radiated calm. "The world is different, but people are clearly the same. This man has an easily defeated spirit. If you had shown what Bulldog called 'pluck,' he would cease annoying you."

I doubt it. Elena got pajamas ("Clothes only for sleeping?") and fixed the futon for the Amazon. When she collapsed on her own bed, she didn't sleep for hours, planning and worrying.

"You'll be my assistant," Elena told Harmothoe over breakfast. "At the museum, I'll teach you about things." *About everything, apparently.* Modern textiles, toothbrushes, Pop-Tarts, Anatolian history, internal combustion engines. Elena talked so much, her coffee got cold. "Okay, let's buy some clothes . . . what's wrong?"

Harmothoe was staring at a bottle of apple juice. "My mother had an apple orchard," she said in a choked voice. But as quickly as the tears appeared, the steely resolve returned. "She is dust, as is the orchard. Let us go."

They didn't leave immediately; Harmothoe didn't want to leave her sword behind. But when Elena pulled out of the garage, the Amazon screamed, "Go back, quickly!" She began choking and turning a funny color.

Elena threw the car in reverse and screeched back. The closer they got to the building, the better Harmothoe looked. "I'll get it, stay there!" *Don't change back!*

When she came back with the sword jammed in a plaid messenger bag, Harmothoe was breathing easily. Elena restarted the engine. "Okay. You have to stay near the sword. Why?"

"Naudar. My husband. A metalworker of renown."

"Amazons had husbands?"

"We can't make babies on our own," Harmothoe snapped. "Are you as ignorant of sex as you are of warfare? Naudar had me shed blood into the molten metal to make it strong and earn the gods' favor. I assume he did the same with the statue. There were enough blood-stained rags . . . when I died." She stared out the window as they neared the mall. "I remember silence . . . then I was in the *agora*. I couldn't see, but I could hear my tribe. I heard them age and die around me. Naudar, Polemusa, and Hippothoe, granddaughter Bremusa, so many more. Whenever one took my sword into battle, leaving Amaseia, silence enveloped me until its return. Bremusa's girl, Alcibe—she had the sweetest voice—must have fallen to the enemy. All was stillness . . . until Rowbotham-Finch found both statue and weapon."

Elena parked the car, searching for something to say. "Did you die in battle, too?"

"Of sorts. I died giving birth to Hippothoe."

When Willard Pomeroy arrived that afternoon, he blinked at the muscular, dark-haired woman carrying a crate. "Our new intern, Thoey Amassian," Elena said.

"Oh? I didn't know we were hiring anyone." His bushy eyebrows furrowed.

"An unpaid position."

Pomeroy relaxed. "Fine! Welcome, uh, Zoe. Elena, get me a coffee and we'll discuss my trip."

Elena switched off her laptop and followed. Harmothoe frowned, then began attacking the crate with a crowbar. When Elena returned an hour later, the Amazon asked, "Why must you stop your work for him? Is your work of lesser value?"

"It's easier to do what he wants," Elena said. "I still get my job done. Now—what's in the crate?"

Harmothoe couldn't read, but she had an unfailing memory of every discussion that took place in the office. "Bulldog's daughter, Budgie, collected items relating to one General Napoleon. A soldier's kit, a partial uniform, a box of coins, a rifle with bayonet, and two letters—one allegedly from Napoleon himself."

"If the letter's real, it's a great find. Napoleon was a mighty conqueror about two centuries ago. Pomeroy will be pleased."

Harmothoe sniffed. "I do not seek his approval, but yours."

That was the start of the busiest—and most enjoyable—year Elena ever spent. During the day, they worked through the collections, Harmothoe discussing provenance, family history, and, in the case of the antiquities, original use. "That is *not* a serving fork," she said, studying treasures Bulldog found in Anatolia. "It was a hair ornament for a noblewoman."

"Well, old Bulldog was bald as an egg. There's his portrait."

"Hmm. His voice was hairy."

At night, Elena taught Harmothoe how to read and explained the modern world. In return, Harmothoe described life in Amaseia. *The Mothers' Council, the battle strategies, the traditions and schooling! This would make a great book,* Elena thought, *but how do I cite my source?*

Harmothoe also got her exercising. "Too much sitting here!" she complained. The next thing Elena knew, they were taking classes (free, at the community center) in aerobics and swing dance with Ian. She drew the line at fencing, afraid Harmothoe would insist on using her *akinakes*. The weapon, obviously, went everywhere with the Amazon, tucked inside the messenger bag.

Not surprisingly, Harmothoe's favorite modern topic was the position of women in the twenty-first century. She appreciated what women could do in America, but hearing about oppression elsewhere got her blood boiling. "These barbarians who are frightened by the idea of women attending school! I would like to show *them* what I learned as a girl!"

"Unfortunately, they've got AK-47s."

"So I have seen. But truly, if I could do anything in this world, I would help such schools. That would be in keeping with the traditions of my tribe."

Elena had a vision of Harmothoe charging through Afghanistan and Nigeria, setting up girls' schools and taking out terrorists' nests. "I'd like to help, too, but that takes money."

"Money. Bah." Money hadn't even been invented in her lifetime.

Elena's salary was barely enough for one to live on, let alone two. Ian helped, as did Elena's dad, but they still didn't have enough for the immigration papers. Fortunately, Harmothoe didn't object to peanut butter and ramen noodles. She also didn't complain when Elena began dating one of Ian's coworkers. "Mitchell is . . . what is the word? Hot!" said Harmothoe with a distinctly modern grin.

One warm night in August, Elena came back late after a weekend in Boston with Mitchell. She was pleased that Igor wasn't around, though he hadn't been so horrible since his thumping. She climbed the stairs, eager to describe her weekend to her roomie. Then she noticed the window had been jimmied open.

She tried the door—*unlocked!* Making as much noise as possible, she barged in. "Hey, Thoey, what's up?" Silence. She looked around the front room. *Her bag's usually on the kitchen chair . . . near that window . . .*

Feeling sick, she opened the bedroom door. A bronze statue lay under a blanket on the futon.

Okay. Think. "Smash-and-grab" is Igor's style. He wouldn't stick around long enough to face Harmothoe. Steeling herself, she walked down to Igor's apartment and peered through the broken shutters. A beam from the street light illuminated the bag, tossed in a corner. *I need back-up—I can't take him on alone.* She looked around in desperation. Fortunately, there were lights in Manny's apartment. If Igor made Elena nervous, Manny terrified her. But if anyone could break down the door, he could. And he didn't like Igor.

Gulping down her fear, she knocked.

"What the hell do you want?" he rumbled. "I'm almost at Level Sixty-two."

"Hi, Manny. Uh, Igor stole my friend's bag, I can see it in his room. Can you help me get it back?"

"Little shit. That ain't right." The enormous young man shut off his PlayStation, eager to pound something besides digital orcs. He banged on Igor's door. "Asshole! You home?" Without waiting for an answer, he kicked it in.

The silence matched that in Elena's place. "Aw, he's cleared out," Manny complained. "All the decent shit's gone. He took his games an' everything."

Elena ran to the bag. *Empty, of course.* But Manny, raiding Igor's fridge, suddenly spotted something on the kitchen table. "What's with the hacksaw?"

Next to the tool, in a pile of iron shavings, was the blade from the sword. Igor had taken the gold and pearl inlaid hilt. Hope flared within Elena. *This is the part with Harmothoe's blood. Is it enough to bring her back?* "It's from the museum where we work," she said, slipping it in the bag. "Igor cut off part of it, but it's still, uh, historical. Thanks for your help, Manny."

"No prob. Wanna Dew? Some Cheez Whiz?"

Elena declined, and ran back to her place. She threw the blanket on the floor. Weirdly, the statue had returned to its previous, time-worn state; she had half-expected it to look as Naudar first made it. She slid the chunk of iron into the palm . . .

. . . the bluish flash returned . . . and so did Harmothoe, looking confused. "What happened? I was dreaming—then I was . . . not."

"Igor stole the sword." As the Amazon stared at the chunk of iron in her hand, Elena added, "I got Manny to break into Igor's place, but this was all that's left. Igor's gone, and so is Naudar's beautiful hilt. I'm sorry."

Harmothoe shrugged. "The blade was the important part." She clapped Elena on the shoulders, which stung. "But you! The little mouse who once squeaked in fear has grown fangs!"

"Oh, I was terrified the whole time. Look, I'm still shaking."

Harmothoe beamed. "You will be a warrior yet! I cannot thank you enough." She studied the blade. "Hmm. I should find a way to bind this to me, so no man can snatch it away again. Perhaps a smith—if there are such nowadays—could hammer it into bracelets."

"Sweet! I know a farrier; she might help." Elena looked around at the shabby apartment. "Leaving this crime zone would be good, too. Getting your papers would be best of all." She kicked off her shoes. Her pleasant weekend with Mitchell seemed like an eternity ago. "It's not your fault you're an alien. It's Bulldog's! I wish we could make the museum pay—at least enough to set you up somewhere. If Bandicoot were still alive, she'd do something for you."

"At least I am here. What is it Ian sings? 'Good times and bum times, I've seen 'em all, and my dear, I'm still here.'"

"Just what this world needs: an Amazon who sings Sondheim."

A month after the break-in, they were cataloging Bandicoot's brother's World War II G.I. magazines. It was likely to be one of their last projects together; the Amazon hoped to find employment with migrant workers picking apples. The farms weren't so fussy about papers and, as she noted with a sad smile, she'd once worked in an apple orchard.

Harmothoe's iron bracelets clanked as she dug through copies of *Stars and Stripes*. "These used to be in the office. Beagle's wife threatened to burn them, so Bandi moved them to the attics . . . " She suddenly stopped. "I've just remembered something. Come with me."

Bulldog's office had a huge fireplace—perfect for chilly New England winters. Harmothoe moved the brass screen and crawled inside. "You're getting filthy!" Elena said. "What *are* you doing?"

The soot-covered Amazon scrambled back out, an iron box in her hands. "There was a hidey-hole in the chimney. Bulldog kept some of his treasures here, hidden from Batty. He told his son and grandson, Badger and Buzzard, about his stash, and no one else." She forced the lid—and both women gasped as the glint of gold met their eyes. Bracelets, rings, necklaces, ornaments sparkled.

"It's Etruscan!" Elena breathed. "Such gorgeous work; they were skilled goldsmiths. But why didn't anyone else in the family know about this?"

"Because all three fell to influenza in 1919. Poor Buzzard, only fifteen. He was so like his forefathers; he had little collections of rocks and such."

Elena fingered the treasures. "I'm terribly tempted to take this for you. You deserve the value of the gold, certainly, but the historian in me wants the world to know about them, not melt them."

"No. We are not like Igor," Harmothoe said.

"Just for fun, let's check the other fireplaces," Elena said. "You're already dirty."

The old mansion had seven different fireplaces, but it was the last, in what had been the nursery, that Harmothoe found another set of loose bricks. "There is something on a ledge, deep within the wall!" she said, her voice echoing as she crawled inside. "Two wooden boxes, both inscribed *Buzzard*."

No gold, however, just a child's treasures—minerals, sea shells, owl pellets, baseball cards. "Worthless, save to poor Buzzard," Harmothoe said sadly.

"Eep," said Elena.

"The expression of surprise?"

"*Not* worthless. There are rarities of all sorts, Thoey. These are very rare pieces of cardboard. They have Honus Wagner on them." She clutched the box. "Put the other stuff back. We're taking this one home!"

Harmothoe frowned. "But should not the world know of this Honuswagner, as with the golden treasures?"

"Those are one of a kind. These are rare, but others exist. They're worth thousands of dollars. And you deserve it. Bandicoot would have agreed."

"Would she?" Harmothoe sounded doubtful.

"Of course. After all, she and my Auntie Tilly started a girls' school themselves."

≈

Three years later, Harmothoe, Elena, Ian, and Mitchell (part of the Amazon cabal after proposing to Elena) gathered in Logan Airport before the women embarked for Africa. They had checked their luggage and were heading for security.

Ian, trying to be gallant, lifted Harmothoe's carry-on. "Oof! Preparing to invade Russia, General Napoleon?"

"Not an invasion, Ian. But we are going to war—against ignorance."

Elena and Mitchell embraced. "I'll join you in June," he said. "Stay safe, love."

"We'll be fine."

Ignoring the looks of bystanders, Ian sent them off with a rendition of "The Quest" from *Man of La Mancha*. *This is an "impossible dream"* Elena thought. *But maybe we'll make it come true.*

Ahead, Harmothoe suddenly set off the metal detector. Behind her, Ian's song came to a strangled stop. The sword-blade bracelets were so much a part of her that they never noticed them any more. The Amazon slipped them off and slowly placed them in a plastic tub. The tub slithered along its conveyer belt, moving farther and farther from Harmothoe's body. Elena held her breath, but her friend calmly stepped back into the scanner, passed through, and retrieved her bracelets.

"Next!" the TSA official barked.

Willard Pomeroy checked his e-mail again. Two months, and still no replacements for Elena and Zoe. Thoey. Whatever. The museum seemed eerily empty without the girls' laughter. What a crazy notion, to leave such good positions—Pomeroy had generously put Thoey on salary after the Etruscan find—to start a girls' school in Africa!

He wandered through the rooms like a lord surveying his lands. *They did do a nice job sorting the junk upstairs,* he had to admit. He liked the weapons hall, the toy room, the neat boxes of ephemera. The one room that gave him the willies, though, was the statuary. He poked his head in. The blank faces stared back at him, especially the painted Etruscan funerary piece. Somehow, that guy seemed really pissed, almost like he was going to slide off his sarcophagus and slug him.

Hey, where's that really creepy one-legged warrior? The one that used to be in Bulldog's office? He stepped into the room, ready to look around. The angry Etruscan now had a definite curl in his lip, an arch to his painted eyebrow. "Ah, the hell with it," he said aloud, trying to dispel whatever ghosts lurked inside.

He'd go down to the kitchen for some coffee. Maybe he could get the damn machine to work right this time.

Saving Private Slime

by Louisa Swann

Staff Sergeant Jillian K. Wilson, aka Jelly the Belly, stared at the scenario before her, wondering just why in the universe she kept pulling Nanny Duty. Yeah, she was good at training recruits, no matter who or what they were, and didn't really mind. In fact, she kind of liked the challenge.

Her first assignment on Centauri VI had been to train a squad of pink blobs—amorphous beings that looked more like oversized mounds of pudding with bulbous noses, beady eyes, and no bodies to speak of—in the art of combat. Not only was her squad now proficient in blob-to-blob combat, they could scale almost any obstacle and could bob and weave like pros.

But were they ready for this?

Jelly shook her head, fruitlessly scratched at an itch beneath her armored vest, and gave a silent groan. "All right, men. Load 'em up." She flashed a series of hand signals, repeating the command to the blobs.

Water splashed in all directions as her men, blob and human alike, plopped into the nearby pond. It wasn't really much of a pond at all, about the size of a movable swimming pool back on Earth. The water-filled depression was big enough to splash around in, but not for doing laps.

It was definitely full now, with six blobs of varying sizes along with their six human counterparts, five men and a woman who made up the other half of her on-planet squad.

"Hey, Buckster," Corporal Murph Ryan wrinkled his freckled nose as he popped open a collapsible bucket. "Careful those babies don't mistake you for their momma!"

"No chance of that, Ryan," Lance Corporal Betty Buckman said with a wry grin. Betty stood six-foot-even, her lean frame all muscle and bone. "Looks like the blobbies have nominated you Momma of the Day."

Ignoring the banter, Jelly scanned the clearing for enemy troops, first studying the enormous, flat-topped, sharp-needled trees growing in swoops and swirls around the pond, then the black granite boulders poking through the rocky soil like newly erupted dragon's teeth. The air reeked of what smelled like a combination of rotten vegetation and monkey feces—the odiferous calling card of the local inhabitants.

Not the friendly blobs. Those particular natives hung out down by the Caribbeanlike oceans. No, this stink came from inside the dirt-and-stick wall surrounding the native compound twenty yards beyond the pond. Jelly suppressed a shiver. The natives reminded her of Chihuahuas gone wild, with bushy little faces, sharp teeth, batlike ears, and a nasty disposition reminiscent of the gremlins she'd seen in an old vid when she was a kid.

They didn't seem to have enough smarts to create anything even resembling a civilization, yet they'd tried to assassinate the blob chieftain—an attempt foiled by her newly trained blob troops—and then managed to kidnap his daughter.

The very pregnant daughter.

Who'd proceeded to give birth to bright pink baby blobbies right here in this very pond.

Jelly's orders were to retrieve the princess and all of her babies. "Come on, men. We don't have all day!"

Something chittered in the trees overhead, making Jelly tense as she squinted up at the branches. The sound repeated amid a sprinkling of needles and bark as the critter—whatever it was—scampered away.

Jelly relaxed her neck, but not her vigilance, returning her attention to the blobs as they splashed around the pond, herding the newborn blobbies into a group. Burp was the tallest of the bunch, coming up to just above Jelly's knees, which put him at about two feet high. Hiccup had the biggest nose. Yawn used to be the littlest, but was rapidly gaining size. When he'd started training, he'd looked like a half-filled water balloon, constantly sloshing from side to side. Now he was almost as tall as Burp and hardly sloshed at all.

Then there was Grumble, Sneeze, Gag, and Barf.

Hard to tell who was who from the backside: they were all as pink and shiny and smooth as a baby's behind, but every single one had proven exemplary on their first assignment, throwing themselves in harm's way and saving the blob chieftain from a nasty gremlin attack.

Her blob squad—and her regular troops—were the best of the best.

"Hey, get back here!"

A cacophony of burps, bubbles, and other strange noises erupted from the pond. Jelly glanced back to see a blob hump its way out of the water. She smothered a sigh.

When she'd first received this assignment, she'd thought the extraction would be simple, especially since she'd just found out that the adult blobs had the unique ability to take an item into their bodies in order to transport that item to a different location. Should be simple to have the adults blobs suck up the babies and hump them back to the transport.

Unfortunately, during the planning stage of the mission, she'd been informed that the blobs transporting ability was limited to inorganic items. Anything organic triggered the digestive system to release some kind of nasty acid that did a number on the "food" in a matter of minutes.

"Ouch!" Buckman screeched. "What the . . . ?"

"In the bucket, Sneeze. In the bucket!" PFC Jason McKenzie roared. At six-foot-five, the big man towered over the other team members. Great for pulling items off high shelves, not so great for bending over and scooping slippery bubbles into a five-gallon bucket.

One after the other, the blobs burped, farted, squeaked, and yawned in ever-increasing intensity as they struggled to herd what looked like very slippery pink bubbles the size of golf balls into the buckets being held by the regulars.

Only one problem: the pink "bubbles," aka baby blobbies, didn't appreciate the rescue efforts.

Water darkened the earth around the pond, turning the dirt into sticky mud, and filling the air with a stench reminiscent of a sewer treatment plant gone bad. Jelly squinted at the viscous tide of babies bobbing up and down in the waves created by all the splashing about.

The little buggers had teeth. Very sharp teeth, judging by the curses and squeals emanating from their wannabe captors.

Baby blobs with teeth. Now why hadn't that been in the briefing?

They'd infiltrated the gremlin compound early this morning and found the princess—alone and drugged—in the first "room" they'd cleared. The compound's interior looked like a bower made of interweaving tree branches with entrances in the form of lopsided archways scattered sporadically around the perimeter wall. Jelly hadn't been happy to find the compound empty—the gremlins who'd kidnapped the princess had to be around somewhere. She'd urged her men to hurry, but getting her royal blobbiness up and moving had proven quite a challenge and had taken way too much time. Locating the birthing pond had taken even more time.

She'd set the slowest blob, Gag, on watch just inside the compound entrance that opened onto the pond area and put the others to work "rescuing" the babies. Now that they finally had everything together, the "babies" had apparently decided it was snack time.

Another blob heaved his bulk out of the pond with an ear-piercing screech, followed by a second blob, and then a third.

It appeared that even giant, pink blobs had their breaking points.

Soon half the squad—the pink half—sat huddled around the edge of the pond, looking for all the world like a bunch of frustrated pudding cones. It didn't take long for the human half to join them.

Grumble's hide looked like someone had been gnawing on his glistening, chewing-gum exterior and Sergeant James "Shark" Mallory's uniform looked like he'd been bathing with piranhas.

A rat terrier-sized slug slid through the arched opening in the compound wall, eyestalks waving in the air like a cheerleader on steroids. Slime came to a jolting stop at Jelly's feet, and straightened up so tall she half-expected the slug to topple over backward. She gave a brisk nod. "Report."

The slug's eyestalks went through a series of contortions and gyrations Jelly found it hard to follow. Shark, Jelly's second-in-command, was also the team's communications expert. He'd taught the little slug how to converse using semaphore, the same language ships used to communicate with each other when radios were down.

"He says the bad guys are coming," Shark translated. Jelly frowned, and Shark shrugged. "His words, not mine."

Slime's eyestalks sagged a little, and Jelly held back a laugh. The little guy tried so hard. So did her blobs.

Tree branches rustled overhead, and suddenly screaming, biting scrawny balls of fur rained down all around them.

Gremlins.

Shots came in quick succession as Jones and Filmore, the human pair guarding the small pile of backpacks stashed among the rocks, fired at the attackers, dropping two of the gremlins, and sending the rest scurrying for cover. Jelly grimaced at the sound of the noisy .45 Martini-Smith automatic pistols, standard issue for her team. Lasers were quieter and more efficient, but her commanding officer had pointed out that most of the native life on Centauri VI was nonviolent, so trendy weapons weren't needed.

As far as she knew, her commanding officer had never set eyes on a gremlin.

Staring at the still-twitching nasties with their pointy teeth, Jelly stifled a shudder. "Ryan, you and Slime head on back and get the transport ready." She ran to the packs, yanked out a small sump pump and hose, and tossed it at Jones, a short, redheaded man with a temper that matched his hair. "Get this in the pond. It's time to stop playing around."

Jones waded into the pond and set the pump in position while Jelly started its portable generator. She stuck the nozzle in one of the half-empty buckets and mentally crossed her fingers. She'd hesitated in using it—didn't want pink hash filling up the buckets instead of baby blobbies—but they were running out of time. Besides, judging by the looks of her team, the baby blobs were probably tougher than the manual implied.

The sump pump chugged, sucking up pond water and vomiting it out through the nozzle. Water splurted into the bucket, followed by a soft *thup, thup, thup*.

"Behind you!" Shark called. Automatically, Jelly whipped the hose around and peppered a gremlin with blobbie-laced water. The fuzzy little beast screamed and skittered back into the compound.

"Yippee ki yay, you fuzzy little . . . " The hose bucked in her hands, and Jelly pointed the end at an empty bucket just in time to send a dozen pink blobbies hurtling into another bucket.

"McKenzie, line up the buckets," she commanded, moving the hose as McKenzie dropped another bucket into line.

According to the blob "manual," baby blobs were born in water so they wouldn't be squished flat as a pancake by the heavy gravity when they left their momma's womb. They remained semi-aquatic creatures until they got large enough to be able to maintain their somewhat-upright, mostly saggy, state.

Transporting the babies in buckets of water wasn't high on Jelly's efficiency list, so she and Shark had put their heads together for a solution. Cook had confirmed their conclusions, and Jelly'd commandeered the camp's entire supply of gelatin mix.

"Filmore, grab the gelatin. Time to make like a pastry chef and mix." Jelly pointed at the bucket she'd just filled. "Throw in three packs, and let's see if Cook's better at chemistry than food prep."

Filmore dumped three packets of QuickGel into the first bucket as Jelly finished filling the second one and moved to the third. Cook had assured her that this particular gelatin didn't need hot water to dissolve or cold temps to harden. QuickGel had been created for use in adverse climates, its sole purpose being to provide a handy energy snack during action-intensive missions.

Figured the flavor of the day was cherry. Pink blobbies in red Jello. Added a rather decorative touch to the mission.

While Filmore opened more packets and dumped them into the next bucket, Jones grabbed the first bucket, tipped it upside down, and shook. One small, pink drop plopped into the mud. Time someone called that gelatin by its proper name—InstaGel.

Jones smacked the bucket's bottom, making it fold up and release the blobby-filled gelatin round with a *slurp*. Shark quickly wrapped the jiggly lump in duraplastique—a breathable food wrap that had been designed to protect supplies slated for drop into inhospitable territory—then sealed the package, and slid it into one of the waiting backpacks. Slick as snot, and twice as tasty.

"Sarge, you better take a look at this," Jones said.

Jelly glanced over her shoulder as she moved the hose to another bucket. Jones held up a freshly wrapped package, wriggling in his grasp. A tiny, pink bubble-face pressed against the duraplastique.

And bit down.

The flexible duraplastique had survived crashes that had practically obliterated everything else—kinda like cockroaches and certain petrified food products—so surely the blobby couldn't chew through the container . . . could it?

Jelly's stomach tightened as she saw the little troublemaker chomp through the gelatin surrounding it. If the blobbies ate all the gelatin, they'd end up flatter than silver-dollar pancakes, and judging by the little blob's voracity, the little buggers would eat their way to oblivion quicker than her uncle demolished a turkey dinner.

Time to get this show on the road.

A crack of thunder split the air just as a tree branch directly over Jelly's head shook and something round and smelling worse than a men's locker room fell into the pond, splashing water in all directions.

"Bomb!" someone shouted.

Jelly had never seen adult blobs—or humans—move so fast. One minute everyone was hanging out around the pond, the next minute she was the only one standing in the clearing, sump pump hose still in hand.

Nice to know her men had such quick reflexes. Not so nice knowing they were so quick to run from a rotten coconut.

Branches rustled again, and more coconuts plopped into the pond. Jelly dodged to one side, signaled Jones to turn off the pump, and circled her hand once in the air. "Round 'em up, boys. Time to move out."

Momma Blob, aka Princess Blobina, pitched a royal fit, farting, burping, and shrieking like a punctured basketball.

"Sounds like the majority of her babies are still in that pond," Shark said with a grimace.

Crap. Jelly glanced at the filled buckets, then at the packs sitting to one side. Her gut was telling her the coconuts had only been a diversion, but for what? "Filmore—how much gelatin is left?"

Filmore held up a small pile of packets and one bucket-size box. "Guess Cook thought we might get hungry."

"Dump 'em all in the pond. McKenzie, Smith—give him a hand."

The three men started dumping packets as Jelly turned to Jones and held out her hand. "Give me your sling and take a position on the other side of the pond."

Jelly picked up several moderately heavy rocks and tied them into the middle of the long, narrow webbing as Jones trotted around the pond. Then she tossed one end of the sling to Jones and watched the rocks sink.

"Shark. Your sling."

She repeated the act, walking around the pond until she stood at right angles to where the first sling lay before tossing an end of the second sling to Shark on the other side.

This time the rocks sank more slowly. Another couple of seconds, and both sling and rocks would've sat on the surface like mermaids waiting for a photo-op.

Less than a minute later, the entire pond had jelled solid.

"Smith—you're opposite Jones," she barked. She used her hands for the next command, flashing signals at the blobs hovering around the princess. Burp, Sneeze, Yawn, and Grumble broke away from the group, taking up position behind the men in charge of the slings. The blobs would watch their partner's backs in case the gremlins decided to show up again.

"Everyone pull on my mark." Jelly said. "If all goes as planned, we'll soon be holding the biggest bowl of jelly you've ever seen."

She switched the generator into air compressor mode, removed the hose from the sump pump, attached it to the compressor, and shoved the other end as deep under the gelled pond as she could. Then she switched the machine on.

And waited.

The air compressor jugged and groaned and air hissed through the hose. Just when Jelly started thinking there must be a leak somewhere, the entire pond heaved.

"On my mark . . . " She raised her hand.

With a ginormous sound somewhere between a hiccup and a burp, the pond exploded.

Bits of pink and red gelatin splatted the tree trunks, branches, and dirt. The entire space stank like an overripe fruit salad. Blobs farted, men shouted, and the princess shrieked.

And that's when the flying, black ninja gremlins attacked.

Jelly drew her pistol and fired, calmly picking off gremlin after gremlin. She flashed a series of hand signals to the waiting blobs. "Grumble, Barf, get the princess to the LZ!"

Slime slithered into the clearing, eyestalks waving once again. It was a wonder the little guy's eyestalks didn't get permanently tangled. It took Jelly a moment to decipher what it was saying: *"Danger! Run! Big bird went boom!"*

Big bird? Jelly flashed on an image of a giant, exploding yellow chicken. "What the . . . "

A gremlin dropped onto Slime's back and sank its teeth into the slug's neck. Slime reared back as Ryan dashed up. Yanking his pistol from his belt, he bashed the gremlin over the head. The gremlin released Slime, turning just in time to catch another blow on its cheek. Ryan kicked the fur-challenged creature away. "The transport— it just . . . "

Jelly's stomach clenched. What they'd heard a moment ago hadn't been thunder. "I've got it, Corporal."

The gremlin attack had stopped for the moment, but Jelly could see spiteful, black eyes glittering high in the trees. Jones, the medic, was still busy attending to the bundled blob babies, so she gathered Slime into her arms, checking the agitated slug's wounds while she determined their next move.

The major portions of the quivering pond were still intact, although it'd been split in four almost-exact pieces, kind of like giant, jiggly pie slices. Lumps of pink and red gelatin skittered around in the dirt. Pain stabbed her ankle and Jelly kicked instinctively, sending a pink bubble flying back into the shaking mass.

"Jones, bag the escapees and toss them in with whatever Filmore's wrapping up." Jelly pointed at the tiny, half-flattened lumps squiggling around on the ground and used her foot to gently send another blobbie flying after its brother, its tiny teeth scratching against her boot before it went airborne.

"Filmore, Buckman, get the DP and wrap the big chunks as best you can. Ryan, gather everyone's slings and ready them to carry the packages." Jelly started as an icy wave spread across her arms—right beneath Slime. Cradling the slug against her body, she pulled her right arm free. Goo ran down her forearm and across her hand, dripping into the dirt. She scowled and scuffed the spot with her boot. The little guy had definitely lost control of some bodily function.

"Slime . . . " Her voice rose in warning, then stopped. The slime-covered dirt was sticking to her boot like she'd glued it in place. She tried to kick the dirty glob off against a nearby boulder.

The dirt glob didn't move.

Jelly stared down at the slug. "Slime?" Both eyestalks, wide with fear, turned her way. "What's going on with your . . . goo?"

The slug's eyestalks drooped a moment, as if thinking. He wriggled and squirmed until Jelly set him down, then crept across the dirt at an even pace, leaving a shiny trail in his wake. His eyestalks waved, forming distinctive patterns that Jelly found she could actually read. "Peace. Calm. Smooth."

Then he raced around, eyestalks waving frantically. Jelly squinted at the slug's trail. It wasn't shiny and smooth anymore. It looked kind of . . . sticky.

Slime signaled frantically. "Anger. Fear. Sticky."

"Well, I'll be damned," she said. "Slug glue."

Slime slowed to a stop in front of her. Jelly frowned. Now was not the time to ponder slug slime. She stored the anomaly in the back of her brain and barked out more commands. "Ryan, take over for Jones. Jones, help Shark with the packs. I want them unloaded and the frames pulled out. Time for everyone to suit up."

As if to confirm her orders, the tree branches swayed and heaved and shook as coconuts started flying again.

Where did they get those things? Jelly wondered, dodging a hard-shelled missile. She answered her own question: *The same place they'd gotten whatever blew up the transport.*

Experience had taught her that battle plans melt faster than a piece of chocolate on a hot day, so Jelly *always* had a backup plan, and sometimes two or three. Shark and she had decided on an alternative LZ during their insertion. Now all they needed was something to distract the furry monkey-demons while the princess and her royal blobbies got to safety—

Jelly got one of those you-gotta-be-insane flashes of inspired craziness that could either save the day . . . or send it right down the tubes. "McKenzie, Smith—take over princess detail. Blobs—you're with me. Shark, get everyone to LZ2. The blobs and I are going to *negotiate.*"

She turned to her scout. "Hey, Slime." The slug lifted its eyestalks and studied her face. "Make a bunch of your trails—the sticky ones— in front of that entrance, then go help Shark." Jelly fired into the heaving branches, and another dead gremlin crashed to the ground.

Slime started racing around. They were going to have to come up with a different name for his—its species. Centauri slugs were definitely a different critter from the slugs back on Earth.

Before Slime could turn the entire breeding ground into a giant fly strip, however, the flying black ninja gremlins pounced again. One of the gremlins near the compound entrance got a surprised look on its pinched face when it tried to move and found its feet glued to the ground.

"Everyone move out!" Jelly cried. "To me, blobs. To me!"

She could stand here and fire into the trees all day, knocking out a gremlin here and there and sending the enemy back into hiding. But she didn't want to take the chance that they would go after the team guarding the princess instead of dodging her bullets.

Jelly snatched a coconut from the ground and hurled it into the trees.

The gremlins went berserk, jumping up and down and hurling coconuts at her as fast as they could find them.

She ducked and signaled for the blobs to follow her as she slid into the depression that used to be a pond. "We're going to play a little game of Catch-and-Return," Jelly said, waving the blobs close. "You guys catch the coconuts, and I'll return them."

Burp *urped* several times, his eyes round and anxious.

"No, they're not bombs. Just plain old coconuts."

The blobs did a great job of stopping the incoming missiles, passing the coconuts through their bodies, and setting them at Jelly's feet. Jelly snatched up the missiles and hurled them back at the gremlins. The distraction worked. Instead of chasing the escaping team, the gremlins screeched in fury and tried to bury the pond in a storm of coconuts. Jelly threw them back as fast and as hard as she could. Wasn't hard enough to keep a gremlin down. Still, she was keeping them occupied, and that was what mattered.

Jones flashed a hand signal before disappearing down a broad path after the main group. Jelly let out a breath of relief. Princess and babies were on their way to the final extraction point. Her arm only had to hold out a few more minutes and . . .

Something wriggled up her leg and she stifled a scream. She started to draw her pistol, then stopped as two eyestalks poked out of the space between her legs and the blob in front of her.

Slime didn't give her time to comment. He pulled his tail free, plopped it on top of the blob to Jelly's right, then plopped his "head" on the blob to Jelly's left.

And waited, eyestalks watching her expectantly.

Jelly got another flash of insight, and wondered if the little slug was some kind of telepath. She lifted a coconut and set it on Slime's middle. His eyestalks waved like a cheerleader on a winning football team. Carefully, Jelly pulled the coconut back until Slime slapped his eyestalks together and let them bounce apart. She let go and the coconut sailed through the air, nailing a gremlin who'd been staring at their strange contortions, and knocking it out cold.

Jelly let out a triumphant shout and loaded the slug sling again, returning the gremlins' attack with a barrage of hard-slung coconuts.

Her mental clock calculated how long it would take Shark to get the extraction set up. That brilliant, adrenalin-addled brain of his had used the blobs' ability to assimilate an object in order to move it from one place to another, and created an escape mode she wouldn't have believed if she hadn't seen herself.

Internal airframes.

Wingsuits were a standard part of the team's equipment, but the blobs didn't have an internal skeleton, and couldn't utilize a wingsuit like a human. Shark had taken care of that. Now the blobs were just as air-mobile as the humans.

And since their squad was paired up blob to man, he'd designed a backpack that could be dismantled into two basic components: airframes for the blobs and wingsuits for their partners.

Today, his system would be put to the test.

Suddenly, the coconuts stopped raining, and the clearing fell silent.

Jelly studied the trees closely. Looked like the gremlins had declared a timeout. No use wasting a prime opportunity to score a goal. She quickly popped Slime off his blob "posts" and set him down.

"Break right," she ordered. The blobs to her right parted and she raced up the bank. The blobs bounded up the bank behind her, humping up the slope like elephant seals on hot sand . . .

Just as the gremlins made a full-out ground assault.

Blobs bleated and burped, and Slime's eyestalks crossed in terror as gremlins swarmed into the clearing like giant hairy ants, stabbing at anything that moved, including each other, with finger-long needles that flashed like miniature sabers—the same kind of needles they'd used during the attack on the blob chieftain.

"Get behind me!" Jelly ordered, pulling her pistol and firing into the advancing horde. The ragged front line dropped like fuzzy stones, but instead of racing off like scared chickens the way they'd previously reacted, the remaining gremlins screeched in fury and darted straight at Jelly. Something flashed to her right, and she snapped a side kick out just in time to divert an incoming needle.

She'd intended to hold off the gremlins by firing strategic shots as the blobs humped out to the LZ, but it looked like the gremlins hadn't been as spooked as she'd thought. They'd just been waiting for backup.

She needed to find another way to get the blobs out of the clearing. And fast.

A coconut plopped to the ground a few feet away and slowly tumbled into the evacuated pond. Jelly stared at the coconut as she ejected the magazine from her pistol and reloaded, a glimmer of an idea gelling in her mind. She fired another couple shots, then snatched Slime off the ground and tucked him under one arm as she fired again, then switched the pistol to full-auto. "Slime, hold tight and help me get these troops moving."

Slime's eyestalks tapped together twice, and then he looked down at the blobs.

"Okay, blobs—pile onto me and flatten out, like you're going to squeeze underneath one of the fence wires back at training camp."

Slime signaled with his eyestalks and the blobs pressed in around her like rippling mounds of duraplastic. Jelly kept her weapon hand outstretched and her finger on the trigger, releasing a short bursts of bullets into the raging gremlins. A mild sense of claustrophobia swarmed over her as the blobs stretched upward, encasing her in shoulder-to-toe blobbiness.

The bullet storm had stopped the gremlins—for now. Some screeched at her from the trees, some poked at the pile of bodies her attack had left behind. The screeches grew into screams as the horde worked itself back into a frenzy. A coconut struck Jelly's stomach and she flinched, expecting to feel the blow, but the blob wrapped around her waist didn't even twitch as the missile bounced off its rubbery skin and fell harmlessly to the ground.

Time to bid their not-so-friendly hosts goodbye.

Jelly backed up a step and winced. Probably should have told the blobs not to wrap themselves around her legs . . . Her foot struck something she couldn't see, and she flopped backward onto her blob-covered butt.

The gremlins surged forward, screeches turning into high-pitched growls.

Jelly took one look at the ugly, snarling faces, pulled her weapon arm tight across her blobby belly . . .

And started to roll.

It took Shark, Jones, and McKenzie to stop Jelly and her makeshift blob armor from rolling right off the cliff. The entire landscape dropped away in a vertical plunge that made her stomach turn. The jagged cliff dropped to a forest of trees far below that looked more threatening than welcoming.

The blobs peeled off her like skin from a fruit, humping over to where their airframes were laid out.

Jelly shrugged into her own wingsuit as the princess farted, burped, and hiccupped like the world was coming to an end. Didn't need an interpreter for that one. Her royal blobbiness was throwing a royal fit.

"You can stay here if you'd like." Jelly pointed at the ruckus in the trees behind them as she fastened her straps. The speed she'd gained during the "rollout" had gained them a little time, but not much. "Or you can come with us."

"Fly the friendly skies," Shark said, keeping a perfectly straight face while Jelly glared at him.

Yawn hopped up behind the princess and banged into her, shoving her royal butt onto her airframe. The princess scowled, wrinkling her bulbous nose up so tight her eyes squeezed closed. Then she let everything drop loose—the blob equivalent of a sigh?—and primly settled down.

As one, the blobs rose, wriggling and shifting until they all looked like rubbery pink kites.

"Sound off," Shark called.

One by one the squad reported in, humans with their names, blobs by sound.

"Launch at will." Shark raised his arm and dropped it.

Jones picked up Burp and hurled the blob off the cliff. The other team members followed at three-second intervals. Then the men each picked up an end of a gel-loaded sling and leapt after their falling comrades. Slime waved his eyestalks at her from his seat in one of the slings.

"No playing around," Jelly yelled as she moved to the princess's side. Slime lifted his tail in answer.

Jelly thought the princess was going to give her a hard time, but her royal blobbiness raised her nose and allowed herself to be flung. Jelly sent the princess sailing out over the tree and studied the horde of screaming gremlins racing towards her.

There was something off about this whole mission. Who had destroyed their transport? Who had supplied the gremlins with stinky, old coconuts? And where had all those pointy needles come from?

Somehow this was all tied in to the attempt made on the blob chieftain's life, she was sure of it. Right now she had more questions than answers, but the answers would come—later. Hopefully, they wouldn't run into any more surprises.

Jelly leaned out over the yawning space . . .

And jumped.

Time seemed to stop as she was suspended in mid-air for a brief instant. Then time caught up, and wind screamed past her ears. She felt the first updraft catch her wings and lift her slightly. Sighting on the river miles below, she took her bearings, and then checked on her team.

This would be the first time any of her team had jumped with a load. The first time the blobs had jumped from this height with the airframes.

So far, everything looked good.

Until she realized the tiny form far below wasn't anyone in a wingsuit or airframe.

It was Slime.

And he was falling.

Damn it! Jelly pulled in her arms, closed up the space between her legs, and dove—

Just as something exploded right where her head had been.

Startled, Jelly pulled her arms in tighter, sending her into a swoop, matching the speed of a plummeting hawk. Another explosion splatted the faceplate of her helmet with pebbles from the rock face.

"Evasive action!" she screamed into her headset. "Cover the blobs!"

The airframes that stretched the blobs into pink kites also made them flying ducks.

And Slime . . .

Jelly had almost reached the little slug when another blast knocked her into the side of the cliff. Pain exploded as a jagged rock slammed into her ribs.

Trees stretched up from the ground not so far below now, looking more like giant spears than places where birds could roost. The river's roar drowned out the air whistling past her helmet.

Jelly set her teeth against the pain and breathed as deeply as she could without passing out. Stretching her arms and legs out wide, she banked hard left just in time to put herself directly below Slime.

"Glue, Slime! Glue!" A cold sensation trickled down Jelly's back. She raised her head just enough to clear a particularly tall tree—

And got caught in a downdraft as she sailed out over the river.

Now would have been the time she'd pull the ripcord and deploy her landing chute, but that wasn't an option, not if Slime were to survive the landing. She should've thought about that before telling the slug to glue himself to her back. If she deployed it now, he'd be ripped away like so much shredded cheese.

She only had a moment to think as the river flashed beneath her.

Water landings had not been recommended when Jelly went through basic wingsuit training, even in an atmosphere as heavy as this one. Yes, velocity was reduced in the heavy, moisture-laden air. But down was down, and once a certain velocity had been reached, flesh-meeting-solid object generally met with the same kind of ending—one that didn't favor the flesh.

There was one way they both might make it. The end of the river flashed by, widening into an enormous fiord that eventually opened out to the sea. She raised her head and shoulders, flared enough to slow her speed as much as she dared, then dropped her head, grabbed her helmet between her hands, brought her elbows tight against her sides, and dropped her feet so her body formed a pike position—

All Jelly remembered was a blinding flash of pain, then she was coughing, struggling to clear water from her nose and mouth. She blinked and blinked again, certain she was hallucinating as a pink kite sailed over her head.

Where the hell was she and how did she get in the water?

She caught sight of a parachute settling down on the water's surface not too far away and memory flooded back.

"Slime?" Jelly thrashed around, struggling to yank the clinging wingsuit from her legs. She took a deep breath and ducked beneath the surface, pulling off her boots and unzipping the wingsuit web between her legs. Then she popped back up and looked around again. "Slime!"

Something tapped the back of her head. Jelly whipped around. "Slime?"

Again the tap on her head. Jelly reached back and felt the slug's wet body. "Hey, little guy. Looks like that glue really works!"

A double tap on the back of her head.

Across the water, she could hear her men reporting in, followed by an astonishing amount of bodily noises. Shark swam up next to her. "Blob Squad, all present and accounted for. I've called for transport."

"And the princess?"

"Her royal blobbiness is safe and sound."

"And the babies?"

"I'd suggest we get out of the water, sir," Jones said, swimming up behind Shark. He motioned all around them with his head. "The immediate environment is about to get extremely uncomfortable." He took off without waiting for her command.

The rest of the squad was headed towards shore, the blobs, for once, leading the way. They'd disgorged their airframes and slithered along the surface like round snakes.

Slime tapped her shoulder as Jelly stared at the pink bubbles bobbing in their wake.

Shark headed toward shore. "I'm not sure what you're waiting for," he said. "Unless you like feeding the fishes."

Two plus two finally added up as Jelly followed Shark. Whether it had been the impact or whether the baby blobs had actually managed to chew through the supposedly indestructible wrapping was immaterial. The squad had accomplished their mission. The baby blobs were back in the water, creating blobby mayhem . . .

She started as one of Slime's eyestalks crept into her peripheral vision, urging her forward with jerky waves. She splashed a handful of water at the little slug still clinging to her back and waded out of the river.

Nanny Duty was over—for now. Life could go back to the same old routine . . . with one exception. "You and I are going to have a long talk about you charging head over pseudopod into trouble, Private Slime."

Unearthing the Undying Armor

by Elizabeth Ann Scarborough

"Welcome to the first episode of Kirsty Kilgore, Rescue Archaeologist," the presenter with the wet face and rain-drenched blonde ponytail said, her voice still holding a trace of soft Scottish burr. She wore a battery-powered microphone that looked a bit like a hearing aid to help her words carry over the traffic din and ambient industrial noise in this part of Glasgow, as well as the thunder rumbling overhead and the pounding rain swelling the Clyde to flood proportions. Over the crew neck of her rain-soaked *I Dig Archaeology* t-shirt, she sported a necklace of mummy beads with an amulet that looked like a replica of the ancient rune for "discovery."

"You see behind me what may look like a construction site, but is in fact the cleared lot of a Victorian shoe factory, soon to be a food court featuring American fast-food stores." (The latter part was added to the script for economic reasons.) "However, there, toward the hole you see in the middle," she said, turning to point to the hole in question. "Two days ago, a backhoe popped the top off what appears to be an ancient tomb. A real bummer for those of us who wish to study all evidence of ancient civilizations, but there was compensation, for the tomb was occupied."

Break for commercial. All about the supposedly culturally conscious purveyors of burgers, pizzas, Pad Thai, and southern fried chicken that would soon be taking over the premises, and how determined they were to preserve national treasures, etc., etc.

Faster than should have been possible, the fast-food stores owning the construction site had not only met their legal obligations by hiring a team of archaeologists to explore and document the site and remove all significant finds, but had contacted the BBC, which had rapidly put together a television show.

The national network already had a team of old duffers rattling on in a scholarly way about tiny finds in pastoral settings, but this one was in the middle of Glasgow. The Americans wanted a "cute chick" as spokeswoman for the dig, the better to enhance their brand identification. Kirsty, a Scot who also held degrees in media presentation and theatre, had been picked as a sort of "Miss Archaeology" from the post-grad students at Robert Gordon University in Aberdeen. The speech training had helped soften her regional accent, but her scrappy Border Reiver heritage had stood her in good stead throughout grad school, and she counted on it to help her navigate the reefs of the television world as well. Her archaeological specialty was ancient jewelry and textiles, and she'd always thought she'd work in Egypt or perhaps Greece, but instead was soaking beside the Clyde, talking into a camera held by a temporary hire.

She was not disappointed by the find, however. The tomb held something—someone—totally unexpected. Possibly it would be so wonderful as to be taken away from her, but she did not intend to see that happen. The network had shifted the duffers from the other show around so they were here as consultants, with the view that they would add erudite authenticity and also provide dialogue.

"Unfortunately, the tomb site is so muddy at the moment that for me to take you there would destroy much of it, and that would defeat the purpose, wouldn't it? Instead, here we have some shots from when it was first uncovered." The narration from the beginning of the dig had already been taped, so she moved while it played. This whole sequence was to be edited and actually shown much later, to avoid gawkers and possibly thieves. The network had rented an adjacent warehouse to provide quarters.

At the door of the posh, climate-controlled examining room the sponsors had provided to preserve the integrity of the find, Kirsty paused dramatically. "No one, *no* one, has ever seen anything like this—at least not in our time." Her voice dropped to a hush as she stepped through the door opened by a crewmember, snapped on a pair of gloves, eschewing the mask customarily worn in such circumstances, and stood beside the examining table and the fabulous figure upon it.

"The tomb was the resting place of this gorgeously clad—armored, actually—woman. Inside this amazing carapace of golden disks and lozenges stamped with talismanic symbols and held together with thousands of small clay beads set in significant runic patterns, is this mysterious ancient Amazon. Queen? Princess? Warrior? Priestess? Goddess? One might even speculate—alien? We'll know more once we've had the opportunity to examine her."

At this point, she faltered. According to the hastily devised script, the duffers should have been standing around the table so she could consult with them, asking such brilliant questions as, "Who might she have been?" "What might she have thought about coming to light—or, okay, rain—in modern Glasgow?"

But no one was in the room except her and the cameraman, one Rob Cruikshank. Something gritted underfoot as she walked across the pre-fab floor of the chamber. Really! The purpose was to prevent contamination, wasn't it? Couldn't someone have been bothered to give the place a wee sweep?

This was the first time she'd seen the figure since it had been moved from the grave. She started to describe it, and stopped when she heard the low keening that seemed to emanate from the corpse. She bent over the head so that the sound would register on her mic. "Hello, this is new," she said. She looked up into the camera lens. "Can you get that, Rob?"

"Get what?" he asked.

"Clean your ears, man! The sound!"

"What sound?"

"That kind of keening coming from her," she said.

"Yer daft," he said.

"Yer deaf," she replied, reverting to her non-TV presenter tones and trusting it would get edited out. Yet she spoke softly, both to allow the keening from the corpse to register and because the sound, enormous development that it was, kind of freaked her out.

True, as a professional student of the past, she was supposed to be on good terms with the dead, but generally they seemed a little deader than the body producing the noise. She couldn't let her nerves get the best of her, however. Now that the tomb's contents had been photographed and measured on site and were in the warehouse, the construction team could get back to work. At least, once the rain stopped. In the meantime, the danger of flooding this close to the river was quite worrying. But if all went well, they'd meet the deadline for the show's debut.

Of course, most importantly, she needed to reap all possible information from the Amazon before the competition could swoop in and make it all old news, if the threatened floods in the Clyde didn't sweep it all out to sea first. So although they'd started shooting, as if they were releasing the news for now, the project was being kept as hush-hush as it could be, and Jaime the producer decided they needed a code name.

"She's the Ancient Amazon," one of the duffers had said.

"A mouthful," Jaime Carter, the producer, had protested. "And we can't call her AA, or she'll be mistaken for the substance abuse program. Call her something easy. Susie. That'll do. We call her Susie from now on, and the dig Project Susie. At least off camera."

They'd finished disinterring her only a couple of hours ago, during a break in the rain, moving her to the climate-controlled area inside the dome just before nightfall. The room's added insulation also muted the outside traffic, industrial noise, and thunderstorms that had moved in almost immediately after the discovery.

The keening noise had begun as soon as Kirsty and Rob entered the room, increasing in volume the longer they were there. For some reason, Kirsty thought of it as Susie's death song. Rob, as was his custom, did not appear to be thinking at all.

"Gotta piss," he said, and left. She suspected there would be input involved from the flask in his pocket as well as the declared excretory function.

"The low, keening sound you hear now seems to be Susie singing," Kirsty told the unmanned camera. "Perhaps some trick in how her body was preserved allows air currents to penetrate certain cavities that emit it as noise, but the hairs on *my* neck are certainly raised.

"The armor is unlike any I have seen before," she continued. "It has some similarities to Asian styles, although they are often lapped to emulate scales. This has fairly wide gaps between the metal bits, where the connecting colored beads are arranged in identifiable runic patterns. These pre-date the Norse runes of the sort available in New Age and occult shops." The runes she could make out were similar to the Norse ones, however, especially the ones meaning "life," "protection," "death," and, like the one she wore around her neck, "discovery." The armor would fetch a pretty penny on eBay, for sure.

Kirsty had no doubt it would end up there, if the sponsors and network execs could manage it, to help defray production costs once the segment was filmed. For all the claims they made in the media about the authenticity of their digs, these people weren't exactly picky about scholarly purity.

"Pretty in a kind of creepy, primitive way, isn't it?" Jaime had asked, putting his arm around her shoulders as they watched the body being gently lifted onto a stretcher.

"Leave off," she told him. She bet Susie wouldn't have put up with that back in the day. Whoever she was and wherever she was from, Susie had obviously been a tough chick with the armor to prove it, even if the armor was not exactly what you'd call sturdy. The average Kevlar vest had it beat by a long shot. The gold in the disks and rectangles was as flimsy and soft as gold often was, and the pretty, runic patterns in the clay beads connecting the metal weren't likely to stop so much as a butter knife, never mind a bullet.

"I want every bead and every link measured and photographed," Jaime said, withdrawing his arm. "We'll need to be able to make an exact copy."

Kirsty rolled her eyes. Examine the body, star in a TV show, decipher the runes in the tomb and reproduce an ancient armor. Piece of shortcake.

So, before Susie could be spirited off site and properly examined by more learned experts with more sophisticated methods, Kirsty was photographing the intricate armor link by link while Rob photographed her photographing it, to further the illusion that Kirsty Kilgore, Rescue Archaeologist, took personal responsibility for the integrity of her rescued artifacts. At least he realized she was capable of real work, and not just a figure and a head.

Before every photograph, she had to delicately dislodge any soil or, um, bodily fluids between the beads and links. "The Ancient Amazons apparently took good care of themselves," she told the camera. "The subject's musculature is remarkably well-defined.

"Bugger. There it is again." She broke off her narrative as the keening grew so loud she could barely hear herself think, much less talk.

Rob had returned to the camera.

"What?" he asked, his voice almost drowned out by the din.

"That sound. It's coming from her. You have to hear it now surely?"

"Yer a nutter," he said.

Kirsty jammed her fingers into her ears, but it did nothing to diminish the sound. It whined through her brain, taking on a rhythm that rose and fell to deeper, gonglike notes. But evidently Rob did not hear the same thing. So, was it all in her head? Toxic gasses from ancient tombs could cause disease or even death, according to the theory about what happened to the victims of King Tut's Curse, but auditory hallucinations from an open pit in Glasgow?

"Excuse me," she said, and left the special chamber for the outer structure. The volume of the keening was dampened somewhat outside the chamber, but it was replaced by a sound much more frightening—thunder, very close. Crivvens! That was some storm! But if the Clyde flooded, and if they were still inside the warehouse, they could be in trouble. And Susie's pit would be beyond salvaging. Which brought up the question of how the ancient Amazon had escaped past floods. The damp climate alone should have caused a great deal more degeneration of the corpse.

With the outer dome empty at this late hour, she and Rob were the only living humans at risk. But Kirsty was appalled at the thought of what might happen to Susie, newly salvaged just in time to be swept out to sea and lost forever without anyone learning the truth about her—and without her discovery having a huge impact on Kirsty's future and fortune.

As she returned to the inner chamber, opening the door, she caught a brief glimpse of Rob draped across Susie's precious, fragile corpse, his hand clutching her armored bosom, before an explosion drowned out the noise in her head. The lights flared and blinked out, and the inner chamber immediately grew warmer. Lightning hitting a transformer? The keening/chanting was louder than the explosion had been now, and she shouted over it, "You are *so* fired!"

But when she fumbled in her bag for a flashlight and clicked it on, Rob was nowhere to be seen. A pile of ash dimmed the golden armor on Susie's left breast and flaked off onto the floor.

Kirsty shined the flashlight beam on the camera, thinking to see Rob Cruikshank behind it, but she felt slightly sick, suspecting why she wouldn't. It wasn't that she'd miss him especially. He apparently had been some kind of a necrophiliac, and she'd been alone with him at night in a deserted warehouse. Anyone capable of copping a feel from a woman at least a millennium old was capable of anything. But the dead cameraman could be a lesser problem than what had killed him.

The chant rose and fell as she worked and, perhaps because it no longer blended into one long sound, she was sure she understood some of the individual words and phrases now, though she had never heard them pronounced before. Although she read ancient runes, they weren't exactly the kind of language one used to chat with friends.

Taking out her cell phone, she pressed the panic button that called Jaime, the producer.

"Jaime, we're going to need another camera operator. Try to get a lassie if you can."

"Where's Cruikshank? Drunk again?"

She hesitated. That was a much more plausible explanation than the one she suspected, and had no doubt been true prior to his atomization. "I suppose so."

"Never mind then. I'll deal with it myself for the rest of this segment and find someone in the morning."

"Or you could stay in bed and I could go to my own and take this up again in the morning."

"No time. The river's rising, and the council is suspicious and breathing down our necks. They'll want to schedule the site once we report our findings, and she'll be lost to us."

She'd tried to stop him, hadn't she?

She looked down at the armored corpse, dead and innocent-seeming, but with its chant still pounding through her head. "If you've something to say, I wish you'd just say it and be done with it," she told the figure. "You are giving me quite the headache."

While waiting, she continued photographing, drawing, trying to decipher the runes. Susie certainly wasn't Roman, Thracian, Dacian, Greek, Norse, or any of the other races that had invaded or passed through Scotland or England, nor was her armor British and certainly not Pictish. "I've no idea who you are or where you're from or what you were doing in a grave beneath a shoe factory. I don't suppose you could give me a wee hint, could you?"

But by then Jaime was there, to take Rob's place behind the camera. "Any clues yet as to the identity of our guest?"

"Offhand, I'd say she's not Scottish."

"Have you peeked beneath the armor?" he asked. "If we had some idea of her coloring or bone structure, it would be a start. The river is already up on the banks, lapping the bottom of the bridge. We'll need to move her to the museum soon to protect the find, but I wish we had a big finish for the show. That armor is incredible, though."

"It is that."

"Let's remove it and make a start on the exam now. Have you recorded it sufficiently that you can mend it if it breaks when we take it off?" He didn't wait for her to answer. He searched for a tool and set to work on the armor.

"I think so, but . . . "

The chant in her ears once more rose to a scream. Kirsty looked from Jaime to the armor-clad corpse. The bit of armor he touched blazed blue suddenly, and Jaime slumped and disintegrated into a pile of ash similar to what Kirsty's Wellies had been tracking all over the room that night.

Without thinking, Kirsty yelled, over the rising chant. "Stop that now, you!"

The chant took on an interrogatory and rather hurt tone.

"See here, I understand that you don't like men, but you're doing me out of a job. That's my boss you've cremated, and while he was a bit of a sociopathic git, this is the best job I've ever had or am ever likely to be offered, so I'd appreciate it if you'd lay off. This 'Mummy's Curse' business is a tad old-fashioned, don't you think?" She realized that the Amazon herself was old-fashioned—extremely so—and she was gibbering at it. Susie lay there, as she had all along, and her armor as intriguing as ever but no longer blue in any respect.

"Thank you very much for not smiting me as well," Kirsty added hastily. "It must have been maddening to lie in the ground all these years, but if you're bored and want something to do, you might explain who you are exactly and what you're doing here."

The chanting rose again, more agitated than before, or was it only Kirsty's own agitation she was projecting onto the Amazon? This whole job had seemed like a dream, especially once they found the body. Instead of a pretty face leading a somewhat dull television show, Kirsty would make history, be asked to publish papers, even books, and give talks for thousands of dollars. She could choose her digs, and possibly have an acting career besides if she wished. But now, because the corpse in question was a wee bit homicidal, it was all not just slipping away, but being yanked from her.

"Really," she muttered, "I do think you owe me some answers. I'm guessing your reaction to Jaime might have been based somewhat on him wanting to part you from your armor, is that right?"

Susie's eyes opened. They were the blazing blue of the armor's death rays, but without the actual blaze. The chanting words shape-changed from one language to the next before settling for an ancient form of Gallic. "Aha!" Kirsty cried. "I know you're not a Scot, but perhaps you were a trader or invader who came up the Clyde and learned the language from the locals, is that right?"

Kirsty put her microphone on again and hoped the camera was still running, even though there was no longer someone to run it.

"This is Kirsty Kilgore, Rescue Archaeologist, live from our temporary headquarters in Glasgow. Something extraordinary has happened. The being discovered in the tomb beneath the shoe factory is not, in fact, dead. She has rendered two men who offended her so, however. I have been hearing her voice in this room, but up until recently, was unable to understand the meaning of her words.

"Since the audience cannot hear the words she speaks in my head, I will translate as she answers a few questions. You don't mind answering some questions, do you, pet?" she asked. "I am assuming, since you disintegrated my producer, and again I am assuming your motives for doing so, but as I understood it, you took exception to his proposal to remove you from your armor and from this place. Is that correct?"

A slightly rattling nod from the figure on the table as the beads on her neck allowed it to move.

"So apparently you understood his words and possibly the words of the similarly disintegrated cameraman well enough without translation?"

Another nod.

"Remarkable! What a talented linguist you must be!" Kirsty really was impressed with the Amazon's communications skills, but also wished to be considered a friend. She felt she had a good chance of surviving, since she was not male, but she didn't yet know any of Susie's other issues, so knew she must tread carefully or be trod upon like the five—she knew now where the three duffers had gone when they vanished—victims before her. "Since your armor appears to be weaponized, you must pardon me, but our viewers will want to know, are you by any chance an alien being of some sort?"

Susie's head shook slightly but decisively from side to side.

"So much for that theory! Well then, if you're not an alien, can you tell us what is the secret of your destructive powers and your long life?"

Susie responded with the Gallic equivalent of, "It's magic, of course. If I told you more, I'd have to kill you."

"In that case, never mind. Magic is good enough for all of us, I'm sure. I couldn't help but notice, from the way you destroyed my producer when he suggested parting you from it, that you are very attached to this beautiful armor in which you're encased. Can you tell us more about that?"

"It's magic," Susie said again. And Kirsty thought that was all she'd get out of her, but then the Amazon added, "It is the Armor of Undying, worn by the Guardian of the Portal."

"The Armor of Undying? Catchy, that! So I take it then that *you* are the guardian of the portal?"

"That is correct."

"Which portal would that be?"

"The portal between this world and the world of fairy."

"Oh, *really?* So it really does exist?"

"Duh," the Amazon said quite clearly, and not in Gallic this time.

"I'm guessing here again, but does the magical nature of this armor of undying, as you call it, account for your incredible state of preservation?"

"Preserving the guardian is its function."

"I see. Little wonder then that you don't want to be parted from it. What is it like, the place beyond the portal?"

"Magic," Susie said. This time in English. She really was a quick study!

"Wonderful. You're speaking modern English with incredible speed."

"Yes," she said, repeating Kirsty's last words back to her almost like an echo. "With incredible speed."

"You say the place is the world of the fairies. Does that make you a fairy as well?"

Susie sat up and faced Kirsty as if she'd been a friend watching TV on the couch. She nodded. "Fairy as well."

"So your armor is fairy-made."

"Fairy-made."

"Why did you call it the armor of undying?"

"Protects guardian from dying so guardian can guard."

"Incredible. So are the runes carved into the gold bits and depicted by the beads are magic spells of protection?"

Another nod. "Spells of protection."

Kirsty was too fascinated to be frightened. "So, did those spells kill the men whose ashes litter this room, or did you?"

"Spells."

"Of course. Why?"

"First men awakened me." This was in Gallic. "They removed me from my post at the portal. They touched me. Second man touched me here." She pointed with her armor-gloved hand to her breast.

"Drunken, lecherous bastard," Kirsty said, and Susie echoed it.

"Third man would take Armor of Undying."

"Of course. But, and I hate to mention it, truly, believe me, and it was in the most admiring and respectful way possible, I assure you, but I have touched it, too."

"Why?"

"It's my job, but also, it's fabulous and I was curious about it, what it means and how it works."

While they chatted, the keening and chanting subsided entirely.

"You heard the Song of Undying. The others did not."

"Lucky for me!" Kirsty said. "It nearly drove me crazy. I thought it was your death song, the kind sung by dying warriors, and it was just the opposite. Fascinating."

The Ancient Amazon pointed to the figured plate helmeting the crown of her head and keened a note, or a word. Her fingers, knuckles guarded by golden rings, golden disk shielding the back of her hand, made beckoning gestures. "Sing," she said.

Kirsty sang, keened, whined, whatever you wanted to call it. She had heard it for hours and hours and found repeating it was second nature. It gave her quite an odd sensation.

Susie pointed to the neck plates and sang another note, encouraging Kirsty to emulate her. Kirsty's ear mic popped off and dropped to the floor. She stooped to pick it up as Susie sang several more notes. Her movements were awkward, her eyes not working properly, and the stupid earpiece had buried itself in someone-or-other's dust pile. No way was she digging through that and sticking the damn fool thing back in *her* ear.

She stood. Was that her bones making that rattling sound? She could hear nothing but the song now. On the other hand, she could see Susie much more clearly. With the armor inexplicably gone from her head and torso, Susie looked a bit like her.

More notes.

As they sang them, her limbs grew heavier, stiffer, more awkward, but nevertheless her feet rose from the floor and her body levitated to a horizontal position. The singing once more filled her skull to the exclusion of everything else. Susie's armored arms slid under her and guided, rather than carried, her out of the warehouse. This time, as the rain beat against her face, she felt it much less, and she heard no more traffic noises. All noise and sensation were drowned out by the Song of Undying.

"Good afternoon," the presenter said, squinting a little from the unfamiliar sun in her eyes. Her voice held a faint hint of some undefined, foreign accent. "Susie Guard, Rescue Archaeologist. As you can see, it's a gorgeous day for the construction work on this disappointing site to recommence. Sadly, the hole the digger uncovered was less productive than we'd hoped, and there was little to be rescued. The bits and bobs found in the earth here were probably washed up by floods over the years. Floods that, thankfully, are no longer a danger at present."

The figure buried beneath the site heard neither the broadcast nor the construction and traffic noises. She heard nothing but the Song of

Undying keening through her brain, her heart, her blood vessels, reverberating within the armor protecting her body from any exterior harm.

But in time—she had no idea how much time—Kirsty's brain began humming beneath the song. So, she'd been tricked. She might have figured that out ahead of time, as soon as Susie admitted to being a fairy, since any folklorist knew them for a tricky race, but like a proposal in a romantic novel, it had all happened so suddenly.

And here she was, the new guardian of the portal. Very well. So she wouldn't see daylight aboveground until the fast-food mall was dozed for a new structure, if then, and she might trick some other poor cow into taking her place, as she had taken Susie's.

Although access to the surface was denied her, she did not know what might lie on the other side of the portal she guarded. It seemed a reasonable hypothesis however that a guardian would have access to the world she guarded. Imagine being the first modern scientist to explore to world of fairy! What an amazing discovery that would be!

The secret must lie in the armor, and she would treat it as if it were a haunted house with secret passages. One of those passages would lead to an ancient and mysterious realm that was sure to be worth the bother of searching for it.

After all, she now had all the time in the world to find it.

Fashion and the Snarkmeisters

by Kristine Kathryn Rusch

You saw it, everyone did—one billion people, if the Nielsens are right (and they so rarely are)—that moment when the statue of a gigantic, naked, golden man toppled onto a scrum of snarky, microphone-wielding "reporters."

Oh, the dithering. Oh, the slow-motion replays. Oh, the terrified faces—right out of a Hollywood disaster movie.

No one was injured, at least not in the Hollywood-disaster-movie way. Expensive clothing was wrinkled and stained beyond repair. Reputations were ruined with little more than a few high-pitched squeals. And way too many people celebrated on social media.

I admit, had I been sitting at home watching the so-called debacle, I might have Tweeted something inappropriate and regretted it enough to delete my Twitter feed the next day.

But I wasn't at home. I was standing about fifty feet to the left, behind the emergency curtain at the edge of the red carpet, some special safety pins clamped in my teeth, a stronger-than-surgical-steel needle in my right hand, and a spool of special glittery metallic thread in my left.

I might have growled a cheer, but I knew better than to open my mouth and take a deep breath before shouting my huzzahs. After all, if I had swallowed those pins and lost my concentration . . .

Well, I get ahead of myself.

The Real Beginning

I have no idea if the snark started on May 16, 1929, in the Blossom Room at the Hollywood Roosevelt Hotel (make that May 17, the day after the Big Event) or if it started back at dawn of time when clothing stopped being optional.

What I do know is this: the word "award" came into common use in the Middle Ages, and if you look at mainstream dictionaries (the ones that don't accept magic), you'll see that award meant "decision after careful observation." Okay, fine. That sounds right—especially considering how much time we all spend watching the nominated films every year.

For the magical, though, the word "award" holds a deeper meaning. The word has the word "ward" in it, and wards, as we magical know, mean "to protect, guard."

You think you know where I'm going—especially since that gigantic golden man fell on those snarky faux-celebrities—but hang on. You have no real idea.

Because once upon a time, awards carried no bling. The bling that you were awarded, back in the day (Ancient Greece, Ancient Rome, Medieval Europe) came in the form of *trophies.*

And the word "trophy" comes from the French *trophée* which means "a spoil or prize of war."

Once trophies got associated with awards—and when all of that moved to Hollywood—the war metaphor becomes apt. Epic battles, gauntlets, victories, and defeats occur throughout award season. Someone's always on top, someone's always losing, someone doesn't fight hard enough, and someone always does something memorable, although not necessarily in a heroic way.

My earliest experiences with awards season came courtesy of my mother, whom you all know as Caro—so famous that all you need is the nickname.

Yeah, that Caro, whose real name had become unwieldy over the decades: Carolyn Sarah Brown Lodge Young Blondell Reynolds Taylor Mellon Torres.

As most of you probably know, Mother was the most nominated actress in the history of film awards—until Meryl Streep took the title a few years ago.

Mother: Beautiful, powerful, award-nominated, always at the top of her game—at least in public. And a mess in private.

The husbands saw that and fled, leaving me alone with her. Me, the only daughter of the most beautiful woman in the world.

I had three reactions to awards season.

> 1. I hated what they did to my mother.
> 2. I loooooooved the clothes.
> 3. I really, really *really* loved the clothes.

I was ten when I realized those things could be melded together.

The Bad Guys . . .

. . . are not the snarkmeisters who got crushed. Honestly, really, as much as we all love to hate them, these so-called "fashion experts" and/or "fashion bloggers" and/or "fashion critics" are really human beings with no real talent themselves (except wit, which, we can argue, is a talent which can be used for good or for harm).

Somehow these slimeballs manage to fill airtime in a way that draws viewers. People like Mother, who have only glamor (actually "glamour"—they're dusted with fairy magic that makes them shine even more than the rest of us), can't see the actual magic that fuels this stuff.

A crack between worlds opened when fashion became important (and much as I love it, I'm not giving you that history), and then the crack widened with each incursion of critics. The International Best Dressed List? Started in 1940, not coincidentally as the world marched to war.

The rise of television, the march of fashion magazines, the plummeting self-esteem of young girls—all a plot that came from the deepest, darkest magics.

Women hold the most innate power, as you all know (or maybe you don't) which is why forces always emerge to hold us down. As each victory occurs, another battle springs up elsewhere.

How do I know all this stuff? Because I inherited almost everything from my father. And no, you have no idea who my father is. In fact, in our house, he's called He Who Shall Remain Nameless, mostly because the press has not yet figured out that he exists. He was a one-night stand between the first Mellon marriage and the second Mellon marriage (Caro and Rafe Mellon divorced, then realized they couldn't live without each other—until they did).

Sadly, I look just like my father—short, squat, big ears, pointy chin. The press, the fashion bloggers, hell everyone on social media mentions this all the time—how sad it is that the daughter of the most beautiful woman in the world (okay, now they call her "one of" the most beautiful women in the world, but still) is an ugly duckling who never turned into a swan.

And no one, not even my mother, thinks that odd.

But I know why I'm here. Because He Who Shall Remain Nameless gifted me with magic—the one that makes things happen. (You don't think it was an accident that a guy as ugly as him slept with the most beautiful woman in the world, do you?)

Part of that magic I inherited is the ability to see other magic. Imagine my fear one night as I watched the clips of Events coverage and saw black shapes glowing behind the snarkmeisters. This was early 1990s, when the awards shows were still in their fashion infancy. In fact, most of the attendees chose their own clothes and the phrase "Red Carpet Fashion" didn't even exist.

The arrivals got shown in a clip montage as the Big Event started— and that's when I saw those shapes, hovering.

I was at home, where every good ten-year-old should be, eating popcorn with my nanny. Events nights were scary nights in the house, because they devastated Mother.

She always had the best *I'm so pleased you won instead of me* face, but when the cameras shut off, she didn't go to the after-parties. She came home and sobbed. By the next day—at least back then—she was all right, ready to return to whatever soundstage they had pried her out of to attend the Event, but the night of the ceremony, my mother was a hurt little girl who couldn't understand why no one liked her, really, really liked her.

The snarkmeisters had little power then. Usually they wrote for newspapers or fashion magazines, weeks after the Event, and their words had little impact. They didn't even hold microphones in those ancient days. Yet the black shadows stood behind them, sparkling with orange glimmers of evil intent.

And I couldn't help myself. I screamed.

Popcorn everywhere, a panicked nanny, a terrified child. Lots and lots of tears, which had to be quelled before Mother came home to indulge in hers.

I wasn't crying because I was sad, but because I was frightened.

That night marked the first time I voluntarily called He Who Shall Remain Nameless.

He chuckled, a raspy unpleasant sound that always reminds me of fingernails on a blackboard, and said, "Kid, the world's rich right now. So the darkness comes to feed. It'll get worse before it gets better. You can do two things. You can let it consume those delicate flowers like your mother, or you can figure out how to protect her."

And then he hung up.

By then, I had stopped crying and started thinking.

I couldn't convince Mother to drag me to the Events. She said They Weren't Appropriate For Children (while thinking that Children Weren't Appropriate For Events).

It took a confluence of things to lead me to my calling.

Thing The First

I turned thirteen. In Hollywood terms, there's nothing worse than hitting puberty as the ugly daughter of the most beautiful woman in the world. (In real world terms, there's a lot worse, but let's go with my reality, shall we?)

I mean, puberty is tough enough for girls. Parts bud, other parts spontaneously bleed, zits appear, and lifelong friends (going through the same hormonal nightmares) sometimes turn into mean girls.

Mother actually helped.

She said, "My darling, you look the way you look. None of us can take credit for our genetics. However, you can control the way that you present yourself. Think of your clothing as your armor. Every day is a battle to be beautiful, and if your face can't achieve it for you, then you make absolutely certain that your clothing will."

She taught me hair, make-up, asset management (not the financial kind) and how to make the most of the best parts and minimize the bad parts.

I surpassed her knowledge within a year, and was actually helping her dress—and about that point I discovered—

Thing The Second

—my talent for creation. If I made clothing, sewed my own dresses, embroidered my own jeans, I added the kind of glamour that my mother had. A wisp of fairy dust made the clothes just that much more beautiful.

It would take years of study, both magical and nonmagical, to actually learn true fashion—but I get ahead of myself.

Because I hadn't realized that I wanted to become one of the best fashion designers in the world until I discovered—

Thing The Third

—photos of a short, not-beautiful woman who died the year I was born. She had everything my mother never had—including eight Academy Awards (and more nominations than anyone except Walt Disney). She was a woman named Edith Head, the best costume designer the movies have ever known.

Not fair. She didn't design *costumes*. She created fashion. The kind that defined eras. Era after era after era.

If she could dress everyone from Mae West to Audrey Hepburn, finding the perfect clothes for those completely different bodies, then she truly was a magician—and one I aspired to be.

And that, my friends, was the true beginning of Warrior Woman Design.

At First . . .

I just wanted the rest of us—y'know, those of us with few assets to manage—to have equal footing in the workplace. Study after study after study has shown that beautiful people get higher pay, better jobs, and more press coverage than folks whose faces (and bodies) aren't symmetrical.

A little glamour on a business dress, and suddenly a plain woman becomes powerful. Or maybe she just thinks she does. Or maybe her inner beauty shines out.

Back then, I had no idea what made it work, but now I know. You feel beautiful, then you are beautiful. It's that simple, that profound.

I learned design at several fashion institutes and donated the clothes to needy women who didn't have the right outfit for a job interview. (We still have a branch that does that.)

And as I grew more confident, the world kept changing. Fashion became relevant. Places like *E! Entertainment Television* began four-hour shows live from the red carpet of every damn award ceremony ever held, and the snarkmeisters gained power. Or, in truth, the shadows that had started to fill the snarkmeisters' eyes and govern their dumpy, jealous, noncreative little bodies gained power.

The last year my mother dressed herself for the award-show gauntlet was the first year I got to accompany her on the red carpet, and now it's time to dump the cutesy little half-screenplay way I've been writing this thing.

Because that night was hell.

Through the magic of television, the red carpet looks big and beautiful and in our collective imaginations, everything around it is big and beautiful too.

But really—No.

Most neighborhoods in Los Angeles are not beautiful, sorry to say. They're flat retail markets with scuzzy 1960s or 1980s or 1990s buildings that look dated in that magic sunlight. The sidewalks are wide, the traffic backs up even on a good day, and the tourists gawk everywhere, expecting a star.

The red carpet is protected space—covered in awnings, guarded by security, usually for days before an Event. Most Events have risers set up on either side of the carpet for "fans" who aren't really fans, more like paparazzi who staked out the turf. (Every Event tries to weed out the paparazzi, but can't, now that everyone wears baggy, low-slung, ripped jeans and some rude t-shirt.)

TV trucks park as close as allowed. A wall covered with the Event's logo goes up beside the red carpet so that the Truly Famous can be photographed properly for the fashionistas and post-game (I mean—Event) shows, and the week-long orgy that is post-Event entertainment television.

We little people, and by that I mean those of us who are not nominated Actors or presenter Actors, get shoved aside by the array of camera-toting assholes who shout, "Caro! Show that fine tush of yours!" "Caro, let's see some leg!" "Caro, lean in for a cleavage shot!"

At that Event, it took me ten minutes to catch up to Mother after the photo gauntlet swept her in and pushed her out, straight into the clownlike mask-face of one of the most famous snarkmeisters, a woman who should have known better, having suffered a lot of snark herself back in the day.

She was, I believe, the first one to ask a question that came from the shadows, a question that in English makes no sense, even though these days it has become common:

"Who are you wearing?"

Never good live and scriptless, Mother blinked in surprise, thinking she had misheard the question. She frowned, and through a camera (as we saw through hundreds of playbacks, usually accompanied by Mother's sobs), she suddenly looked old and befuddled.

Then the tide swept her away. Her moment in the sun—as a presenter that year—wasn't to her advantage either. She had chosen a dress from her closet that dated from before I was born. Yes, it still fit, and without the lights, it looked gorgeous, but someone (a shadowy someone in make-up, perhaps?) hadn't extended the make-up from her face to her neck and onto her bosom.

She looked like an elderly woman wearing a Caro mask whose color didn't match her sun-wrinkled skin tone.

At the time, Mother was forty years old. Everyone said she looked eighty.

Show after show after show, recap after recap after recap, there was Mother, front and center: Red Carpet Fashion Victim, worthy of the jibes that our culture gives women no longer in their prime.

Men have it easy when it comes to clothing—even on the Red Carpet. They get props for wearing a white tuxedo jacket with black pants or for wearing a scarf instead of a bowtie. Every now and then, some idiot wears shorts or scuffed jeans and gets dinged for being too casual for "the biggest night of the year" (or what passes for a big night that week), but mostly, the men have little choice, so they can do little wrong.

But for women, it's a nightmare.

Wrong color, wrong shape, wrong hair, wrong jewelry, wrong posture, too much leg, not enough leg, too much cleavage, too see-through, not see-through enough, too daring, too bold, too reserved, too refined, too short, too long, too wide, too narrow, too—

Oh, you get it.

And with each little snarky phrase, the shadows grow. They get bigger and blacker and even more powerful. They absorb glamour like an alcoholic sucks down beer, and they prey on women—in our culture at least (I have no idea what happens in those cultures where the women are robed and covered all day)—because in our culture, women have the plumage, the glory, the most glamour and the most instinctual magic.

He Who Shall Remain Nameless sent me books on shadows and darkness and creeping bad things. I learned that the creeping, shadowy, bad things always, always arrive twenty years before the world turns on itself, and the way they accomplish that turn is to eat all of the world's innocent beauty.

And bury it under snark.

After that devastating fashion-victim Event, I thought Mother would never leave the house again. So, I slowly rescued her.

First I made her a pair of 1930s movie pajamas—the kind of exquisite silk top and bottom numbers that Ginger Rogers made famous before the Second World War. They were the first project I made for Mother in which I added a little magic—comfort magic, to calm her, and remind her that she was more than a pretty (well, beautiful) face.

The pajamas worked—and they gave me an idea.

Next year, when the shadows asked that stupid question: *Who Are You Wearing,* she would answer—vaguely, because shadows must always be answered vaguely (there's too much magic in names) that she was wearing an original—designed by her daughter, the ugly duckling.

Me.

The following year, Mother was nominated for her thirteenth Oscar, and of course, she didn't win. I had hoped she wouldn't—thirteen is one of those numbers you should live through, not call attention to.

She wore a flowing, pale lavender gown with piping that made it look vaguely Egyptian, placed in a pattern that warded away bad magic and amplified protective thoughts.

I accompanied her that year, not as her "date" because, by then, she had a new man, but as her dresser.

I followed along, adjusting her train. I primped, I plucked, I made sure no make-up artist screwed up the lovely glow we gave her. (And sure enough, I saw a tiny harassed blonde who, when I viewed her with magical vision, looked like she had been swallowed by a black, shadowy Category 3 tornado.)

I got Mother to her seat, and then hovered at the edges, so I could touch her up if need be.

All went well, through the too-long dance numbers and the lame jokes (although I did have to touch up her eye make-up after the Dead-Roll because she had some friends on it). But I wasn't prepared for the moment Mother's category got announced.

Mother's dress flared as it tried to keep her tension down (I put some comfort magic in the thread as well), and then—

She lost.

No surprise there.

But that was the category where the winner—a twenty-something with a plum indie role (right before her big debut as the Heroine of A Saga) tripped going up the stairs to get her award. And remained sprawled for the longest time.

I couldn't run to the winner; I didn't dare. Because I hoped no one else magical was watching. The energy above her, the lavender energy that tripped her—well, that had come from my mother.

Mother had been jealous of the winner throughout the entire awards season. And honestly, I understood it even if I hadn't encouraged it. A twenty-something, beautiful, witty woman actually making more money per picture than Mother made in her entire career—and already stamped with a trademarked series of award wins.

Well, Little Miss Award-Winner-Above-The-Title managed to pick herself up and go on, giving a good speech if not a great one, and the show continued.

But I had some revamping to do.

The dresses couldn't just send out magical "protect" energy. The energy had to be addressed at the shadows—the true magical threat, not a talented young woman who just happened snag the role of the season.

I didn't yell at Mother. After all, she had put on her marvelous best *I'm so pleased you won instead of me* face, and had outwardly done the right things. Never once has she expressed the mean-girl jealousy that appeared via the dress that night.

And believe you me, I did some serious magical cleaning to make sure that the dress hadn't been infected with shadow energy.

Nope. The dress had done its job. It had protected my fragile mother from the crushing disappointment that accompanied her every loss.

At least, this time, she wasn't excoriated on the fashion shows. And every single night thereafter, she was listed as one of the best-dressed with only one snarkmeister mentioning that Mother was a Woman Of A Certain Age.

I would have thought victory was mine, if it weren't for the humiliation the poor twenty-something had inadvertently suffered at my hands on her big night.

I had to make sure that sort of thing would never happen again.

I refined the dresses, gave them away for free, test-ran them at minor awards venues such as the Pawtucket Film Festival, and then offered them to starlets for bigger festivals like Sundance. No one fell, no jealous energy attacked another winner, and if the snarkmeisters didn't mention the dress positively, then they didn't mention it at all.

Mother married (happily) in one of my dresses, divorced (happily) in one of my dresses, and lost every award she was nominated for in the next five awards seasons, without ever attracting any more snark. Plus, her appearances got her ranked in the top five at least once a season—and she was becoming known for wearing Warrior Woman Designs, which had rehabilitated her.

Snarkmeister 1: *Everyone should be so lucky as to have a daughter like Caro's. The girl never had the looks, so she studied how to make* *fashion accessible even for the not-so-beautiful. When you apply that fashion to the unbelievably beautiful—well, [my only-for-today-friend Snarkmeister 2], you can see the results.*

Snarkmeister 2: *You certainly can [Snarkmeister 1, my current-and-future rival, whom I'm only talking to because we're getting paid a few thousand and we get to wear free clothes]. Who knew that ugly ducklings knew how to swan along a red carpet?*

The positive press grew, and soon everyone wanted to wear Warrior Woman. I only have so much staff, however, and only have so much magic, so I had to choose who needed my help.

The women I dressed were too old by Hollywood standards (meaning barely over thirty), too fat by Hollywood standards (at least a size six), or too ugly by Hollywood standards (think Streisand, who [even now] gets referred to as a success despite her lack of looks).

The dresses didn't make these women younger or thinner or prettier. The dresses made them feel protected, and warded off the snarkmeisters and their increasingly more powerful shadow puppetmasters. My women were untouchable and, over time, the dresses let them relax enough that they saw what was going on with their own friends (and rivals).

I like to think the dresses let them see an echo of those shadows that haunted me.

The women talked to me about making dresses for everyone.

I couldn't do that, but I started developing a plan.

I couldn't get rid of the snarkmeisters and their all-powerful shadows. Complaining about them only made them stronger.

But I could send the shadows back where they came from—if I could only get my hands on some undelivered little golden men.

Here's something no one tells you about awards shows until it's too late. The awards themselves are protected better than the gold at Fort Knox. (Is there still gold at Fort Knox? Oh, you get the idea.)

Seriously, I don't think the president is guarded as well as those little trophies.

So, I had some setbacks. All I wanted to do was ward the trophies—have them repel the snarkmeisters and band together to send the shadows back through that crack in the world from which they slimed forth.

I tried everything. I worked backstage. I even volunteered to be on the trophy committee (which has a different name at each ceremony). Nada.

Finally, I decided to pay for inclusion in the goodie bag. Eighty thousand dollars' worth of swag compiled just to give free stuff to already rich people. I gave a little gold man to everyone, with a coupon for a free post-Oscar collectible t-shirt wrapped around his tiny little tush.

Those shirts, which I worked on for months, sent a little bit of positive energy into the world.

But more than that, they allowed me into the dress rehearsals, partly because I extended some of that swag to the hard-working artists who put on the show.

I didn't get to see any gold trophies, but I did see something rather horrifying.

Where the red carpet met the marble floor inside one of the most famous theaters in the world, a slight crack had formed. Not one that a structural engineer with no magic would see. A crack in the fabric of reality, the kind shadows slip out of.

And there were shadows slipping upward, like smoke from an underground fire.

I backed away, and then I called He Who Shall Remain Nameless, not because I needed his more powerful magic, but because he knew who the magical were among the electricians, contractors, and set designers in our industry.

Together, my father and I found a group with more than glamour, and who were willing to work on short notice.

I needed them to add a layer of glittery, clear paint to the gigantic gold statues that stood near the front door—and I needed them to do it legitimately.

And they did.

Now, realize that none of the magical truly knows how magic will work. And none of us truly understands the mechanism that makes magic do what it does. We can predict, but we're like TV weather anchors. We can get it wrong.

I expected that magical glamour, added to the statues, to suck up the shadowy forms and hold them prisoner inside those gigantic trophy replicas.

Instead, the glittery coating reflected the protective magic from the dresses worn by the actresses who had just completed the red carpet gauntlet and who were feeling a bit—Cranky? Weary? Terrified?

Terrified. Because the moment they walked away from the snarkmeisters' microphones, those women knew the snarkmeisters—under the influence of their dark shadows—would find something to snark about, ruining a night that was supposed to be about the honor of being nominated and making it into a night about whose dress fit best.

I stood just behind the emergency curtain at the edge of the red carpet, armed for a magical emergency. I had some special safety pins clamped in my teeth, a stronger-than-surgical-steel needle in my right hand, and a spool of special glittery metallic thread in my left.

I was going to repair a few dresses, reinforce the magic, and coordinate the removal of the shadows after the glare of the cameras moved inside. Instead, the glowing dresses and their lovely stars queued up, air-kissing before they mounted the stairs for a drink and a little relaxation before an usher found them and settled them in their seats.

I could feel the magic of the dresses—my magic—thrumming. Those dresses were working overtime, like all armor does in battle, protecting those fragile human bodies hidden deep inside.

I just didn't expect the armor to link up, like protestors facing the police—using magical arms threaded at the metaphorical elbows—to hold off a darkness that was growing increasingly worse.

These women had no magic besides the kind my mother had. Just a little something extra to make them glow before the cameras. Yet, to a person, these women looked toward the snarkmeisters, lined up for a final "interview" as if the shadows had become visible.

Maybe they had.

They had certainly become powerful.

And that coating on the golden statues was doing absolutely nothing.

So I spit the pins into my left hand, took the needle, and was about to lob my magical gold thread at the shadows when the crack in the ground widened.

The statues opened their eyes, and looked—truly looked—at the shadows.

And the shadows blinked.

They started to flee, but one of the statues toppled sideways so fast that no one could move out of its way. It hit the snarkmeisters—yes—but if you look at all those replays, which you see over and over again, you'll see that it landed on top of the place where the red carpet met the tile.

It blocked the crack into the other world.

The shadows floated around the statue in terror, and that was when the second statue seemed to absorb them. But what I saw wasn't the absorption. It was the dozens of gold, manicured fingers, which came from the dress magic, that shoved the shadows into that statue, inside the ward that the trophy truly was.

I crouched at the toppled statue's base, and grabbed my thread, using it and the needle to stitch the edges of the crack closed.

Then I used the last of my magic to spell that thread. It would continue sewing itself after the teamsters got the statue upright again.

The crack would—and did—close.

And our little part of the world was safe again.

I wish I could say that snark died that day. Or that the snarkmeisters vanished.

That group did, actually. They were humiliated and/or terrified, some of them coming to their senses.

New snarkmeisters immediately rose in their wake. But honestly, I didn't see any shadows around them.

Now, I see shadows around cell phones—in the hands of ordinary people who somehow think themselves snarkmeisters. They blog, they post, they Tweet. They have absorbed the culture of critics, and they initiate online battles as harmful as any that go over the airwaves.

I would organize an anti-snark campaign, but I have no ground to stand on, really, as you can tell from my tone.

Snark happens when you don't respect someone, when you want to control and ridicule them to show your own superiority.

I think I might have absorbed some of the shadows on my own.

Mother tells me I need the shadows for battle. Weapons make us stronger, she says. It simply depends on how they're used.

But I don't like the shadows within, and I'm vowing to purge them.

After I watch that instant replay of our miraculous victory—one last time.

About the Authors

Robin Wayne Bailey is the author of numerous novels and series, including the FROST adventures, the *Dragonkin* trilogy, the *Brothers of the Dragon* trilogy, and other stand-alone works including the Fritz Leiber-inspired *Swords Against the Shadowland*. He's written over 150 short stories, some of which have been collected in two volumes: *Turn Left to Tomorrow* and *The Fantastikon: Tales of Wonder*. His most recent work includes stories in the anthologies, *The Raygun Chronicles*, *Stars of Darkover* and *Shattered Shields*. A former two-term president of the Science Fiction and Fantasy Writers of America and a founder of the Science Fiction Hall of Fame, Robin lives in Kansas City, Missouri.

Linda L. Donahue, an Air Force brat, spent her childhood traveling. Having earned a pilot's certification and a SCUBA certification, she's been, at one time or another, a threat by land, air or sea. For eighteen years, she taught computer science, mathematics and aviation; now she teaches tai chi and belly dance. Among her published twenty-plus short stories are her stories in Esther Friesner's anthologies, *Strip Mauled* and *Fangs for the Mammaries*. Her work can also be found in novels published by Yard Dog Press. She and her husband live in Texas with their pet cats, rabbit, and sugar glider.

Laura Frankos has had stories in a few other *Chicks in Chainmail* collections, as well as *Analog* and other places. She's also written a mystery novel and a humongous compendium of musical theatre trivia, *The Broadway Musical Quiz Book*. This is what comes of listening to way too many show tunes as a child. She dedicates her story to Kurt Weill, Ogden Nash, and S.J. Perelman, for their inspiration.

❧

Nebula Award winner **Esther M. Friesner** is the author of more than forty novels and nearly 200 short stories. She created and edited the first *Chicks in Chainmail* anthology, published in 1995, which is one heck of a way to use a Vassar College B.A. and an M.A./Ph.D. from Yale University! She is also the author of the popular *Princesses of Myth* series, the most recent titles being *Deception's Princess* and *Deception's Pawn*. When not writing about young women with that certain Can-Do/Can't-Stop-Me attitude, she's found in Connecticut, attended by her delightful family and epic cat.

❧

Jim C. Hines is the author of eleven fantasy novels, including the *Magic ex Libris* series about a magic-wielding librarian, a dryad, a secret society founded by Johannes Gutenberg, and a flaming spider; the *Princess* series of fairy tale retellings; and the humorous *Goblin Quest* trilogy. He's an active blogger, and won the 2012 Hugo Award for Best Fan Writer. Jim lives in mid-Michigan with his wife and two children. Online, he lives at *www.jimchines.com*.

❧

P.C. Hodgell writes: "I inherited my interest in creativity from my parents, both artists, but my images have always come in words. In a sense, my heroine, Jame, and I grew up together. There are seven novels in the *God Stalk* series so far. Two or three more should do it. 'Knot and the Dragon' is a departure for me, lighter and less dense than my usual work. It was fun. I hope you find it so, too."

❧

Sarah A. Hoyt is the author of a dozen novels in various genres, including the Darkship science fiction adventure series and the Shifter saga, which includes previous entries *Draw One in the Dark*, and *The Gentleman Takes a Chance*, as well as her acclaimed Shakespearean fantasy series, which started with the Mythopoeic award finalist *Ill Met by Moonlight*. An avid history buff and longtime reader of sci-fi, fantasy, and mysteries, Hoyt has published more than three dozen short stories in esteemed magazines such as *Asimov's, Analog, Amazing, and Weird Tales*, as well as many anthologies. She lives in Colorado with her husband, two teen boys, and a pride of cats.

Kerrie L. Hughes loves art, history, science, animals, people, and all things having to do with books. She has edited thirteen anthologies, her favorite being *Chicks Kick Butt,* co-edited with Rachel Caine from TOR. Her upcoming new favorite is *Fierce,* co-edited with Jim Butcher, to be published by Penguin in 2016. She has also published eleven short stories, most recently, "Do Robotic Cats Purr In Space," appearing in *Bless Your Mechanical Heart,* from Evil Girlfriend Media. Kerrie has also been a contributing editor on two concordances: *The Vorkosigan Companion* and *The Valdemar Companion*.

Julia S. Mandala (*www.juliasmandala.com*) holds degrees in history and law, and is a freelance editor, scuba diver and belly dancer. She edited *The Anthology From Hell: Humorous Tales from WAY Down Under*, and has three published novels, *The Four Redheads: Apocalypse Now!, Redheads in Love* (with Linda L. Donahue, Rhonda Eudaly and Dusty Rainbolt), and *House of Doors* (Yard Dog Press). Her works appear in Esther Friesner's *Witch Way to the Mall* and *Fangs for the Mammaries,* and in *The Mammoth Book of Comic Fantasy II, The Four Redheads of the Apocalypse, Dracula's Lawyer* and many small press anthologies.

Lee Martindale's short fiction has appeared in numerous anthologies, including *Turn The Other Chick* and, most recently, a collection of her work entitled, *Bard's Road*. She's edited two anthologies, *Such A Pretty Face* and *The Ladies of Trade Town*. When not slinging fiction, Lee is a Lifetime Active member of SFWA (where she is serving her second term on the Board of Directors), a member of the SCA, a fencing member of the SFWA Musketeers, and a Named Bard. She and her husband live in Plano, Texas, where she keeps friends and fans in the loop at *http://www.HarpHaven.net*.

⁓

Jody Lynn Nye lists her main career activity as "spoiling cats." She lives northwest of Chicago with one of the above and her husband, author and packager, Bill Fawcett. She has written over forty books, including *The Ship Who Won* with Anne McCaffrey; eight books with Robert Asprin; a humorous anthology about mothers, *Don't Forget Your Spacesuit, Dear!*; and more than 115 short stories. Her latest books are *Fortunes of the Imperium* (Baen Books) and *Dragons Run* (Ace Books).

⁓

Steven Harper Piziks was born with a name that no one can reliably spell or pronounce, so he usually writes under the pen name Steven Harper. He sold a short story on his first try way back in 1990. Since then, he's written twenty-plus novels, including *The Clockwork Empire* steampunk series. Currently, he's writing *The Books of Blood and Iron*, a fantasy trilogy. *Iron Axe*, the first one, came out in January, 2015. For this anthology, he resurrected Dagmar and Ramdane, his brother-and-sister team from *Turn the Other Chick*, so he could say good-bye to them. The story is dedicated—and why not?—to Esther's cat, Lulu, and her fondness for turkey. Steven also teaches English in southeast Michigan. When not writing, he plays the folk harp, wrestles with his sons, and embarrasses them in public. Visit his web page at *http://www.stevenpiziks.com*

⁓

When **Jean Rabe** isn't tossing tennis balls to her moose-of-a-mutt or sharing a lawn chair with her pug, she writes and edits. She's the author of thirty fantasy, SF, and adventure novels, and boatloads of short stories. She's edited a couple dozen anthologies and more magazine issues than she cares to count. She lives in a tiny town in Illinois surrounded by railroad tracks. Visit her at *www.jeanrabe.com*.

⁓

Laura Resnick is the author of the popular Esther Diamond urban fantasy series, whose releases include *Disappearing Nightly, Doppelgangster, Unsympathetic Magic, Vamparazzi, Polterheist, The Misfortune Cookie*, and *Abracadaver*. She has also written traditional fantasy novels such as *In Legend Born, The Destroyer Goddess*, and *The White Dragon*, which made multiple "Year's Best" lists. An opinion columnist, frequent public speaker, and the Campbell Award-winning author of many short stories, she is on the web at *www.LauraResnick.com*.

⁓

Kristine Kathryn Rusch's novels have hit bestseller lists worldwide, including *USA Today*, the *Wall Street Journal*, and the *Times* (London). She's won or been nominated for every major award in the science fiction and fantasy field. She's an award-winning editor as well, currently with *Fiction River*. 2015 marks an experiment she's conducting with WMG Publishing: every month, from January on, she's publishing a brand new novel in her Retrieval Artist series. The novels complete a story arc that began with the novel, *Anniversary Day*. To her knowledge, no one else in SF has ever done such a thing. When she completes that, she will return her attention to her worldwide bestselling fantasy series, *The Fey*. For more information on her work, go to *www.kristinekathrynrusch.com*

⁓

Elizabeth Ann Scarborough is the author of 39 novels, including the 1989 Nebula Award-winning *Healer's War* and sixteen in collaboration with Anne McCaffrey. Best known for her versatility in subject matter and humorous writing style, Scarborough is also a former army nurse and served in Vietnam. She never had to wear armor, however, just a flak jacket and helmet when her hospital unit was under fire. She is currently working on *The Dragon, The Witch and The Railroad*, a spinoff of her popular *Songs from the Seashell Archives* series.

❧

Alex Shvartsman is a writer and game designer from Brooklyn, New York. Over 60 of his short stories have appeared in *Nature, InterGalactic Medicine Show, Galaxy's Edge, Daily Science Fiction*, and many other venues. He edits Unidentified Funny Objects, an annual anthology of humorous SF/F. His fiction is linked at *www.alexshvartsman.com*

❧

USA Today bestselling writer **Dean Wesley Smith** has published over a hundred novels in thirty years and hundreds and hundreds of short stories across many genres. He wrote a couple dozen *Star Trek* novels, the only two original *Men in Black* novels, Spider-Man and X-Men novels, plus novels set in gaming and television worlds. He wrote novels under dozens of pen names in the worlds of comic books and movies, including novelizations of a dozen films from *The Final Fantasy to Steel* to *The Rundown*. He now writes his own original fiction under just one name, Dean Wesley Smith. His new thriller *Dead Money,* came out in November 2013, and since January 2014 he has published ten original novels in science fiction and mystery. His new monthly magazine *Smith's Monthly,* premiered on October 1, 2013, and contain an original novel in every issue, and at least four short stories plus articles and serial stories. Dean also worked as an editor and publisher, first at Pulphouse Publishing, then for *VB Tech Journal*, then for Pocket Books. He is now the executive editor for *Fiction River*.

❧

John W. Campbell Award Winner, **Wen Spencer** resides in paradise in Hilo, Hawaii, with two volcanoes overlooking her home. Spencer says that she often wakes up and exclaims, "Oh my god, I live on an island in the middle of the Pacific!" According to Spencer, she lives with "my Dali Llama-like husband, my autistic teenage son, and two cats (one of which is recovering from mental illness). All of which makes for very odd home life at times." Spencer's love of Japanese anime and manga flavors her writing. "Dark Pixii" features the characters from her most recent novel, *Eight Million Gods*.

Born on an Indian reservation in northern California, **Louisa Swann** spent the first six months of her life in a papoose carrier. Determined not to remain a basket case forever, she escaped the splintered confines, finally settling down on a ranch where she spins tales that range from light to dark and back again. Louisa's writerly eccentricities have resulted in numerous short story publications in various anthologies. Find out more at *www.louisaswann.com*.

Harry Turtledove is an escaped Byzantine historian who writes alternate history, other science fiction, fantasy, and (when he can get away with it) historical fiction. Recent and upcoming books include *Joe Steele* and *The House of Daniel*. He is married to fellow writer, Laura Frankos, who also perpetrated a story for this book. They have three daughters, one granddaughter, and the required writer's cat.

Elizabeth A. Vaughan is a *USA Today* bestselling author who writes fantasy romance. Her first novel, *Warprize*, was re-released in April 2011. You can learn more about her books at *www.eavwrites.com*. Beth has dedicated this story to Robert Wenzlaff, friend and fellow author, whose own story ended far too soon.

About Esther Friesner

Nebula Award winner, **Esther M. Friesner** is the author of more than forty novels and nearly 200 short stories. She created and edited the first *Chicks in Chainmail* anthology, published in 1995, which is one heck of a way to use a Vassar College B.A. and an M.A./Ph.D. from Yale University! She is also the author of the popular *Princesses of Myth* series, the most recent titles being *Deception's Princess* and *Deception's Pawn*. When not writing about young women with that certain Can-Do/Can't-Stop-Me attitude, she's found in Connecticut, attended by her delightful family and epic cat.

About John Helfers

John Helfers is a full-time freelance writer and editor, and is the president of Stonehenge Art & Word, an editorial/literary management company. He shares a long history with the *Chicks* series of anthologies, having assisted on the previous four volumes during his sixteen years at Tekno Books under Martin H. Greenberg. On his writing side, he's published more than fifty short stories in anthologies such as *Fiction River: Risk Takers* (WMG Publishing), *Schemers* (Stone Skin Press), and *Shattered Shields* (Baen Books). His media tie-in fiction has appeared in anthologies, game books, and novels for the *Dragonlance®*, *Transformers®*, *BattleTech®*, *Shadowrun®*, *Warlock II®* and *Golem Arcana®* universes. He's also written fiction and nonfiction, including a novel in the first authorized trilogy based on *The Twilight Zone™* television series, the young adult novel *Tom Clancy's Net Force Explorers™: Cloak and Dagger*, the original fantasy novel *Siege of Night and Fire*, and a history of the United States Navy.